Who Killed Michael Douglas?
A Chambers Elliot Mystery

Michael Paulson

BooksForABuck.com
2010

Michael Paulson
Who Killed Michael Douglas
Michael Paulson

BooksForABuck.com
March 2010

ISBN: 978-1-60215-114-7

Chapter 1

Chambers Elliot, a tall man with gray hair and dark smears beneath his blue eyes from habitual lack of sleep, looked up from the brief on his limed-oak desk to focus upon the black-clad figure entering his private, well-appointed office.

"Good morning, Father Zamoyski," Elliot said in his usual, reassuring manner. His deeply-timbered voice resonated from the rosewood walls. He arose from his swivel chair and with a finger indicated one of the brown Harvard chairs fronting his desk. "Please sit down."

The stooped, white-haired Priest took a ragged breath. Then he moved unsteadily across the brown carpeting toward the lawyer's desk, not unlike a sailor on the deck of a ship in heavy seas.

Below the Priest's thinning hairline was a pale, deeply-lined, wet face set off by hollow eyes with constricted pupils, a generous nose, and a heavy jaw. Lodged in one ear was an old-fashioned hearing aid. The wire from the ancient device dangled across the priest's tunic into an inside pocket. His short legs joined large feet encased by scuffed, black shoes. Despite the unusually warm weather for June his hands were sheathed in thin, black leather gloves.

"You're a trial-lawyer?" The priest's voice was ragged, like the sound of tearing canvas.

"Litigator," Elliot corrected, and resumed his seat. Then the lawyer leaned back in his chair and smoothed his gray, pinstriped vest. "What can I do for you?"

The Priest sat down with great reluctance, like a prisoner expecting execution. Then he looked into Elliot's curious eyes. "I talked to your receptionist."

The lawyer crossed his arms. "Maggie Sharp."

"She sent me to see your legal-assistant."

"Lydia Marshall."

"Neither explained my need?" asked the priest, his voice despairing.

Elliot pursed his lips. "Lydia told me your name is Father Aleksey Ivanovich Zamoyski. You want to speak with me concerning a murder; the details of which you would disclose only to me." The lawyer's voice trailed off slightly upon noticing the erratic vibration of the priest's carotid artery. He quickly tilted forward resting his forearms upon the desk. "Do you need a doctor, Father Zamoyski?"

"Doctor? There's nothing a doctor can do for me once…" The priest left the words hanging as he paused to clear his throat. Then he said, "It's been so many years since the incident that brings me to you. However, I feel I must make an effort to right a terrible wrong." His lips thinned at the end of the last words, as if the statement fouled his tongue.

"Right what wrong?" Elliot's voice rose slightly with his quickened interest.

After taking several choking breaths the priest replied. "The wrong man was charged. He hanged himself while in jail rather than face the humiliation of a public trial." There was another pause for breath. Then Zamoyski added in a worried whisper, "I am concerned, however, that I have waited too long. The murder occurred nearly thirty years ago."

"Thirty years?" Elliot's bushy, gray eyebrows furrowed with sudden disappointment. "There is no statute of limitations on murder," he muttered, making a vague gesture. "However, if the perpetrator is deceased…"

The priest's shaggy head shook. "He isn't."

The lawyer licked his lips with renewed curiosity. "You know who the killer is?"

"Of course."

Elliot splayed his hands in confusion. "Then why have you waited thirty years to right this wrong, as you put it?"

"Rules of my profession, Mr. Elliot." The priest's voice took on a weary tenor. "There are many rules. So many, many rules."

Father Zamoyski glanced around Elliot's office, his eyes pausing as if with purpose or envy at each of the several Joan Miro wall-hangings. "You enjoy abstraction," he eventually remarked.

"I enjoy all sorts of puzzlement." Studying the priest, Elliot concluded that opium-addiction—possibly taken in treatment for chronic pain—explained the man's sickly pallor. "If these rules have kept you silent for thirty years, what has changed?"

The priest jerked toward the attorney's voice with a start, as if having been awakened from a dream. "I'm dying. There are even rules for that. Did you know? We are constricted at every turn, from womb to coffin. I…" His voice faded, again, as if confusion's talons were plucking at the folds in his brain.

"Why don't you tell me about it from the beginning, Father Zamoyski?" Elliot urged. "Take your time."

"Yes," Zamoyski muttered, uneasily. "The beginning. It's always best to start from the beginning. But beginnings can be very difficult." He composed himself, brought his knees tightly together and then leaned slightly toward the lawyer; his wrists rested upon his lower limbs, his gloved hands gripping his knees.

"As you must realize I am privy to a great many secrets. The majority are trivial matters. But some would blight even the most tarnished of souls." The priest looked around the office for a second time, the lines in his face deepening as if he were having trouble concentrating.

"A few are horrendous tales of violence. Others are infected with loathsome depravity. Then there are…" He made a despairing movement with one hand. "Then there are those so filled with blood-lust I shudder to make recollection."

Elliot said slowly, evenly, "I give you my word that whatever you confide will remain between us."

Zamoyski raised his gloved hands to his face as if in shame. Then between the fingers he gasped, "I feel such despair!" The priest's voice faltered, into a sob. Then his hands fell away and he stared teary-eyed at Chambers Elliot. "Had I broken my vows of the confessional and come forward, that man would be alive."

"Possibly," Elliot said with faint impatience. "But there can be no certainty. Thirty years is a very long time, Father. Illness and accident take their toll. Who was murdered?"

"Michael Douglas."

"Who do you suspect killed Mr. Douglas?" probed the lawyer.

"I don't suspect, I know!" The priest's chin fell to his chest, his body quivering with grief.

The lawyer considered the tormented man a moment. Something was not quite right. What it was, Elliot had not yet pinpointed. But something was definitely wrong. He said, "I assume, based upon what you've disclosed that you came by this information through a parishioner's confession?"

Zamoyski nodded, blinking back tears. "In part."

Elliot folded his hands on the desk, still assessing the priest. "What is the killer's name?"

"God help me, I can't break my vows."

The lawyer twisted his mouth sardonically. "Father Zamoyski, unless you are willing to disclose what you know, then *nothing* can be done."

The priest gave Elliot a small, sad smile. "To speak means the revocation of my ordination. Even at this low point in my life, I could not bear such a disgrace."

Chambers Elliot flipped his arms wide in exasperation. "Father Zamoyski, I am bewildered as to what you expect me to accomplish. Your silence shackles me."

The priest squirmed in the chair as if suddenly feeling the scrutiny of his maker. "All I want you to do is clear the accused man's name based upon information I have gathered outside the confessional."

"To what end? You said the man was dead."

"Surely you realize his family shares this unwarranted shame!" exclaimed Zamoyski. "It is for them, that I come to you."

"Each of us has a predecessor of dubious character, Father," Elliot remarked. "It is the nature of mankind." Then the lawyer stopped, his face darkening with remorse. "I'm sorry for those remarks. They were uncalled for. But my point was well meant. Whatever's been done by our forbearers hardly reflects upon us, good or evil. We are who we are—no more, no less."

Zamoyski seemed mildly amused. "For a man of strength like yourself, perhaps. But for the rest of us…" The priest's unfinished words hung in the air. After taking a ragged breath he said, "Shame is the most powerful of emotions, Mr. Elliot. It tears at our hearts like a ravenous beast whose hunger can never be sated."

Elliot scowled in silence for many seconds. The he said, "I cannot possibly meet your expectations."

"But you can," Zamoyski insisted.

"How?" The attorney's hands flew apart. Then he leveled a long forefinger at the priest. "Without the killer's name, I am stopped before I begin." Chambers Elliot leaned back in his chair. "I'm sorry, Father. But there is nothing I can do."

"At least hear me out?" the priest pleaded. "I beg you."

There was a long pause. Then Chambers Elliot smiled as he suddenly realized what was wrong. The man sitting before him was not a priest. The cassock Zamoyski wore was double-breasted. Therefore it was not of a Catholic priest, but that of an Anglican. Further, in this country, that garment was traditionally worn only in church or at a seminary. In public, Catholic priests were never attired in it.

"Nothing would give me greater pleasure—*Father Zamoyski.*"

The priest's gloved hands became animated, his voice confidential. "You see, I have devised a scheme to get around my obligation to the cloth."

"I don't understand," Elliot said, purposely baiting the man into disclosing as much as possible about his real purpose.

The priest glanced about for a few seconds. Then he tilted confidentially toward Elliot. "You will identify the killer without my disclosing the name."

Elliot chuckled grimly. "Surely you don't take me for a mind-reader?"

The priest wagged his head. "I'm serious, Mr. Elliot. You will know who the killer is—when he kills, again."

"Again?" The lawyer's eyes widened with mock alarm. "Are you saying you've concealed the name of a serial-killer?"

"No," declared the priest.

"Then what are you saying?"

Father Zamoyski's spread his lips into a leering grin, giving Elliot a peak at decay-blackened teeth. "I've set a trap for him."

"Trap?" Elliot echoed, still baiting.

The priest nodded. "He is going to kill me, Mr. Elliot. At which time, you will deduce his identity. Whereupon, you will have all you need to clear the wronged man."

"Nonsense. You have referred to the killer as 'he' and 'him'. Can I assume this killer is a man? Or are you leading me down the garden path in that respect, as well?"

"As well?" asked Zamoyski, tilting his head askance as if suddenly caught in a lie.

Elliot leaned back and crossed his arms, staring fixedly at Father Zamoyski. "Have you been threatened, after all these years?"

The priest giggled, "It is I who have threatened him—with exposure."

"Then the killer is a man?"

The priest looked down at his gloved hands. "I can admit nothing."

"Father Zamoyski, the best legal advice I can give you is to go to the police." The lawyer once more leaned his arms upon the desk. "Tell them all you know. Including whatever you're planning by way of entrapment…"

"I have the wherewithal to pay your fees, Mr. Elliot," the priest quickly interjected. "I am not here seeking charity."

Chambers Elliot gaped a moment in surprise. "Nevertheless, my point of concern is for your safety."

"But you need not worry, Mr. Elliot. I am not seeking protection. In fact, you must agree not to take any action along those lines. Otherwise my plans may be thwarted."

Elliot got to his feet. "Plans?"

"To entrap the real killer."

"Ah, yes, *those* plans."

"My passing is of my own choosing, Mr. Elliot. Its timing and method are that of my assassin." The priest's countenance became anxious. "When we complete our arrangements you and I will not see each other, again—at least, for what remains of my life. Your duty is to the wronged man—not me."

"A dead man." The lawyer moved to the front of the desk and took a perch on its edge, facing the priest, still suspicious. "For whom you expect to die?"

"Death is my penance, Mr. Elliot." Father Zamoyski's pinpoint pupils peered desperately up at the lawyer, from beneath craggy white brows. "I beg that you accede to my request?"

Elliot shrugged. "Should I choose not to, what do you propose to do?"

"I had not considered that possibility. You see, what has been set in motion cannot be stopped. Even as we speak, my assassin makes plans. By the close of this week—no later—I shall be with my maker whether you assist, or not."

Elliot elevated his lean height, his eyes studying the priest's ghastly pallor. At this close proximity he could see the makeup being used to create the man's deathly complexion. "Before we march you to your grave, Father, tell me the circumstances of Michael Douglas' death."

"A liquor store," said the priest, leaning back in the chair. One hand went to his chest as his breathing became short and rapid. Then, when his breaths normalized the hand fell away and he said, "The clerk— Michael Douglas—was shot during what the police foolishly believed was a robbery."

"The murder was motivated by other reasons? You are certain?"

The priest nodded. "A woman."

"Indeed? What was the name of the store?"

Father Zamoyski paused, his brows furrowing deeply as if he was searching his deepest memories. "Winston Liquors."

"I don't recall the incident." Elliot returned to his chair, taking a yellow notepad and pen from a desk drawer before making a notation.

"I'm not surprised," Father Zamoyski observed. "Doubtlessly, there have been thousands of liquor-store robberies since that terrible time thirty years ago. We humans are such horrid creatures. Each of us is infested with the promise of violence and avarice."

"And deceit. Did the killing take place inside that store or outside?"

"Inside." The priest cast a sideways glance at Elliot as if testing for a reaction to his tale.

"Is this store still in business?" Elliot asked, still taking notes.

"Yes. It is in Georgetown."

Chambers Elliot nodded as he wrote, recollection pushing at him, fast and hard. Suddenly his eyes widened and he looked over at the priest in genuine surprise. "Douglas was killed execution-style."

"Yes. Exactly." The priest quickly brightened into a smile. "You do remember."

"The man charged with the crime was Jerome Petty," Elliot continued, the incident now becoming clear. "I was working for the Public Defender's Office, at the time. In fact, Petty's defense was assigned to me."

The priest nodded. "Which is why I came to you rather than another attorney."

The lawyer set down his pen, now more curious than before about the man sitting before him. "As I recall there was no mistake as to Jerome Petty's guilt. Petty was a career-criminal. Two eyewitnesses of sound character identified him as the shooter. The Jensens, Mr. and Mrs."

Father Zamoyski shook his head in refute. "Those witnesses lied, Mr. Elliot."

"Why would they?"

Father Zamoyski's eyes narrowed. "We all have our price."

The lawyer shoved the notepad off to one side scoffing, "That robbery, as best I recall, netted less than two hundred dollars. Lies may be bought, Father—yes. But they don't come cheaply—as you are aware."

Father Zamoyski laboriously straightened his body in the chair, his gloved hands gripping the arms. "I'm not lying, Mr. Elliot," he declared, fervently.

Elliot said grimly, "Aren't you?"

"Mr. and Mrs. Jensen were killed in a helicopter crash during their vacation to Samoa, shortly after Douglas' murder. Convenient—at least for Michael Douglas' killer—wouldn't you agree?"

"So it would seem." Chambers Elliot rested his elbows on the desk. "You said Michael Douglas was killed over a woman. Can you tell me her name?"

"I was not able to discover that."

"So, this unnamed killer who you referred to as 'he' and 'him' but could be of either sex, took personal offense to Mr. Douglas' philandering with a particular woman who remains unidentified?"

Zamoyski hesitated. "I realize it must sound a bit odd..."

"That is an understatement. But what makes this incredible is that you expect me to believe this brutal killer sought absolution."

"It was not his confession that I heard."

The lawyer's face fell. "Come, again?"

The priest's very faint smile hardly moved his mouth. "It was another who made the confession."

"A witness?"

"Not directly. More along the lines of a confidante."

"Then how can you be certain that what you heard was not just fools-play?"

"My certainty is absolute, Mr. Elliot. I, through subsequent investigation, determined the real killer's identity and, thereby, the motive."

Chambers Elliot leaned back laughing. "I strongly suspect your inquiry was flawed, along with the rest of your portrayal."

"I assure you it was not."

"If you concluded the killer's identity on your own, then you are not barred from disclosing it."

"But I am, Mr. Elliot. You see, the confessor's identity would also disclose that of the killer."

Chambers Elliot chuckled under his breath, for a moment. Then he said, "You're quick. I'll grant you that. But if you are murdered, what makes you think the police won't botch their investigation and charge the wrong man, again? In this state, it is a frightfully common occurrence."

"I have every confidence the authorities will not repeat their mistakes of thirty years ago," Zamoyski declared. "The science of crime is far more advanced."

"So is the sophistication of criminals. Your death may be interpreted as an accident. Or worse, considering your calling, as a suicide. Dare you risk being denied absolution over a man like Jerome Petty? No sacrament of any kind may be administered after such a death."

Suddenly a conflict of emotions was expressed upon the sickly man's face. "I had not considered that."

One eyebrow arched the merest trifle in the direction of the priest, as the flawed statement about sacraments failed to garner a correction from Zamoyski. "Father Zamoyski or whatever your..." Chambers Elliot began. Then he caught himself. "On second thought, I'm willing to pursue this matter inasmuch as you intend to pay my fees. But I want it understood that I cannot guarantee success."

"Thank you, Mr. Elliot!" Father Zamoyski took a brown banker's envelope from within the recesses of his suit, and set it upon the desk. Then he took out a pair of extremely thick eyeglasses and put them on. "Within the envelope are two certified checks. One is for sixty-five thousand dollars, to cover your fees. The other is in the amount of twenty thousand dollars and is to be handed over to my brother, upon my death. It is my hope you will take care of that bequest, as well."

"Acting as executor for your estate is not a problem," Elliot declared. "Did you give Lydia the details on your brother and any other assets?"

"There is only the check. My brother—Daniel—will contact you, in a day or two. Naturally, he will have the appropriate documents to validate his identity." The priest made an embarrassed gesture. "I have been out of the country for a number of years. Therefore, I cannot recall my brother's address."

Chambers Elliot pursed his lips in thought, remaining silent for nearly a minute. Then, with decision written upon his brow he said, "I want to add a codicil to our agreement. The understanding is that I have freedom to pursue this investigation in any fashion I choose."

"To the extent your best-efforts are directed toward the cause of justice, for all concerned."

"You can count on that, Father Zamoyski." Chambers Elliot picked up the envelope and tore it open. Within were two certified checks in the amounts stated by the priest. "I'll have my legal-assistant give you a receipt for these. I will be in court, this afternoon and tomorrow morning. Consequently, I won't have the executorship forms and the contract covering my efforts on your behalf finalized, until late tomorrow. But…"

"I will return tomorrow afternoon, then." The priest glanced at his wristwatch. "I'm late for an appointment."

"Where can I reach you between now and your return tomorrow, should the need arise?"

"St. Michael's Rectory. I gave your receptionist the address and telephone number."

Father Zamoyski struggled to his feet like a newborn calf, turned toward the door and then turned back. "The check for my brother… You do have a safe, I presume?"

"Of course."

"Would you humor me by putting my brother's bequest in there while I am present? Daniel is my only living relation. I know it must sound foolish. However…"

Chambers Elliot got up without remark, turned and pulled aside the Joan Miro painting hanging on the wall behind his desk. A cylinder-safe came into view, which he quickly opened. After putting the envelope given by the priest within, Elliot shut the safe and gave the dial a spin. Then the lawyer turned to face Zamoyski. The priest nodded his approval, removed his glasses and stuffed them into a pocket. Then he hobbled away.

Elliot watched his client's departure with special interest. "Why," he reflected, "was that man willing to spend so much money to retain my services under false pretenses?"

Seconds later, Lydia Marshall, Elliot's legal-assistant, entered his private office.

"Was that priest on the level, Chambers?" she asked, with dubious grin. Lydia was tall, blonde, slender, mid-twenties and attired in a pink suit.

"You obviously think otherwise, Lydia."

She shrugged. "For a priest, he didn't ring true to me."

"You're a Baptist. Why should he?" Elliot went around to the front of his desk. There he stopped; legs splayed, hands balled at the bottoms of his trousers-pockets, eyes on Lydia. "I must admit, however, you are quite correct. He is not a priest."

"Then who is he?"

"I don't know. But I intend to find out."

"Why didn't you confront him with it?"

"I nearly did. But my curiosity got the better of me."

She pointed at the exposed safe. "I hope you demanded an advance for services?"

"That is what makes it all the more curious. He supplied eighty-five grand in certified monies," Elliot said, thoughtfully. "At least the checks *appeared* to be genuine. He'll return tomorrow to sign the executorship documents and the contract covering our efforts on his behalf. Sixty-five thousand is our fee. The remainder is a bequest to his brother. I'll give you the details later. In the meantime get in touch with the Taggart Detective Agency. Tell Jason Taggart to drop whatever he's doing and come to my office."

"No can-do, Chambers," she said. "You have an *ex-parte* hearing before Judge Kereru on the Simpson case in less than an hour, remember? You'll be lucky to get to the courthouse before it convenes."

"Then after that." Elliot studied her blue eyes, rubbing his chin with one paw. "Say four o'clock?"

"Okay." Then Lydia wrinkled her high forehead. "Zamoyski talked to me about a murder. In fact, the man was in tears when he spoke with me."

Elliot gave out a lazy laugh. "The murder was a teaser, along with his role. Zamoyski's purpose for seeing me, or so he claimed, is to hire me to find *his* killer. In so doing, I would be able to clear the name of the man blamed in that thirty-year-old murder. Do you see why I became so curious as to his real purpose?"

Lydia blinked rapidly in confusion. "For a dead guy he talks pretty good."

The lawyer's face darkened. "That's the part of this game that worries me." Elliot returned to his chair. "I don't think Zamoyski was lying about having a killer on his tail."

"I'm not kicking about the chunk of change he dropped off. We can use that. But if Zamoyski's playing us, we could be in for more trouble that it's worth. What is that old saying about curiosity and cats?"

"Zamoyski claims he's dying," said Elliot, ignoring her. "Based solely upon his appearance, I would agree. If my recollection of medical jurisprudence is accurate, constricted pupils and clammy skin are symptomatic of opium-addiction. But he was made-up to have that appearance. Why?"

"Maybe he's an actor hired by someone else?"

Elliot rocked her question back and forth in his mind before slowly saying, "I would agree that he is an actor. But you're missing the point. Why pose as a sickly priest? Why not a healthy dentist? It would've been a role easier to succeed at."

"Who did he say was murdered?"

"Michael Douglas." Elliot waggled a finger. "That's another part of his ploy that I found so curious. You see, I was assigned as defense-counsel for the man charged in the killing Michael Douglas—Jerome Petty."

"So whoever this guy is, he knows a great deal about you."

Chambers Elliot nodded.

"Perhaps Petty put him up to it?"

"Petty committed suicide not many days after his arrest."

Lydia rested her weight on one leg. Then, she put her hands akimbo at her hips. "Is it possible Petty's relatives are taking revenge on you?"

"What for? I wasn't responsible for Petty's suicide. No. I'm more inclined to think that Zamoyski's purpose has nothing to do with Douglas or Petty. But I'll be damned if I can figure out what he actually intends."

She went over to the desk and leaned her hands upon it, staring into her boss' face. "Chambers, you're just asking for trouble with this. Let me send the checks back to him. I'll tell Zamoyski that your schedule simply won't allow you to accept another case."

The lawyer shook his head. "Why not play his game?"

Lydia folded her arms defiantly. "Good, old fashioned common sense comes to mind."

Elliot smiled. "Something dramatic is about to occur, Lydia. Something very dramatic. I want to be in on it."

She eased erect, her arms dropping. "What if his plan is to kill you? Did you consider that? Your legal wrangling is behind more than one prisoner's presence on death row. What if one of them hired Zamoyski? It's possible, isn't it?"

The attorney pondered her question a moment as if searching for reassuring response. "Possibly. But I still want to know what's going on."

She moved around the desk to stand next to him. "At the cost of your life?"

Elliot said with a reassuring smile, "You worry too much, Lydia. Nothing bad is going to happen."

She leaned back a little and regarded her boss with a childlike seriousness. "Jason Taggart's no fool, Chambers. He'll hear two words about that priest and head back to his own offices faster than he left."

"I don't think so, Lydia. Thirty years ago, Taggart was a homicide detective. It was he who arrested Jerome Petty for killing Michael Douglas. That gives Jason a vested interest in Zamoyski's motives."

"You're assuming Jason Taggart can remember that far back."

Chambers Elliot stood up and gave his legal assistant a fatherly smile. "Anything else on the agenda?"

"I telephoned the university about the summer-intern we hire each year. The woman I spoke with claims we were assigned an intern. But she's not sure which one. She thought it was either the girl with the green-stalked hair and no underwear, or the lanky guy in the gold chinos with the greasy, black mop and pencil-thin moustache."

Elliot made a disbelieving face. "Pencil-thin moustache?"

"Apparently it's making a comeback among young, romantic males who have no idea what a woman wants."

"Magistrate Elmo Whitaker has a moustache like that," said Elliot, with a shudder.

"As I recall," she said, "Magistrate Whitaker also wears silk suits, has a silver-capped front tooth, and dangles lots of gold jewelry. He reminds me of a Tijuana pimp."

Elliot grinned. "I'm not so sure he wasn't."

"The University is supposed to call back as to the intern's name and telephone number."

He made a meaningless gesture. "If they give you a choice, Lydia, take the one without underwear. I'm not sure I can cope with being reminded of Magistrate Whitaker every day for an entire summer."

Chapter 2

At 4:15 that afternoon, Private Investigator Jason Taggart slid into one of the Harvard chairs fronting Chambers Elliot's desk. The detective's eyes were sleep-smeared. His face was unshaven. His blond hair was matted. His dark suit a mass of wrinkles.

"You look like death warmed over, Chambers." The detective dug a pack of cigarettes and a Zippo lighter from his rumpled, brown suit.

"I think it's my blood-pressure," Elliot said, as he rummaged through desk-drawers. "I've been sweating like a pig all week. When was the last time you slept, Jason? You've got eyes like a raccoon."

Taggart shrugged, wearily. "This week, I think." He sloughed up a cigarette and caught it between his lips. Then he twisted in the chair to drape a leg casually over one of the arms, before smiling at the lawyer. "Tall, blonde and beautiful mentioned that you may or may not be working for an opium-addicted priest, who may or may not have conned a killer, and who actually may be an actor. Is Lydia hallucinating because of another fad-diet? Or is this for real?"

The lawyer glanced up, his brow furrowed in thought. "We've got a bit of a mystery on our hands."

The P.I. watched Chambers Elliot with small, blue eyes set within a rugged Nordic face. "Meaning Zamoyski is not on the level?"

"That's part of what I want you to determine." Elliot jerked a file folder from his desk, set it down in front of himself and tilted forward in his chair. "Do Private Investigators carry life-insurance?"

The detective gave out a languid laugh. "Is that a rhetorical question? Or should I heed the resulting urge to leave?"

Elliot grinned. "I was just curious." He rested his elbows on the desktop, his eyes level on the detective, and his chin supported in the palms of his cupped hands.

Taggart's smile went bleak. "Sounds like I'm already late for a safe departure. Never mind, Chambers. Hit me with the worst of it."

"Think back thirty years to when you were a cop in Austin-Homicide." The lawyer scratched the back of one hand. "Jerome Petty? Michael Douglas?"

The Zippo in Taggart's hand flicked to life. But the detective he did not bring the dancing yellow flame to the cigarette. His mind raced back through time.

After many seconds Jason Taggart touched fire to tobacco, flicked off the lighter, dropped the Zippo and cigarette-pack back into his pocket, and then slowly exhaled smoke.

"Winston Liquors," the detective said. "What about it?"

Elliot smiled at Taggart—a small dry smile that moved the corners of his mouth slightly but left the rest of his face stoic. "According to Zamoyski, Jerome Petty did not kill Michael Douglas."

"Nonsense." Taggart shifted into an upright, seated position. "Two eye-witnesses of good character fingered him. The case was cut and dried before I had Petty booked."

"Considering only the Jensen's identification, yes." The lawyer impatiently rattled his fingertips on the desktop. "But we both know how unreliable eye-witnesses can be."

"When identifying strangers, mistakes *are* common—particularly if that stranger is of another race. But that wasn't the case in the Douglas killing." The detective brushed cigarette ashes from his trousers. "The Jensens lived in the same neighborhood as Jerome Petty. Both Jensens had known Petty for years and vice versa. Jerome Petty had a lot of misdemeanor history, Chambers. He was also a two-time loser in the felony department. He was guilty."

"What about the Jensens? Anything criminal in their backgrounds?"

Taggart shook his head in silence.

"What about Michael Douglas?" the lawyer asked.

"Nothing. But there was plenty of history between Douglas and Petty, and it was not good. Add that to the fact that one more felony-conviction would've put Petty behind bars for the rest of his life as a habitual criminal, and the motive for killing Douglas is clear." The detective took a long draw on the cigarette. Then he blew a stream of smoke toward the ceiling. "Get to the juicy part," he said, with a sharp grin. "You know. Where I risk life and limb to give your law-firm another batch of money-making headlines."

"Zamoyski claims Mr. and Mrs. Jensen were bribed to identify Jerome Petty as Douglas' killer."

The detective gave a tired head-wag. "Not a chance. That robbery netted a hundred and eight-seven bucks. I admit that inflation has always been a big pain in the ass. But risking an accessory-to-murder-charge came a good deal higher than that, back then."

"Zamoyski also claims the robbery was a ruse." Elliot folded his arms and leaned back in his chair. "He said the real motive for Douglas' murder was revenge—over a woman."

Jason Taggart eyes glistened as he studied the glowing coal on the end of his cigarette. "On that point there may be some validity. Both men considered themselves high-fliers with the fairer sex." He took another drag. "In fact, they were often rumored to be pursuing the same

16

woman—usually one who was married and well-heeled."

Elliot tilted forward with interest, resting his wrists on the edge of the desk. "Any particular woman?"

"Chambers, I'm not likely to remember thirty-year-old gossip." Then Taggart added with cynical laugh, "Let's say some idiot did bribe the Jensens. That first bribe would've become a lifelong blackmail payout. Did your Zamoyski give you the name of anybody with that kind of money to toss around?"

Eliot spoke very quietly, adjusting the lay of his tie. "Zamoyski claims he knows who the killer is, but he would not disclose the name. Further, he told someone—presumably the real killer—that he, Zamoyski, was going to expose the facts of the killing." The lawyer looked over at Taggart questioningly. "Did the Jensens report the shooting?"

Taggart shook his head slightly. "No. It was the night janitor—Billings. I think that was the name. Yeah. Junior Billings. He came to the liquor store to do his usual cleaning and found Douglas on the floor, dead. Billings telephoned the police. I arrived on the scene a few minutes later."

"Then how did the Jensens get involved?" Elliot scratched the end of his chiseled nose.

"It wasn't until the next day," the detective explained with a casual wave of one hand. "They came by the precinct and reported what they'd witnessed. I spoke with them later at their home to confirm their claims. Everything they said to me was consistent with what they'd told the desk sergeant."

"Did the Jensens say why it took them a day to take responsibility?"

The detective shrugged. "The usual—not wanting to get involved and then deciding they had an obligation to the community." Taggart leaned forward and flicked the ash from his cigarette into the ashtray on the desk. "I think it was more likely that Petty threatened to kill them if they talked. That was his style of bullying. It just took the Jensens a day to get their courage up. Chambers, if you suspect Zamoyski is playing you, why bother with this?"

"Because I want to know why I was selected for his game." Chambers Elliot tugged at one ear as he took another trek through his memories. "As I recall, Jerome Petty offered to take a lie-detector test."

The detective thought and then he nodded. "He might've even passed it. Petty was consistent enough in his story. But it wouldn't have changed my opinion. Chambers, he killed Michael Douglas."

"Did Forensics find anything incriminating?"

"They found nitrates on his hands. Petty explained that by claiming he'd been shooting rats at the dump, earlier in the evening." Taggart took a handkerchief from his pocket and blew his nose. "That may have been the case. There was a .32 caliber revolver in the trunk of his car that had been fired very recently."

The lawyer gave him a swift, flickering glance. "I remember that, now. In fact, wasn't Petty stopped a few blocks away from the liquor store?"

"Not more than ten minutes after the call came in about the murder, Petty was given a citation for speeding—which put him in the vicinity." The detective stuffed the cloth back into his pocket. "The gun gave him the means, his ongoing conflict with Douglas gave Petty plenty of motive, and being near the store gave him opportunity."

The lawyer's brows furrowed with confusion. "The gun in his trunk wasn't the murder-weapon?"

"We couldn't be sure," Taggart said.

"You mean the bullet wasn't recovered?"

"It was—some of it, anyway. The round had been cast from a lead-zinc alloy. That made the projectile extremely brittle. It shattered on impact." The detective dragged his hands across his face sleepily. "Some of the pieces lodged in Douglas' brain. Most went out his eyes and got busted to hell and gone on the store's inventory. Consequently, we were unable to prove or disprove it. But as near as we could tell—based upon the weight of the projectile-pieces—Petty's gun was the right caliber."

"Lead Zinc? Is that usual for bullets?"

The detective wagged his head. "It's what some recreational shooters use to cast inexpensive rounds. They take discarded wheel weights from vehicle-tires and melt them down. Those cost about one-tenth that of pure lead. They don't damage the barrel because they're softer than copper. So for plinking they make sense."

Elliot nodded in understanding. "Did Jerome Petty have that type of ammunition?"

"He did, indeed. Further, the metallurgy report on the pieces taken from Douglas matched that of the ammunition recovered from Petty's apartment. Which is another reason we were certain we had the right guy."

Elliot frowned. "I don't remember Jerome Petty saying anything about reloading ammunition."

"He didn't," Taggart said, shrugging his shoulders indifferently. "Petty claimed he got the bullets from Michael Douglas."

The lawyer's eyes widened in surprise. "But you said they were enemies."

"The pair had an off and on friendship. The only time they were at odds was when a woman was involved. They'd known each other since grade school."

"So, Michael Douglas was a shooter as well?"

"Douglas was licensed to carry a concealed handgun. He owned a gun of the same make, model and caliber as Petty. But we never found it. We think he was carrying it at the time of his murder because his shoulder holster was empty. At the time, I assumed that Petty had gotten the drop on Douglas, disarmed him, and then shot Douglas—taking the pistol with. And before you ask, I did verify that the pistol found in Petty's trunk was not the gun owned by Douglas. We also found reloading equipment in Douglas' garage—including wheel-weights that had been cast into bullets of the same caliber as Petty's pistol."

"Did Douglas reload specifically for Petty?"

"I doubt it. He had several hundred rounds of ammunition at his place, in various calibers. I think it was a business sideline where he sold to anybody who had the price to buy."

Elliot considered that carefully. Then he asked, "What do you remember about Junior Billings?"

"He was the handyman-cum janitor at St. Michael's rectory, for most of his working life," the detective replied slowly. "Junior also provided janitorial services to a few of the small businesses in town—including Winston Liquors. He had some criminal history—shoplifting, petty theft—that sort of thing. I don't remember if he actually served time. But when Douglass died, Billings had been clean for over a year."

The lawyer winked. "As far as anyone knew."

"Agreed. Junior Billings was a cagy character." Taggart flicked more ash. Then he said, "I read where he died last week."

"Could Billings have killed Douglas?"

"Look, Chambers, no matter what Zamoyski says all the evidence—be it circumstantial—pointed to Petty. Petty had a long criminal history going back to when he was a kid. And, most importantly, he and Douglas argued the night before the murder—during which Petty threatened to kill Douglas." His breath labored, as he reached over and snuffed out his cigarette in the ashtray. "Even if we ignored the nitrates on his hands, the revolver in his trunk, ammunition in his apartment, the Jensens' identification and his lack of a verifiable alibi, that murder threat alone would've convicted him."

"Maybe. But as I recall, Jerome Petty never denied the argument."

"No point," the detective said with a shrug. "It took place at Winston Liquors and was witnessed by at least half a dozen customers—who came forward with what they'd heard when the news of Petty's arrest hit the airwaves. Jerome Petty killed Michael Douglas—end of story."

"Was that argument over a woman?"

Taggart nodded. "But Jerome Petty refused to name her."

"If my memory serves, there was some question as to whether Billings reported the shooting timely."

Taggart scratched his head impatiently. "We had only Billings' claim as to when he found the body. Back then, time of death was a very broad estimate based upon a lot of variables that weren't very reliable. Regardless, if there had been a delay it wouldn't have changed anything."

"Of course it would have," Elliot returned in a flash. "It would've put Petty elsewhere when Douglas died."

The detective jabbed the air between then. "Or put him right on the scene."

"People don't change. Coming into a store where the owner was dead would have offered Billings an opportunity for theft, which, in turn, would have delayed him from reporting the murder. It may have been he who took the money. For that matter, it may have been he who killed Douglas."

"Chambers, there's no point in trying to change my mind on this thing," the detective said.

"How was the amount of money taken determined?"

"We knew that based upon the sales tally kept by the cash register. Douglas was very methodical. When he opened for the day, he recorded on the cash register the amount he'd put into the till. He did that by entering a value and then pressing a special button on the machine. Thereafter, the cash register tracked each sale made."

"Less than two hundred dollars in the till doesn't sound right for a liquor store."

"Whenever the cash in the till exceeded a thousand, Douglas would dump the money into the floor-safe in the back room less the original seed-money." Taggart's eyes got the dullness of slate, as his impatience grew. "Douglas also placed the printout of the till's tally in the safe— which he did that night. Based upon the date and time on the printout we recovered from the safe, Douglas had done that approximately half an hour before he died."

The lawyer frowned with confusion. "My recollection of the case is that Michael Douglas died on a Friday. Fridays, in the off-sale liquor business, are usually pretty busy."

"Which explains the thousand bucks he put into the safe."

"Yes, Jason," Elliot conceded dubiously. "But a busy night likely means there must have been others who saw what happened."

"If so, they never came forward."

"Was an inventory done?"

"To what end?" The detective breathed audibly between his teeth. "We had no way of knowing what should be on the shelves."

"What about a video camera?"

"There were two security cameras in the store. But the video-tapes were missing."

Elliot's eyes widened and he tilted toward the detective. "I don't recall being told of that when I was assigned Petty's case."

"There was nothing to tell. Back then, it was not uncommon for security cameras to be nothing but show. Companies would hang up equipment, but not turn it on to save a few bucks. For the average gun-toting punk, the sight of a camera was enough to keep them from pulling a robbery." There was a moment of silence. Then Taggart suddenly bolted to his feet shouting, "Shit!"

"What's wrong?" demanded the lawyer, in surprise.

The detective's nostrils quivered and got sharp. "Damn! Damn! Damn!" Taggart exploded. "I might as well blow my frigging brains out!"

The lawyer jerked upright, growing more and more concerned over the detective's agitation. "What in hell is the matter, Jason?"

Taggart waggled a finger at Chambers Elliot. "You were right to ask about my insurance."

The lawyer laughed, finding irresistible humor in the detective's remark. "It took you this long to realize you weren't insured?"

Taggart rolled his eyes in despair. "When I did the original investigation there were a number of statements taken that suggested Old Frank Portello actually owned Winston Liquors. See what I mean? If your priest is right, that Mafia-Don was behind the Douglas' killing." Taggart began to pace. "Which means the Portellos will take offense to my nosing around. Which means, I'm as good as dead unless I pass on this gig. Which means…"

Elliot's brows furrowed, anxiously. "Jason, you're overreacting."

"Overreacting? Have you forgotten the dip-tank?" The detective flung his arms wide.

"There is no vat of acid in some secret warehouse where the Mafia dips its enemies."

The detective thumped his chest. "That's easy for you to say! You've never been on the Portellos' kill-list."

"Have you?"

"No. But I've heard rumors I was close."

Elliot's mouth moved in a sardonic grin. "No way did Old Frank Portello—*Capo de Tutti Capi*—hire Jerome Petty to kill Michael Douglas."

"You're assuming the Jensens were lying when they fingered Petty. Well, I don't think they were." Taggart turned and strode over to the lawyer's desk, tapping the side of his nose as he spoke. "As for Old Frank... Well take it from me, Frank Portello might've had good reason to order the hit on Douglas."

"Why?"

The detective spread his arms. "Like Rita Portello, for why."

"Rita?"

The detective held up a hand and began raising counting fingers to emphasize his words. "Slinky brunette? Beautiful face that hides the world's nastiest disposition? The only woman in the Texas with a toddler who can pick pockets, and play darts with a switchblade? The only woman in the world with more missing former-fiancés than the average black-widow spider? Am I ringing any bells in your head, yet?"

"I know who Rita Portello is," Elliot, blurted. Then his forehead knitted with a puzzled frown. "But she couldn't have been more than ten or twelve, at the time of Douglas' murder."

The detective fanned the air with his hands. "You're missing the point, Chambers."

"You haven't gotten to it."

"Thirty years ago, several of the witnesses I interviewed claimed that Rita Portello had a crush on Michael Douglas. At the time it didn't seem relevant to the killing because she was just a kid."

The lawyer folded his hands and began twiddling his thumbs. "Young girls fall hard, so the saying goes."

"Hard, hell! I spoke to Jerome Petty about it. As far as Petty knew, Douglas would never take a sexual interest in any kid, let alone Rita Portello. But Petty did say that Michael Douglas had been seen with Rita and Dominic Portello frequently over the month before the murder. See what I mean? If Douglas trifled with Rita... Mary Mother of God, Chambers! Whatever that priest paid you, it ain't enough."

Elliot's nod was perfunctory but noncommittal. "I agree that Old Frank would've taken severe action—not excluding murder—if what you suggest is true. But when did you ever hear of Frank Portello leaving a body to be found? His style of murder invariably meant the victim disappeared without a trace."

"But if Rita was molested..." The detective ran his hands through his hair in nervous anxiety. "Look, Chambers, Old Frank may have made an exception in Douglas's case. He may have wanted to send a message to anyone else with designs on Rita. Please let this thing go?"

"If Old Frank wasn't dead I might agree with you about this being risky. But he is dead."

The detective's arms flew wide. "His sons aren't! Salvator and Dominic Portello are not going to want their little sister's name dragged through the dirt; I don't care how long ago Douglas died."

"Stop shaking. It makes the wrinkles in your suit look like crawling snakes."

"I can't. Not with the prospect of riling the local Mafia on my mind." Taggart thumped the desktop with one palm before adding fervently, "Chambers, you know I'm willing to take on any investigation you toss to me. But this is suicide. In case you've forgotten, Dominic is a goddamn lunatic. Salvator isn't much better—although marriage seems to have mellowed him, slightly." Then Taggart tilted closer, shaking a warning finger at Elliot. "As for your client… If Zamoyski threatened that Mafia-family with exposure to a murder charge… Well take it from me, he's as good as dead and there's no reason for the two of us to join Zamoyski at heaven's gate."

Chambers Elliot calmly leaned back in his chair, folding his hands across his chest. "According to Zamoyski, the actual killer did not confess to the crime. Instead it was someone who knew about it. If Frank Portello ordered the hit on Douglas only he and those actually involved in the killing would've known the details. Would Old Frank or any of his men have done anything so foolish as to confess a murder to a priest?"

"Jerome Petty might've."

Elliot wagged his head. "Jerome Petty was a Baptist."

"The Sicilian Brothers?" the detective asked, despairingly. "They're always running to church for one reason, or another."

"They're too young to have been involved. It would've been done by one of the old-line torpedoes." Elliot paused a moment in thought. Then he tilted forward and spread his fingers upon the desk. "Fat Tony Vincennes was Old Frank's lieutenant, in those days."

Taggart went over to his chair and slumped into it, his emotions somewhat placated. "It couldn't have been Fat Tony. I remember seeing him in the hospital the day after Douglas bought it," he muttered, scowling, breathing hard. "Tony'd had surgery because of a perforated ulcer. That's clear in my mind because I had to bring Jerome Petty to the emergency room after he jumped out of his bedroom window and broke a leg."

"Petty resisted arrest?"

"That's how it went in the report," the detective said.

Elliot crinkled his nose for a moment. "I think we can agree the Portellos had nothing to do with this."

The detective shook his head. "I'm still on the fence, Chambers. With Tony in the hospital, Old Frank might've delegated the hit to Joey the Whop Barbagelata. Joey was one of Frank's bodyguards, back then. Not too smart and a religious-freak to-boot. Which fits in with the confession Zamoyski heard."

Chambers Elliot batted the air with both hands in refute. "Joey confess to a killing? Not a chance."

"It could've been him," Taggart protested. "If it was, our troubles are only beginning. Chambers, Joey may be retired but he's still alive. That means my digging might hook him to the Douglas' hit. And if that happens…"

"Just how wide is that yellow streak running up your back, Jason?" the lawyer snapped.

The detective leaped out of the chair fuming. "Now just a minute, Chambers…." His voice had taken on the metallic twang of a thin wire in a high wind.

Elliot stood up waving one hand. "I didn't meant it, Jason."

"Like hell you didn't." Then the detective faltered, "Look, Chambers, accept my advice—for once. Pretend Zamoyski never existed."

Chambers Elliot shook his head. "I can't. I've accepted his retainer."

"For God's sake, Chambers, you weren't fully informed on the details when you made that acceptance."

"I'm going to see this through—whether you help me, or not."

Taggart started toward the office door. "Then get yourself another investigator."

"No hard feelings, Jason?" Elliot called to his back.

"No." The detective abruptly stopped, turned and gave the attorney an apologetic look. "All right. What exactly do you want me to do—and may my death be on your head."

Elliot smiled appreciatively. "I need to know the histories of Father Zamoyski, Michael Douglas and Jerome Petty. There must be a link between them. After that, we'll reassess the situation."

"By reassessing you mean planning my funeral because I've turned up dead?"

"Nonsense, Jason. Salvator Portello follows in his father's footsteps, faithfully. You're body would never turn up." Then with a chuckle, Chambers Elliot raised his right hand, rising to offer Taggart the palm. "On my honor you will not have anything to do with the Portello Crime-

Family."

"I'm in either way," muttered Taggart, as he went back to his chair. "God help me." Then, Jason Taggart gave his tired eyes a roll. "The only time I was ever shot happened after I ate a prune Danish."

"What has that to do with anything?" Elliot gave the detective a bewildered look.

"That's what I had for breakfast, this morning—the first in over twenty-eight years," the detective explained, unhappily. "Christ, it's probably an omen."

"I never realized you were superstitious."

"It comes from being friends with you."

"Zamoyski said he was staying at St. Michael's Rectory," the Lawyer said. "He has a brother by the name of Daniel. Start with him. There cannot be that many Daniel Zamoyskis in town. That's where you should start. He does business with a bank…" Elliot suddenly stopped, turned and drew aside the painting over the safe. "Wait. I'll get you the bank's name and address. That'll save you some time." He opened the safe with a spin of the dial and looked inside.

"Gone!" Chambers Elliot cried out, in shock.

"What's gone?" Taggart got to his feet.

Elliot turned back to the desk and pushed the buzzer on the intercom. A few moments later Lydia hurried in.

"Your five o'clock showed up early," she said, with an allergic sneeze. "She brought one of the cats along, again. How much longer will you and Jason be? Maggie's eyes are starting to close and I can barely breathe."

"Cat?" Taggart asked in confusion.

Elliot's eyes flicked with pity as he noticed Lydia's red nostrils and watering eyes. "Mrs. Hanson has an *Inter Vivos* Pet Trust, Jason," he explained. "I'm afraid each visit gets the better of Lydia and Maggie, due to cat-allergies."

"A trust that changes with the wind I might add," said Lydia, with a cough. "Mrs. Hanson gets clawed or bitten or suffers some other slight by one of her cats and the next day she arrives, wanting the trust changed to exclude the fuzzy transgressor. A week later she relents and wants the offending animal added back in. Then another cat falls out of favor and she's back here once more. It's a round-robin, some months. Today she requested that I become the Alternate Caregiver to her fur-shedding beasts. Me, with my allergies? I don't think so. My luck she'd drop dead on the way home and I'd be stuck with her damn cats for the next ten years."

"Mrs. Maratha Hanson?" the detective asked. "The old girl who's worth billions?"

Lydia gave a nodding sneeze.

"How much does an Alternate Caregiver get paid?" asked Taggart, with sudden greed.

"Nothing," said Elliot. "It's the Remainder Beneficiary who ends up with anything left-over after the animals die. That, by the way, is me —God bless the old girl." Then he said, "Lydia, did you take the bankers envelope from the safe?"

She wagged her head, after letting go a horrific string of sneezes. "I was planning to make the bank-deposit on my way home, this evening."

"Was anyone here during lunch?" pressed Elliot.

"Nope," she replied, with another cough. "I locked up when Maggie and I went out."

"I thought you were on some special diet?" remarked Taggart. "You know, eat greens and stay thin without going bald?"

"I am," she assented. "But Maggie and I won a free meal at the diner, across the street. We had to use the gift certificates, today or lose out. Waste not, want not."

Taggart stifled a small chuckle. "You've been had, Chambers. What else was in that safe?"

Elliot turned and rummaged through the steel-walled hole, glancing at piles of papers and computer disks. Then he faced Taggart. "Nothing else appears to be missing."

"Let me rephrase the question, counselor," said Taggart, his smile widening slightly. "What was in there you would not want someone else to see?"

"DVD's containing our tax records for the past five years," Lydia declared.

Chamber Elliot shook his head. "Those wouldn't be of interest to anyone."

"The Pierce documents might," she said. "George Pierce wanted his will changed to add Sheila Clifford, as his granddaughter."

"You mean George Pierce finally verified that Sheila Clifford was his granddaughter?" Taggart scoffed. "That must've put Sydney Pierce, the ne'er-do-well son, into a tailspin."

"I don't know about her lineage," Lydia stated. "But Mr. Pierce insisted upon adding Sheila to his Will with the proviso that she could not inherit until she was confirmed as a member of his family."

"But how in hell did the thief get into the safe without blowing it open?"

The pause that followed was perceptible. At length, the lawyer gave out an embarrassed groan. "It was Zamoyski. The bastard had me open the safe so he could get the damn combination! Then he got Lydia and Maggie out of the way with a free lunch, and came back for a casual rummage. The bastard took the envelope to keep the checks, probably figuring I would not suspect him."

"Are you certain it was your priest?" Taggart asked.

"The checks are of no value to anyone else," Elliot said. "Only he could get them refunded."

Lydia made a disappointed face. "We could've used that money."

"You shouldn't have let him stand right beside you, when you opened the safe," Taggart chided.

"I didn't," protested the lawyer. "Zamoyski was standing about where you are."

"How in the world could he see the numbers on the dial from that far away?" Lydia asked.

The detective thumbed his lower lip in thought for a moment before saying, "With the right type of eyewear, he could've."

"He wasn't wearing glasses," she said.

"Zamoyski put them on in here," Chambers Elliot said, ruefully. "He took them off as he left. The lenses looked like the bottoms of glass ashtrays."

"Telescopic specs," Taggart remarked. "Well, considering that you've been robbed by the bastard, I say we forget this whole investigative gig."

"Find Zamoyski, Jason. And not too gently bring him to me."

"He said he was staying at St. Michaels Rectory," chimed Lydia. "Near the capitol building, in Austin."

Taggart nodded and puffed. "Six, two and even they've never heard of Zamoyski."

Elliot nodded, grimly. "Nevertheless, I have questions for the venerable Father. I don't care if I have to take a lesson from Salvator Portello to get the answers I want, and dip that phony Priest in acid! Lydia, you'd better telephone George Pierce. Tell him our safe was burgled and that the terms of his Will and other privileged information he provided may have been compromised."

"What I don't understand is why Zamoyski gave out that song and dance concerning the Winston Liquor Store killing," the detective mused. "Why not simply ask you to be executor of his estate?"

"Exactly, Chambers," Lydia agreed. "You would have put the envelope in the safe, as he requested. So he'd still have gotten the combination."

"He probably…," Elliot began pensively.

"Sweet Jesus!" Jason Taggart interjected. "He's pulled something on the Portellos by posing as Father Zamoyski, and they're hot on his heels. By showing up here, he's forced the Portellos into a stall. They'll grab you to find out what you were told before killing you and the real Zamoyski. While your phony client—whoever he really is—leaves town safe from future pursuit because the Portellos will think he's dead."

"You mean there actually is a Father Zamoyski?" Lydia gaped.

"Bank on it," Taggart declared.

"I'll call the Rectory and warn them." Lydia hurried from the office.

The detective looked over at Chambers and arched his eyebrows in question. "From the look on your face you don't buy my theory."

"You have Portellos on your brain, Jason," Chambers Elliot scolded. "Anything Zamoyski might've disclosed about the Portellos to me is privileged information. I cannot reveal it to anyone without my client's permission."

"You know that. And I know that," said the detective, tapping his own chest. "But does Salvator Portello know that?"

"Of course he does. He's a member of the Bar." The lawyer's lips pressed together tightly. "It's more likely this whole thing revolves around George Pierce and Sheila Clifford. Find her, Jason. I want a little chat with the alleged granddaughter of George Pierce."

"To what end? A DNA test would tell the tale on Sheila Clifford, not the information George Pierce gave you." The detective clucked his tongue, thoughtfully. "Why go to all this trouble just to get a look at the Will?"

"There are a hundred million reasons – all in cash and securities." Then Chambers Elliot made a face. "No. There has to be more to it. Otherwise, there'd have been no reason to go into detail about the Michael Douglas murder."

"The song and dance concerning Winston Liquors was to make sure you'd agree to do as he wanted—namely, open the safe." The detective rubbed his chin thoughtfully.

"If so, why choose that particular murder? Why not something more recent? Something where he would be assured that I would take on the task, instead of a thirty-year-old killing? No. Zamoyski selected Michael Douglas for a reason. That means it must fit with George Pierce. But how?"

Taggart shook his head. "When I investigated the Douglas killing, George Pierce's name was never mentioned."

Elliot began to pace. "What do we know about Sheila Clifford? Has she the brains to orchestrate something like this?"

"Not according to what's been rumored," the detective replied dryly.

"She's been busted for soliciting and shop-lifting."

"But her cut of the Pierce estate would be enough to get the best brains in the crime-business involved."

"Enough to fix a DNA comparison, and then kill George Pierce so she could inherit? I'd agree with that. But I'm still telling you…"

Elliot suddenly held up a hand to silence the private detective. "Why did he take the checks? Why not leave them?"

"Because when they bounced you'd have realized you'd been taken."

"And I would not be concerned by the checks' disappearance? No, Jason. The checks were taken to get us chasing him. ."

Lydia hurried back into Elliot's office. "There is no Father Zamoyski at the rectory," she announced.

"Then who in hell is Zamoyski?" demanded Taggart.

"But get this…" Lydia continued. "There *was* a priest by that name at the rectory about thirty years ago. He was of Russian descent. But he had family in Poland. That's where he is now—assuming he's still alive."

Elliot said, "Get all you can on the real Zamoyski, Jason. In particular, the names and addresses of any family or friends he may have in this country. The pastor at the rectory should be able to provide that. I'm thinking our Zamoyski is relative of the real one. Otherwise, why choose that particular name?"

"I'm on it." Taggart hurried out.

Chambers Elliot returned his attention to Lydia Marshall. "I want you to place advertisements in every paper in the tri-county area. Headline in bold capitals: *WHO KILLED MICHAEL DOUGLAS?* Then request that anyone having relevant information, contact our office. Offer a reward but don't mention an amount. Make sure the ad is big enough to catch greedy eyes."

"Do you want me to mention when the murder took place?"

He shook his head. "If there were witnesses, they'll remember. Not disclosing the date will give us a way to weed out the crank calls."

"What about your five o'clock appointment, Chambers?" Lydia asked. "Maggie and I can't take much more of that cat."

"Give me ten minutes, Lydia," said Elliot. "Then send Mrs. Hanson in. Why that woman keeps disinheriting one cat or another, is beyond me."

"She's filthy rich, eccentric and can afford your fees."

The lawyer rubbed his hands together and grinned. "Sounds like I should raise my rates."

"After I place that advert in the papers, you'll have to. It's going to cost a fortune."

"Any news on our summer intern?"

"I'm still waiting for the university to give me the details."

Chapter 3

The next morning, when Chambers Elliot arrived at his offices, Lydia Marshall greeted him by offering the telephone. "Taggart's on the line. He says we've got big trouble but won't say what."

Elliot pressed the handset to his ear. "What's the problem, Jason?"

"Chambers," said Jason Taggart from the other end of the connection, "I'm at the Double Oak Hotel. You'd better get over here, right away. Your phony Father Zamoyski is dead. It looks like he was tossed off the hotel's roof."

"Are you certain it was a homicide?"

"Absolutely."

"Who's in charge of the investigation?" Elliot asked.

"Lt. Herbie Mann," the detective said. "But don't expect any favors. His wife's got him on another diet and Herbie's a real bear."

"I'm on my way." Elliot rang off and glanced at his watch. "Lydia, reschedule today's appointments for tomorrow or thereafter."

"What's happened?" she asked.

"Zamoyski—our erstwhile client—murdered."

"Zamoyski," Lydia echoed, her face going dead-white.

The lawyer reached out and grabbed her shoulders as she started to teeter. "Don't faint on me."

"I'm all right," she said, her color returning. "We've never had a client murdered, before."

"You'd better break the news to Maggie. I don't think I could—considering her delicate emotional temperament."

Lydia gave her boss a worried look. "Chambers, if the Portellos are behind Zamoyski's killing… That means you could be next. Or me. Or Maggie. They must know Zamoyski came to see us."

Elliot gave her a fatherly smile. "You're letting Jason's wild assumptions take control of sound logic. I'm certain the Portellos had nothing to do with this. Regardless, you know I'd never let anything happen to you or Maggie."

She nodded. "It's just that with the other problem, this morning…."

His brows arched in surprise. "Other problem?"

Lydia wrinkled her nose. "Our summer intern arrived."

"Why is that a problem?"

She made a face as if seeing something utterly revolting. "It's Mr. Pencil-thin moustache."

"Surely, things could be worse?" the lawyer chuckled.

Her head shook. "He's got greased-back hair, a diamond-stud earring in his left lobe, one gold-capped canine, and prefers a heavy dousing of bay-rum as an accessory to his peach-colored Zoot-Suit."

"Did you say, Zoot-Suit?" he frowned, certain he'd misunderstood.

Lydia nodded. "Fedora, padded shoulders, two-foot watch-chain, brown and white wingtips: the whole nine yards."

Elliot gave her a crooked grin. "I admit he doesn't sound like the other interns we've hired. But I think we can overlook the man's appearance for a few months."

She crossed her arms. "What if I told you our intern's name is Ramón Whitaker?"

"Dear God!" the lawyer whimpered, both hands clamping over his eyes as if he had been blinded. "Not, Magistrate Elmo Whitaker's idiot son?"

She nodded grimly. "The same."

The lawyer's hands dropped. Then he staggered over to one of the customer-chairs, and slumped down. Chambers Elliot shook his head as if trying to blot out a dreadful image emblazoned upon his brain.

"So far Ramón hasn't torn off his clothes in the name of peace, if that helps," she declared.

"Not much," he muttered, staring blankly at the floor. "I keep having this horrible flashback about a hairball wearing nothing but running shoes, bursting into my office and spouting antiwar propaganda."

Then Elliot jumped up. "Well, what does he have to say for himself? Was Ramón sick? Was he arrested for indecent exposure, again? Does he have any explanation for not being here six days ago?"

Lydia made a diffident gesture. "Apparently Ramón's love-life got in the way of his desire for legal experience."

Elliot blinked at her for several seconds. "You don't mean some poor, desperate woman actually married that twit?"

"Close." She crossed her arms. "Ramón belongs to a dating service. It requires that he meet at least four prospective compatibles, each month. His latest encounter, or so Ramón intimated, was very aggressive."

The lawyer tilted toward Lydia in confusion. "What has that to do with him not showing up at the agreed-upon date?"

"He claims she kept him forcibly chained to her bed and busy—for nearly three days, and nights."

More blinking. "Did Ramón notify the police about this illegal and probably deranged detention?"

"I asked Ramón about that," she said. "Not only did he not report the incident, but Ramón went all dreamy-voiced as he announced his plans to send her roses for the rest of his days."

Elliot gritted his teeth before asking, "Did our less than contrite Casanova explain the other three days of absence?"

"Ramón was recuperating from exhaustion and chafed body-parts." Her face took on the revolted expression again. "I thought I'd let you gather any necessary details."

The lawyer shuddered with disgust. "Don't even suggest it."

She jabbed a thumb over one shoulder. "Shall I tell our Lothario we no longer need an intern?"

Chambers Elliot dragged one hand across the back of his neck as if it ached. "Being Magistrate Elmo Whitaker's son removes that option, Lydia. I'm afraid we're stuck with Mr. Pencil-thin-moustache for the entire summer."

"What shall I do with Ramón?" She indicated the reception chairs with a sweep of one hand. "I can't let him deal with customers, looking as he does. They'll think we're running a brothel."

"For starters, put him to work in the law library researching all rulings related to the 2005 Texas Marriage Amendment. I'll need that for the Shelton adoption when I go before his father, next Friday." Then the lawyer gave a heartsick shake of his head. "I don't suppose that highly disturbed woman left Ramón feeling suicidal? It's a common occurrence after being sexually degraded."

"Not a chance, Chambers." She reached down and tapped the top of the desk. "Two minutes after arriving, Ramón was making moves on Maggie."

"Why that disgusting animal!" His arms flung wide. "Has he no business acumen?"

"It gets worse."

Elliot's eyes bugged. "Dear God, he assaulted her?"

Lydia shook her head. "Worse than that."

His hand clutched at his chest. "Sweet Jesus! Ramón killed our little Maggie?"

"Worse. Maggie thinks Ramón is God's gift to women." She tilted her chin toward the office entrance. "I had to send her on a cooling-off errand for donuts, after locking him in my office. That woman was panting after Ramón like a bitch in heat."

"Our Maggie—the fearless virgin—has the hots for Ramón Whitaker?"

Her eyes rolled. "Chambers! You and Taggart have to stop calling her that."

His hands went into a flurry of apologetic movements. "I wasn't being derogatory about Maggie's innocence. It's just that I can't picture someone as sweet as her having sexual inclinations for someone with family-ties to Magistrate Elmo Whitaker." He gave Lydia a beseeching look. "Couldn't you have forced Maggie to put on her glasses?"

"She did put them on—to get a closer look at all that is weird-and-wonderful, from Zoot-Suit central." Her hands went akimbo at her hips. "I'm telling you, Chambers, as disgusting as Ramón is, Maggie's got his number and loves every digit."

"I can't deal with him, now. I have to get to the Double Oak hotel. But I'll be back as quickly as I can. At which time, I will sit down with Ramón Whitaker and set him straight about his duties and impulses with respect to this office, and its personnel. In the meantime, keep Maggie busy and him away from her."

"I received a telephone call from Richard Gerber of the Gerber Beauty School. He claims the Texas Attorney General sued him over a leak of student information."

"How was the information stolen?"

"It wasn't. Gerber abandoned his leasehold on a location, leaving the student's files behind."

"Which is why he is in trouble," said Elliot, with a grimace. "Under Texas statues 35.48(d) and 48.102 companies must adopt reasonable procedures to protect and safeguard sensitive information. These procedures must include some way to make personal information, unreadable."

"Like shredding the stuff?"

He smiled. "Exactly. Is Gerber still on the line?"

"I said I'd talk to you and get back to him."

"Tell Gerber he can be fined up to $50,000 for each violation. Further, that abandoning those files is akin to a confession of guilt."

Her eyebrows arched. "Are we interested in the case?"

"Not if he put a gun to my head," proclaimed Elliot. "Gerber's better served to admit his culpability and claim extenuating circumstances. He'll likely be fined a few thousand and given a slap on the wrist."

"In his case, those extenuating circumstance would be stupidity?"

Chambers Elliot went over to the door, grabbed the knob and jerked it open. "That would be my interpretation." Then he looked back at Lydia. "This office is four floors up."

"It has been for at least as long as the building's been here. Are you having another flashback, Chambers?"

"If Ramón should develop suicidal symptoms put him in my office—and open the window."

* * * *

The drive to the Double Oak Hotel took nearly an hour. When Chambers Elliot arrived, the police had cordoned off an area along the front of the building. In the morning sunlight, the yellow police-barrier appeared bleached-white. It was nearly as lifeless-looking in the rising heat, as the corpse lying on the asphalt several yards beyond.

Elliot hurried from his 1938 silver Lagonda into the hotel to find Jason Taggart waiting in the lobby.

"Lt. Mann is as closed-mouth as ever," confided Taggart, as Elliot came over to him. "Well, as closed as one gets gnawing on a carrot. But one of the uniforms claimed there are marks on the dead man's wrists." He glanced around as if worried he might be overheard. "These indicate that your Zamoyski had been tied up for a period of time just before he died. That is how I know it was a homicide."

"How did you hear about this?" asked Elliot.

"On the police-band radio in my car," explained Taggart. "When I heard a priest had been murdered I followed a hunch, and came here. Zamoyski's room is on the third floor." The detective gave his head a dismal wag. "It didn't take the Portellos long to move on him."

"What did you learn at St. Michael's Rectory?"

Taggart tugged one of his earlobes. "I spent several hours there after leaving you, yesterday, talking to everyone. As Lydia told us, the real Father Zamoyski had been there thirty years ago. Why he went to Poland —nobody could recall. I got a phone number from the rectory's pastor and telephoned Zamoyski. As expected, he denied knowing you."

"Does the real Zamoyski have a brother in Austin?"

The detective wagged his head. "No brother—Daniel, or otherwise. No relatives in this country, at all."

"Did you explain the situation to Zamoyski?"

"As subtly as I could," Taggart acknowledged. "But, when I mentioned the possibly of him having been told about Michael Douglas' murder in the confessional, Father Zamoyski abruptly ended our conversation."

Elliot's eyes widened. "Then a murder-confession actually did occur."

"That's my assumption—which does not make me feel any easier about this whole thing." The detective pulled Elliot to one side of the room so he they would not be eavesdrop on before saying, "I've been giving this a rethink, Chambers. I agree with you that Old Frank Portello wasn't behind Douglas's killing. But I am convinced his sons were."

"It won't wash, Jason. Not if the information about the Jensens is true."

The detective scowled at Elliot, fished in his pocket for a pack of cigarettes, sloughed one up and stuffed it between his lips. "Just hear me out, okay? If either Dominic or Salvator discovered that Douglas was messing about with little-sister Rita, I don't think they'd tell Old Frank." Taggart returned the cigarette-pack to his suit and dragged out his Zippo. "I think they would've taken it upon themselves to mete out revenge, rather than shame their sister. Rita was the apple of Old Frank's eyes."

The lawyer shook his head. "If they killed Michael Douglas on the Q-T to keep their father from finding out about what had been going on, they wouldn't have left his body. They'd have made it appear that Douglas ran off. Otherwise, Old Frank might've had his people dig into matter—which, I'm certain, he did. No. Michael Douglas was killed by someone outside the Portello camp."

"What about this?" persisted Taggart. "What if the Jensen's saw the Portello brothers kill Douglas? They might've been foolish enough to finger Jerome Petty, for a financial consideration from Old Frank." He lit the cigarette and returned the lighter to its keep. "It would certainly explain that accident they had while vacationing in Samoa."

"I don't buy it, Jason. I think whoever killed Michael Douglas also killed the phony Zamoyski."

"Which is as good a reason as any to back away from this." The detective indicated the front of the hotel with a tilt of his head. "Your client's dead. Therefore, you have no obligation to continue on his behalf."

"Whoever killed the phony Zamoyski may assume he told me who killed Michael Douglas. He'll assume I divulged that to Lydia and Maggie. That means he's not done with his killing. I can't leave them at risk."

"Then let's tell Herbie. Let him deal with it."

Elliot glanced around then said in a low voice, "Tell him what? We don't even know our Zamoyski's real name, let alone why he got me involved. Everything we've discussed so far is purely speculative."

"Chambers…"

The lawyer jabbed a thumb toward the front exits. "Did you get a look at the body?"

Taggart nodded, took a deep drag on the cigarette and blew smoke to the ceiling. "Pasty-faced and hollow-eyed, exactly how you described your client. At least what was left of him." He made a disgusted face. "The poor guy landed head-on."

The lawyer swallowed thickly. "Do you have a contact in Forensics who would be willing to inform us if Zamoyski's fingerprints are on file?"

An elderly woman wearing a green hat hobbled over to Taggart and banged his shin with her cane. "You're not allowed to smoke in here!"

He dropped the cigarette to the floor and crushed it under his heel. She snorted contemptuously, and hobbled away.

"I hate old women," Taggart grumbled.

"Never mind that," said Elliot. "What about the fingerprints?"

The detective shrugged. "I've got a contact, yes. But I also got a look at the dead man's palms and fingers. They're nothing but old, rippled scar-tissue. If those injuries occurred after the last time he was fingerprinted, Forensics won't find a match."

"Self inflicted burns to conceal his true identity, if arrested?" asked Elliot.

"Not from what I saw."

"That would explain why our Zamoyski wore gloves," the lawyer reflected. "I thought it odd at the time, considering the warm weather. But if his hands were badly scarred he might have wanted to conceal them. Does Herbie know the dead man was my client?"

"Not yet," said Taggart. "I thought I'd leave that little declaration to you."

"Have you located Sheila Clifford yet?"

Taggart shook his head. "I've got Popovitch on it. He met with the landlady at Sheila's last-known address. The old girl mentioned that Sheila Clifford had recently taken up with a man and woman—both a number of years older."

"Friendship? Romance?"

"The landlady wasn't sure."

"Did Popovitch get the names of this couple?"

"No. But from the general description of the man, your Zamoyski could've been him."

Chambers Elliot tugged at an earlobe, thoughtfully. "Did you notice any makeup on the dead man's face?"

The splayed his hands. "Look, Chambers, if Sheila Clifford was involved with the phony Zamoyski, that pretty much confirms George Pierce as their target. So if the Portellos didn't kill Zamoyski…"

"George kill Zamoyski to stop whatever feeble attempts were being made to get Sheila into George's Will?" Elliot scoffed. "I hardly think so."

"George is known for his short temper."

"Temper flare-ups, I agree with. But George isn't killer material. He's too smart to pull something like that."

Taggart raised eyebrows so high it looked like his entire face was working to keep them arched. "What about Sydney Pierce? I wouldn't put murder past George's ne're-do-well. If Sheila is a Pierce, that means Sydney will be losing half of his father's estate when George dies. For lots of folks, fifty million is worth killing in order to hang onto it."

"But why kill Zamoyski? Why not Sheila Clifford?"

"Maybe she was there and got away." The detective lowered his eyebrows and tugged at one of the long hairs that grew out of his nose. "Or maybe he killed her and got rid of her body."

"Sydney Pierce doesn't have the guts for a cold blooded killing, Jason."

"I don't agree," Taggart said, wagging a warning finger. "Where that much money is involved, anything's possible."

The lawyer fumbled with his lower lip. "Can we take a peek at the Zamoyski's room?"

Taggart took a key-card from his pocket. "It cost me a c-note."

The lawyer nodded agreeably, still thinking.

"One more thing…" the detective said. "Your dead client had a visitor last night. Something brunette, tall and very slinky. She was such a hot number the clerk followed her out and caught the plate-number on her new Corvette. 'XVB859'. That, also, cost me a c-note."

"And?"

"I had the plate run. The car is registered to a Kathy Martin, of Leander. Her address is 3456 Chilton Street. I sent Von Drake over there to keep an eye on the place."

"Right now you're billing me for two operatives?" asked Elliot, one eyebrow rising slightly. "Popovitch and Von Drake?"

Jason Taggart grinned. "Three. Don't forget yours-truly—which is another good reason for you to walk away from this thing."

Chambers Elliot said flatly, "If these costs keep rising, Jason, I might have trouble paying your bill."

"Don't worry, Chambers," Taggart said, pointing to the elevators. "I'll hire a *good* attorney to sue you."

Elliot followed the detective over to an elevator. Taggart jabbed the call-button and glanced around to see if they were being observed.

After a moment, the car-door opened and the two men quickly stepped inside. Jason Taggart pushed the button for the third floor. Then the elevator shot up, ticking off red floor-numbers in a liquid-crystal display. At three, the car stopped and the doors opened.

"Herbie isn't going to like not knowing that corpse was your client, Chambers. He's seen me." The detective's chin came out until his jaw muscles rippled like worms. "Which means, he'll know I kept that from him."

"Stop worrying," scolded the lawyer. "I'll give Herbie a call. For the time being, I don't want him to know I'm here. You know how suspicious he gets."

"With you involved, I don't blame him."

Taggart led and Elliot followed down a wallpapered corridor, to room 302. A yellow crime-scene tape was tacked up across the doorway.

Taggart slipped the key card into the lock, pushed the door open and then the two men crept under the tape.

The suite looked like a pair of elephants had tussled in it. A chair was overturned. The glass globe for the floor lamp was smashed into a myriad of frosty, shards. These twinkled up from the green carpet like diamonds on grass. The bedcovering was rumpled. Several stains added a rusty hue to its green fabric.

"Looks like dried blood," remarked Taggart.

"My stomach and I are trying not to notice, Jason."

The two men split up, searching the suite.

Chambers Elliot went over to the closet and opened the door. "There's no suitcase," he announced. "No change of clothing. Nothing."

Taggart came out of the bathroom dusting his fingers together. "No shaving gear, either. None of the towels have been used."

"So our phony Zamoyski arrived here without luggage," mused the lawyer, scratching the end of his chin. "Which means this was a meeting-place. Possibly for a blackmail payoff? In any event, he lives somewhere else. Perhaps in Leander?"

The detective nodded agreement. "Which means there's a good chance Kathy Martin is also dead."

"Then we'd better get over there," the lawyer said.

"As long as we're here, let me check one more thing."

Taggart strode over to the desk and pulled out each drawer; examining its interior, and the alcove from which it came. Then he got down on all fours and crawled beneath the desk to look at the side facing the wall.

"Eureka!" the detective cried after a few seconds.

Elliot hurried over to the desk. "What did you find?"

A moment later Jason Taggart crawled out from beneath the furnishing, holding up a spindle of paper. "There was a hole between the desk and one of the legs. Just the tip of this was sticking out. You'll never guess what they are."

Elliot unrolled the spindle. "The missing checks. I guess that proves Zamoyski was the one who rifled my safe."

A cunning light came on in Taggart's eyes. "And you can bet he's passed-on whatever he saw to Sheila Clifford."

"After which she and Kathy Martin of Leander killed him?" snorted Elliot.

The detective spread his arms. "You keep refusing to believe the Portellos are involved. So why not? A two-way split beats a three-way, hands down."

Jason Taggart glanced around as if expecting the room to collapse upon them. "If I was shaking somebody down, I sure as hell wouldn't pick a quiet, out-of-the-way hotel room to collect the payoff. Would you?"

Elliot shook his head, stuffed the checks into his pocket and then headed for the hotel-room door. "I'd want some place very public, preferably with a police presence."

Out in the hallway the lawyer asked, "Do you still have a good contact in the coroner's office?"

"Good or not, it'll cost you."

"I want a copy of Zamoyski's autopsy."

Taggart shrugged heavily. "I'll see what I can do."

The lawyer started toward the elevators, but abruptly stopped. "Was the dead man wearing a hearing aid?"

Taggart nodded. "The old fashioned kind with a wire. Your car or mine, to Leander?"

"Yours," said Elliot. "Jason, we need to know if the Jensens' deaths in Samoa were actually accidental."

"After thirty years who's to say?" Taggart said, pointedly.

"There must be someone alive who was involved in that investigation."

"Chambers, time does not stop just because you want it to. If there are survivors of that era, they've long forgotten about the Jensens."

"Give it a try, anyway." Then Elliot added slowly, "I have the nagging feeling I'm being led down the garden path."

On their way out, Taggart and Elliot passed Lt. Herbie Mann entering the hotel. The bulky police investigator paused to look after them, suspiciously. Then, he continued his trek toward the elevators.

"So much for Herbie Mann not knowing about you being here," remarked Taggart, as they crawled into his old Chrysler.

Elliot grinned. "We'll claim we met here for brunch."

The detective rolled his eyes. "Herbie will believe that like he'll believe I'm a priest."

"Things could be worse, Jason."

"Not much," Taggart said as he started the car.

"You could have Ramón Whitaker working for you."

"Nobody in his right mind would hire that…" The detective looked over at Elliot in horror. "You mean he's this summer's intern?"

"Just drive, Jason."

"You have my deepest condolences, Chambers."

Chapter 4

Ninety minutes later, Jason Taggart pulled his car to the curb on Chilton Street in Leander, half a block down from number 3456—a small, blue, frame house with a single-car garage beside it. They were parked directly behind a plumber's van.

"Not much of a living-space for a woman driving such an expensive car," remarked Chambers Elliot, as he studied the house. "It needs shingles and paint."

"The cost of the car probably precludes her from renting a nicer place," reflected the detective. "That's why I hang onto my Chrysler."

Elliot rolled his eyes. "You hang onto it because it's paid-for and you're cheap."

"I am not cheap," protested Taggart, giving the lawyer a hurt look. "I just know the value of a dollar."

"Cheap."

The detective's eyes narrowed. "What about that nineteen-thirty-something you drive?"

"That Lagonda is a collector's item."

"Collection of rusty bolts you mean," Taggart snorted.

The lawyer tapped the forefinger of one hand into the pal of the other for emphasis as he said, "It cost me nearly two hundred thousand."

The detective gaped. "That rolling deathtrap doesn't even have air conditioning."

A tall, lanky man dressed in jeans and plaid shirt climbed out of the van and strolled back to Taggart's car. Jason Taggart and Chambers Elliot got out to talk with him.

Jason Taggart introduced the man to Elliot as David Von Drake. Von Drake was of medium height and build with rusty hair and a round, boyish, freckled face.

"I've heard a lot about you, Mr. Elliot," Von Drake said in greeting. Then he indicated the old house with a jut of his dimpled chin. "Kathy Martin lives in the blue house. Her Corvette's in the garage. I talked to the neighbors. Kathy rents the place. Been there about three months. Lives with a guy named Milton and another woman—no name for her. Kathy Martin is a brunette. The other woman is blonde. The blonde is about twenty. Kathy is thirty-something. The man is about forty-five or fifty. Milton is described as being of medium height, and with a very pale-face. The neighbors haven't heard a last name, for him. Both the blonde and Milton left for parts unknown last night and have not been seen since."

"Sheila Clifford's blonde and about twenty," remarked Taggart. Then with a decisive nod he added, "Milton must've been Zamoyski."

"The three of them have lived there the entire three months?" asked Elliot.

Von Drake's head wagged. "Kathy Martin and Milton—yes. The blonde is a recent addition, been there just a few weeks. According to the neighbors, those three don't keep regular hours. Nobody knows how they earn their money. Quiet people. No parties. Keep to themselves. The blonde, however, dresses like the party-type."

"I'm surprised two women and a man living together doesn't raise eyebrows," Elliot remarked, glancing around at the older, low-income houses.

"According to the neighbors, there's nothing going on between Kathy and Milton. They don't argue. But they don't hold hands, either. There are two bedrooms in the house. So the sleeping accommodations are adequate for a platonic arrangement. However everyone I spoke with implied there may be action between Milton, and the blonde. Those two are frequently seen playing slap-and-tickle."

"I'm surprised he has interest—considering how ill he appeared to be." Then Chambers Elliot mused, "Making Kathy Martin a likely suspect for having shoved Milton off that Hotel roof."

Taggart said, "Hang loose, David. When Kathy comes out like I'm expecting, tail her. We're going in for a chat. Oh, you'd better let Popovitch know that you may have located Sheila Clifford. Have him come by ASAP. I want him to touch base with the neighbors showing them Sheila's photo to get verification."

The operative nodded and hurried back to the van.

Taggart noticed Chambers Elliot checking out the vehicle. "In Texas the most common repair-truck on the road is from a plumbing shop. This country's worst plumbers congregate, in Texas. So, somebody always needs repair-work because of previous repairs."

Elliot grinned in agreement. "I can relate to that."

The two men headed across the street to the tiny house. Elliot rang the doorbell.

"How are we going to play this?" asked Taggart.

The lawyer glanced around to see if they were being observed. "Just follow my lead."

Taggart gave his head a dismal wag. "That usually means a strong potential for being arrested."

"You worry too much, Jason."

The detective nodded. "After years of you, I've got damn good reason."

There were footsteps from within. Then the door opened a crack and a brunette with green eyes peaked out. Elliot pushed the toe of his shoe between door and the jamb. The woman gave out a frightened squeal and tried to slam the door. Taggart put his weight against it, forcing the door open, and her into retreat.

Elliot followed the detective inside, and closed the door.

Kathy started, gasped, and then managed to get control of herself. "Who are you?" she demanded, in a quivering voice. "What do you want?"

Her dark hair was cropped short and curled thickly about her ears. She was slender, well-formed, athletic, and nearly as tall as Elliot. Her face was just a trifle too long and thin to be considered beautiful. But she had a smooth complexion and was very pleasant to a middle-aged man's eyes.

"Relax, Kathy," cooed Elliot. "All we want is conversation."

The place was an interior designer's nightmare. The main room was square, its walls and ceiling a flat white. The furnishings in the front room were Mission, in style. A wide double door at one side of the room led to the bedrooms. Directly across was another door leading to a bath. To the right was a doorway into a small kitchen. There was a window on the left. Another straight ahead that was large and square—the one they had seen from outside. A clock on one wall displayed 1:45. Below it rested a davenport, an armchair sitting five feet in front of it. A narrow, pine coffee-table. A blue-shaded drop-light hung above the chair and a scalloped, mahogany table half-blocked the doorway leading into the kitchen. On it a small radio was playing an old Louie Armstrong tune about a shark.

Chambers Elliot noticed closed suitcases standing next to the coffee table. "Leaving town, Kathy?"

Her eyes whitened. Then they darkened until only the pupils showed. "I'll call the police if you two creeps don't get out of here."

Elliot pointed to the phone on the coffee table. "Feel free. I'm certain they'll be interested in your relationship with the man who came to my office posing as Father Zamoyski—considering he was just murdered at the Double Oak Hotel."

Her eyes darted toward the phone but Kathy did not move. "Murdered? Milton?"

The detective was standing on the balls of his feet, as he smirked, "Your friend took a fast six-floor tumble followed by an abrupt session of asphalt-kissing. What's his full name? Milton what?"

"Milton Raintree," she choked. The tip of a pink tongue came out between her lips and furtively tasted the air.

The lawyer glanced questioningly at Taggart.

"I've heard the name. But I've never run into the guy," said the detective. "Grafter, as I recall. But as far as I know, he's never been tagged."

"I'd like to look through Mr. Raintree's possessions," said Elliot.

Kathy Martin's face became a rigid white mask. "I didn't think it'd end like this."

"Did you hear me, Kathy?" prompted the lawyer.

"There's nothing of his here," she murmured. "All gone."

"He lived with you didn't he?" demanded the detective, impatiently.

"Let it go, Jason," said Elliot.

Kathy Martin staggered over to the chair across from the davenport, and slumped. Her face was so drained of color that her unpainted lips looked dark and bloody in contrast to her skin. Her eyes were clenched shut with horror.

"We tried telling Harry it wasn't worth it," she continued. "But he wouldn't listen. Said it was the action he'd waited a lifetime for." Then she gave the detective a pleading look. "Were they both killed? Harry, too?"

"Harry, who?" demanded Taggart.

"Harry Farmer," she replied, glancing over at Elliot, obviously surprised they did not know who she was talking about.

Chambers Elliot gave the detective another questioning look.

Taggart said, "Harry Farmer is no-talent grafter. He's been out of Austin for a number of years."

Elliot returned his attention to Kathy Martin. "There was only one body. Which of them came to see me, yesterday?"

She picked up a pack of cigarettes from the coffee table, and sloughed one up. "You're the lawyer?" she asked, looking up at Chambers Elliot.

Elliot nodded.

"Milton," she said.

Kathy caught the upright cigarette from the pack between her lips. Then she pulled out the book of matches pinned behind the pack's cellophane and struck a match by dragging it along the friction strip, without tearing the match from the book. After lighting the cigarette she held up the burning match and blew a soft gray smoke ring across it, snuffing the flame.

As the circle of smoke drifted, she dropped cigarette pack and matchbook onto the table. Then just before the smoke ring floated beyond her reach, Kathy poked a finger through it. The action twisted the circle into snaking wisps that slithered toward the ceiling.

"Harry was supposed to go," she added. "But Milton didn't think he'd carry off the priest impersonation."

"What did Milton Raintree want from my safe?" asked Elliot.

Kathy Martin wiped her hands on her jeans, leaving damp traces. "I don't think he wanted anything. The Father Zamoyski gig was Harry's, not Milton's. Milton was just helping Harry out by playing the part. Harry's not been well."

Chambers Elliot passed his hand over his eyes. "Help Harry with what?"

Kathy gave out a vague shrug.

Taggart pulled aside his coat to display a holstered Glock pistol. "Now would be a good time to tell what you know."

She crinkled her eyes as if she might cry. "Harry was running a game on the Portellos. Milton told Harry it was the same as suicide, doing a thing like that." Her voice faltered. "But Harry didn't listen."

"Sweet Jesus!" groaned Taggart. "I knew it! The Portellos probably have goons outside waiting to make a move."

Kathy's head jerked toward the detective. Her eyes got wide. She held the smoking cigarette rigidly in front of her gaping mouth.

The lawyer wiggled a thumb toward a window. "Take a discrete look around, Jason," Elliot said, in a low, strained voice.

Taggart unholstered his Glock and went toward the back of the house.

She spoke rapidly, breathlessly. "The Portellos killed Milton, didn't they?"

Elliot walked up and down the room, his hands clasped behind him, a lectern-expression on his face. "Apparently so. Why was I selected as the attorney to contact?"

"You have a reputation. Milton thought if he went to see you it might put the Portellos in reverse. Harry wasn't moving too fast, lately."

"Reverse? Meaning what?"

"They'd fingered Harry's gambit and were closing in on him." She took a draw on the cigarette and blew smoke toward the ceiling.

"What gambit?"

Kathy shrugged. "Something about an old murder."

Elliot stopped and looked over at her. "Michael Douglas?"

Her eyes rounded in surprise, and then she nodded.

The lawyer resumed his pacing. "Were you with Harry when he

contacted the Portellos?"

"All's I know is, Harry mailed Dominic Portello a package," she replied. "Then Harry phoned somebody from a phone-booth in a roadhouse outside of Georgetown. I don't know what was in the package. I didn't who Harry called or what he said." She took another drag on the cigarette. "I didn't want any part of hustling the Portellos."

Chambers Elliot stopped and went over to face her. "Did Harry claim that Dominic Portello killed Michael Douglas?"

Kathy made another shrug. "You got me." She wiped her nose on her arm. "Poor Milton. He never wanted any part of it, but he felt sorry for Harry."

"You're certain it was Dominic to whom Harry Farmer sent a package, not Salvator?" Elliot pressed.

She splayed her hands. "What do you want from me, Lawyer? That's the name I saw on the envelope."

"How did Raintree know that I was defense counsel for Jerome Petty?"

"Never heard of Petty." Kathy examined the nail of her index finger. "But *she* might know."

"She?" Chambers Elliot asked.

"Sheila." Kathy looked up at the lawyer woodenly.

"Sheila Clifford?"

Kathy nodded. "We were roommates in Houston, 'til I moved to Austin. Harry was mad as hell about it—Sheila and Milton getting it on."

"Raintree had a romantic relationship with Sheila Clifford?" Elliot asked, dubiously.

She considered his question with a frown. "You might call it that." Then her face became distant. "I don't think they ever went to bed. Personally I thought Milton would prefer money over bottled blondes."

The lawyer tugged at an earlobe in thought. Then he snapped his chin down. "Why did their relationship upset Harry?"

"Harry's Sheila's old man—father—adoptive father, I guess you'd call him," she replied, with a shrug. Kathy studied his face as if trying to decide how to proceed. Then her words came out like a flood. "That's how Harry got tied up with Milton, and me. Through Sheila. You don't think Milton Raintree would partner with a loser like Harry out of choice, do you?"

Taggart returned to the front room, still holding his pistol. "I couldn't see anybody outside, Chambers," the detective said gravely, his left hand going to his cheek in a nervous movement. "But that doesn't mean the Portellos aren't out there. I think we'd better get clear while we can."

Elliot looked at the detective in stern reproof. Then he indicated the davenport with an impatient finger. "Take a load off, Jason."

The detective let go a nervous sigh, lifted his eyebrows resignedly and holstered the pistol. Then he went over, sat down and tried to get comfortable. Elliot moved closer to Kathy Martin. The woman glanced from man to man, her green eyes still uneasy.

"You and Milton are scamming George Pierce about Sheila Clifford's paternity," declared the lawyer. "Don't deny it."

She spread her palms. "There's no scam. Sheila is a Pierce."

"She can prove it?" Taggart scoffed.

Kathy nodded. "A few weeks ago some detectives showed up at her apartment, in Houston. They said George Pierce had changed his mind and wanted to see her."

"George had spoken to Sheila before?"

"Six or seven months back, Sheila came to Austin after finding her birth certificate and a letter from Edward Pierce among her mother's paper," explained Kathy, making a vague motion with one hand. "Edward Pierce was listed as her father's name on the certificate."

"Edward Pierce isn't a common name," Elliot remarked. "But it isn't unusual either. There must be several in Houston. Why come here?"

"The return address on the letter's envelope listed the Pierce Ranch."

"Did you see this letter?" Taggart asked.

She took a draw on the cigarette and blew smoke toward the ceiling. Then her head wagged.

"George didn't believe her, I take it?"

"He sent her running, claiming the birth certificate and letter were forgeries."

"Who were the detectives who approached Sheila?"

"Never heard."

Kathy put a forefinger to her lips and touched it with the tip of her tongue. "Milton's been helping Sheila collect the proof she needs to convince George Pierce that she is his granddaughter."

"Collect what proof?" the lawyer demanded. "A DNA test will decisively prove or disprove her claim."

Another shrug.

"Where can we find Harry Farmer?" Taggart asked. "The hotel was just a front."

"With Sheila, I suppose." Her tone was almost flippant.

The lawyer forced a weary grin. "I was under the impression that Sheila lived here."

"She did. But me and Sheila had a fight. She packed and walked out. Milton packed and followed." Kathy Martin indicated the suitcases. "I was getting ready to leave town when you jokers arrived."

The attorney glanced over at Jason Taggart. "If Harry Farmer is with Sheila, is there any danger to your operative?"

Taggart crossed his legs and studied the glistening toe of his left shoe. "Nobody messes with Popovitch."

"You visited someone at the Double Oak Hotel last night," Elliot said to Kathy Martin. "Harry Farmer or Milton Raintree?"

She put her elbows on her knees and rubbed his eyes with his fingers, dusting the floor and table with cigarette ash. "They were both there. I pawned some jewelry Sheila'd copped the last time she visited George Pierce. She was afraid that if she got caught selling it, it would queer her plans for inheriting when George kicked off. So I agreed to hock the stuff."

"Sounds like you're down to rubbing nickels," remarked Taggart.

She nodded carefully, snuffing out her cigarette in the ashtray on the table. "Time to move on."

The telephone rang. Kathy looked over at it and then at Elliot, seeking approval. He nodded, and resumed pacing. She leaned over and grabbed up the receiver. After a moment her eyes brightened, she let go a sigh of relief. Then Kathy dropped the handset back into its cradle.

"Good news?" asked Elliot, stopping to look over at her.

"Sister's in town," she replied. Kathy stood up, stretched. "If there's nothing else, I'd like to go get her. She's at the bus-station."

"Sister?" Taggart echoed suspiciously.

Elliot gave him a warning glance. "Did Harry or Milton mention how the money was to be received from the Portellos?"

She rubbed her eyes, yawned. "Not to me."

"Have you met George Pierce's son, Sydney?" asked Elliot.

Her cheeks flushed. "I guess I must've." She smiled, showing a lot of very white teeth. "He lives at the ranch, doesn't he?"

"Well, if that doesn't…" muttered the detective.

"I think we've taken enough of Kathy's time, Jason," Elliot said, and motioned the detective to follow him out.

"But Chambers…" protested Taggart.

"I wouldn't want to leave *my* sister stranded at the bus station," the lawyer declared. "You know the sort of men who work there."

"My brother-in-law works there," the detective protested. "And those charges were dropped—eventually."

Chambers Elliot winked at Kathy. "Nice talking with you."

Jason Taggart reluctantly trailed outside after the lawyer. When they got to the sidewalk, Taggart grabbed Elliot by the arm and pulled him to a stop. The detective's voice was emphatically incredulous.

"Chambers, if she's got a sister at the bus station I'm overdue for a leg-waxing. And if Salvator Portello didn't kill Milton Raintree, then I'm in need of a sex-change. As for the rest of her lies... Didn't you see her face when you asked her about Sydney Pierce? If ever a woman told a tale with a blush, it was her."

"I agree about the blush." Elliot glanced up with concern at the purple-black clouds overhead, as thunder let go a crackling rumble. "But right now I want to get my hands on Harry Farmer. I think it was he, who just telephoned Kathy. Come on, before it rains. We'll let Von Drake tail her to Farmer. When they get together, we'll make our move."

"But Chambers..."

"You said Harry Farmer was a grafter, Jason?"

"A small-timer whose run every scam out there—and not very successfully. He's spent more time in the joint, than out."

"Dig into Milton Raintree's background," said the lawyer. "Get everything and anything. I want to know what his favorite color was and where he scratched himself when no one was looking."

"It just occurred to me, Chambers," said Taggart. "How would Raintree know what was in your safe?"

"If you're implying that Maggie or Lydia have loose tongues..." started the lawyer, protectively.

"Not at all," interjected the detective, with a placating wave of both hands. "My point is Sheila Clifford was living with Kathy Martin and Milton Raintree. Therefore, there's no ongoing direct contact between her and George Pierce. So how did Raintree know you represented George? And how did he know George's documents were in your safe? See what I mean?"

Chambers Elliot twisted his lower lip in thought for a moment. "You think Kathy is funneling information from Sydney Pierce to Raintree?"

"Who else would know what George was up to besides Sydney?" Taggart answered gravely. "And I'll take any wager she and Sydney are as close as close can get."

Chambers Elliot glanced at his watch. "Nearly two. Drop me off at the office. I think I'll send my new intern to the library."

"Library, hell! If Ramón Whitaker was my intern I'd send him out to measure the width of I-35... during rush-hour."

"That's my backup plan. Right now I want Ramón to gather all there is on Michael Douglas' death."

Chapter 5

Lydia Marshall was seated at Maggie Sharp's walnut, kneehole desk when Chambers Elliot entered his offices.

"From the wan look on your face, Lydia, you're still a believer in Taggart's theory concerning Zamoyski," Elliot scolded.

Something hard prodded his back. With a start, the lawyer looked over his shoulder. Behind him was a thickset, dark-haired man in a pinstriped, navy suit.

"Gun," the man grunted.

"As you see, I have other things to worry about." Lydia spread her shaking fingers across the desk's inlaid leather top. "The not-so-nice man behind you and his boss showed up an hour ago. The others of that party are in your office."

Concern crinkled his face as Elliot turned back to her. "Are you okay?"

She nodded. "So far. Lt. Mann telephoned. He wants to see you."

"Where's Maggie?" asked Elliot, glancing around.

"Maggie had a dental appointment and left before they arrived."

Elliot let go a sigh of relief. "Don't worry I'll take care of everything."

"I'm not so sure," she said. "Ramón decided to make a run for it when they got here."

"They killed him?" the lawyer asked, hopefully.

The gunman snickered, "Not your lucky day, is it?"

Lydia said, "They strung him up by his heels in the elevator-shaft after he threatened to sic his father on Mr. Portello."

"Mr. *Salvator* Portello," chimed the gunman. "We must be precise."

"Why the elevator?" Elliot asked.

"There they could tie his—his tattoo—to the elevator's cable," she explained.

The lawyer tilted toward her. "Tattoo? Tied? What am I missing?"

"That woman who kept Ramón busy is a tattooist. She decorated his —his personal appendage—sometime during their not-so-brief interaction."

"Roses 'n thorns," chuckled the man with the gun. "Never seen anythin' like it."

"Personal appendage?" Elliot echoed in confusion.

"Men have one and women don't," explained Lydia.

"Ah, that personal appendage."

"He'll be okay unless somebody takes the lift to the basement," she continued.

"You mean…" Elliot interjected.

Lydia nodded. "Ramón's tattoo is likely to be stretched beyond human endurance."

Chambers Elliot let go a sympathetic groan, and tilted his knees together.

The door to the lawyer's private office opened and a tall, gaunt, bearded man dressed immaculately in a gray suit stepped into view. Even his shoes were gray. The only hint of color was a ruby tie-tack that winked blood-red when he breathed. He stood there politely, one hand touching the doorknob at his back, his eyes curiously upon the lawyer.

"That is Mr. Salvator Portello," said Lydia.

"Chambers Elliot, I presume?" Salvator's lean, bearded face seemed to blend with the color of his gray clothing. "I would've made an appointment. However, people are often reluctant to receive me. Surprise visits usually work best." Then he indicated the office behind with a sweep of one hand. "Won't you join us?"

Elliot tilted his head toward Lydia. "My legal-assistant has business elsewhere, as does my intern—the one you have in the elevator-shaft."

"I can stay if you need me, Chambers." Lydia's voice trembled with fear.

He shook his head. "Mr. Portello and I have private matters to discuss. The less people involved the better. I'll see you in the morning." He took the checks from his suit and dropped them upon the desk. "On your way home try to deposit the one made out to us."

"You found them?" she gaped.

"Things have way of turning up unexpectedly." Then he glanced over at the Mafia Don. "As do people. Try to have a nice evening, Lydia."

Salvator signaled the man behind Elliot to allow her to leave.

After she went out, Elliot insisted, "My intern as well, Mr. Portello. Or our discussion is at an end before it starts."

"Are you sure?" Salvator asked. "That screaming bastard is more trouble than he's worth."

Elliot gave an understanding nod. "I won't take issue with your assessment of Ramón. Nevertheless, I want him released."

Salvator snapped his fingers.

The man with the gun holstered the weapon and quickly departed.

Elliot strode over to Salvator, passed the gangster without remark, and entered his private office. Then he went directly to his desk and settled into the swivel chair behind it.

In addition to the Mafia-Don, there were four other people in the room. Two were obviously the Portello family guardians. They stood like olive-skinned sentries in black suits, guarding either side of the doorway. The other two occupied customer chairs in front of the desk. One, Elliot recognized as Dominic Portello, the mobster's younger brother. His skin was pale and Dominic looked like he needed a shave. He had the type of heavy stubble that would make him always look like he needed a shave. His hair was curly and black hair. His heavy eyebrows met over his thick nose and . Hhis small ears lay flat against his head. His eyes had a shine close to tears, as if he were in constant emotional turmoil. He looked much older than Elliot knew him to be.

The occupant of the other chair was a slender, beautiful, brunette Elliot had only seen in newspaper-photos—Rita Portello.

"What can I do for you, Mr. Portello?" Elliot gritted impatiently, to Salvator. "Or should I address you as, *Capo de Tutti Capi?*"

"Don't push your luck, Shyster."

Elliot glanced at his watch. "I do have appointments this afternoon. The quicker we finish your business, the better for both of us. Shall we proceed?"

Salvator shut the office door. Then he went over and took a perch on the corner of Elliot's desk, tilting toward the attorney in a menacing manner. "You had a visitor yesterday."

"As, I'm sure, did you," said Elliot. "It's a frequent occurrence, for both of us. Are we finished?"

"Don't fuck with me, Shyster!" the gangster shouted. "You were hired to do a job."

"That is why people come here, Mr. Portello. In my case, they almost always leave in a better emotional state than when they arrived." Elliot shrugged one shoulder and his brows arched in taunting. "Unfortunately, you cannot say the same. Now, get out of here."

Dominic Portello jumped to his feet. "Don't get cute, Shyster!"

"Sit down, you idiot!" bellowed Salvator, to his brother.

Immediately, Dominic slumped back into his chair, looking like a little boy who was about to wet his pants.

The Mafia Don folded his hands in prayer fashion as he addressed the lawyer. "A priest called upon you."

"Any particular priest?" demanded Chambers Elliot, not concealing his growing irritation. "Or are you talking about the one you had tossed off the roof of the Double-Oak Hotel? Lt. Herbie Mann took a dim view of that situation. Unlike you, he's a staunch Catholic and regards murdering the clergy as unconscionable."

Salvator leaned across the desk shouting, "Like Hell I put a hit on that guy!"

"I'm sure it was Hell for Father Zamoyski," Elliot quipped. "At least during that brief flight to earth, before joining his maker."

Salvator eased to his feet and shoved his hands into his pockets. "His name ain't Father Zamoyski—that bastard. And, he ain't no priest. His name's Harry Farmer."

Chambers Elliot could not help but gape in surprise. "Harry Farmer? You're certain?"

The gangster reached down and tapped the desk with one manicured forefinger, for emphasis. "The burned hands cinched the I.D."

Elliot said, "I take it Mr. Farmer was a business associate?"

"Never mind what he was," growled Salvator. "What did he give you?"

"Nothing," snapped Elliot. "Is there anything else?"

Salvator angled toward Elliot. "Count on it, Shyster."

"Shall I assume you killed Mr. Farmer because you thought he gave me something?" demanded Elliot. "I want to get my facts straight before I talk with Lt. Mann about your visit."

The gangster made an impatient face as his hands coiled into fists. "Ain't no cop gonna' show here 'til me and mine leave, no matter who calls 'em."

"It must be nice to have police-presence controlled so precisely."

"I pay through the nose for that privilege. Now, you're gonna' tell me what I want. If you don't, my boys will get tough. Clear?"

"Can't we do this some other time, Sal?" Rita interrupted. She was dressed in a red suit, with matching shoes, earrings, necklace and purse. "Constance is waiting for us."

"She can wait some more!" Salvator growled over one shoulder. Then he glared at Elliot. "Give!"

"Anything my clients tell me is privileged, Mr. Portello," said Elliot, politely. "Anything they might assign to my care is equally so. As a member of the bar, you know that."

"Are you deaf?" Salvator, stooped farther over the desk to further menace Elliot. "Farmer gave you a DVD. Well, I want it and you're gonna' give it!"

"Mr. Farmer did not pay a call on me." Chambers Elliot checked his watch; the curve of his mouth was like a smile. "Now, if you and yours will be on your way, my next appointment is due any minute."

"Your appointment can wait!" Salvator shouted. "Now you listen to me… I know he was here. My people followed him here. Talk or so help me God…!"

Elliot looked over at Dominic. "I understand the police are

reopening their investigation into the murder of Michael Douglas. Why don't you elaborate on that for the benefit of your brother?"

Dominic flushed, the scar on his chin becoming livid and wormlike. Rita Portello shifted uneasily in her chair, her hands forming into white-knuckled fists upon her purse-strap.

"What the fuck do we care what the cops do?" demanded Salvator, flinging his arms wide. "We own this fucking town!" Then he jabbed a finger through the air at Chambers Elliot. "Hand over that goddamn DVD!"

"You're missing a rare opportunity, Salvator," Elliot pinged. "Dominic is about to explain how finding Michael Douglas's killer will impact your entire family."

Dominic's mouth dropped open. His eyes rounded. He was scared. He was thinking. Thinking, clearly, was difficult for him.

Salvator suddenly jerked erect and glared over at his brother. "What in hell is he talking about?"

"Nothing, Sal," whimpered Dominic. "He's full of shit. Just blowin' smoke. You know them lawyers."

"Since your brother doesn't have the guts to tell you, why not ask your sister?" Elliot crossed his arms in defiance. "I'm sure Rita can fill you in on Michael Douglas—and how he died."

Rita's face went as gray as a potato dumpling. She bit her lip and cocked her head slightly to look at Elliot. Then she lowered her lashes until they feathered her cheeks. A moment later, she slowly raised them, like a shade, still staring askance at the lawyer.

Salvator twisted further so he was facing his sister. "Well?"

Rita tossed her head angrily, and the nearly-black of her hair glistened under the office lighting like a sheet of freshly chipped basalt. "Like Dom says," she replied, in a quaking voice. "The lawyer's blowing smoke." Then Rita set her mouth stubbornly.

Salvator returned his attention to Chambers Elliot, his face now awry with confused exasperation. "What the fuck are you playing at?"

"Why don't *you* start the explanations, Dominic?" Elliot suggested. "For example, tell Salvator how you killed Michael Douglas."

The Mafia-Don whirled back toward is brother and gave the chair Dominic sat in a vicious kick. "You whacked some bastard, you goddamn idiot?"

"No!" whimpered Dominic, his eyes going wide and white. "I swear to God, Sal! The lawyer's runnin' you up a tree."

"I swear to God, I swear to God," Salvator mocked. "That's all I fucking hear from you!" The Mafia-Don's angry face made a squint as he tilted closer to his brother. "You told me Farmer gave that DVD to his lawyer. You told me he came here to see this bastard. Did you lie to me?"

Dominic jerked his head back in forth, his eyes blinking rapidly in panic. "The lawyer's lyin', Sal."

Rita jumped to Dominic's defense, stepping between her brothers. "Leave him alone, Sal!"

Salvator pushed her back into the chair and glowered at Dominic. "What's on the DVD? Tell me, damn you!"

"It's just like I said, Sal," whined Dominic.

"Shuttup!" shouted Salvator. Then he returned his attention to Chambers Elliot. "You tell me, lawyer."

Elliot shrugged. "I don't know. As I explained, Harry Farmer did not visit my office." The lawyer grinned up at the fuming gangster, unruffled by the glowering man. "I do have very reliable information, however, that Mr. Farmer did send a package to your brother. I cannot attest as to what that package contained. But there may have been a DVD in it." Then he gave Dominic a taunting sneer. "Since you know what is on that DVD, obviously you received it."

Dominic started to rise, his face wooden. "I'm gonna' kill you."

Salvator tossed his brother a warning glance that dumped the younger mobster back into his seat, quivering like a terrified puppy. Then the Mafia-Don turned back to Elliot.

A faint smile pulled at the shadowed corners of the Salvator's mouth. "Somebody's jerking my pud, Shyster. If it's you, I'm gonna' spend a week dippin' your ass."

"I have no reason to lie, Mr. Portello." Elliot made a placating gesture with his hands. Then he smiled over at Dominic and Rita. "But your brother and sister do."

"I didn't get any DVD, Sal!" whimpered Dominic. "I swear to God!"

The lawyer focused upon Rita. "Why don't you enlighten Salvator about Michael Douglas and his relationship with the Portello family—you in particular?"

Rita curled her lip into a snarl but said nothing.

Salvator jerked around to face her. "Do you know about that hit? Was there something between you and this Douglas creep? Tell me!"

"It was thirty years ago, Sal," she murmured, softly. "It was nothing. Nothing happened between me and Michael Douglas."

"Thirty years?" The Mafia-Don twisted back to Elliot sneering, "Thirty fucking years?" The tone of his voice was incredulous. "Is that what this is about? That idiot Farmer figured he could shake us down for something that happened thirty fucking years ago?"

"Some things endure forever," taunted Elliot. "Like the memories of a one's first sexual experience, and the statute of limitations on murder. Wouldn't you agree, Rita?"

Rita started to get up, but caught herself. After settling back into the chair her lip curled again, this time showing a canine. Then she hissed, "Dom didn't kill Michael."

Salvator studied his sister a moment as if suddenly realizing there was more than implication in Chambers Elliot's words. "Who was Michael Douglas, Rita?"

She shifted away from her brother's scathing gaze. Her eyes further distanced themselves by focusing upon the ceiling. "Nobody."

"Rita was the reason for the killing," Elliot chimed. "She had a crush on Michael Douglas—at least that's part of the rumor. Douglas allegedly despoiled her innocence. Then there's the rumor that makes Dominic the shooter—trying to avenge his sister's honor."

Salvator let go a low growl as he lunged at Dominic, gripping his younger brother by the throat, and dragging him from the chair. "You killed the fucking bastard! Don't lie to me!"

"No!" choked Dominic. "I swear on our mother's life I didn't do it, Sal!"

The Mafia Don shoved his brother back into the chair and then glared over at his sister. "What went on between you and Douglas?"

"Nothing, Sal. Nothing. Michael never laid a hand on me." Her voice was low and mournful.

"Did you know about this hit all these years, Rita?" demanded Salvator. "Was it Dom? For Christ's sake, Rita, tell me so I can take care of things!"

Elliot cocked his head and grinned as he listened to the torment in Salvator Portello's voice.

"If that lawyer knows so much, ask him," Rita said in a quivering tone. She looked at Elliot, her eyes seemingly far away as if reliving a near-forgotten moment. "Ask him about Michael. I'm through talking about him."

Salvator returned his attention to Dominic. "So help me God, if the cops show up with a warrant for you on this Douglas hit, you're as good as dead—because I'm gonna' kill you myself."

The younger brother wagged his head as if refusing poison. "I didn't cap him, Sal! I swear to God, I didn't!"

"Who the fuck is Michael Douglas, anyway?" demanded Salvator looking from his family back to Elliot. "How come I never heard of him?"

"He worked for Pa." Dom flinched. "You remember him, Sal. The high-flyer with the hot car and the broads. Winston Liquors."

"Rumor has it," Elliot chimed, "that Old Frank financed that liquor-store as a front to his early money-laundering efforts. You probably still carry the business on your books."

"Winston Liquors…" Salvator echoed. A curious expression abruptly flitted over his gaunt features. Then he pointed to the office door and roared at Dominic, "Take your sister out to the car."

Dominic got to his feet like a frightened old man. "We can't let that Shyster talk to the cops, Sal."

"Why is that, Dominic?" pinged Elliot, with a cocky grin. "Are you worried I've found the gun? You were smart enough to use a zinc-alloy bullet. It shattered on impact when you blew out Michael Douglas' brains. But I think today's computerized forensic techniques will match-up the pieces so it can be compared."

Rita cast Elliot a warning glance. "I'd cut your throat just to watch what runs out."

Elliot leered at her politely. "Not at the price of your brother's life, you won't."

She spat at him. Then Rita strode out, with Dominic following closely on her heels; his shoulders sagging; his hands trembling.

Salvator trailed them as far as the door. Then he motioned the two bodyguards to go out and wait in the reception area with their compatriot. After the men left, Salvator closed the door and then went over to face Chambers Elliot.

"All right. Maybe I took the wrong approach with you." The pulse in his lean throat throbbed visibly. "No more threats. In return I don't want any bullshit. Agreed?"

Elliot indicated the chairs fronting his desk, with an open hand. "Please sit down, Mr. Portello."

Salvator slumped into a chair like a man who was seconds from exhaustion. "Just between you and me and the walls, what the fuck's going on?"

"I did receive a visit from someone who posed as a priest," said Elliot. "He did identify himself as Father Zamoyski. He retained my services on two matters, neither of which I can discuss. He did not—I repeat—he did not give me a DVD. He was not—I repeat—he was not Harry Farmer. He made no mention—I repeat—he made no mention of anyone in your family. He did, however go into great deal over Michael Douglas's murder."

The gangster clapped one hand at his chest, forming a fist. "My men spotted him coming into this building…"

"The man they saw was disguised to look like Harry Farmer, I grant you. But he was not Harry Farmer. I want that clear in your mind, Mr. Portello." Then Elliot leaned forward, casually resting his forearms on the desk. "Do you recall Michael Douglas?"

Salvator Portello half-closed his eyes. "I didn't like him."

"As you probably remember, Michael Douglas was killed execution-style," Elliot said. "I don't know who actually shot him. But, according to my informant, Harry Farmer suspected your brother. As for the DVD, I think it is safe to assume that it is a replication of the videotape that recorded Douglas' murder. There was a camera in the liquor store, wasn't there?"

"Maybe. We had 'em installed in some of the stores." The mobster stared at the lawyer, half-frowning. "Why would Farmer get you involved?"

"Again, I was not visited by Harry Farmer. It was another man posing as Zamoyski."

He flung one arm toward the office door. "My brother may be an idiot. He's fucked-over everything his whole life. But the Sicilian Brothers—those two you saw guarding the door—told me for a fact that Harry Farmer came to see you. The Sicilian Brothers do not lie, Shyster."

"I'm not alleging they do, Mr. Portello. I'm saying they were mistaken. The man who visited me is still alive. Harry Farmer, by your own statement, is not."

"Then who the fuck was it who came here?" the mobster shouted, in exasperation.

"I can't say with absolute certainty and I'm not about to speculate."

Salvator eased forward expectantly. "So you do suspect?"

Chambers Elliot shrugged. "Regardless, I shall not disclose my suspicions to you, or anyone else."

The mobster thrust a finger toward the lawyer. "You'll tell me or—"

"What you should be concerned about is Dominic's culpability in Michael Douglas' murder. If he did kill Douglas, and that DVD shows him doing so and it ends up on the prosecutor's desk, your brother will be arrested. Considering Dominic's murderous reputation you can bet the prosecutor will treat the Douglas killing as a capital crime."

The Mafia Don slumped back in the chair, again clutching at his chest. "Everybody knows that bastard Petty killed Douglas."

"Jerome Petty was arrested," agreed Elliot. "But new evidence strongly suggests that he didn't kill Douglas. Did you know the real Father Zamoyski?"

The Mafia-Dom made a disgusted face. "Yeah. Rita spent half her time in prayers and the other half in church making confessions to the bastard."

"Why did Zamoyski return to Poland?"

Salvator suddenly looked nervous. "He…" Then his voice went soft as if he were speaking only to himself. "Look, they were just kids. Kids don't gun down clowns like Douglas."

"Dominic was two years from being of draft-age. Rita was old enough to have romantic ideas. All girls do at that tender age. And we both know that kids commit murders every year in this country. It's one of the curses of life."

Salvator lunged out of the chair to lean across the desk and scream, "They didn't do it!"

"That's not for either you or I to say, is it?"

The mobster staggered back to the chair; one hand gripping his chest, his face twisted in pain. "I got a bad heart," Salvator grunted, as he slumped. "I got it because I got nothing but aggravation every minute of my fucking life. And now I got you on my Goddamn ass over something I never knew about."

"You can easily get rid of me, Mr. Portello."

Salvator shook a threatening finger at Chambers Elliot. "You damn well better believe it, Shyster!"

Elliot chuckled. "I'm not on a crusade against your family, Mr. Portello. I am, however, looking for honest answers. Perhaps we can help each other? What do you recall about Michael Douglas?"

"Nothing much. Nothing good!" The gangster's forehead wrinkled and the pain in his eyes gave way to disgust. "Douglas was always after the women, always chasing around. That dirty bastard… If I'd known he'd touched Rita…" He hesitated, his gray eyes busy with thought. Then Salvator glared at Elliot. "Let's get something straight, Shyster. Maybe you got that DVD. Maybe you don't. But if I find out you do, there won't be anywhere on earth you can hide from me."

Elliot flexed his lips. "Instead of threatening me, consider that I'm trying to help you with your brother's defense. Think back to when you had those security cameras installed at Winston Liquors. Did they actually cover the entire store? Could a recorded tape show who killed Michael Douglas?"

Salvator's jaws snapped shut, with a click. "At the time I was interested in how Douglas was handling the till. Women are expensive. And he had lots of women." He pulled his lips back against my teeth. "So I had one camera directly above the cash register in case he decided to skim. There was another camera mounted in the ceiling above the front door. It focused on the counter. Cash registers of that day did not have inventory systems. By seeing what the customers were buying I could to predict inventory needs."

"So you viewed these recordings frequently?"

Salvator nodded. "Daily. I hired this whiz-kid to cut out all the action from each tape except sales and till business. That's all he did, all day long. When he got through editing the tape from the day before, I viewed it at high-speed – an hour or so of my time"

"Did Harry Farmer contact you about Michael Douglas?"

Salvator's head wagged. "He knew better than that. Harry used to work for me. I'd have recognized his voice."

"What was his demand of Dominic?"

"Dom said he'd been hit up for a shakedown over some shit he'd pulled a few years back. He said it had to do with—never mind what it had to do with. The bottom line is, the price was five million." The gangster flung his arms wide. "You think I'm gonna' lay out five mill when I can cap the blackmailing bastard for free?"

"Not with any expectation of being correct."

The mobster shrugged his wide sharp shoulders. "I put feelers out. That's when the word got back to me that Harry Farmer was in town. Harry was one of the truck-drivers on that action Dom claimed was behind the shakedown. I said to myself, 'that asshole Harry set this up'. He figured he'd rattle my cage. So I sent my boys nosing around. Sure enough. They came back with information that Harry was about to make a big score."

"I'm surprised you didn't hunt Harry Farmer down."

"We did. My boys cornered Harry. After some chitchat, he admitted he'd done a number on Dom. My boys dumped Harry in a car and headed for my office." Salvator moved his thin gray eyebrows slightly. "But before they could get there, Harry jumps one of my men and gets a gun. He caps both—right there and then. The car crashes. Harry gets out and makes tracks. We didn't find his trail until he was spotted going into this building."

"Did your people see Mr. Farmer leave this building?"

Salvator made a vague gesture. "Somehow he slipped out without my men seeing. It took us until now to pin down who he met here—you." He leaned forward shaking a threatening finger at Elliot. "So you see why I'm upset. I'm being jacked around for five mill and two of my men are dead and now you're giving me shit about a thirty year old killing."

"If you didn't kill Harry Farmer who did?" asked Elliot.

Salvator stood up grinning like a bear about to devour a Salmon. "You think I'm stupid enough to leave a body around for the cops to find?"

Elliot shrugged. "If I were you, I'd concentrate on who Harry hired to pose as Zamoyski. Whoever it was, that man had acting experience." Elliot glanced at his watch. "Now I must end our meeting. Lt. Mann is expected. Unless, of course, you would care to remain? I'm certain he would be keenly interested in your recent experiences with Harry Farmer."

Salvator scratched the back of his neck. Then he gave his gray head an angry shake. "If that fucking DVD shows up, you'd better bring it to me. Understand?" He looked at Elliot obliquely. "If you don't, there won't even be memories of you in this town."

Elliot stood up, unmoved by the threat. "If I receive such a package you can count on me sending it to the police – along with a quote of all that's transpired between us. If for no other reason than to show you I don't kowtow to anyone."

Salvator Portello spoke in a harsh, guttural voice. "*Vaffanculo!*"

"*Nessuno me lo ficca in culo!*" Elliot quickly countered, with a taunting grin.

Salvator's faced flushed with rage. "This ain't over, Shyster."

"No, indeed, Mr. Portello. I'll give your regards to Lt. Mann."

Mafia-Don glared at Elliot with white-rimmed eyes. Then he turned, and stormed out.

Elliot followed him as far as the reception area. Then he went over to Lydia's desk and picked up the telephone. But before he could dial, Jason Taggart rushed in with his Glock pistol at the ready. The detective's chest was heaving, his eyes were bugged out, and sweat was dripping from his face.

Taggart croaked as he gasped for air, "Lydia. Portello had you cornered. Tattoo stretched. Elevator out of order. Think I'm having a heart-attack."

"Take a deep breath and calm yourself, Jason." Elliot dropped the phone back into its cradle. "Salvator and his family of fun-seekers are gone. But I expect to chat with Mr. Portello sometime soon. Is Lydia safe?"

Taggart nodded, still gulping air. "In my car. Planning my funeral."

Elliot gave him a confused stare. "Funeral?"

The detective holstered his gun, leaned over and gasped, both hands supporting his upper body, from his knees. "Complications. Tattooed–dick. Blood."

"Dear God, you mean that Ramón lost his…?"

Jason Taggart wagged his head as he forced his body upright. "But he waggled it at me when I asked if he was hurt. I misunderstood his intent and slugged him. I may have busted his nose."

"You mean Ramón was walking around on the street with his schlong hanging out?"

Taggart shrugged. "Until the cops pulled up."

"He was arrested?"

Another nod. "And they nearly busted Lydia."

"Why?"

"After I hit him he was screaming and holding his bleeding nose," explained Taggart. "That's when a prowl car pulled to the curb. Lydia, in an effort to keep the police from seeing Ramón's dick hanging out, squatted down and tried to zip up his pants. That, as you know, can be tricky, when done by someone in a hurry who is not used to male equipment."

Elliot winced and pinched his knees together. "I take it that extremely sensitive skin was painfully pinched in the zipper?"

"Blood-curdling-scream type pinching," said the detective with a sympathetic shake of his head. "Well that pretty much focused the officers on Ramón and Lydia. Then, what with Lydia on her knees in front of him, his dick in one of her hands as she tried to jerk it free of the zipper while holding onto his crotch of his pants with the other… Chambers, as you can imagine the cops assumed that Lydia had beaten the hell out of Ramón in order to forcibly… purloin his seed."

The lawyer clapped one hand over his eyes. "Oh, my God."

"I did my best to clear things up, Chambers," pleaded Taggart.

Elliot scowled. "Couldn't they see she was just trying to help?"

"Seeing was part of the problem." The detective coupled his hands at his chest as if holding something. "You know who people sort of twist their mouth to one side when they're having trouble getting something to work? And the more difficult it becomes the more dramatically the mouth gets distorted?"

Elliot nodded, impatiently. "Your point being?"

"That mouth positioning tends to look like a pleased grin, in many cases. And Lydia was having a great deal of trouble."

"Why in hell didn't you stop her?" the lawyer demanded, his arms going wide.

"I tried." He held up a bruised finger. "But she bit me when I started to pull her away from him. She thought I was going to slug Ramón again. Unfortunately, that was not what came to mind with the police officers.

Her attack on me pretty much made up the officers' minds about her and her intent. Fortunately, after Lydia got Ramón zipped up and explained the situation, both the officer's agreed that no woman would be that desperate—not with Ramón, anyway. Not in the middle of the afternoon on a busy sidewalk. Unfortunately, one of the uniforms has a real hard-on for Magistrate Elmo Whitaker. It was she who insisted Ramón be charged with indecent exposure. I tried, but I couldn't talk her out of it. That was when Lydia went over the edge chewing me out, because she thought I had instigated Ramón's arrest. I've tried to explain. But she refuses to listen."

"There will be hell to pay when I go before Magistrate Whitaker on that adoption matter," muttered Elliot.

"I take it Ramón did not get to the library and weed out the details on Michael Douglas' murder?"

"No. And I suspect after this afternoon's outrage he'll likely end his internship—at least, one can hope. Have one of your people search the archives on the mysterious Michael Douglas." Then he pointed to the door. "In the meantime, let's get Lydia some food. I'm sure she'll forgive and forget once her stomach is filled."

The detective's eyes widened. "Do you think that's possible?"

"Despite your less than amiable relationship with Lydia, she is not an ogre."

"I didn't say she was."

"Then why do you assume she's not going to hold Ramón's arrest against you, forever?"

"I was talking about her stomach getting filled."

The lawyer declared, "There's not an ounce of fat, as far as I can tell, on that young woman."

The detective tapped Elliot's chest with a finger. "This is how Lydia keeps suckering you and me into buying her meals."

Elliot reached and patted the detective's shoulder. "Relax, Jason. Tonight's dinner is on me."

Taggart grinned. "That's why you and I get along so well, Chambers. We understand each other."

"Yes, we do, Jason. We both know that I'm brilliant and you're so cheap you squeak."

"I'm not cheap!"

"Then I'll give you two options. One, you pick up the check or two, you drive."

"I'll drive."

"Cheap."

"Have you seen the price of gas, lately?" Taggart scowled. "Cheap, cheap, cheap."

Chapter 6

"Jason looked worried when he went to answer the phone-page," Lydia Marshall remarked after Chambers Elliot ordered another round of cocktails.

It was an hour later and they were seated at a table near the dance-floor at the Top Hat Club, in Austin's West Side. On a dais at the far end of the main room an orchestra played a torch song from the forties. Couples dressed in mixed garb swayed romantically across the dance-floor in time to the music; sharing smiles, words and kisses.

"The rising rate of inflation preys heavily upon that man's mind, Lydia," Elliot returned.

She looked over at her boss in amusement; her eyebrows were up and half her mouth was smiling. "What you really mean is, Jason is a cheapskate."

Elliot gave her a wink. "Is there any other way to describe our favorite P.I.?"

Rita wrinkled her nose. "He's your favorite, not mine."

The lawyer scowled. "What have you got against Jason?"

"For starters, he's always referring to Maggie as 'the fearless virgin'. That's derogatory."

He shrugged, somewhat embarrassed. "Sometimes it just slips out."

"Maggie's choice to remain celibate is nobody else's business." Her eyebrows came together. "Then there's what happened tonight with Ramón. What's Magistrate Whitaker going to say when he has to bail Ramón out of jail again?"

"I didn't think you were very keen on Ramón."

Lydia's ears pinked. "He sort of grows on you."

Elliot noted her reaction and smiled. "In any event, things could've been worse than Ramón being arrested." He tapped the table. "You, for example, being arrested for forcing Ramón to submit to—shall we say, a romantic impulse?"

Lydia stared over at her boss confusion. "Impulse?" Then her eyes widened sharply and her neck reddened. "I was trying to zip up his pants, not forcibly—impulse," she snapped. "I told the police that. If Taggart hadn't hit Ramón, Ramón wouldn't be in jail and nobody would be thinking—impulse."

He waggled a scolding finger. "Nevertheless, it was Jason who went to your defense with the police, wasn't it?"

Her hands flurried above her glass in flustered embarrassment. "Maybe I do owe Taggart an apology." She let out a thin sigh. "A very small one.”

Elliot jumped his eyebrows. “Offer Jason a couple bucks for gasoline. You’ll move right to the top of his best-friends list.” The lawyer glanced about for a few seconds. “When Milton Raintree, A.K.A. Father Zamoyski came into your office, what did you notice about him?”

“His face, of course,” she replied, with a shudder. “I’d never seen anyone look like that. Maggie was horrified. She thought he was going to die. That’s why she sent him to me instead of dealing directly with his request.”

“Were Raintree’s hands gloved when you first saw him?”

Lydia thought for a moment before nodding. “Yes. I noticed that, too. It was a warm morning. But he wore gloves, anyway.”

“Think carefully,” urged Elliot. “Did he remark about anything you haven’t told me?”

Another pause as she considered. “He came into my office and said Maggie had sent him to see me, but he really wanted to see you. I checked your appointment book. Your first was not for another hour. So I asked the reason for his visit. He said his business was private, but that it pertained to an old murder. He insisted it was something he could discuss only with you. I told him to sit down. Then I went into your office.” Her brows furrowed with concern as she asked, “Chambers, were you expecting him to say something in particular?”

The lawyer shook his head. “But the master to the DVD Salvator is after is somewhere, and I want it. I was hoping Raintree might’ve made an offhand remark that would lead us to it.”

Her shoulders jerked. “Zamoyski wasn’t carrying anything that I could see.”

“I doubt he would’ve brought it, considering who was after Harry Farmer.”

“Perhaps Raintree didn’t realize the danger he was in?”

“Kathy Martin said that Raintree knew the Portellos were closing in on Harry,” said Elliot. “That’s why Raintree disguised himself to look like Harry Farmer—albeit dressed as a priest. She claimed that Raintree intended to make the Portellos think Harry had contacted me. In her words, ‘To put the Portellos in reverse.’” He let out a soft sigh. “Obviously, that did not work since Mr. Portello paid a call on us this afternoon.”

She gave him a bewildered look. “How can you be certain those gangsters did not kill Harry Farmer?”

“I am certain Salvator Portello *intended* to kill Harry. That was why his men abducted Harry Farmer and were later killed by Harry—that, per

Salvator. But I'm equally convinced that Salvator had nothing to do with what occurred at the Double Oak hotel." One of his feet began to tap restlessly. "Having said that, I must admit that Jason might've been correct when he suggested Dominic as Harry's killer. Dominic Portello was in a panic about that DVD. He was also terrified about what I knew concerning the death of Michael Douglas."

"From what I've read, Dominic is impulsive and uncontrolled."

"I saw that first hand," Elliot agreed. "He may well have dragged Harry Farmer up to the roof intending to frighten the DVD's location out of Harry. Then things got out of hand."

She shivered. "I didn't like those people—none of them."

The lawyer made a grimace. "I'm in complete agreement with you."

"What do we do if they come back?"

"Not if, when." He pursed his lips and gave his head a shake. "I don't want you or the others worrying about that. This is between Salvator and myself."

"Not worrying is good advice but hard to take." Lydia looked around for a moment. "I don't understand why Raintree posed as a priest."

"To add credibility to his story," said Elliot. "And to begin with, it did."

She thought for a moment, weighing her boss' explanation. "Then there was no confession?"

"Quite the contrary. Taggart spoke to the real Zamoyski. Although the priest did not admit anything, his reaction indicates a confession did take place." His lips twitched. "However, who made that confession is still up for grabs. I certainly don't see Dominic seeking absolution after committing murder."

"He was very young at the time. Killing someone must be terrifying."

He shook his head as if trying to dislodge the cobwebs of confusion. "That might explain it. Still…"

"You're convinced he killed Michael Douglas, too?"

"I'm convinced that both murders were done by the same person. Based upon my meeting with the Portellos this afternoon, I know that Dominic and Rita had something to do with Michael Douglas death. Their reactions to my taunts and questions made that clear." He drew a long slow breath and let it out. "I also know that Salvator Portello had nothing to do with either killing. Again, based upon what I observed and heard. I know that Dominic received a copy of the DVD, despite his denials. That DVD frightened him. So I assume it shows him killing Douglas. But it's all surmise."

"A very risky surmise." She ran one finger around the rim of her glass. "Why would Milton Raintree put himself into such a dangerous situation? He is trying to scam George Pierce, isn't he?"

"On Sheila Clifford's paternity? I think he's doing his feeble best to collect something from her. He must realize a DNA profile will tell the tale regardless of anyone's claims. But you made a good point. With the potential for tens of millions coming down the pike, why risk his own neck for Harry Farmer?"

"Do this favor and I'll let you marry my daughter in case she might inherit fifty million from George Pierce's estate?" Lydia suggested, with a casual wave of one hand.

He nodded. "Under normal circumstances I would agree. But grafters are not normal people. Everything they do has a purpose. Posing as Harry, wearing a priest's Cassock…"

Lydia's eyes narrowed a moment in thought, and then opened again. "And the Michael Douglas murder?"

"Exactly. The reasoning behind that, however, I still cannot fathom."

"What will you do if you find that DVD?"

Elliot gazed at her. "Look at it, of course."

Lydia glanced down at herself. "And if it shows Dominic Portello killing Michael Douglas?"

The lawyer adjusted his tie. "As an officer of the court, I am obligated to make any evidence of a crime available to the police. Which I shall do."

She tilted toward her boss. "But Dominic Portello isn't just anyone."

Elliot scratched his cheek. "Which will make the DVD's disclosure all the more delightful for me."

"Chambers, the Portellos are not going to let you get away with putting a member of their family on death-row. They'll retaliate."

He gave her hand a fatherly pat on the hand. "I suspect he's planning that as we speak."

Lydia shook her head ever so slightly. "It's no joke."

He hesitated before nodding ever so slightly. "How did George Pierce react when you told him our safe had been burgled?"

"He wasn't concerned. He actually laughed, when I gave him the news. I got the impression he thought it was a good joke on you."

"You did tell him that Sheila Clifford might actually have a copy of his will?"

"Of course," she said with a raise and fall of her hands. "George said to tell you not to worry. That anything she might have done will be moot, shortly."

"That must mean he's gone ahead with a DNA profile. I wonder what changed his mind?"

"Can a DNA profile be rigged?"

His head wagged. "Not as such. The results could be contaminated and therefore invalidated. Or DNA from someone else could be substituted. But the process itself is always precise. The report, however, could easily be reworked to someone's advantage."

Her lower lip went in under her teeth, and drew down sharply at the corners. "The report is all that George would see, correct?"

His fingers interlaced and he stared down at the table, considering. "Yes."

"So if I dummied up a report that claimed Sheila Clifford was his granddaughter," she pressed, "even though she was not, George would believe it?"

"Unless he had reason to suspect something was wrong." There was another pause as his head rose. Then in a grim voice he murmured, "Lydia, tomorrow when you get to the office telephone George Pierce. Tell him it is imperative that we meet as soon as possible, either at our offices or at his ranch."

She nodded. "You said Milton Raintree was having an affair with Sheila."

"That was what Jason and I were told by Kathy Martin; yes."

"And Harry Farmer disapproved of it?"

With a dip of his chin Chambers Elliot said, "Again, according to Kathy Martin, Harry is or was Sheila's stepfather. Apparently Harry had hopes that his daughter would not follow in his footsteps."

"What about Milton Raintree as the killer? With Harry objecting, there was a chance that Sheila might not cut Raintree in on part of what she would inherit. Raintree was alive and old enough when Michael Douglas was killed, wasn't he?"

Chambers Elliot gave her a smile of admiration. "So you're saying by bringing the Michael Douglas murder to my attention he was blatantly admitting to it?"

"It would fit a grafter's psychology, don't you think?"

The lawyer's eyebrows arched sharply. "Yes, it would." Then he slowly asked, "What do we know about Sydney Pierce?"

"He's a lazy, forty-something playboy," she replied. "From what I've gathered, Sydney's never held a job in his life—other than that of an actor in local stage productions. He does that quite often, but to mixed reviews."

Elliot offered her a remote smile. "Anything else?"

"He attended the University of Texas where he took a degree in chemistry. He likes fast cars and belongs to a number of clubs—shooting, golf, cars and exercise." Her tongue went to one cheek as she paused in thought. "Sydney and George do not get along. From what I've been told, they have an ongoing verbal war. Always it is about Sydney being lazy as a tic."

"Has Sydney ever married?"

Lydia folded her hands on the table. "Not that I recall. Why?"

"I think he and Kathy Martin might be romantically involved—at least she is with him. I'm wondering if Sydney's the type to marry or if he'll continue to remain a bachelor?"

"Once he inherits the family fortune?"

Chambers Elliot nodded.

"Men like Sydney Pierce don't make for good marriage material." Lydia looked into her glass, rattling the ice. "They also don't make good losers. If Sheila Clifford is a legitimate heir, George might give Sheila preference over Sydney. George might even cut Sydney out of it."

Elliot stared bleakly.

"Couldn't Sheila pursue a claim against George Pierce's estate after he dies by getting her own DNA analysis done?" Lydia asked.

"The point of doing so would be questionable," said the lawyer. "If there is a valid will—even assuming she actually is a Pierce—she would be entitled to nothing. Simply because we are related to the deceased does not guaranty a bequest." He raised his eyebrows slightly. "There are circumstances when preferential treatment in a will can be contested. But George was a man of integrity and sound thinking. His will would stand. If Sheila is not a Pierce, then the court would immediately toss out her claim has not having merit."

"What if there was no will?"

Chambers Elliot eased back in his chair, suddenly grim. He crossed one ankle over his knee and rubbed the anklebone as if it ached. "That is another matter, entirely. If she can prove her paternity, she could make a claim that would stand." He fingered the air between them with a forefinger for emphasis. "As to how much she would inherit would be up the court. However that claim could be substantial."

Lydia raised her glass and sucked an ice-cube into her mouth. Then her eyes widened in surprise and she spat it back into the glass. "Remember a few weeks back when I told you I thought the cleaning people were snooping through my desk?"

He nodded, pinching the softness at the end of his chin.

"I think Milton Raintree went to work for the cleaning people so he could have a look around our offices," she continued. "When he didn't find anything relating to Sheila in the filing cabinets or desks, he assumed that information must be in the safe."

Chambers Elliot smiled in amused agreement. "I think you are now inside Mr. Raintree's head, Lydia."

From across the room came a shrill, spasmodic laugh. Lydia glanced in that direction before saying, "I don't think I like Mr. Raintree."

"Grafters are universally unloved people."

Lydia opened her mouth to speak but abruptly fell silent as Jason Taggart returned to the table.

Chapter 7

"That was Von Drake on the phone," Jason Taggart said as he sat with Chambers Elliot and Lydia Marshall. "He was following Kathy Martin but she tumbled to him. Kathy ran a light." The detective paused and cleared his throat. "Von Drake followed and got pinched by a motorcycle-cop. The bottom line is he lost contact with her."

The lawyer looked at the detective sharply and immediately looked away. "I guess that's to be expected."

Jason Taggart nodded, licking his lips. "We'll find her again."

"Any news on Milton Raintree?" the lawyer asked.

"There's a warrant out for Raintree's arrest. But it dates back three years to when he pulled several scams in the panhandle area, mostly against the elderly. His favorite was the 'arrested relation'."

"What's that?" asked Lydia, looking from detective to lawyer.

"The caller claims to be the grandson or granddaughter of the intended victim," explained Elliot. "They beg for financial help. The victim wires the money as requested, not realizing it's a hoax."

"A simple telephone call to the parent of the alleged grandchild would verify," chimed Taggart. "But many times that does not take place."

"What a creep," she said tartly.

"All would agree with you," said the detective. "Raintree also favors the Bank Examiner Scheme."

"Bank Examiner?" Lydia echoed.

"That's an old scam that continues to work each year despite warnings from every law enforcement agency in the country. It involves two grafters. Way back when this scam began, these people often posed as Bank Examiners—hence its name. In more recent times, it's become effective to representative themselves as members of law-enforcement. These scammers contact you—they prefer elderly women—and pretend to need your help in an investigation. They invariably explain that you were selected as one of the bank's most valued customers or because you are well-known in the community as being an upstanding citizen." He tilted his head on one side and rubbed the back of a finger along the lower edge of his chin. "Once the schmoozing is accomplished, these guys ask you to withdraw your money from the bank, and hand it over to them. The cash, according to the grafters, will be used as bait to trap a thief. Naturally, they promise to redeposit or return your money after the investigation is completed."

"Which means you'll never see the green again," chimed the

detective. "So far there are no photos of Raintree. And there are about a dozen descriptions of him—all different. It's like he's several people all rolled into one." Taggart tilted across the table toward Elliot. "After talking with Von Drake, I touched base with Quigley—the man I have digging into Michael Douglas' background. Douglas was, as expected, quite the Romeo—often keeping three or four women dangling at the same time: always, married women."

Lydia smiled, but very faintly. "Expensive hobby."

"Agreed," said Elliot. "So how does a clerk in a liquor-store finance such a demanding preoccupation?"

"At the time of his murder, Douglas was the legal owner of Winston Liquors," Taggart replied.

The lawyer's eyebrows arched in surprise.

"But you said the Portellos own it, Chambers," Lydia interjected.

"They do now," said Taggart. "But when it first opened, Salvator was not of legal age and Old Frank had a felony conviction." His mouth made a downward, sickle curve. "The Feds nailed him for narcotics distribution. Old Frank cut a deal to get the charge reduced to felony-possession. He served eighteen months—his one and only stretch behind bars. But that kept him from owning a liquor store."

"Why?" Lydia asked.

"Felons cannot get an off-sale liquor-license—it's illegal," Elliot added. "So, Frank Portello hired Michael Douglas to front as the store's owner. It's a common enough practice."

"After the Douglas' killing," said Taggart, "Salvator Portello immediately became Winston Liquors legal owner—he was of age, by then."

"Why would a mafia-boss bother with a liquor store?" Lydia asked, her eyes darting from Taggart's to Elliot's.

"Money laundering is the Portellos' bread and butter," Elliot explained with a greedy rub of his palms. "They sell that service around the globe. A cash-business like off-sale liquor makes a wonderful washing-machine, for illicit funds." He fluttered his left hand. "That is also why Salvator Portello owns laundries, movie-houses, restaurants and quite recently nightclubs. He owns this one, for example."

"Not to mention the Lester Hampton Building in downtown Austin," added the detective. Then he gave the lawyer a questioning look. "Since tonight's debacle takes away any doubts as to the Portellos' involvement, are you ready to walk away from this? Or shall I arrange a group funeral?"

Elliot grinned. "Right now it is the Portellos who are on the run. I led them to believe the Michael Douglas murder-case is being reopened. That put Dominic and Rita into a panic and Salvator nearly ended up in a coronary-care unit."

Taggart rolled his eyes in despair. "You and your bluffing, Chambers…"

The waitress brought over the second round of drinks and took their meal orders.

After she left Taggart said, "Can we assume that Rita did more than flirt with Douglas, despite his reputation for married women?"

Elliot shrugged. "Salvator confronted Rita over it. She flatly denied any wrongdoing. If I'd heard her statement on the witness stand, I would've assumed she was telling the truth. But, I'm equally certain she and Dominic know a great deal more than they've admitted about Douglas's and Farmer's deaths." Elliot looked over at Lydia and asked, "When did you have your first crush on a handsome older man?"

"Don't get Lydia started on her love-life," Taggart complained. "We'll be here all night."

She tossed the detective a dirty glance. "I think I was about ten," Lydia said. "The older man, as you put it, was twenty. He lived next door. Nothing came of it other than my wonderful fantasies about him carrying me off to his own private island." The glitter of her eyes almost disappeared between suddenly drooped lids. "But I would've done anything for him."

"How long did it last?" asked Elliot.

"For a year I loved him heart and soul," she replied. "Then my first love got married and I met Ricky Jabloski. Ricky had red hair, freckles and a bug-collection. He sat next to me in Math class." Lydia chuckled. "For an eleven-year old, Ricky was considered quite a catch."

"I think Rita loved Michael Douglas," mused Elliot.

"According to what my operatives discovered," Taggart interjected, "Douglas was not one to offer love in the real sense. He used it as bait to keep the women in his life on a string. From my original investigation, I can tell you that any woman drawn to Michael Douglas had better be a bit on the exhibitionistic side."

Lydia tilted toward the detective. "What, exactly, do you mean by that?"

Taggart grinned. "Michael Douglas was a camera buff—of the private-studio kind."

"You mean some of the photos still exist?" asked Elliot.

The detective wagged his head. "Not that we know of. But Michael Douglas was more than an amateur at it. He rented a studio above a café.

When I initially began the investigation into his murder I wasn't aware of the place. Then, nearly a week later, we got a tip. But by that time the studio had been ransacked. That doesn't mean whoever got to the studio first didn't take the photos and negatives that were there."

"Someone like a night-janitor?" suggested Chambers Elliot.

Taggart nodded. "I questioned Junior Billings about the studio. He denied all knowledge of it. But I took it for granted that he was lying. In any event, we didn't find any fingerprints indicating that he had ever been there. But we did find a lot of prints from a lot of different people—all females. However, none were ever identified."

"Any rumors as to whom those dalliances included?" asked Elliot.

"Only one, so far," replied the detective. "I was stunned when Quigley told me. Barbara Pierce."

Lydia chuckled, as she looked over at her boss. "What does that do to your single killer theory, Chambers?"

"Not much in the way of supporting it," muttered the lawyer.

"A romance does not make her a killer," Taggart declared.

Elliot stared down at the table in silence for a few seconds. "No."

"But it might give George Pierce the impetus to commit murder in an effort to protect her," suggested Lydia. "What happened to Barbara Pierce?"

"She committed suicide not long after the Douglas' murder," said Taggart. "The papers blamed her death on a history of mental-illness."

Chambers Elliot shook his head. "I never believed that. Barb had bouts of depression, yes," he said, white lines forming at the corners of his mouth. "But as far as I know she never considered suicide."

"Which makes the fact that there was no real investigation into her death something to think about," the detective said.

Elliot rocked his cocktail glass back and forth between his fingers. "I don't like where this is going."

"There's more," Taggart said. "A neighbor of George Pierce claims that Barbara asked George for a divorce, several times. But, as a good Catholic, George refused."

"George never mentioned that." Elliot looked over at the detective with a start. "He and Barb lived together until she died. I just assumed…"

"As may be," continued Taggart. "But back then, fault was necessary for a divorce decree. Barbara Pierce's romantic involvement with Michael Douglas could've been her way to embarrass George into filing for divorcing."

Her long lashes twitched. "How did she die?"

"Another interesting tidbit," said Taggart. "Cause of death was due to an overdose of sleeping pills—pills without a prescription. Pills George Pierce could not explain, when asked about the drugs during the inquest."

"I refused to believe that George murdered Barb for being unfaithful rather than agreeing to a divorce," said Chambers Elliot, impatiently.

"Chambers, I know George is your friend," said the detective. "I know you don't want to hear speculations that decry him. But what people believe isn't going to change simply because you don't like what you're hearing."

"I'm sorry, Jason," Elliot said.

"The photo-studio suggests that Douglas's women willingly posed," Lydia enjoined.

"Or he drugged them for the photos—that's another thing we have to consider," said Taggart.

"Is it possible Michael Douglas blackmailed these married women using their photos?" Lydia suggested.

"Very much so," Elliot said.

"Which could explain how Douglas financed his flings," Taggart added. "Now here's something interesting. Despite his philandering, Michael Douglas was a devoted employee, according to several sources. More than anything, he wanted to expand his business-holdings under Old Frank Portello. That meant keeping on the good side of the Mafia Don."

Elliot reflected, "Which meant, not doing anything stupid with the boss's daughter."

"Douglas doesn't sound Sicilian," commented Lydia.

"Which is why Douglas couldn't have been a 'made man' in the mob," Taggart explained. "He would always have continued as a member of Old Frank's business-front team. Not that being relegated there was a bad deal. Frank Portello took good care of his people."

"What if Rita Portello is our confessor?" Lydia Marshall asked.

"Where'd you come up with that?" the detective fired back.

She shrugged. "After what Chambers told me Salvator's remarks about Rita's frequent church visits, it made sense."

Elliot nodded, "I think that's a logical conclusion."

"Nonsense," Taggart declared. "It's more likely she helped kill Douglas. Rita's got the reputation enough for it."

Lydia gave her head a determine shake. "Rita didn't kill Michael Douglas. Not if she loved him. Not at that age."

"Think back to your first crush, Lydia," said Elliot. "How did you feel when it didn't pan out, because you were too young?"

"Hurt, of course," she replied. "But I didn't consider shooting the guy. And neither did Rita—I'm certain of that. Love at that point in a girl's life is far too pure for such a thing. It's far more likely she would've killed herself."

"Say what you like, Lydia. But Rita Portello is known for unmitigated vindictiveness," declared Taggart. "God help any man who trifles with her affections. That woman gets even at all costs—ask any of her former suitors. Those, who are still among the living—which as, I recall, are not many."

"Dear God," Lydia said under her breath. Then she glanced at the men's questioning eyes. "A horrible thought just came to mind. If Rita shared her feelings with Michael Douglas, he might've rejected her outright as being a child." The curve of her cheek stiffened. "At that age, such a remark would've been crushing. Rita might've lied to Dominic about Michael Douglas and what went on. He would've… Oh, that poor woman."

"Poor woman!" scoffed Taggart. "Rita Portello tried to castrate the last guy who jilted her – with her teeth."

Lydia continued impatiently, "I'm thinking about her carrying the guilt of a murder all these years. Vindictive or not, as a young girl she loved Michael Douglas. Living with an angry lie that caused the man she loved to be killed would be horrible."

"Horrible enough to commit murder in order to protect Dominic from prosecution?" mused Chambers Elliot. "Perhaps my single killer theory is not so far-flung after all."

She shook her head earnestly. "Rita didn't do it," insisted Lydia.

Taggart said, "One last thing, Chambers. My contact in homicide told me that Dominic Portello was seen leaving the Double Oak Hotel minutes after Harry Farmer bit the asphalt. Although forensics found nothing to link Dominic to Harry's murder, Herbie Mann plans to question Dominic about his presence at the hotel. Herbie also intends to question you."

Chambers Elliot folded his hands and rested his elbows on the table. "Which means things could get very interesting for me, very soon."

"If you're worried now, wait until you see my expense report," said the detective. "I arranged for a copy of Harry Farmer's autopsy report, as soon as it's completed. The cost of which will probably give you heart failure."

Lydia's lips parted slowly until her teeth caught the light and glittered, as she watched her boss grit his teeth. Her breath made a harsh sound as she stifled a laugh.

Chambers Elliot refocused upon Jason Taggart. "Did your people find a link between Kathy Martin and Sydney Pierce?"

"Other than the blush we saw on Kathy's cheeks when she talked about Sydney?" Taggart wagged his head.

Elliot frowned. "When George Pierce initially contacted us about Sheila Clifford, you ran a background check on her, didn't you Jason?"

"And my people have hit all the bases, again. But so far she's not to be found," said the detective.

"Why is she hiding?" Lydia asked.

"Probably for the same reason I'm a nervous wreck," Taggart said. "The Portellos. Salvator probably assumes that Sheila, as Harry's stepdaughter, has that DVD—which could very well be true."

"I was just thinking," Elliot said. "With the man she knew as her father murdered, Sheila might abandon Raintree—particularly, if her claims of being a Pierce are nothing but air. Did Sheila ever have a pimp?"

"Sheila Clifford's a prostitute?" Lydia gaped. "Does George Pierce know?"

"If Sheila is family, her history won't make any difference to George," Elliot declared.

"She did have a pimp," the detective said. "Mazy Wilson. I'll see if I can run him down."

"That is so disgusting!" Lydia gave the detective a disbelieving look. "How do you know Sheila had a pimp? It's not like those creeps advertise."

"We know because he paid her bail after she was arrested for soliciting." The detective redirected his attention to Chambers Elliot. "My people did find out how Harry Farmer became Sheila Clifford's adoptive father. Sheila's mother, Maria, married the old boy in a fit of drunken lunacy. Then she divorced Harry and promptly ran off with some rich guy she met during one of her nights killing time in the various bars around Houston. However the affair was short-lived and Maria came back to Harry with apologies and a baby on the way. Harry took her back without question. After Sheila was born, he adopted the baby."

"Sounds like Harry had more character than he's been given credit," remarked Elliot, staring down at the table broodingly. "It also means it's not likely that George Pierce's deceased son, Edward, is Sheila Clifford's father."

"But it's not beyond possibility, Chambers," said the detective. "Edward Pierce was not fussy about his playmates."

Elliot stood up and looked over at Lydia. "I think we have time for one dance before our meals arrive. Interested?"

"Give me a second to check my makeup." Lydia adjusted her face with the aid of a compact and its duster. Then, after dropping the makeup-gear back into her purse, she stood up. "I'm ready whenever you are, Boss."

Elliot led her out on the dance floor where they blended with the other couples.

"Are you really going to notify the police about Salvator Portello's visit?" she murmured into his ear. "I mean if he's going to think Lt. Mann's upcoming talk with Dominic is because of you…"

"I want Mr. Portello to understand that there is a big price to pay for threatening us."

She tilted back her head to look her boss squarely in the face. "Chambers. He might counter-attack."

"Salvator was angry and not thinking when he came to call. Since leaving me, he's had a great deal of time to reflect and interrogate." He pulled her closer. "Relax. Whatever involvement Dominic and Rita had, as far s Michael Douglas and Harry Farmer are concerned, Salvator now knows all. And, I suspect, he knows that I would be worth more to him alive as Dominic's defense counsel than dead."

She tilted back, again, to give him a surprised look. "You wouldn't serious consider such a case would you? I mean, those people are killers!"

"Of course I would," he said, drawing her against him, once more. "The fees from such a case would set us up for years. And, each of us— no matter our history—deserves a chance at justice. That includes the Portellos."

She drew her blonde brows together in thought. "I hope for the sake of your reputation you would refuse at least once."

He nodded, grinning. "That's to be expected in all negotiations—in order to up the ante."

"Will Salvator be arrested for what his men did to Ramón and his threats against you?"

"Not likely. I have no doubt that Mr. Portello will produce a hundred witnesses claiming that he was miles away from our office at the time. The exercise isn't to get Salvator incarcerated. It's to bring his bullying tactics against us to task. He'll react more slowly, next time, after I've curbed him a little."

The song ended and they returned to their table. Their meals had arrived and Jason Taggart was devouring his salad.

"Jason, you've got dressing on the end of your nose," Lydia scolded.

The detective daubed at the offending smear with his napkin. "Your trouble is, Lydia, you don't know how to enjoy a good supper. You're too busy dieting."

"Bathing in Roquefort isn't my idea of enjoyment, thank you very much," she said quickly, and sat down.

"I've been thinking, Chambers." Taggart munched. "About Father Zamoyski and how information privy only to him might come to guys like Harry Farmer and Milton Raintree."

"Mind reading?" grinned Elliot.

The detective made a dismissive wave with his free hand. "The way I figure it, those clowns must've been pals with Zamoyski."

Elliot wagged his head in disagreement. "Grafters like Harry and Milton wouldn't wait thirty years to cash in on that type of knowledge. They learned what was said, recently."

"Assuming Rita is the one who confessed," suggested Lydia, "it's a good bet she sought advice before talking to Zamoyski."

"I'm still not convinced that's the case—" Taggart began.

"Hear me out," Lydia said cunningly. "Rita wouldn't have gone directly to Father Zamoyski. Not at that age. Not on something so personal as Michael Douglas' murder."

Elliot asked, "But, who would she trust other than her family and priest?"

"A neighbor," suggested Taggart.

"Another girl," declared Lydia, cocking her head on one side. "Rita would've confided in her best friend."

"But if she did that, why did it take thirty years for this best-friend to talk?" asked Taggart. "And why would this best-friend tell all in the first place?"

"That's what we'll have to find out," said Elliot. "Start in the old neighborhood where Rita grew up, Jason. Talk to the women there."

"You'd better leave that to someone who understands, Chambers," interjected Lydia.

"What do you mean by that?" demanded Taggart. "I'll have you know I'm adored by women all across Texas."

"The desperate ones," Lydia taunted as she began devouring her steak.

"See what I mean about feeding her, Chambers?" Taggart said. He tilted his head towards Lydia. "She doesn't even come up for air."

Lydia glared over at Taggart, her mouth stuffed with meat, her eyes wide.

"Pay no attention to him, Lydia," encouraged Elliot. "I adore the way

you enjoy your food - especially how you get those dribbles of steak-
sauce on your chin."

Chapter 8

Three days later, after court recessed for the afternoon, Chambers Elliot was walking along the sidewalk toward his offices when Jason Taggart pulled his Chrysler to the curb in front of the lawyer and got out.

"Slumming, Jason?" asked Elliot, with a faint crooked smile.

"Lydia told me where to find you," the detective said brightly. "Von Drake contacted me about half an hour ago. Kathy Martin is registered at the Forty Winks Motel. Not only that but a man appeared at her door and she welcomed him in with open arms. It's no guaranty. But I'm thinking we finally have Milton Raintree."

"So Kathy and Milton Raintree are not as distant as she led us to believe?" Elliot mused.

Taggart shrugged. "I'm on my way over there, now. Do you want to come along?"

Elliot's eyes glistened with anticipation. "Absolutely."

Two hours later, Taggart's Chrysler parked across the street from the motel, the plumbers van Von Drake drove. He and Elliot got out.

Von Drake crawled from the van and gave his cigarette a toss before strolling back to where Elliot and Taggart waited.

"Don't you ever sleep?" asked Eliot.

Von Drake laughed. "In this business, you sleep only when you have to." He tilted his head toward the collection of brown-painted cottages. "That's her Corvette under the tarp, next to number seventeen. She's registered under the name of Carpenter."

"Any movement since you last contacted me?" asked Taggart.

"I'm afraid so." Red dots formed on his cheeks as he glanced around before continuing. "The guy who was visiting her left, about ten minutes ago. He went off on foot. Hendricks hadn't arrived, yet. So I had to make a decision. Follow a guy who might be Raintree, or sit tight." He extended his hands in front of his body, parallel and close together, as though he was measuring the risks of a wager. "I decided on tailing him. After a couple of blocks he spotted me and ducked between some houses. I gave chase, but he slipped away. I just got back."

"He'll have warned her," said Elliot, absently.

"Sorry, Jason," said Von Drake.

"You did the right thing," said Taggart.

From across the street, childish laughter bubbled. The men looked over and noticed a couple of girls playing a game of catch with a red ball between the first two cabins.

"Are you certain the man was Raintree?" asked Elliot.

Von Drake shook his head, still watching the kids. "Nothing to go by other than Kathy Martin gave him a kiss at the door, and he patted her ass."

The lawyer glanced over at Taggart. "That little scene could mean Sheila Clifford is no longer cooperating with Raintree."

"Or they'd spotted me watching the place," put in Von Drake. He squinted at the lawyer sideways. "And gave me a show."

Taggart studied the house for many seconds. "Is Kathy Martin is still in there?"

Von Drake shrugged. "Not if they had me pegged before he left. If he didn't spot me right away, there's a chance I got back before he warned her. But I've not seen anyone moving behind the curtains since returning."

Elliot balled his hands at the bottom of his trouser pockets. "Was he the only one visiting Kathy?"

"As far as I could tell," Von Drake said, a little obscurely.

Jason Taggart glanced around as if expecting to see someone. "Where's Hendricks?"

"Parked where he can watch the alley," the other detective replied.

Behind them, the sound of an approaching car floated over the street. Taggart glanced toward it with disinterest and then returned his attention to Von Drake.

"We're going to try and pressure Kathy Martin into fingering Raintree," Taggart told his operative. "Call Beatrice. Have her come out with another vehicle. Drive down to the drop-point she suggests and switch with her." He paused as the car roared past. Then he continued with, "Find a spot where you can tail Kathy when she leaves. If she hooks up with Raintree, grab him. We want Raintree no matter what. We'll worry about justifying your actions to the locals after we get our hands on him. Give Hendricks the same order in case Raintree comes back here."

"Gotcha'," said Von Drake over one shoulder as he trotted back to the van.

Elliot and Taggart crossed the street and hurried over to number seventeen. Taggart tapped lightly on the door, rattling the plastic, numeric medallions mounted upon it.

There came no answer.

He knocked again, more loudly.

Still, there was no answer.

"Kathy ran for it," Elliot muttered.

"Von Drake did the right thing by tailing Raintree, Elliot," Taggart said.

Elliot looked at him without expression. "I'm beginning to feel like a cat trailing a mouse that's got eyes in the back of its head."

Somewhere not far off, a church bell began to toll in low, plaintive notes.

The detective indicated the door with a thumb. "She could still be in there. Kathy wouldn't just abandon her Vette."

Elliot whispered, "I've got an idea." Then he took out his handkerchief and stuffed it into his mouth. After which he leaned close to the door and garbled, "It's me, baby. Open up."

They waited. Again, there was no response.

Taggart dropped to his knees, took out a pen and a penlight. Then using the pen to lift the door-sweep and using the penlight to illuminate the cabin's interior, he peered beneath the door. After a few seconds he stood up shaking his head.

"I can't see anyone, Chambers." There was a swift shine as detective's eyes moved from the lawyer, down to the floor and back to the lawyer.

"That is what I was afraid of," Elliot returned, glancing at a fingernail.

Taggart stuffed the pen and penlight back into his suit. "Hang tough. I'll go around back and check for another door. If these cabins are separated into bedrooms, she could be holing up in one, until we leave."

Elliot stared at the door in silence. Taggart hurried away.

A few minutes later, the detective returned, panting from exertion. "There's no rear door. There are, however, two back-windows." He held out his hands giving a two-foot span between the palms. "Both are big enough to crawl through. Both are locked from the inside. Both have their curtains drawn."

"I have to be certain either way," reflected the lawyer.

Taggart produced a leather-bound tool-kit from his pocket and took out a lock-pick and pry tool. "Which will it be?" he asked. "Legal or illegal?"

A vague smile moved the corners of Elliot's lips. "There's no guaranty a phone-call would get the police here. Then there's the risk of filing such a false report..." He gave the end of his nose a tug. "Naturally, as good citizens, we would not want to do such a thing."

The detective gave worried roll of his eyes. "Us good citizens who could lose our licenses over such an irresponsible act, you mean?"

"So," Elliot continued, once more glancing around to check for observers, "let's consider this a legal effort by two good Samaritans who heard a muffled cry for help, and rushed to assist."

Taggart scowled. "What you're really saying is, this is where you cover your eyes and I discover the door is open—after I pick the lock."

"I think that's best, don't you?" Elliot laughed.

"I hope they give us adjoining cells, Chambers." Taggart sighed. "I want to be able to remind you of this moment for the next three years as we perform hard labor for the State of Texas."

He fitted the pick and pry tool into the lock. A few seconds later, there was a distinctive click as the lock yielded to Taggart's illicit efforts. "I suppose you want me to go in first? In case she's armed and disinclined toward uninvited guests?"

"Our fair State is known for its shoot-first policy with respect to intruders," Elliot remarked. "That's how we limit the number of executions each year."

"Don't remind me," Taggart groaned, as he put his toolkit away. "Lights, or otherwise?"

Elliot tugged on one earlobe thoughtfully. "We may as well give whoever might be in there and armed a clear shot."

"Why don't I just paint a bull's-eye on my chest?" complained Taggart.

"Wait until we're both inside and the door is closed before throwing the light-switch. I'd hate for some poor innocent to get killed by a stray round passing through you and the open doorway."

The detective's breath made a rushing sound. "Always concerned for the other fellow, aren't you?"

Elliot nodded, grinning. "It's a curse, Jason."

"Why do I get the feeling you're not taking Harry Farmer's murder seriously? " Taggart jabbed a finger at the door. "For all we know she was in on it. If so, Kathy Martin won't appreciate this Good-Samaritan ploy of yours."

"Just how wide is that yellow streak down your back, Jason?"

Taggart looked at the lawyer sharply. "Now, don't start that again."

Chambers Elliot patted the Taggart's shoulder contritely. Then he nudged the detective aside, pushed the door open and stepped into the cabin.

Jason Taggart followed close on the lawyer's heels and shut the door. Then the detective fumbled along the wall until he found the light-switch.

A second later an overhead fluorescent affair flickered to life. The bluish glow made the small living space appear to be a distortion of lights and shadows.

The cabin's main room was meagerly furnished with twin beds, a bureau, a table and two straight-back chairs. Women's clothing lay strewn upon the beds. The suitcase they had seen at Kathy's home was open in the center of the room, and partially unpacked. The bureau drawers were all open, and empty. Atop the bureau sat a rattail comb, a round hairbrush and a Styrofoam manikin's head for holding a wig.

"No bedrooms," said Taggart, staring at the beds.

There was a musty odor about the place. Both men's noses wrinkled in disgust as they looked around. Although, there was scarcely a place in which a cat could hide, they split up; one going into the tiny bath, while the other looked beneath the beds. Moments later, both came face to face by the door.

Elliot said in a low voice, "We're right back where we started."

"I'll have Von Drake put a GPS tracking device on her car." Taggart's forehead took on the appearance of rippling water. "When she comes back for it, we'll know exactly where she goes."

Chambers Elliot made a sweeping gesture. "Did you notice anything unusual?"

The detective put one hand out and turned it slowly, fluttering the fingers, with an effect almost like a butterfly taking flight. "Other than the air smells like something I really dislike finding on the heels of my shoes?"

The lawyer shook his head, went over to one of the beds and picked up two pieces of female clothing. "There's nothing here for a man. And the garments left behind are in two different sizes."

"What of it?" Taggart cracked the knuckles on one hand with the fingers of the other.

"It means that Kathy is living with another woman—probably Sheila Clifford." Elliot dropped the garments back onto the bed. "That scene Von Drake witnessed might have been genuine after all—if it was, Sheila was who he saw, not Kathy."

Taggart dropped the corners of his mouth and looked sideways at Elliot. "Sheila was wearing a wig, you mean?"

Elliot eyed the manikin-head. "Possibly. I think I would if I thought the Portellos were searching for me. It could also explain why the car was left behind—Kathy was not here to take it when this flop was vacated." The lawyer paused a moment and fumbled with his lower lip in thought. Then he said, "Drop by my office in the morning. Get there about my usual arrival-time."

"What gives?" the detective asked.

"After what happened with Von Drake, I think Milton Raintree is going to try an end-run."

"I don't get you, Chambers." Taggart leaned toward the lawyer. "What does a football play have to do with anything?"

"Raintree's got to be worried, after that little race to get away from Von Drake. He doesn't know if Von Drake is part of the Portello mob or somebody I sent. He's got to find out which it is." Elliot dug a nail clipper from his pocket and nipped a hangnail off his thumb. Then he returned the clipper to his pocket. "If the Portellos are onto him, survival means leaving town until things cool off—possibly forever. If I'm his only worry, he can afford to hang around and keep dodging me. I expect he'll send Sheila Clifford to my office to find out where he stands."

"Why would he send *her*?"

"Kathy Martin and he are at odds over Sheila. Therefore, Kathy is not likely on his 'trust-list'." Eliot smiled with confidence, as if he had found a crystal ball that actually worked. "Check with Maggie when you get to my office, tomorrow. If she tells you that Sheila's come, wait for Sheila to leave and tail her. Raintree will want to know what she found out immediately. So she'll make a beeline to him."

"And if she isn't there?"

Elliot sighed, "I'll call you when she arrives."

"What now?"

"I don't know about you but I'm ready to call it a day."

Chapter 9

"For the fifth time, Ramón, *amicus curiae* has nothing to do with your Friendship-Dating Club!" Chambers Elliot shouted from behind the door to his private office, the next morning. "*Amicus curiae* refers to someone, not a party to a case, who volunteers information in an effort to assist the court in deciding the matter before it. And stop scratching! I don't care if it was stretched beyond human endurance."

Maggie Sharp glanced toward the verbal tirade and gave Sheila Clifford, the svelte blonde seated in one of the reception chairs, an embarrassed grin.

"Your boss I take it?" snickered Sheila.

"Ramón is our new intern." Maggie nervously raked her fingers through her curly red hair. "He's a first-year law-student from the University of Texas. Mr. Elliot is usually a very patient man. But Ramón sort of irritates him. Actually, Ramón sort of irritates everyone—almost, everyone."

"Sounds like Ramón is too self-involved."

"He's pretty much obsessed with the decorated part that got stretched, anyway," Maggie said with a blush.

"I guess I can relate," declared Sheila. "I over-stretched my back doing exercises once. It gave me so much pain all I could focus on were aspirin and my back."

"In Ramón's case it's more of a frontal concern."

The door to Elliot's office banged opened and the lawyer stormed out. "I've sent Ramón out for sweet-rolls and coffee. Hopefully, he'll get lost and never return!"

"This is Sheila Clifford, Mr. Elliot," said Maggie, pointing to the blonde. "She didn't have an appointment. But since Sheila might be George Pierce's granddaughter, Lydia said you would be willing to speak with her. Oh, and Mr. Taggart stopped by a few minutes ago to say he would meet with you later, as planned."

Chambers Elliot's blue eyes gave the blonde woman, who was now rising to her feet, a quick assessment. She was a languid creature with a broad, vacuous face. Her mascaraed eyebrows arched upward, haughtily above dark eyes. Large jade danglers hooked to the lobes of her ears. Her hair waved back smoothly from behind them. The smile she offered him had a frozen, tailored quality. Her skin indicated she was no older than twenty-five. She had long, smooth fingers with nails lacquered a jade-green. Her clothing—a sleek, green, dress—suggested she was neither shy, nor retiring. The matching green handbag was new, and expensive.

A shiny new wedding band sat on the ring finger of her left hand.

"I was expecting you, Sheila," he declared, pleasantly.

"You were?" she gaped in surprise.

"You must be an early riser like me," Elliot remarked. "Most females of my acquaintance are night-people. Some rarely get out of bed before noon." With a wink he added, "That, I must admit, has certain advantages."

Sheila Clifford gave Chambers Elliot bright smile as she oozed over to him in the manner of one desirous of sexual attention. "I'm always ready for anything on the rise," she cooed. The fingernails from one hand toyed with the hair over one ear. "No matter how often I peak."

Her nearness bathed him in body-warmth and Shalimar perfume. "Better and better," he said. "In fact, I'm feeling a rising right now." Chambers Elliot indicated the open office door with a generous sweep of his right hand. "Shall we go in?"

As the blonde swayed past, Elliot gave an astonished Maggie a smile before following Sheila into his private office.

"Please sit down," Elliot said as he shut the door.

Sheila settled into one of the customer chairs in front of his desk, opened her purse and took a cigarette from an engraved silver case. Then she withdrew a silver lighter. It was an expensive match to the cigarette case. With a flick of her thumb the lighter became alive, and she lit the cigarette.

Elliot strode over to the desk and took a clean ashtray from one of its lower drawers and slid it across the desk to her. But instead of smoking the cigarette, Sheila snuffed it out in the ashtray after one puff.

"I keep forgetting I'm wearing one of those damn patches," she muttered, irritably. "They say you can die if you wear one and smoke." Then Sheila forced a smile. "I'm trying to quit. But it's tough."

"You're from around here?" He set the ashtray to one side.

"Houston. A friend is putting me up while I'm in Austin," she replied, dropping the cigarette case and lighter back into her purse. "Or was." Her eyes twinkled coquettishly.

He put his elbows on the desk and propped his chin on the backs of his hands. "How is it you contacted George about being his granddaughter?"

Her smile became uncertain. "After my mother ran out on Harry and me, I found a letter written to her from an Edward Pierce. The return address listed the Pierce Ranch. In the letter was an apology for getting her pregnant." She paused and arched an eyebrow to see the effect of her words on his face. "Sadly, Edward died in a car crash, not long after I was born. So…"

Elliot's forehead corrugated with confusion, as he sat upright, letting his hands rest upon the desk. "I'm surprised George took you seriously based solely upon a letter."

"He didn't, at first." Sheila hesitated, and spoke more slowly. "In fact, he told me right were to go. Then, a few months after that this detective showed up at my apartment." Her face became politely serene. "He said I was George Pierce's granddaughter and that George wanted to speak with me." She shrugged her shoulders, slightly. "So I came here and saw George, again." She lowered her head and looked at him from underneath, on the slant. "This time he didn't toss me out."

"What is the name of that detective?"

"I don't remember." She popped her knuckles and looked down at her purse.

His eyes darkened with disbelief. "Do you know where your mother is?"

Sheila's blonde head shook as her eyes rose to his. "Mommy was always running off with somebody. Harry Farmer adopted me. I guess I should be grateful. At least I had a father when I was growing up—if you can call Harry a father. He was in jail most of the time, leaving me in foster homes." Her lower lip trembled slightly and her mask of contentment crumbled into a façade of genuine grief. "Poor Harry."

"Did your mother ever speak to you about Edward Pierce?"

"No," she replied, trying to reform her happy-face. "I don't think Mom realized that Edward had the bucks. You can't tell with men. Some come on like they own the world. Later you find out they've only got pennies in their pockets."

"Have you ever been married?" Elliot asked, casually.

"No." Then her eyes dropped to her hands and she giggled nervously. "Actually, I am. We were married this morning."

"Your husband, I take it, is Milton Raintree?"

Her head jerked up and she gave the lawyer a look of blank amazement. "How—how could you know that?"

He shrugged. "I'm a mind reader. What does Milton look like without the stage makeup?"

She laughed, nervously. "I don't know what you mean."

"It's not important," he said, noncommittally. "Where do you plan to honeymoon?"

"That's still up in the air," she replied, sourly. "So's our wedding night. You wouldn't believe it, but the guy's never even touched me."

"I thought nobility had gone out of style."

She shot a furtive glance toward the door. "I wouldn't call Milton noble."

"Where is he?"

"My husband had to leave town. Business, you know."

"Not really. What type of business does a grafter like Milton Raintree have?"

Sheila eyed him with sudden apprehension. "Grafter?"

"Where do you work?" Elliot asked.

"I don't—now that I'm married," she asserted, lightly.

"Then you've got a rare husband. Most women are expected to assist with the economics of marriage these days. Where did you work last?"

"Houston." Her fingers tightened briefly on her purse. "Don't you want to know why I'm here?"

"Where in Houston?" he pressed.

"Does it make a difference?" The fingers went white-knuckle tight, but she did not notice.

"To me it does."

"Iverson Oil-Drilling." There was a taut reluctance to her voice.

"What was your job with them?"

She forced a smile. It was a plastic, bad-girl smile this time as if she were hiding a dirty secret. "Bookkeeper."

"Bookkeepers are in short supply," he remarked, offering her a reassuring nod. "At least the honest ones. I'm certain you'll have no trouble finding a job, should the need arise. You and your new husband have a place in Austin or in one of the outlying towns?"

Her smile hardened a little. "Austin."

Elliot stroked his brow with a gesture of infinite weariness. "Address?"

Sheila nervously cleared her throat. "I—I don't know the address. I'm staying at the Double Oak Hotel. Milton said he'd pick me up there when he got back in town and we'd drive to our apartment together. Look, Mr. Elliot…"

"You're registered at the hotel under your own name?"

"No," she said. "Milton said I should register as Alma Dickerson."

The lawyer gave her a curious look. "Why that particular name?"

"I don't know," she snapped, impatiently. Her face took on a haggard appearance. "Look, I didn't come here to discuss my personal—"

"What's your cell-phone number?"

"I don't have one. My phone was stolen." Her words sounded as if they were made of glass, brittle, ready to shatter. "Wouldn't it save us both a great deal of time if I told you why I needed a lawyer?"

Elliot shook his head before saying, "You're requesting my services, Mrs. Raintree. You may or may not be able to pay what those services cost in advance. Therefore I would be extending credit in anticipation of future payment. Such a financial arrangement necessitates my assessing your ability to pay. Does the name, Kathy Martin mean anything to you?"

"Yes," she replied, after several nervous gulps. "She's a friend of mine. How does Kathy fit into your concerns about getting paid?"

"She doesn't," replied Elliot, with a shrug. "I was just curious if you knew her. What about Mazy Wilson?"

Sheila flushed all the way down to her elbows. "I don't know him—anybody, by that name."

Elliot pursed his lips in thought. "It was my understanding that Mazy was a business associate of yours. One might even describe him as your pimp."

Her mouth moved as if her tongue were growing too large to be contained. "So you know?"

"I know a great many things, Sheila."

She squirmed under Elliot's stare. "I suppose you told George?"

The lawyer shook his head. "Do you own a car?"

"No." Her chin tilted scornfully. "Do you plan to put a lien on it if I did?"

He bowed his head in thought. "You came to my office by taxi?"

"Yes."

His eyes rose up to hers. "Does George Pierce know you're married to Milton Raintree?"

Sheila answered in a lifeless tone. "I didn't want to tell him until everything was settled—that he had accepted me as his granddaughter." She leaned back in her chair and crossed her legs, trembling like she was locked naked in a freezer.

Chambers Elliot gave a grunt of satisfaction. "What you're really saying is, you didn't want George to take one look at Milton Raintree and change his mind about making you one of his money-grubbing heirs."

Tears puddled in her eyes and she dipped her chin to avoid the lawyer's suspicious glare.

"How did you meet Milton Raintree?" Elliot asked.

"Kathy introduced us," she sniffed.

He frowned reflectively. "Before or after the detective contacted you?"

"After." She tilted toward the lawyer. "Kathy called me up the weekend I saw the detective. I told her about him. That's when she suggested I come to Austin. Milton was with her when I got off the bus.

He was very nice to me. He…"

"What has Mr. Raintree told you about the Pierce family?"

Her eyes went wide with sudden worry. "Things."

Chambers Elliot made a gesture of impatience. "Did he tell you how much you might inherit after George's death—should you be in George's Will as his granddaughter?"

She grinned greedily. "Fifty million, give or take—if I get an equal share."

"Fifty million which will become community property—now that you and Milton are married," he said, dryly. "Fifty million that will automatically come to him, should your death follow George's. Consider my last statement as free legal advice."

She blanched at the implication in Elliot's last statement. "Milton loves me. He told me. He'd never do anything to hurt me." She smiled bitterly. "Milton's really very nice." She paused, as if in conflict with herself. "You just need to get to know him. Once you do…"

"Yes, yes, yes," Elliot said, the tenor of his voice clearly taunting. "The adoring Mr. Raintree loves you." He stood up. "How did Harry Farmer get that DVD?"

Sheila seemed almost in pain, her mouth twisted, her eyes closed. "I don't know. He went to stay with a sick friend after the Portellos nearly killed him. When his friend died, Harry came looking for me. He had the DVD, then."

"What's the name of that friend?"

"Billings."

The lawyer's eyes widened in surprise. "Junior Billings?"

She nodded, with another sniff.

"What motel was Harry living at when the Portellos caught up with him?"

She drew a deep breath. "The Forty Winks."

Elliot settled back into his chair. "Does Harry still have a room there?"

"Not that I know of."

"Milton Raintree was living with Kathy Martin, then, wasn't he?"

She nodded. "But they didn't have anything going on between them. It was strictly business. Both Milton and Kathy told me that."

Elliot's thin lips curled. "I'll just bet they did." He looked at her long and thoughtfully. "Why did the detective think your paternal father was Edward Pierce? Did Raintree feed him that information?"

Sheila was shaking her head slowly. "No. Milton wouldn't have known anything about me, then. Like I said, I didn't meet him until

Kathy asked me to move here." She opened her purse, took out a piece of gum, unwrapped it, and stuck the gum into her mouth. Then she squeezed it around a few times between her teeth before saying, "Look, Mr. Elliot, I'm not going to claim I'm some girl-scout who deserves a pile of money. But, if I'm entitled to a better life I want it."

Elliot leaned back in his swivel chair and said, "Do you want it bad enough to kill for?"

Sheila stiffened. Her eyes were hostile. "Of course not."

"I don't believe you."

She reached over and dropped the gum-wrappings into the ashtray. "Why would I lie when I'm here asking for your help?"

He tilted forward rattling his fingertips upon the desktop. "We have the death penalty for capital murder in this State," he growled irritably. "You might want to consider that. You might also want to remind Milton Raintree of it."

She twisted away from his stare.

The lawyer smiled derisively. "Do you understand what being an Accessory After the Fact means?"

"I'm not a killer, Mr. Elliot," she declared, glaring back at him.

"It means anyone, while knowing an offense has been committed, who receives, relieves, comforts or assists the offender in any way in order to hinder or prevent his or her apprehension, trial or punishment, is an accessory after the fact and punishable accordingly. Murdering George Pierce for gain is a Capital Crime. Are you sure you don't know where I can find Milton Raintree?"

She chewed her gum faster and faster as if her tongue were in a race with her molars. "If I did, I'd tell you."

Elliot shrugged his shoulders and said, "Tell me about your time with Harry Farmer after your mother left."

Sheila took a deep breath. Then she began her tale. As she spoke Chambers Elliot stopped her from time to time to ask questions, or get clarification. When she finished, Sheila raised her hands and let them fall back to her lap.

"Not much to brag about, is it?" she said, wearily. Her voice sounded like lead slugs falling on a piece of stone.

Elliot regarded her in slow appraisal before asking, "Have you told the police you're Harry Farmer's stepdaughter?"

"No. Milton said…"

"Are you still a prostitute? Is that how Raintree's financing his life until George's money comes to you?"

She tightened her lips into a thin line. Then she said, "I don't do that

95

any more." Her eyes searched Elliot's face and then she offered a pleading smile. "Does George have to know that about that?"

"Not if you've been honest with me. But…"

Sheila's eyes never wavered. "I have, Mr. Elliot. I swear to God, I have."

The lawyer's brows arched in surprise as he recalled Dominic Portello's repeated use of that same statement. "How well do you know Dominic Portello?"

She took a sudden interest in her purse. "Never heard of him."

"A man as infamous as Dominic Portello and you've never heard of him."

The subtle irony his voice expressed caused her to look at him quizzically.

"Your husband's visit to my office, the other day, as Father Zamoyski was entertaining," Elliot said. "Please extend my congratulations to Raintree for his characterization of the priest. I must admit, he almost fooled me. I am curious, however, as to what he wanted from my safe?"

"Safe? I don't anything about a safe." Her voice was suddenly high, out of control.

He gave her a doubting look. "The two of you are running out of time, Sheila. Salvator Portello and his people are fervently hunting the DVD Harry had. I think you have it, now."

Her throat bobbed. "No. I never saw it."

"You're lying."

"You told the Portellos that I have the DVD?" she choked. The words came between mumbling lips, like those of a little girl waking from a bad dream.

"Not yet."

"Well, I don't have it," she declared, her eyes darting away from his as eyes do when lies are told.

His brow knitted with puzzlement. "Of course you do," Elliot insisted. "Harry was at the hotel to receive payment. He'd been a grafter for too many years to have what he was peddling with him. There was too great a chance he would be overpowered by his blackmail victim and end up with nothing. He would've arranged for a third party to deliver the DVD once Harry was satisfied with the amount of money brought as payment. He wouldn't have trusted Raintree or Kathy. Therefore he left it with you. What was the arrangement? He would telephone your room at the Double Oak once the money was counted, and you would stroll down to his room to witness the swap?"

She gulped, but said nothing.

"You were there when Harry was killed," he said slowly. "Did you know who Harry was expecting?"

"Dominic Portello," she murmured.

"I want that DVD, Sheila." He folded his hands on the desk and grimaced with impatience. "I want it very much. You're courting death by hanging onto it."

"But I told you the truth. I don't have it. Not any more. I gave it to Milton." She sounded like a child repeating a lesson.

The lawyer rubbed a thumbnail on his jaw. "It is my understanding the DVD shows Michael Douglas' murder. Is that true?"

Her eyes blinked rapidly, her amazement growing; her tongue stunned mute by his words.

"Milton Raintree agreed to help Harry," said Elliot. He narrowed his eyes. "Therefore it follows that Raintree realized the importance of the DVD. Harry didn't trust Raintree. So it also follows that Harry showed him what was on the DVD with someone else present. You."

"I saw it," Sheila admitted in a quivering tone. She caught himself on the downbeat, and held steady. "But it didn't show much. Some kid about sixteen was yelling at this guy. Then the guy dropped. After that, the kid ran out carrying a gun. Then maybe a minute or two later, someone wearing a hooded sweatshirt came in and went over to the cash register. He took the money and left. Then this woman came in. After a few seconds, she left. That was it."

"The kid, as you described him, was Dominic Portello?"

"That's what Harry said. But the picture wasn't all that clear."

"What about the man wearing the hooded sweatshirt?"

"He kept his face hidden, like he knew the camera was watching," she said vaguely.

Elliot scowled at her. "Then how do you know you were watching a man?"

She showed Elliot her palms. "I saw his hands."

Elliot nodded slightly. "What about the woman? Did Harry tell you who she was?"

Her head wagged. "I don't think he recognized her. But Milton knew her. His eyes got real big when he saw her."

A tiny flash of triumph highlighted the lawyer's face as he asked, "Did you ask Raintree who she was?"

"Yeah. He wouldn't tell me her name. He just said she was somebody dead."

"Could you hear what was said? The shot? Anything?"

"No," she said with a light toss of her head. "There was no sound."

Chambers Elliot stood up smiling. "Well, it was nice chatting with you, Mrs. Raintree. Give my regards to your husband. Now, you'll have to excuse me."

She looked at him in surprise, her eyes wide with disappointment. "But I haven't told you what I need done," she bleated.

"I'm afraid my time is booked for the foreseeable future, and…"

Sheila Clifford jumped to her feet. "But you have to help me! Milton said…"

Elliot stopped smiling and looked serious. "I'm certain he gave you detailed instructions. Unfortunately, unless I can speak with your husband directly there is nothing I can do for you."

There was anger, a volcano-burst of anger behind the cold blue eyes as she spat out the words, "You *have* to help me!" She sneaked a look at him to see if Elliot had been swayed be her demand. Their eyes met. "I am George Pierce's granddaughter. Shouldn't you help me for his sake?"

"How are you to contact Raintree after leaving here?"

A shadow of anxiety crossed her face. "He said he'd call me."

"On the phone line at the hotel? Or will you receive that call on the cellphone that was stolen?" the lawyer mocked.

Words seemed to be struggling to her lips. But instead of uttering them, Sheila leaned mutely back in the chair, looking very ill at ease.

The lawyer sat back down in his chair. "Whatever Milton Raintree's promised you, Sheila, forget it. It's not going to happen. And if anything should happen to George…"

"Milton said I was to hire you to defend me in case I was arrested," she interrupted.

"Arrested for what?"

"Murder." Her arms flew upward in a supplicating gesture.

"Whose murder?"

Her voice had taken on an empty, frightened tenor. "George Pierce's."

Chambers Elliot reached over to the intercom and pressed one of its buttons repeatedly. A moment later, Lydia Marshall rushed into his office.

"Get George Pierce on the line. Tell him I have to talk to him, now. Don't let him put you off."

Lydia cast a glance over at Sheila Clifford and then hurried out.

A fleeting look of cunning replaced the concern in Sheila's face, a half-smile came and vanished on her lips almost in the same instant. Then her lips parted. A low hum of delight came forth.

Chambers Elliot returned his attention to Sheila Clifford. "Raintree is going to kill George?"

She shrugged. "Milton just said that I was to hire you in case something happened to George."

"Tell me the rest of it?" demanded Elliot. "What's the plan? When will it happen? Tell me!"

She gave her blonde head a frantic wave. "I don't know!"

Chambers Elliot stood up and indicated the door with a tilt of his head, signaling the end of their interchange. "I'm certain I'll see you again, Mrs. Raintree."

She got to her feet looking dismal. Then with a parting glance she started across the room.

"One last thing, he called to her back. "So help me God, I will cut a deal with Salvator Portello to take revenge upon you and Raintree, should anything happen to George. Make that clear to your husband when you see him."

When Sheila reached the door she paused, and looked back. Her hand was on the knob, tension vibrating through her. Then she turned and left, abandoning the door to its hinges.

After Sheila left his office, Elliot pressed the intercom button twice. A moment later, Lydia Marshall came into view. Chambers Elliot regarded his legal-assistant for several long seconds, before saying, "Did reach George Pierce?"

"Not yet. The butler—Armistice—said George was out."

"Out of town?" Elliot asked with alarm.

"No. Just out. I left a message for George to telephone. What's up with the painted blonde?"

Chambers Elliot sucked in air, held it a moment. "Raintree sent her as I anticipated. But not for the reason I was expecting. Did Jason follow her when she left?"

Lydia nodded. "I saw him on the sidewalk across the street keeping pace as she stormed off. What did she want?"

"She wants me to defend her against a murder-charge."

"Raintree's?" asked Lydia.

"No. She married him. It's George's murder we're talking about."

She put the back of her hand to her mouth. "Dear God."

"Dear God, indeed," said Elliot. "We don't know what Milton Raintree looks like and I'm convinced he's planning to murder George." He closed his eyes, held them shut a brief instant, and then opened them wide. "How do you stop a man who's invisible?"

"Taggart will follow her to him…"

"I'm not so sure. He held both his hands out in front of him and looked at the backs of the fingers, as if checking the quality of a manicure. "Sheila claimed Raintree is out of town. He even missed their wedding night." Elliot gave her a questioning look. "I find that very unusual, don't you?"

Her brows jumped. "Maybe he doesn't go for bottled blondes?"

The lawyer shrugged. "With all that's the rest that is Sheila? I doubt that very much."

"Could be Raintree's gay. For fifty million I think a gay grafter would pretend an interest in marriage."

The corners of Elliot's mouth drew down. "I'm worried that Raintree's got murder on his mind."

Lydia's eyes narrowed rather prettily, like a cat's. "Chambers, killing George makes no sense."

He made a hoarse sound in his throat. "It could if Sheila was in his will."

"But she isn't, yet. And even if she was, why would Milton Raintree marry Sheila only to set her up for a murder charge?" Lydia an aimless gesture with both hands outspread. "She would not be able to inherit, if she's convicted of killing George. Therefore he could not benefit as her spouse."

"So one would logically assume," he agreed. Then Elliot pointed to the ashtray on his desk. "When Jason checks in, tell him to send one of his people over with an evidence bag. I want the cigarette-butt Sheila left in the ashtray submitted for DNA profiling. It will be a long shot. She only took one puff. But I have to follow that possibility. Also, tell him to send someone to the Forty Winks Motel. I want to know if they're holding anything for Harry Farmer. Whoever he sends will have to describe Farmer. Harry was probably living there under an assumed name."

"You think Harry Farmer left that DVD there for pickup later?"

"No," Elliot said. "He entrusted it to Sheila. Whereupon she gave it to Milton Raintree who…." He rubbed his jaw with a finger. "But there might be something else, there. Something that will lead us to the mysterious Milton Raintree."

"Loving daughter, this Sheila Clifford," smirked Lydia.

"Not very. But her meeting with me was not a total waste of time. I learned that Dominic Portello is on the DVD." He ran his fingers through his gray hair. "Him, another man whose face is hidden, and an unnamed woman who Milton Raintree recognized but would not identify."

Lydia pressed the heels of her hands together and said very softly, "Then Dominic did kill Michael Douglas?"

"If she wasn't lying, it would seem so."

Lydia Marshall went over to the window. "Did you notice the car down the block when you arrived this morning?"

Chambers Elliot went over and looked out. "What car?"

"That black sedan down the block." Lydia tapped the glass in its direction. "See it? I walked past it on my way to the office, this morning. The man driving works for Salvator Portello." She opened her large eyes a little wider. "He's the one who stuck the gun in your ribs. I didn't recognize the other one."

"Get Lt. Herbie Mann on the phone."

She drifted away from the window. "Are you going to have him roust those two in the car?"

Elliot nodded. "Damn right I am."

Lydia stared at her boss uncertainly. After a moment she said, "What if Herbie asks you about Harry Farmer?"

"Harry wasn't our client—assuming Herbie's identified Harry. Milton Raintree was, so far as we know. Therefore I am under no obligation to say anything about Mr. Farmer. Except, of course, as a good citizen trying to assist the police."

Lydia twisted toward Elliot, crossing her arms. "You're going to wish you'd taken my advice and passed on this case, one day soon."

He glanced at Lydia and smiled. "After you get hold of Herbie, give George another try. If he's still out, leave a message to the effect that if he can't take time from his busy day to telephone, I shall be out at his ranch tonight—whether he likes it or not."

"Do you want me to come along?"

"I think not," Elliot said. "I don't plan on pulling any punches with George. So it might get a bit crusty, in the conversational sense." He frowned. "You being there would only inhibit my vocabulary."

Chapter 10

That evening, the sky above Austin opened up and let go a torrential downpour. Chambers Elliot managed to arrive in his Lagonda sedan at the Pierce ranch outside of Leander, despite the weather. After beating his way through gray sheets of rain to the front door, Elliot was let in by an elderly man clothed in a swallow-tail tuxedo.

"Is Mr. Pierce expecting me, Armistice?" Elliot asked the butler, as the lawyer took off his wet trench coat.

"Yes, sir," the white-haired man calmly replied, taking Elliot's coat. "He had planned an early night. I hope you won't keep the master any longer than necessary."

Elliot nodded agreeably. "Armistice is a very unusual name," he remarked. "Is it a family tradition with your people, for baby boys?"

"No, Sir," said the butler. "I was born on Armistice Day." He tilted his head indicating the long hallway across the walnut-paneled foyer. "Mr. Pierce is waiting for you in the library."

Elliot hurried off down the hallway.

He paused at the door to the library to look in. The room was more or less wall-to-wall books with bits of oak wainscoting in between stacks of shelving. Spotlights embedded in the copper-paneled ceiling provide lighting for the collection of leather chairs dotting the brown floor-tiles, as well as for the austere man seated behind the massive oak desk, at the room's far end.

"You picked one hell of a night to come calling, Chambers," Pierce called, in a voice that sounded like gravel being dumped from a steel bucket. "Come in and take a seat."

George Pierce was in his seventies, with a thatch of gray tousled hair and a round face whitened by beard-stubble. He had a pair of square, gold eyeglasses perched on the bridge of his big nose. He was short and fat with several gold rings adorning the fingers on each hand. A tattered, multicolored bathrobe nearly covered the silky-red of his Chinese pajamas.

Elliot walked into the room, and over to one of the wingback chairs fronting the desk. His eyes stared steadily at the man. "I thought it was important enough to make the trip, George."

The rancher smirked, staring lazily at his guest. "What sort of trouble am I in that worries a lawyer like you?"

Elliot gripped the back of the chair in front of him; his shoulders squared, his feet planted and spread slightly apart. "I think you're going to be murdered."

Pierce made a vague movement with one hand indicating the chair in front of the lawyer. Elliot moved around it and sat down, crossing his legs.

"Is somebody in particular going to kill me, Chambers?" Pierce scoffed. "Or am I on a public-shooters list?"

"It's no joke, George. I'm convinced that Milton Raintree is behind it."

The rancher's eyes flickered with recognition at the sound of the name. His tone was no longer one of amusement. "What makes you think he's got a grudge against me worth killing over?"

The lawyer's eyebrows arched in surprise. "Then you know Raintree?"

Pierce nodded. "He visited me one night, a few months back. I sent him running." He smiled wryly. "I put some private detectives on his tail, figuring to get enough on him to involve the police. I did." He shrugged his shoulders. "There was no need. There already was an outstanding warrant against him." The rancher pulled a briar pipe from his robe and a book of matches. "So far he's not been arrested. But everybody's luck turns bad, once in awhile. What makes you think he's planning to take revenge?"

"It's not revenge, George. He wants your estate."

George Pierce chuckled nastily. "Let him try to get it."

"He married Sheila Clifford. Did you know?"

Pierce leaned back in his chair, taken aback. "Married Sheila? Are you certain?"

"I have not verified it," said Elliot. "But that's what she claims."

The rancher struck the match to ignite it. Then he lit the pipe slowly before waving the match until it went out. Afterward, he blew a plume of smoke and stared through its haze at Elliot. "When did you speak with her?"

Chambers Elliot gave George Pierce the gist of his meeting with Sheila Clifford. When he finished speaking, Pierce looked worried.

"But until she's in my Will…" the rancher began, waiving the hand holding the smoldering pipe.

"I can't explain Raintree's reasoning, George. It doesn't make sense to me, either."

Pierce set down the pipe, shoving it off to one side as if having lost all taste for it. "Forget about it Chambers," he said, batting the air with one hand. "It's nothing but a grafter's bluff."

"When was Raintree here?"

"Six or eight weeks back—maybe longer. I don't recall, exactly."

Pierce removed his glasses and wiped them with the inside of his pajama top. Without them on, his face looked putty-like and powerless. "He showed up with some fool's tale about finding Edward's daughter."

The lawyer's eyebrows narrowed with concern. "Raintree claimed that he'd found Sheila Clifford?"

"Not as such," said Pierce, putting his glasses back on. "Raintree wouldn't give me a name. That was the information he was selling."

"But I was under the impression you hired a detective to locate Sheila Clifford."

"Nonsense. Why would I hire anybody for that? I knew where Sheila lived." Pierce yawned. "I got all that the first time she came here."

"Why didn't you tell me about her visit" asked the lawyer.

"There was nothing to tell. Sheila came to me with a story that her mother had been put in a family way by my son, Edward. Sheila told me where she lived. She even showed me a letter she claimed had been written by Edward to her mother." His lips pressed back against his teeth. "But at the time I didn't believe her. I told Sheila she was offering up a bunch of hooey and sent her on her way."

The lawyer knotted his hands, twisting at his fingers as he weighed what he was hearing against what Sheila had told him. "What changed your mind about her?"

"The letter," returned Pierce. "Sheila was so angry when she left, she dropped it. It looked so much like Edward's writing that I hired a handwriting expert to look it over, and compare it to letters I had from Edward. Surprisingly, the letter she'd dropped was genuine." His weary eyes looked at the lawyer, probingly. "However, that still didn't prove she was Edward's child. Regardless, I felt she deserved a better hearing than I first gave her. So I sent Sydney to Houston with an invitation, to see if she was still interested in talking to me."

Elliot tilted toward Pierce in surprise. "Sydney drove her here?"

"Nope. As usual he subcontracted the whole deal out to some flunky and the poor kid had to take a bus to Austin." Pierce made a vague gesture. "But it all worked out in the end."

"Did Sydney tell you who he sent to get her?"

Pierce weighed the question a moment, and then shook his head. "I was so steamed when I learned what he'd done that I just told him to get out of my sight."

"When you had Raintree investigated, did those detectives find where he lived?"

"Nope. He comes and goes not staying anywhere for more than a few days. At each motel, he pays cash for the room so there's no paper trail to follow." He studied his fingernails a moment. Then he said, "I suppose I'll have to tell the police about her marrying him."

"Have you submitted Sheila's DNA for profiling?"

Pierce nodded. "I should get the results in a few more days. There was some screw-up at the lab and I had to resubmit the samples. But they claim they've got it worked out, now."

Elliot made an impatient gesture. "Did you tell that to Raintree?"

"It took place after his visit. In any event, it's none of his business."

"Why isn't Sheila living here?"

"I offered her accommodations, but she refused. Sheila said she wouldn't move in until it was a certainty that she was my granddaughter." His eyes narrowed. Then a glaze came over them, a hard defensive glaze. "Nothing wrong in that type of thinking, Chambers."

"Do she and Sydney get along?"

"As far as I know, he's never met her. Sydney's always gone when she stops by. Damn car club he belongs to or some other foolishness." He curled one lip. "That was why I wanted him to bring her here from Houston. So they'd get acquainted in case she was Edward's daughter. But as usual…"

"Did Sydney know about the handwriting analysis?"

"Of course," the rancher replied softly. "There was no need to keep it a secret."

"How did he take the news that it was written in Edward's hand?"

The rancher thought for a moment. "Not very well, I'm afraid."

"Has Raintree talked to you since that first enticement—about anything?"

George Pierce shook his head.

"Do you know Kathy Martin?" asked Elliot.

The other man's eyes brightened. "Sheila's friend. Sure. Sweet young woman."

"Does Kathy visit you often?"

The lights in the rancher's eyes died as he grimaced. "What do you mean?"

"You're being evasive, George," Elliot scolded.

"I've chatted with Kathy Martin a number of times, with her sitting right where you are." His voice became colder, sharper "And, yes, I know she used to work for Milton Raintree." He flung his arms wide. "But she's clear of him now."

"Have you given her any money?"

The rancher laughed, with exasperation. "She's never asked for a nickel."

"That doesn't answer my question."

"What's going on, Chambers?" Pierce said thickly, harshly. "First you imply there's some murder plot, and now you're pinging on Kathy."

"Are you providing Sheila with an income?"

"Of course," said the rancher. He made a pleading gesture. "Until I know different, I'm assuming she's family. What's wrong with that?"

"Should the DNA profile support your assumptions, will you increase that allowance?"

The rancher nodded. "Substantially."

"To an amount large enough to make you more valuable to Raintree alive than dead?" the lawyer asked.

A trace of a smile twitched the lips of the man sitting behind the desk. "Okay," he conceded. "You've made a valid point of concern." The smile extended, stretching thin its corners. "But you're forgetting the warrant that's outstanding against him. If he shows up here I will notify the police and that will be the end of Mr. Raintree."

"Raintree's marriage to Sheila indicates he does not foresee any problems in you accepting Sheila as your granddaughter," Elliot said thinly. "It could be she is Edward's daughter and Raintree knows it. Or he has a confederate at the lab where the DNA profile is being done."

The rancher looked at him woodenly. "Now, you're talking foolish."

"I concede that the science cannot be altered. But the resulting report could be along with whatever is provided as documentation."

"Chambers, if Raintree married Sheila as you say, then he obviously did so to hedge his bet." He shrugged wearily. "If she is my granddaughter he hopes to profit by that. If not, he'll leave her high and dry."

Elliot fumbled with his lower lip. "Or forge your will and kill you."

The rancher batted the air with both hands. "Don't be ridiculous. He hasn't the brains God gave baby geese. Him kill me and expect to get away with it? Not a chance."

"What's Raintree holding over you, George?"

Pierce looked up sharply. "What in hell gave you that idea?"

"You're being evasive, again."

Crimson rose up the rancher's neck and into his face. "Dammit, Chambers, you're wearing my patience thin."

"And you mine. I think there's a link between Sheila and Dominic Portello. Did she ever mention him to you?"

Pierce started to stand up, his face purple with rage. But he caught himself and settled back into the chair. "Now hold on Chambers. If you're saying that Sheila's been some mobster's moll…"

"Did you know a priest named Zamoyski?"

"What of it?" A muscle twitched in his cheek. "He was the pastor of my church, a lifetime ago."

"What about a man named Junior Billings?"

The rancher nodded, his jaw muscles working, his breathing rapid and noisy. "I used to have a string of hamburger joints. Billings did the cleaning at a couple of them. What are you digging for, Chambers?"

"Anything." The lawyer gave a frustrated wave of both hands. Then in a changed voice he added, "I've been roped into something that I don't understand, George. Milton Raintree is behind it. Also involved is the Portello Crime Family. Somewhere in the middle of that mess is you. I have no way to link the situations, yet. But I'm certain there is one."

"Like I told Lydia, there's no reason for you to concern yourself with Sheila Clifford any further. The DNA results will settle the whole matter."

"How is her DNA profile to be compared? To yours?"

"Against Barbara's – I was told it would be the method least prone to error."

"But Barb's been dead for..."

"Barbara had tissue removed for biopsy, shortly before her death," the rancher interjected. "The physician intended to have it analyzed for cancer. Fortunately, the tissue was still being stored in a frozen state. Barbara's DNA has been successfully extracted from it."

"Sheila made no mention of providing a DNA sample," Elliot remarked.

He looked at the attorney patronizingly. "I had it gathered surreptitiously. I wanted to be certain there was no hoax involved."

"You're certain of the collector's integrity?" Elliot asked, his face remaining stoical.

"I'm no fool, Chambers," Pierce said, watching him shrewdly. "I personally gathered it by collecting the cigarette butts she left behind."

"Do you know a man named Mazy?" Elliot demanded, his exasperation showing.

The rancher shifted uncomfortably in his chair. "Never heard of him."

The lawyer's lips thinned at the sound of the lie. "Do you know Harry Farmer?"

"Not personally."

"Harry is dead: murdered."

"So I read." George Pierce clenched one hand, unclenched it slowly. "Farmer was a lowlife. So what?"

"Harry Farmer was not a classic Texas resident," snapped Elliot. "But he had the same rights as you and me, George. He didn't deserve to die in that fashion."

"Chambers, I didn't mean anything derogatory against the man," Pierce protested.

"Harry Farmer was Sheila's adoptive father. Did she tell you?"

George Pierce stiffened, his eyes wide in shock.

"Harry Farmer was attempting to extort money from the Portellos," continued Elliot. "Did she tell you that?"

"Sweet heaven come for me," whispered the rancher, as if he was looking into the face of Satan. "Blackmail a Portello? The man must've been crazy."

"Sheila was at the hotel at the time Harry died. She claims she does not know who killed him. But I think she does. When I asked who Harry was waiting to meet when he died, she told me it was Dominic Portello."

The rancher shifted slightly, looking uncomfortable. "Obviously, that's who killed him."

"Perhaps, a little too obvious."

"If you're implying that she lied…" Pierce stood up stuffing a pipe into his mouth. "Is there anything else, Chambers? I'm really pressed for time."

"Has Sydney mentioned any interest in Kathy Martin?"

Pierce flushed profusely. "Sydney? Don't be ridiculous."

"Are you certain he's not dating her?"

Pierce's head jerked as he hammered out the words. "Of course, he isn't."

Chambers Elliot studied the other man's telling color for a few moments before asking, "Are you involved with her, George?"

"Don't be an ass, Chambers!" The rancher made an angry fist. "She's young enough to be my daughter."

"People get lonely," the lawyer observed. "Barbara's been dead a long time. Kathy is an attractive woman. There's nothing wrong with it."

"Look, Chambers, Kathy is a very charming woman. But…"

"How charming?"

Pierce batted the pipe from the desk; his voice becoming belligerent; his face screwed into an embarrassed knot. "Kathy… Miss Martin… she… we… I'm not having an affair with her. Okay? Frankly, Chambers, I find your questions concerning my private life a breach of our friendship."

"I apologize, George." Elliot got to his feet. "Did Edward tell you about the pending birth of his child?"

"No." Pierce pushed his tongue around inside one cheek. Then he said, "I suppose it was his way of punishing me."

"You and Edward had a falling out?"

Pierce's chin tilted downward as he wet his lips. Then he said, "Women were Edward's downfall." He tapped the desk absently. "I told him if he didn't stop whoring around I'd disinherit him. Then he had that damn car wreck." The rancher looked up at Elliot for several seconds in frowning concentration. "I know how to protect me and mine from the likes of Milton Raintree, Chambers. Let's just leave it at that."

"Not hardly, George."

Pierce stood by the desk, his fingertips stroking the top of it, his eyes on the floor. He remained like that for many long seconds. Then he returned to his chair, grim and stiff.

"I'll talk to Sheila," Pierce muttered. "Perhaps you've misunderstood about her and Raintree getting married."

"There was no mistake," the lawyer said flatly.

Pierce frowned in concern. "Sheila's not a complete fool, Chambers. Killing me before she's in my will would get her nothing."

"She's not the one who's planning it. Milton Raintree is. And I think he's cold-blooded enough to wait until everything is settled before killing you." Chambers Elliot took a folded document from his pocket, and set it down on the desk near Pierce. "This is your revised will. As I told you when you sought these changes, I think it is grossly premature to incorporate any bequest to Sheila Clifford—regardless of conditions—until you verify paternity. Nevertheless, it was drafted as you stipulated."

Pierce picked up the document, unfolded it, glanced at its contents briefly, and then dropped it into the desk's center drawer. "I'm too tired to deal with this tonight. I'll go over it in the morning."

The lawyer said emphatically, "George, in my opinion you must disallow Sheila—regardless of what the DNA proves. Only when Raintree realizes there is no chance for receiving any benefit will he abandon his plans for you, and leave her. Once he's out of her life..."

"I can't do that, Chambers." The rancher scratched one ear for a moment. Then he asked, "What about establishing a revocable living trust for the entirety of my estate, with you as trustee? That should motivate a quick exit by Raintree if he's all you claim. Can you take care of it?"

"Of course. But I'm not sure that's the answer."

"You're a pessimist, Chambers." He rubbed his mouth with the back of one hand, as if the lawyer's response had been a slap. "Nevertheless, that's what I want done."

Elliot gave a reluctant nod. "With whom as the beneficiary to this trust?"

"My son, Sydney, and Sheila Clifford on an equal basis—her right to make a claim predicated upon the outcome of the DNA profiling. The proceeds from my estate for both beneficiaries will be lifelong annuity—I'll give you the monthly payouts for each in a few days." He sighed and stretched himself. "Upon their deaths, any residual will be given to—I'll have to get you a list of the organizations I want benefited."

"You understand that anything included becomes part of the trust? In other words, the trust will take ownership of everything you now control. Are you certain you want that?"

"It's a trust I can revoke at any time." He smiled at Elliot strangely, as if deciding whether to say anything further. "I fail to see the risk, Chambers. You'll be running the trust, remember?"

Elliot nodded. "There isn't any risk… assuming you are capable of managing your own affairs. But—"

He laughed. "You doubt my sanity?"

"No. However greed can create complications you might not like. Your beneficiaries, for example, could join forces and attempt to have you declared *Non Compes Mentes*."

Pierce laughed again. "I'm hardly likely to be dragged into a hearing and proven incompetent, Chambers."

"The right to a competency hearing is not absolute, George. You could be forcefully hospitalized by your kin and held without right of regress for an evaluation period. During that time you could be kept out of contact with everyone except those approved by your kin, and the physician attending you. If that physician decrees that you need further hospitalization, your heirs could get a court order enforcing it."

"No judge in the world would…"

Elliot smiled indulgently. "George, even if I was able to bring you before a judge, it would fall upon you to *prove* competency. It wouldn't be assumed."

Pierce fidgeted. "But I'm not incompetent."

"Proving that is not as easy as it sounds, George. You see, a judge's observations could become the entire basis for that determination. Considering the implications of drug side effects, such an assessment could, depending upon the drugs used in your hospitalization, prejudice the judge against you." Elliot gestured emptily. "As a result, you could be held indefinitely against your will without recourse for release—except by catering to the financial whims of those who instigated your incarceration. And believe me, George, once you're safely locked away, your heirs will take legal action against me claiming that your incompetency began before you established the trust and, therefore, I must be removed as trustee."

"Now, you're exaggerating," scoffed Pierce.

"Admittedly I am portraying a worst-case scenario," Elliot said grimly. "However, stranger things have occurred. If nothing else, efforts to have you declared *Non Compes Mentes* might keep you from retaining control of your own financial holdings for an extended period of time. That, in turn, could create catastrophic business outcomes." The lawyer rubbed the lobe of one ear. "Take my advice about Sheila Clifford, George. She must be disallowed from—"

Pierce cut him short, but talked very quietly. "You've made your concerns clear, Chambers. But I prefer to proceed in this fashion."

"Very well," said the lawyer, with a dismal wag of his head. "I'll draft the initial documents tomorrow. Then I will personally bring them here for your review. Once we've agreed upon the verbiage and you've given me the necessary details, I will return with the final documents for your signature."

"Will a trust create any negative tax implications?" asked the rancher.

"You mean Inheritance Tax?"

Pierce nodded.

"When you die," explained Elliot, "the property in the trust would become part of your estate. Whatever tax implications might exist in the normal course of inheritance would apply based upon the property's market-value."

The rancher smiled confidently. "I think that should safely secure my future as well as that of my heirs, don't you?"

Elliot said, "No, George, I don't."

"What can Milton Raintree possibly do once the trust is established?" Pierce smiled faintly and leaned far back in his chair. "Raintree's a wanted man. If he shows his face anywhere to make a claim, he'll be arrested."

"I know," sighed Elliot. "But I'm not going to underestimate him. Milton Raintree's a man you should fear—not mock."

Pierce's eyebrows arched in surprise but he remained silent.

"What laboratory is doing the DNA profile?" asked Elliot.

"The Midland Laboratory in Dallas." George Pierce put his glasses on the desk and dragged his hands wearily over his face, as if wishing Chambers Elliot would leave. "Are we finally done?"

"Nearly," said Elliot. "Harry Farmer's extortion of the Portellos was based upon a murder that took place thirty years ago. Michael Douglas was the victim. Jerome Petty was arrested for the crime. Did you know either of those men?"

"I don't recall the names," muttered Pierce, with an impatient wave.

Elliot gave his head an exasperated shake. "There's a link between Michael Douglas and Old Frank Portello. It was Frank who financed the liquor business Douglas purportedly owned."

Pierce's hands fell away his eyes clenched, his jaw muscles taught. "I said I didn't know the names!"

"What about Barbara?"

"What are you suggesting, Chambers?" Pierce took a breath and let it go slowly, as if trying to curb his fear. "That Barbara or I killed Douglas thirty years ago?"

"Was Barbara having an affair with either Douglas or Petty?"

Pierce stood up slowly, his mouth a slit, his expression withdrawn. "That tears it," he growled.

"I know Barbara asked for a divorce, George. It's reasonable to assume her desire to leave was to go to someone else. Did Barbara ever mention either man?"

The rancher's chin dipped, his eyes averting Elliot's stare tellingly. "Barb and I weren't getting along. Yes, I knew she was involved with Michael Douglas. But right after he was killed, she changed."

"Barb tried to rekindle your marriage?"

"Yes. But at the same time she became obsessed with things."

"Like what?"

"Helicopters for one thing. She was determined to learn to maintain one of the damn things. Can you imagine? Barb covered in grease? But she never finished the course. After that, she became obsessed with the South Seas. She took Sydney and the two of them went to Samoa." Pierce lifted a hand and rubbed the side of his nose. "They must've been there for almost two months. Then they came back. At that point she simply fall apart—emotionally. She started drinking. I tried to get her to a sanitarium. But before I could talk her into it, she killed herself."

"Do you recall when she was in Samoa?"

George Pierce considered the question and then nodded. "Approximately. Most of that September and at least all of October, possibly part of November. It's been so many years."

"How do you and Sydney get along?"

There was no sign of emotion upon Pierce's face as he spoke. "Not well. Sydney's pushing fifty and hasn't worked a day in his life. He spends his time sponging off me and whoring around with his friends. His only accomplishment in life is becoming President of the La Gatos Canyon Car Club—what a waste!"

Chambers Elliot went over to George Pierce and shook his hand. "I'm sorry I upset you. But believe me when I say that my concerns have your best interests at heart."

"I've never doubted your integrity, Chambers. Just your damnable tactics."

Elliot turned and left the room.

Pierce regarded the lawyer's departure coolly.

In the foyer, Armistice appeared from the shadows offering up Elliot's raincoat.

"How's the weather, Armistice?"

"Fit neither for man nor beast, Sir."

The lawyer nodded in understanding. "In Texas it is either numbing cold, broiling hot or pissing down rain—at least whenever I have to face the elements."

Rain beat down in slashing torrents and the wind whipped the surface of the asphalt drive into miniature whitecaps as Elliot dashed from the Pierce Ranchhouse. The trees surrounding the stone structure twisted and swayed as if alive; their branches, like grotesquely twisted arms, battled the storms wrath.

"Christ, it's gotten worse!" he complained, to the darkness.

The loose ends of his coat flapped wildly about his knees as the cold wet wind bored at him relentlessly. He jumped a puddle near the Lagonda only to have his foot slip in a pile of wet leaves and slide him into an ankle-deep pool. Immediately, cold water flooded his shoes.

With a curse, Elliot shook his feet disgustedly. It was one hell of a night to be out playing lawyer. Then he jumped into the Lagonda and slammed the door. It was not until then he noticed the middle-aged man wearing a yellow rain-slicker sitting in the passenger's seat.

"What the hell…" gasped Elliot, in surprise.

"I'm Sydney Pierce," said the man. "Sorry. Didn't mean to startle you, Mr. Elliot."

"You sure as hell did," Elliot said, looking into guileless blue eyes.

"May I speak with you?" asked Sydney Pierce.

"What about?"

The younger man rolled his eyes as if thinking. "Sheila Clifford."

"That's what I get for coming out on a night like this," Elliot muttered, and started the engine. "What's your interest in Sheila?"

Sydney grinned at Elliot. "I suppose my father told you I'm the black sheep of the family?"

"Not as such."

His chin came down an inch. "What did he say?"

"Your father should address your inquiries on that topic," Elliot said.

Pierce's face became conspiratorial. "Did you talk to him about Sheila?"

The lawyer smiled thinly. "If we did discuss her," Elliot told him, "I'm not at liberty to say anything concerning the conversation. Let's get to what brought you into my wonderful, wet world."

"I might be able to help." Sydney tried to smile. Then all expression went out of his face, like he had just gotten his brains flooded by a low-flying duck with a bad case of diarrhea. "From what I understand, she's going to need it."

"Help, how?" Elliot asked carelessly.

Pierce's tilted toward Elliot, the younger man's eyes brightening. "With Sheila's paternity claim, of course."

"Of course. Well, I've never been one to turn down help," Elliot said, cagily. "What did you have in mind?"

Sydney picked at the material of his jacket. "Sheila's entitled to a share—assuming she is my niece."

"You think she might not be?" Elliot inquired.

"I only meant if it's proven," Sydney explained, making a casual gesture with one hand. "I'm trying to keep my distance on that topic."

"Is that why you sent someone else to meet with her in Houston, on your father's behalf?"

Pierce nodded. "I'm sure my father ranted about that."

"Who did you send in your stead?"

He shrugged. "I don't recall his name. I met him in a bar. He claimed he was a detective." He licked the corners of his mouth with the tip of a pink tongue. "So I thought, who better than to run dad's errand? I paid him, of course"

"Of course." Elliot said slowly, "It doesn't bother you that Sheila's share, as you put it, will diminish your own?"

A slow flush crept up his throat. "Of course not. There's more than enough for both—should the worst happen."

For a moment Elliot just stared at Pierce. "You're assuming you won't be cut out of your father's will in favor of Sheila Clifford."

Sydney's head turned so he could look out the side window as if the downpour was turning the ranch into a wasteland. He said, with his face averted, "Is my father's going to cut me out of his will?"

"That's something else you must talk to him about. Tell me how you think you can help?"

Sydney twisted in the seat to face Elliot. "Whether I'm disinherited or not, I still love my father. The fact is, he's in trouble. I've told him as much. But, as usual, he doesn't believe me."

"In trouble, how?" Elliot asked, his tone bemused.

Sydney's hands clenched with indignation. "I happen to know that Edward had no children."

"What about the letter Sheila brought to your father? I'm told it mentions a pregnancy of his making."

"That's phony." His shoulders jerked. Then his eyes got furtive. "I even know the man who forged it. His name's Milton Raintree."

"You know Raintree?"

Sydney's chin went up and down. "I'm afraid I do."

"But your father had the letter authenticated by an expert."

"Raintree's a genius. Not only at forgeries. He's worked out an arrangement with the laboratory that's doing the DNA profile on Sheila." For a moment Sydney's body became quite rigid, his breath held rigidly. Then he let it out slowly and relaxed. "A technician at the lab has agreed to alter the DNA report so it confirms Sheila as a Pierce."

"Such an arrangement would require a great deal of money, considering the risk. Where did Raintree get it? I'm reliably informed that he is down on his haunches when it comes to money."

"That's because he bribed the technician."

"What's the name of the technician?"

"That, I don't know." Sydney sucked in his breath and straightened toward the window. "Is what I'm telling you going to help?"

"If it can be substantiated, yes. How is it you know all this? If Raintree is the genius you claim, I hardly think he would share such damaging information with others."

Sydney turned toward Elliot, the younger man's dark eyes in glittered with pride. "He's a member of the car club I belong to—I'm its president."

"Congratulations. Was his membership at your club happenstance or planned?"

"Planned, most assuredly." Sydney Pierce leaned back in the seat and pasted an amiable expression onto his face. "Milton Raintree joined with the intent to make contact with me. He was hoping I would be willing to help in his scheme."

"In what context?"

"He wanted me to intercept the DNA report and give it to him— Raintree." The peaks of his dark eyebrows formed in arches and made corrugations in the white skin of his forehead. "Naturally, I refused."

"Naturally. But what did Raintree hope to gain by seeing the report before your father?"

"He didn't say. I assumed that he wanted to personally verify that the technician had done as requested."

"That would make sense. Still, I find it odd that Raintree would think you might accede to such a request. It's to your financial advantage to make certain Sheila isn't a Pierce."

"Which is why Raintree suggested a monetary arrangement," explained Sydney Pierce. The younger man pushed his chin forward a little. His eyes were vaguely troubled, as if he was now sorry he had offered to help. "Sheila and I would enter into a contract whereby she would pass over half of her inheritance—at whatever point my father died."

"The idea being if she actually was your niece, you would end up with half of her birthright. If she wasn't, then you would only be risking half of what she might otherwise inherit. Although a contract like that would not be enforceable, it must've been a terrible temptation. Why did you refuse?"

"Integrity, mostly. But logic played a part, as well. As you said, the contract would not be enforceable." He looked at the lawyer quizzically, as if trying to read Elliot's mind. "You do see my point?"

"You mean about your integrity? Absolutely."

"No. That Sheila is not Edward's daughter and Milton Raintree knows it. Otherwise, he would not attempt such a bold plan."

"Ah, that point." The lawyer nodded, noncommittally. "What it during this chat that Raintree disclosed his plans to fake the DNA results?"

Sydney spread his hands. "When I heard what he was going to do, I couldn't believe the audacity of the man."

"I'm sure it came as a severe shock to you. Nevertheless, Raintree must've realized you could perform your own testing to refute his forged results. So why forewarn you of his intentions?"

"That is where the man's genius comes into play," said Sydney. He drew a long breath and let it out with a rush. "You may not know it but my father and I don't get alone—we never have. So which report would my father believe? That of the reliable laboratory? Or the results his wayward son tossed at him? You know my father. What do you think?"

"I think George would take you quite seriously," said Elliot.

Sydney considered Elliot's words sullenly. "Obviously, you don't know my father as well as I thought."

"Did you tell any of this to your father?"

He worked his tongue along his lips. "Of course. But he refused to believe me."

"That must've been disheartening."

His eyes got tight and his mouth got stubborn. "I've never been so disappointed in my father in my entire life."

"What would concern me, had I been approached by Raintree, is when he expected to collect. Your father could live another thirty years."

"The implication I got from Raintree was that my father was not long for this world, Mr. Elliot." He twisted away from the lawyer again, as if the Elliot's remark was weighted. "That's why I felt it was so important to speak with you."

"I'm very glad you did. Do you know where I might find Milton Raintree?"

He glanced back. "I have no idea. I got the impression he wanted me to make a commitment right then and there because he was headed out of town until things cooled off."

"Cooled off, how?"

"Rumor has it the police are after him for something he did a few years back."

"Did he talk to you about anyone else who might be working with him to make this scam work?"

Pierce pursed his lips in thought. "I did hear one name… Mazy."

"Mazy Wilson?"

"Possibly." Sydney smiled, rather softly, as if his hand held aces. "I don't recall a last name being mentioned."

"Did Milton Raintree discuss a DVD with you?"

"No," Sydney said without hesitation. "I'm not much of a movie-buff."

Elliot looked at him coldly, slowly nodding his head in understanding. "Have you spoken to Sheila about Raintree's plans?"

"Actually, I've never met or spoken with Sheila. As I told you, I want to keep a distance from this thing."

"Yes, of course. But surely under the circumstances it would be wise to determine her position with respect to any complicity in Raintree's plans?"

The younger man shrugged. "To what end? My father wouldn't believe me even if she was involved."

"Sheila married Milton Raintree this morning. Did you know?"

Sydney Pierce looked startled. He sat in gaping silence for many seconds before saying, "I guess we all have our price."

For a nearly a minute, both men fell silent. The only sounds were the rain drumming on the car, the rattling tree-branches, and the howling wind. Finally Elliot asked, "When can you come to my office?"

"I'm not sure. I don't want my father to find out about this. I'm on the outs with him, as it is."

"Why?"

"The usual." He jerked his head and his nostrils flared angrily. "Me, going to work for him."

"Something wrong with that? You're not exactly a young man."

Pierce looked over at Elliot indignantly. "Why should I work when he has a hundred million doing nothing but gathering interest? It's not as if he can take it with him."

"Going to work would be a shrewd way of keeping yourself in the running for his favors, Sydney. Continuing to refuse employment in his business could mean you end up inheriting nothing. Give it some thought. Uh, I understand that you and Kathy Martin are an item."

Pierce's face darkened. "She a great kid," he said with a crooked grin. "But I'm not interested in anything long-term."

"That will come as a disappointment to her."

Sydney raised his hand in good-by and as he climbed from the car. His sleek, silent smile was the last thing the lawyer saw as the younger man faded into the darkness.

Elliot turned on the headlamps. The rain looked like snow in the lights. He threw the car into gear. Then with his foot lightly dancing between accelerator and brake-pedal he negotiated the sharp curve of the drive's turnaround. After which, with foot heavy on the throttle he roared away from through the storm.

Chapter 11

Three hours later the storm was beating the bedroom windows of Chambers Elliot's home in Georgetown, as if the raindrops were a whip made of steel beads. Despite the incessant rattling he managed to drift off. But not many minutes into his slumber, the telephone's sharp ring from the bedside table roused him.

He groped for the lamp blindly, his eyes blinking rapidly in the darkness. As his fingers found the lamp's base he fumbled around for the switch, and eventually turned on the light. The resulting blaze of incandescence burned his eyes.

With a groaning curse, the lawyer jerked back. Then he grabbed the telephone-receiver and clamped it to one ear.

"This had better be good," he growled into the handset, his throat rough with sleep-thickness. "I was at the point in my dream where my hands were closing around Ramón Whitaker's neck."

"We got complications, Chambers," Jason Taggart said glumly, from the other end of the line.

Elliot blinked several times trying to clear his head, as his memory searched for a name to put to the voice. When he finally recognized it he grumbled, "What's happened? Where are you? What in hell time is it?"

"A little after midnight," Taggart said. "I'm sorry to break it to you this way, Chambers, but George Pierce's dead."

"Dead?" Elliot croaked, jerking into a seated position, his legs dangling over the edge of the bed. "When? How did you hear this? I just talked to George a few hours ago. Are you certain?"

"Von Drake contacted me," explained the detective. "There's no doubt that it's murder."

"Give me the details."

"Von Drake said Kathy Martin came back to that motel around ten. She jumped into her Corvette and raced off. Von Drake lost her almost immediately. But he spotted her car later on and managed to tail it to the Pierce ranch. When you spoke with George did he mention he was expecting her?"

Elliot's hand flexed on the handset. "No. In fact he was planning an early night."

"Von Drake couldn't get onto the property because of the gates across the entrance. They operate by remote control. She got past, however, apparently having been given a remote-control box. Anyway, Von Drake parked out on the highway and waited. But after twenty minutes passed he began to get edgy. So he headed for the gates on foot."

"Did anyone turn up in the interval between Kathy's arrival and Von Drake going to the gates?"

"Not according to Von Drake. But the butler says otherwise. And here's where the timeline confusion gets real serious. According to Von Drake, he heard shots as he was approaching the gates. At about that same time, the gates opened and the Corvette came roaring out. A woman was driving, he's certain of that. But he couldn't see her face or if anyone was in the passenger seat. However, when he questioned the butler, Armistice claimed the shots were fired much earlier."

The peaks of Elliot's eyebrows made sharp angles against the white skin of his forehead. "How much earlier?"

"About the time the Kathy arrived. The butler also claimed some woman he had never seen before, forced her way inside the house. She demanded to use the phone to report a car accident."

"But I thought you said no one but Kathy drove in there," said Elliot. "Exactly."

The lawyer scratched his chest. "According to George, Kathy Martin had been there several times. Therefore Armistice would've recognized her. So why is the butler lying?"

"It gets more confusing," said Taggart. "Von Drake got past the gates while they were open and started toward the house. That's when he saw a woman rush out the ranchhouse's front door. It was too dark to see who she was. But she apparently spotted Von Drake and did not want to be seen. She ran toward the rear of the house. He followed. But she disappeared amongst the trees.

"Von Drake gave up his search after a few minutes and went back to the house. At the front door he rang the bell. When the butler answered Von Drake identified himself as a police officer and asked about the shots. That's when the butler told him about George being dead."

"Identifying himself as a cop might not have been the smartest thing to do," remarked Elliot.

"I told him as much," said the detective. "But Von Drake felt so bad about losing Kathy twice on tails that he wanted to make amends. Anyway, Von Drake went in and the butler took him up to George's bedroom. But there was nothing anybody could do." There was a pause. Then the detective said, "George was shot once in the back of the head with a small caliber gun. Von Drake estimated it to be a .32 caliber based upon the size of the entrance wound. It was done execution-style, Chambers."

"Your man must have a strong stomach," observed the lawyer. Then he stopped, his brows pinching down. "You said there were shots—more than one?"

"Five of them. But Von Drake said as far as he could see, George was shot just the one time."

Elliot made a disgusted face. "Your man inspected George's entire corpse?"

"Von Drake takes his work seriously, Chambers."

"So it would seem." The lawyer's hand involuntarily gripped his stomach. "Did the butler describe the woman who wanted to report the accident?"

"All Von Drake could get out of Armistice is that the woman was hideous and very militant. From what Von Drake heard, the old boy thought he was going to be assaulted. And I don't mean punched."

The lawyer smiled, slightly. "Did this woman actually make her call?"

"No idea. The butler also could not say when she left. Von Drake said the old guy seemed to be in a fog, like he'd had a stroke."

"That could explain the timeline variances. Where's Von Drake, now?"

"When he heard the police-sirens he told the butler to meet the locals at the door. Then Von Drake slipped out the back of the house. That's when he phoned me and gave the lowdown. I told him to hang around and find out all he could."

"Where are you?"

"On my way to your house."

"I'll be ready by the time you get here."

After ringing off, Chambers Elliot stripped off his pajamas, and pulled on slacks and shirt. Then he hurried into the front room and grabbed his trench coat from the closet. It took several uncomfortable attempts before he managed to struggle into the damp garment. His bare feet squeaked as he forced them into his soggy shoes. With a complaining whimper, he wiggled his toes within the shrunken leather, hoping to redistribute the flow oozing from the soggy soles.

"I'll have webbed feet by this time tomorrow," he grunted.

A horn blared from the curb in front of his house.

Elliot opened the door and hurried outside. Seconds later he was sitting on the passenger side of Taggart's Chrysler, listening to the detective complain about the latest inflation figures.

"Is Von Drake still at the Pierce Ranch?" interjected Elliot.

Taggart nodded. "Parked outside on the highway." The detective paused for a moment before saying, "I'm sorry about George."

"I didn't think Raintree would act so quickly," Elliot sighed.

The detective's eyebrows arched. "There's no evidence suggesting he did."

"It had to be him." Elliot paused a moment, thinking. "Jason, I'm certain Milton Raintree was holding something over George."

"What? If ever a man walked the straight and narrow, it was George Pierce."

The lawyer shrugged. "We all have history. Including Mr. Raintree."

"Chambers, there's no proof Raintree was even there, tonight."

"Who else could it be?"

Taggart wagged his head. "As you said, we all have history."

"Dammit, Jason, George is dead because I overplayed my hand."

"It's no good to snap at me."

The lawyer said very slowly. "I didn't mean to. I'm sorry."

The rain drummed on the hood, roof and glass of Taggart's Chrysler as they drove. The thick drops came in at an angle, flattened out and washed down the windows in tiny waves. At one corner of the windshield, the rain leaked in. The trickle ran across the dashboard, and dripped down onto the lawyer's shoes.

"Did Sheila Clifford approach you as expected?" Taggart asked.

Elliot wagged his head. "Sheila claimed that Raintree had predicted George would be murdered. Further, Raintree expected her to be charged in the killing. Now do you see why I'm convinced he's behind this?"

Taggart's eyebrows came together as he pushed his chin forward slightly. "I admit the circumstances strongly suggest Raintree. Nevertheless, there's nothing you could've done to protect George."

"I should have done something! I should have…" The lawyer stopped to get his emotions under control. Then he asked, "Do we know what Kathy Martin was doing at the ranch?"

"Not yet," the detective replied. His lower lip went in under his teeth and his eyebrows drew down at the corners. "I've got Henderson covering that motel. But as yet she hasn't returned. He has orders to contact me when she does."

Chambers Elliot dragged his handkerchief and wiped his damp cheeks. "How did that woman who wanted to report the accident get to the ranch?" he reflected.

"We won't know that until we find her. If we find her."

The detective filched a pack of cigarettes from inside his coat, sloughed one up and caught it between his lips. Then he tossed the pack onto the dashboard and punched in the car's cigarette lighter.

"How long was she there?" asked Elliot.

"Armistice doesn't recall."

"So we don't know who she is or how she got to the ranch or when she left," mused the attorney. "But we do know she was on the main floor of the house when the shots were fired."

Taggart wagged his head. "When Armistice spoke with Von Drake, the old boy claimed he was in the foyer when the shots were fired. Then he claimed he was upstairs. So anything the butler claims is suspect. We do know there was another woman because Von Drake saw her leave the house." Taggart pulled a folded piece of paper from inside his coat and handed it to Elliot. "This is the autopsy report on Harry Farmer. It looks like he was dead when tossed off the roof… shot with a .32 caliber pistol. Part of the round split off as it when through his skull. But they have enough to match it to a gun, should the weapon be found. Forensics says the rope used to restrain Harry was the vinyl type frequently found on boat anchors."

Chambers Elliot stuffed his handkerchief into a pocket, opened the document and turned on one of the car's interior reading lights. Then he quickly scanned its contents, from page to page. "Bone-cancer."

"That probably explains the opium addiction." Taggart grabbed the cigarette lighter when it popped, touched the cherry-red end to the cigarette, and puffed. "Farmer must've been in terrible pain."

"Any news on Raintree?" the lawyer asked, as he stuffed the report into his pocket.

"All we know is that he's not made contact with Sheila Clifford." Taggart glanced over at Elliot. He shoved the lighter back into its hole. Then he drew a long drag on the cigarette and exhaled a cloud of smoke. "I followed her from your office to the Double Oak Hotel. She was already registered there, but under a phony name."

Elliot nodded. "So she told me. Apparently, that was Raintree's idea."

"I remained at the hotel until Popovitch arrived," continued Taggart. "He's been there since. But so far Sheila Clifford's stayed in her room." The detective sucked on his upper lip for a second. "Are you sure Sheila and Milton Raintree actually got married? I mean, considering what she looks like, you'd think he'd want to be with her."

Elliot shut off the reading light. "That's a big hotel. How can Popovitch be certain she's still in her room?"

"Because I rented the room next to hers," explained Taggart, impatiently. "He's been in there listening through the wall. He heard her on the phone, once, ordering room service. Since then, other than the room service waiter, nobody's been in or out of her room."

"Was Kathy Martin alone in her car when she drove away from the motel?"

"Von Drake thought so. But when he spotted her he was parked down the block. With all this rain it was hard to see clearly."

"Kathy might've picked up Raintree after losing Von Drake," Elliot mused.

Taggart glanced over at Chambers Elliot. "You're thinking Kathy drove Raintree out there, waited in the car while Raintree went inside and shot George?"

"What else can I think?"

"Then why didn't Von Drake see him in the car when Kathy drove out? I'll tell you why, because he wasn't there. Because there wasn't time for him to shoot George and get back down and into Kathy's Corvette in the time-delay between the time Von Drake heard the shots, and spotted her driving out."

The lawyer's hands fluttered with frustration. "She must've left him, then

Taggart flicked the ash from his cigarette into the Chrysler's ashtray. "Chambers, what if Raintree didn't do it?"

"No one else had a motive."

"George was not universally loved," the detective protested. "He was a tough businessman who stepped on more than his share of toes, making his hundred million." Taggart glanced over at Elliot. "What's that old adage about revenge being a dish best eaten cold?"

"I agree that George had enemies. But it's too coincidental to what Sheila Clifford told me not to be Raintree." The lawyer fell silent. After several minutes he said, "I think George was romantically involved with Kathy Martin."

The detective took another drag on the cigarette. His voice became dry, cool, sardonic. "That must've been cozy—considering she's hooked-up with Sydney Pierce."

Elliot grimaced. "George denied any involvement with her. But I think he was embarrassed by his feelings for so young a woman. Do we know if anyone got inside her car after Kathy drove onto the ranch property? That woman who forced her way in, for example?"

The detective wagged his head. "Why would that woman do so if she was already at the house?"

"You being irritatingly rational, Jason."

"Did you warn George that Milton Raintree was planning something?"

"Of course," said Elliot. "He didn't take me seriously, at first. Then we talked at length discussing several options to keep Raintree from the

Pierce fortune." His eyes flicked at the detective. "Finally, George told me to put the whole kit-and-caboodle into a revocable trust—something I advised him against. But he insisted. I left him with the latest draft of his will."

"So at this point George Pierce died intestate?"

"No," replied Elliot. "Testate. His old will—the one last executed—is still binding."

Taggart gave Elliot a confused look. "Is it possible that George executed the new will after you left?"

"What would be the point? The trust was George's idea." Elliot made an unhappy gesture. "Once it went into effect I would have to redo the will anyway. George knew that."

The detective nosed the Chrysler onto the freeway, pressing the accelerator to the floor. "I can't remember the last time you ventured out in a storm to meet with a client."

Elliot's smile was reluctant. "George was more than just a client."

Taggart rolled the cigarette around in his fingers. "You're still convinced that Sheila Clifford's claim is phony?"

"With Milton Raintree involved, it's hard not to. But George was convinced she was Edward's daughter."

"But killing George before she was in the will is tantamount to Raintree shooting himself in the foot."

"I agree. Which makes this all the more confusing. Unless…"

Taggart tossed a glance at Elliot. "Unless, what?"

"Wills have been forged."

The detective thought for a moment. "Maybe that woman Armistice let in was Sheila in disguise? Maybe she killed George instead of making the call?"

Elliot nodded, thinking. "As confused as Armistice sounds, she may well have been able to get upstairs without him realizing it."

"Could Sheila collect if she was in the will even if she was not who she claimed?"

"Assuming such a will exists and passes muster, that would depend on the verbiage. In the case of the latest draft, George stipulated she would collect only if she was proven to be of his bloodline. Consequently, Sheila would still have to face a DNA profile comparison before benefiting."

"That, I imagine, would not please Sydney Pierce."

"Sydney could still contest it claiming Sheila used undue influence over George. But under such circumstances it would be difficult for him to prevail."

"Did George know Sheila had married Raintree?"

The lawyer hunched his shoulders. "Not until I told him."

Taggart chuckled. "I'll bet he went through the roof."

"No," said Elliot. "George was actually blasé about it. He showed more emotion when I asked about Michael Douglas and Jerome Petty."

Taggart blinked in surprise. "He knew them?"

Elliot nodded. "Michael Douglas, anyway. Initially George denied it. But, later he admitted knowing that Barbara had been involved with Douglas."

"That could mean he killed Michael Douglas," Taggart remarked.

The lawyer waved that aside. "Not, George."

The detective gave Elliot a defensive look. "More than one man thought incapable of murder has killed to save his marriage."

"I wonder what Douglas' intentions were toward Barbara Pierce?" the lawyer mused.

"Considering that man's history, not long-term."

"There was one unusual aspect to my visit with George," the lawyer remarked. "Before I left his ranch I had a chat with the Sydney Pierce—who was waiting for me outside in my car. He wanted to help me with Sheila Clifford."

"Sydney? Help?" the detective scoffed.

Elliot smiled slightly. "He claimed had had concerns that the DNA profile being done would unjustly prove she's Edward's daughter."

Taggart snorted, "If I had options on a hundred million and was worried about losing half, I guess I might've told you the same thing."

"In any event, he did make a good point. With that much money up for grabs it might be possible to bribe one the laboratory technicians into falsifying results by using DNA from a member of the Pierce family."

"We all have our price, old friend."

"So I keep hearing," said Chambers Elliot, thoughtfully. "But that's not the interesting bit. You see Sydney's concerns reflected my own when I spoke with George."

"Ah," grinned Taggart. "Sydney has his old man's bedroom bugged."

"If so, Herbie's men will discover it."

"Still, rigging a DNA profile makes no point," said Taggart. "A second test by another lab would refute the first. That's the beautiful part of today's science. There is no guesswork. Well, as along it's not the Dallas County Sheriff's lab doing the testing. With them, anything's up for grabs." Then he glanced over at Elliot and said, "If you were involved with a much younger woman, would you secretly meet her in your pajamas?"

"I wouldn't, but… Oh, I see what you mean. Now that you mention it, George had not shaved, either. He was also wearing a rather worn robe over his nightclothes. No. He wasn't expecting Kathy Martin or any other woman."

"What about a private meeting with Milton Raintree? One he didn't tell the butler about."

"Or a lazy son?" Chambers Elliot gave Jason Taggart a questioning look. "Do we know the whereabouts of Mazy Wilson?"

"Nope. His last address is at that same motel we visited looking for Kathy. But he moved from there a few weeks earlier with no forwarding address. Could be he left town."

Chambers Elliot squirmed against the confines of his wet raincoat. "What about the Portellos? Anything on the street about them?"

"I was going to hold off on that bit of bad news until tomorrow," said Taggart. "But since you asked, my sources tell me that Salvator Portello's put out a reward for the delivery of Milton Raintree—alive." He jerked his chin toward the windshield. "That can only mean he's found a link between Harry Farmer and Milton Raintree and suspects the latter to have that DVD. In my opinion, the dip-tank will be put to use, shortly."

"I have to hand it to Salvator," Elliot said begrudgingly. "He doesn't let moss gather on his stones."

"Don't give him too much credit, Chambers. He owns most of the police in this town, not to mention several high-ranking politicians right up to the top man in this State. Half the State's employees are unknowingly working at tasks that assist Salvator, in one form or another." The detective whistled between his teeth. "A hundred million. I wonder if Sydney would like to adopt a P.I. type as a stepfather?"

"Based upon my limited exposure to Sydney Pierce, I don't think you'd enjoy the association."

"What do you mean? Sydney's more or less a playboy, isn't he?" Taggart grinned. "Hell, I'd fit right in with his idea of high-living."

"Midland Laboratory in Dallas. Are you familiar with them?"

Taggart nodded. "Very reliable."

"I want you to confirm that they are doing the DNA profile on Sheila Clifford."

Taggart nodded his head. "No problem."

Chambers Elliot thought for a moment before saying, "George said he expected to have the DNA results any time. Would they be hand-delivered or sent by post?"

"The results will be sent by certified mail."

"See if we can get a copy of the DNA results."

"That's not going to happen, Chambers, and you know it."

"Not across the counter," agreed the lawyer. "But I was hoping you would use your special tact to get us a copy."

"You've become a very corrupting influence, of late," Taggart muttered.

Rain spattered across the windshield and rattled on the roof. Sheets of it flew across the headlight beams. The windshield wipers thumped monotonously back and forth. The rubber-edged blades could barely keep up with the incessant downpour as Taggart kept the Chrysler accelerator near the floor.

By the time they reached the Pierce Ranch, the entrance was blocked by two police cruisers. A quarter of a mile past, Taggart spotted Von Drake's car. They drove over and parked behind it. Taggart flashed the Chrysler's headlights.

Von Drake scrambled out, hurried back to the Chrysler and crawled into its rear seat.

"Lt. Mann's hot as hell," Von Drake said. "Somebody tipped his wife to him having a burger for lunch instead of the yogurt coleslaw she packed for him."

"Did you actually see Kathy Martin driving away?" Elliot asked.

"Yes," Von Drake said. "Check that. I saw a woman driving the Corvette. But I could not see her face clearly through the rain-choked windows. But I don't see Kathy Martin lending that car to anybody. I wouldn't—especially on a stormy night like this."

"Can we be certain there was no one else in the car?" Elliot pressed.

"Not that I could see," Von Drake replied. "I only had two or three seconds."

"Call it a night, Von Drake," Taggart said. "Tomorrow morning check out the house Kathy Martin and Raintree rented. Talk to the neighbors, again. See if there's any leads we've overlooked."

Von Drake nodded and crawled from the Chrysler. Then he leaned in the open door. "One thing," he said. "When I first got here, a wrecker was pulling a car out of the ditch, just down the road."

"Before or after you heard the shots?" asked Elliot.

"Before." With that, he raced back to his car through the downpour.

"That could explain the woman wanting to report an accident," said Taggart. "That could also explain how she got to the ranch."

"But why would she want to report it if she was involved and the wrecker had already come?"

"I've never claimed women were overly endowed with common

128

sense."

Chambers Elliot looked back through the rear window at the flashing lights. "I've got to get in there, Jason."

"Herbie's not about to allow that." Taggart twisted in the seat to follow the lawyer's stare.

"It's all a matter of how we approach the situation," Elliot returned. "Drive further along. Maybe there is a way we can get through the fence, on foot."

"If they catch us sneaking in we'll be arrested."

"For what? I came to visit my client. You drove me here. We took the entrance my client instructed. Therefore our presence is completely justifiable."

The detective tapped the side window. "How do we explain not seeing that? Those flashing lights are hard to miss, even in the rain."

"We came from the other direction. Now, stop prevaricating and get going."

"And the reason for our visit?"

"George's will, of course. Use your imagination, Jason. Do I have to lie for both of us?"

"Chambers, I prefer you do the lying because you're so much better at it than me."

The lawyer rolled his eyes in aggravation. "Just drive, Jason."

Taggart put the Chrysler into gear and nosed it along the asphalt until he spotted a gravel road that wound through a clutch of cottonwoods in the direction of the Pierce ranchhouse. "There's no guaranty it's going to get us there, even if we don't get stuck in the wet gravel."

"It's as good as we're going to find."

The detective eased onto the narrow road and let the Chrysler roll forward. Despite the heavy rain, the ground remained firm under tire and several minutes later they were parked near a gate in the fence at the rear of the Pierce ranch-yard.

"Just so our stories are in concert," Taggart said, "why was the change to George's will so important that we had to come out at this time of the morning in this weather?"

"I was working on the will and needed clarification as to what assets were to be distributed between the beneficiaries."

"And George's reason for expecting you at this hour?"

"I often call upon clients at this time of the morning. Ask anybody."

"I hope I get the chance, Chambers—before Herbie reads me my rights. But just one more thing. Why am *I* here?"

"You were passing, saw a light on in my house, stopped and offered to drive me because of the bad weather."

The detective gave his head a dismal wag. "Lies just roll off your tongue, don't they?"

"It's a criterion for my profession."

Jason Taggart and Chambers Elliot got out of the Chrysler and slogged through the rain toward the gate. The cast-iron hinges let go a soft creak as Taggart swung the entry-point open. Then the pair moved through and followed a stone path to the grove of pecan trees at the rear of the ranchhouse. When they reached the back door, Taggart tried the knob. It was unlocked.

"Just for arguments sake, Chambers, what if Herbie doesn't believe our story?"

"Then you'll likely spend the night in jail."

Taggart looked over at Elliot in shock. "Why me and not you?"

The lawyer grinned. "Because, I'm a better liar. Stop stalling, Jason. George's bedroom is on the second floor."

The door took them into the kitchen. Elliot pointed toward the hallway leading to the front of the house. Then he led and Taggart followed. As they headed for the stairs, Elliot noticed partially dried footprints on the floor. Based upon the size and shape of the sole, the tracks looked to be made by a woman.

"Once we get to the second floor, I'll head to the left," whispered Elliot. "Third door down on the right. You follow but keep an eye peeled."

"In case you haven't noticed, Chambers, we're leaving a trail of water and mud for the police to find."

Elliot nodded. "As did someone before us."

When the pair reached George Pierce's bedroom, they stopped in the doorway. George's corpse was lying on the floor near the foot of a canopy bed. His eyes were open, clear, dark. The pupils were blown wide, indicating that whatever had been played behind them behind them before was over. One of his hands was flung out in a frozen, defensive gesture. The fingers were curled as if he had been trying to make a fist. His other hand was beneath his body. His robe was twisted as though he had been thrown by a giant, and rolled. His gray hair was matted with blood, black as boot polish. There was more of it on his face and on the floor beneath his head. A grayish ooze was mixed in with the blood, there. Lt. Herbie Mann stood near the body, making notes. His face looked drawn and tired. Herbie needed a shave and a change from his wrinkled brown suit. Several forensic technicians were gathering fingerprint and other evidence from various areas of the room.

"I don't care what I have to do, Jason, I'm going to nail Milton Raintree for this," Elliot whispered.

"I think Salvator Portello will finish Raintree well before you," the detective responded.

The bedroom was spacious. In addition to the canopy bed, there was a nightstand supporting a telephone and an ashtray, a highboy dresser, and desk topped by computer hardware. Vivid watercolors hung on the plaster walls, dragon-embroidered black curtains were drawn across the windows, and, scattered about the carpet were sheets of typed papers.

Elliot called out to Lt. Mann, "What happened, Herbie?"

Mann whirled with a start toward Elliot. "How in hell did you two get up here?"

"Insomnia," Taggart blurted.

"I had an appointment with George Pierce." Elliot made a casual shrug. "He asked that we come in through the back of the house rather than disturb the family. We didn't realize anything was wrong until we saw George's body."

"Stay put," Mann ordered. "There's been enough traffic through, here." Then he walked over to Elliot, his face twisted with suspicion. "Appointment for what, Chambers? It'll be dawn in a few hours."

"Clarification." Taggart nodded.

Mann gave Taggart a disgusted glance before asking Elliot what needed clarified.

"At George's request, I was preparing a change to his will," Elliot explained. "I needed to know the distribution of assets. How did George die?"

"Unpleasantly," Mann grumbled, taking himself very seriously.

"Suspects?" Elliot asked.

Mann glared over at Taggart. "Is Von Drake still working under your license?"

Taggart began hemming and hawing.

"If you're planning on enticing him to the police force, Herbie," Elliot interjected, "you'll have to wait until Von Drake gets back from vacation. He's got me penciled in for at least three Bass for grilling."

"I didn't know Von Drake was a fishing enthusiast," said Lt. Mann. "I thought he was more the roulette-wheel spinner."

"When will the M.E. get here?" Elliot purposely changed the subject.

Mann turned and went back to the body, still making notes. "He's been called."

"Head shot?" Taggart asked.

"One round," replied Mann, still making notes.

"How close?"

"Contact wound," Mann replied.

"Small caliber?" Taggart asked.

Mann gave Taggart a suspicious look. "What made you say that?"

Taggart pointed at the corpse. "George is still wearing his head."

"Was George restrained in any way when he was killed?" Elliot asked.

Mann wagged his head. "No evidence of it."

"Any visitors this evening?" asked Elliot.

Lt. Mann jabbed the air between he and the lawyer. "You. And some woman who forced her way in to report an auto accident. She apparently arrived in a Corvette. As suspects go, I'm discounting you for lack of motive and her for lack of time. She'd just gotten in the house when the shots were heard."

"Have you spoken with that woman?" Taggart asked.

"As far as we can tell, she must've left in the Corvette that brought her here. We're hoping she'll come forward tomorrow."

"A Corvette brought her?" asked Elliot.

Lt. Mann nodded. "That's what the butler claimed." Then his eyes narrowed on Chambers Elliot. "What were you birds doing at the Double Oak Hotel the other day?"

Taggart gave Elliot a worried look. To Mann he said, "Brunch. Why?"

"The corpse on the asphalt out front is why." Lt. Mann tapped Taggart on the chest with his pen. "You seemed inordinately interested in the dead man, according to one of the uniforms at the scene."

"Old habits die hard," Taggart mumbled.

"Where was Sydney Pierce when his father was killed?" Elliot asked.

"In his bedroom," Mann said.

"A pretty lame alibi, isn't it?" Taggart remarked. "Considering Sydney Pierce did not get along with his father and is now about to collect several fortunes."

"Not really," Lt. Mann said with disinterest. "The butler was with him."

"Butler?" gaped Taggart. "But I thought…" The words became a loud yelp of pain as Elliot stepped on the detective's foot.

"I beg your pardon, Jason," said Elliot.

Then Mann looked over at Elliot. "I understand you represent Sheila Clifford."

Elliot wagged his head. "Who told you that?"

Lt. Mann grinned. "Rumor has it she went to your offices."

"Have you questioned Sheila?" asked Elliot.

"Not yet," replied Mann. "She seems to be missing. I'd hate to think her disappearance is your idea, Chambers."

Elliot grimly wagged his head. "Such an action would be highly unethical if not illegal, Herbie."

"Since when do lawyers have ethics or worry about legalities?" countered Mann. "Who is Kathy Martin?"

"I've heard the name," Elliot said vaguely.

Herbie Mann asked, "Is it true Sheila Clifford is Edward Pierce's daughter?"

"That's still an unanswered issue," Elliot replied. "Just so my interruption of your duties is not a complete waste, I think you should talk to Milton Raintree about George's death."

"Raintree? Is he back in town?" Mann demanded.

"He predicted that George Pierce would be murdered." Elliot pointed at the body.

"Do you know Raintree, Herbie?" Taggart chimed.

"What do you mean predicted?" Mann demanded.

"He sent…" began Taggart, before Elliot stepped on his foot, to illicit a cry of surprise.

"I'm sorry, Jason," Elliot said. "My feet keep getting in the way of your big mouth." Then he turned to Mann. "What's your take on this, Herbie?"

"We don't think robbery was a motive," Lt. Mann replied. "The deceased is still wearing this rings."

"Anything in George's pajama pockets?" Elliot asked.

Mann wagged his head. "What are you expecting to be there, Chambers?"

"Perhaps some notes with respect to the changes George wanted for his will."

"Herbie probably forgot to look," Taggart jeered.

Lt. Mann turned and stalked over to Taggart. "How would you like to spend the next three days being interrogated about your presence here?"

"I would like to speak with Sydney Pierce," Chambers Elliot interrupted.

"It won't be today," Mann said.

"What about the windows?" Elliot asked.

"What about them?"

"Could George's killer have escaped by crawling out one?"

"They were locked from the inside—no chance. His killer walked out of the house—probably the same way you clowns walked in."

"In that case, is there any way we can assist in your investigation, Lieutenant?"

"Did you know Father Zamoyski?" Mann asked suspiciously.

Chamber Elliot shrugged. "I can't say that I ever met the man."

"Father Zamoyski is killed and you two are there," Mann said. "Now George Pierce is killed—and you two are here. I'm not a whiz with numbers. But the odds must be pretty high against you guys coincidentally being present at both scenes."

"For your information," Taggart gloated, "Father Zamoyski is in Poland. The corpse at the Double Oak was Harry Farmer."

"How do you know that?" demanded Lt. Mann.

Jason Taggart raised his hands, his palms toward Mann. "I knew it when I saw the scars. But I could be wrong, Herbie. Us untrained P.I.s are prone to mistaken identities."

The lawyer gave Taggart a dirty look. "Harry Farmer was an associate of Milton Raintree as well as of Salvator Portello."

Mann pointed at Taggart as he said to Elliot, "Take your monkey and get the hell out the way you came in. If I need any more information I'll stop by your office."

"I thought that went surprisingly well," Taggart surmised after he and Elliot got back to the Chrysler.

"Considering your lack of tact," agreed Elliot.

"What do you mean?"

"You were supposed to let me do the lying."

"I did."

"Well, you should've kept quiet about Harry Farmer."

"What for? Herbie will find out in time."

"I agree. But once he knows Harry was associated with Kathy Martin and Sheila Clifford, Herbie will learn about Raintree's impersonation of Zamoyski in my office."

"You give Herbie too much credit, Chambers. By the time he ties that all together you and I will be ten years in heaven. Where to?"

"Home. I'm beat. But first call whoever you've got watching Sheila and find out if he's still got her cornered."

Jason Taggart took out his cell-phone. But after putting it to his ear he gave Elliot an embarrassed look. "The damn thing's dead."

Chambers Elliot took out his phone and handed it to the detective.

Taggart punched numbers and then waited. "Popovitch? This is Taggart. Have you still got Sheila Clifford under surveillance? Oh. My phone's been acting up. Sometimes it works. Sometimes it doesn't. No. Okay. Better call it a night."

"He lost her?" Elliot asked dismally.

Taggart handed back the phone. "Apparently. He doesn't know when she left her room. When he thought things had gotten too quiet, he slipped the lock on the adjoining doors and went into her suite. She was gone, bag and baggage. Sorry, Chambers."

"It's my night for things going wrong."

Chapter 12

Chambers Elliot no sooner got home than the telephone rang. The woman on the other end of the line identified herself as Kathy Martin.

"Where are you?" Elliot asked.

"The Grove Ridge Apartments, number 312, Anderson and 183. I'm in trouble."

"More than you probably realize," Elliot said dryly. "It'll take me about an hour to reach you. Will you still be there?"

"Yes."

After ringing off, he turned and headed back out into the rain.

A cold, wet dawn was turning I-35 into river by the time Chambers Elliot parked his Lagonda in the Grove Ridge Apartments lot. He climbed out and made his way through the icy downpour to the apartment building's front door. In the foyer, he pressed the buzzer-button beneath apartment 312.

Immediately, the electric lock on the door rattled, and he was able to get inside.

Elliot gave his soaked raincoat a feeble shake, and then made his way down the hall to the elevator. His shoes were soaked through, and each step squished out a trail of water.

When the elevator doors scraped open on the third floor, he stepped out to the sounds of a baby crying from one of the apartments. The child's wail melded with the beat of rain on the roof and the growling wind. He walked nearly the length of the corridor before stopping in front of apartment 312. There he knocked, lightly.

A woman's frightened voice said, "Who's there?"

"Chambers Elliot," he replied, impatiently.

There were several seconds of rattles and thumps as the woman on the other side of the door released locks and latches. Then Elliot heard the scraping motion of a heavy bolt being slid back. After that came the rattle of a chain.

Elliot tilted forward expectantly. A moment later the door opened a crack and Kathy Martin peered out. She was clad in Pooh-Bear nightgown, and slippers. Large, pink curlers were stuck in her dark hair. Her face was devoid of make-up. Around her neck draped a double choker of imitation pearls. Her weary eyes anxiously contemplated Elliot.

"If we're going to chat, it would be easier if I came inside," Elliot remarked.

She hesitated in the doorway, saying nothing. Her darkly circled eyes watched him with frightened suspicion.

Elliot gave his head an irritated shake. "I'm too tired to rape and too old to plunder. Do I come in or go home?"

Kathy backed away with a toneless, "Come in."

"Is Milton Raintree here?" Elliot entered the apartment.

She went behind him and shut the door, setting the heavy bolt into place. "He's run out on us."

The attorney glanced around Kathy's meager accommodation with its open Murphy bed, littered kitchenette counter, tap-dripping bathroom sink, condensation-filmed windows. An old fashioned radiator, on one side of the room, ticked softly as hot water expanded it slightly. On the other side was a Hollywood bed with the covers thrown back, one pillow and the sheet wrinkled. Past the bed was a low, glass-topped vanity almost bare on top. One side held a cut-glass flagon. On the other side was a pair of silver-topped men's hairbrushes. Near the door, resting on a section of newspaper spread atop the floor, was a pair of women's shoes, mudcaked and still damp. The atmosphere of the room was suffocatingly warm, the smell of fried bacon filled the air.

"Us?" asked the lawyer.

She nodded. "Sheila and me."

"I thought he and Sheila were married." Elliot removed his wet coat and dropped it on the floor, in front of the door.

"They are." Kathy smiled wanly. "But Milton's not one for sentiment when trouble comes to call."

"Are we talking about the murder of George Pierce as the trouble, or something really insidious like Salvator Portello perched on your windowsill?"

Kathy Martin moved away crossing the room to take a seat in a stained, yellow loveseat. "George is dead?"

"Surprise, surprise," he snorted. "As if you didn't know."

"I didn't know."

"Of course you did. You drove Raintree to the Pierce Ranch so he could kill George."

She jumped, her face white with worry. "I didn't!"

Chambers Elliot closed his eyes, drew down the corners of his mouth, and moved his lips as his mind worked. Then he opened his eyes and demanded, "Where were you tonight, let's say between nine and now?"

Kathy pointed at the floor. "Here."

"The entire time?" he asked, moving over to where she stood.

She nodded.

"How curious. You see, a woman was seen getting into your

Corvette, earlier. Your Corvette was followed—to George Pierce's ranch. Whereupon, shots were heard. Then your Corvette raced away with a woman driving it. If you were here all night, who was driving your car?"

She shrank away from him instinctively, taking a perch on the loveseat. "Milton. He took my Vette."

"Stop playing me, Kathy. I said a *woman* was seen getting into your car - you. I said a *woman* was seen driving it out of the Pierce Ranch—you. I said a woman was seen driving it away after the shots—*you.*"

"I'm not lying, Mr. Elliot. Look, I knew you'd have somebody watching me. So did Milton. That's why he dressed as a woman when he took my car."

"A woman's muddy footprints left at trail from the Pierce ranchhouse's back door, across the kitchen, down the hall and up the stairs to George Pierce's bedroom."

"It wasn't me!" She gulped. "It must've been Milton. He wore women's shoes."

"The feet were too small." Chambers Elliot tugged thoughtfully at an earlobe, his eyes glancing over at her muddy footwear. "Was anyone with Raintree when he left in your car?"

"Not with him," she said, her voice breaking off. "Sheila was waiting for him a few blocks away. Those footprints you saw must've been hers."

"That would be convenient for you." Elliot sidled over to the overstuffed armchair across from the loveseat and slumped into it. "I want Milton Raintree, Kathy. Where is he?"

When she next spoke it was without looking at him. "Milton said the Portellos were on his case and he had to bail. That's why he took my Vette."

"You just handed him the keys never expecting to see that expensive car again?"

"I didn't give him the keys. He just took them."

The lawyer purposely looked at his watch, indicating a growing impatience. "When you telephoned, you said you were in trouble. What trouble?"

Kathy collected herself before shaking her head. Then her eyes rose to his. "I think Milton's steered the Portellos in my direction."

"If they were onto you, we wouldn't be chatting. You'd be dead; your body dumped somewhere quietly and permanently out of sight. I would be tucked away in bed, once more dreaming about strangling Ramón Whitaker."

She tilted towards him, her voice becoming sharp and brittle. "But I saw a man following me."

"Perhaps he was simply drawn to your bright and cheery attitude? When was the last time you visited George Pierce?"

"A few days ago." Her hands were shaking, so were her knees. "Do the police think I killed George?"

"Not yet. Were you and George romantically involved?"

She twisted away from his stare, but said nothing.

"Don't play me, Kathy. Or I'll hand you over to the police with a long list of reasons to make you suspect number one in George's murder. Were you involved with George?"

"Yes."

"Did Raintree make any threatening remarks concerning George? Overt, implied? Anything?"

She looked down at her feet, her eyes half squinted, worry lines gathered around her mouth. "He was upset that George had gotten Sheila's DNA without telling her."

"How upset? Enough to kill George?"

She looked up with a start. "Of course not. Milton knew that if George died before Sheila was in the will, she'd get nothing."

"But, Sydney would benefit," the lawyer reflected. "Did George say anything to you about feeling threatened by Sydney in any way?"

"Sydney would never kill his father," she declared.

"So you admit you know Sydney Pierce? Were you putting a smile onto his face as well?"

Her cheeks reddened. "You have a dirty mind."

"Only when it's warranted. Did either man know you were involved with the other?"

She looked away from Elliot's stare. "Sydney suspected it."

"If not Milton or Sydney, who do you think killed George?" he asked.

She hesitated. "I guess it doesn't matter any more. George didn't want me to tell anyone. But the Portellos were trying to force George into signing over his business holdings."

"Force George, how?"

"Dominic Portello threatened to kill George if he didn't agree to stock transfer it."

"You heard this?" Elliot asked in surprise.

She nodded. "Dominic came to the Pierce Ranch late one night. George met with him in the library."

"How did you know that?"

"I was staying at the ranch—in George's bed," she replied. "When George got out of bed I woke up. I couldn't get back to sleep. A few minutes later I heard arguing voices. I got out of bed and followed the sounds to the library. I peeked in and saw Dominic Portello pointing a gun at George and threatening to kill him."

"What happened?"

"George told Dominic to do what he liked, that nothing would change his mind. Dominic hit George and left."

"Did Dominic see you?"

"No. When I saw Dominic turn, I hid in the laundry room. It's across the hall from the library. After Dominic went past where I was, I ran into the library to help George. That's when he told me to tell no one about what I'd seen and heard."

"You're certain the man you saw was Dominic Portello?"

She nodded. "Absolutely."

His eyes arched slightly. "Didn't Sydney realize there was trouble in the house?"

"No. He was out of town that night."

"Sheila Clifford told me that she gave the DVD Harry was using to extort Dominic Portello, to Milton Raintree. Did Raintree give it to you?"

Her eyes darted to him and just as quickly dropped to her hands. "No."

"But you know where he's hidden it," Elliot snapped impatiently.

"No!"

"You're lying. According to Sheila there are four people on the DVD. Dominic Portello, Michael Douglas, an unidentified woman and an unidentified man. You saw it. Who is the man wearing the hood?"

Her eyes darted back to his with a start. "I don't know, I tell you."

"You're lying again. What about the woman? Who is she?"

Kathy shrugged.

Again, Elliot checked his watch. "My how quickly time flies when one is being told tall tales." Then he grinned coldly at her, and got to his feet. "I wish you well, Kathy. Don't fret. I'll send flowers to your funeral." He turned and started for the door.

"Wait!" she called to his back.

Elliot stopped and turned to face her. "Well?"

Kathy became quiet and thoughtful. At length she said, "I know who the woman is. I saw her photo in George's bedroom. She was George's wife—Barbara Pierce."

The lawyer looked surprised. "Barbara?"

"I'm telling you the truth, Mr. Elliot."

His mouth became a thin line. "So that was what Raintree was holding over George." Then he looked at her suspiciously. "How is it

Harry Farmer got the DVD from Junior Billings?"

"I didn't know he had."

"You're lying again, Kathy."

Kathy twisted her hands. "No! I swear."

The lawyer's head shook decisively. "You were in on it from the beginning. You would've asked questions. Harry and Raintree would've given answers."

Kathy stood up. "All right. Milton said they bought it from Billings' daughter, Elvira after Junior died."

"How would she know to contact them?"

"Harry was living there at the time. Elvira approached him. But Harry didn't have the cash, so he contacted Milton. Then those two worked out a deal with her."

"Who else is in on Raintree's scams?"

"Mazy Wilson."

"Anybody else?"

"No," she said. "That's it."

"I've been told the profile George Pierce ordered on Sheila's DNA will be a sham. How is Raintree managing that?"

She gave him a surprise look. "He never said anything about that to me."

Elliot grimaced with growing irritation. "Where can I find Sheila Clifford?"

"With Milton, I suppose." There was a short pause before she bitterly added, "He tossed me aside as soon as he saw Sheila. Said she was wedding-night perfect."

"How curious. Sheila intimated that he put off their wedding night. What's Mazy Wilson's contribution to Raintree's schemes?"

Her eyes widened. "He's the muscle."

"If I had any brains I'd get out of this business," Elliot grumbled. Then he pointed over at the silver brush up on the bureau. "Does Raintree live here?"

Her head wagged. "I rented it when I first came to Austin—before I met him. I kept up the rent because I know how men operate. Those brushes are his. He hides out here when the cops are onto him. He left them behind when he took off."

"Yes. We poor stupid men hate and abuse all women. Especially the ones who lie." There was bitter sarcasm in his voice. Elliot strolled over to the brush set and picked up one; noting the blonde hairs clinging to it. "Do you live here alone?"

She half-closed her eyes, her voice becoming dulcet. "Yes."

He set down the brush and turned to face her. "You're lying, again."

"I—I used to have a roommate."

"Sheila Clifford?" he inquired, with his cross-examining smile.

"Yes—until she married Milton." Her eyes were cool, her lips slightly parted.

"Something's out of whack. I'm being conned, I know I am." Elliot returned to where she was standing. "Where can I find Mazy Wilson?"

Her head wagged. "I don't know. He only shows up when Milton needs an enforcer."

"Have you heard from either Sheila or Milton since he left in your car?"

Kathy hesitated a moment as if carefully forming her reply. Then she turned, offering Chambers Elliot her back, before saying, "With George murdered, I figure they're a couple hundred miles away."

He passed a hand tentatively over his stubbled chin. "Is Sheila actually Edward Pierce's daughter?"

Kathy started to open her lips to form the words of a reply. But, as if she found it impossible to say anything, she gave another nod.

Chambers Elliot drew down the corners of his lips, raised his eyebrows. "How can you be certain?"

"Milton said she was." She was staring abstractedly at the floor. "He had no reason to lie to me."

Chambers Elliot pointed at her muddy shoes. "If you were here all evening, how did your shoes get in that condition?"

She twisted her body to stare in the direction he was pointing. "That was from yesterday."

"Lies pass so easily over the lips of a grafter," he muttered. "I don't think you can tell the difference between fact and fiction. All right, I'll give you one simple fact. When I get back home I'm going to telephone Mr. Portello and tell him where you are."

She gasped, one hand darting to her throat. "Dear God! No! Please?"

"Then stop your damn lying!" He turned away. "While I was at the Pierce ranchhouse, Lt. Mann asked if I knew you. It follows, therefore, that someone mentioned you to him. He's going to find you, Kathy. He'll ask questions. You'd better have answers."

Her eyes dipped to the floor.

Chambers Elliot turned to face her. "Mazy Wilson killed George?"

Her eyes came up with a start. "No. He couldn't have."

The lawyer eased forward, his hands on his hips. "Why not? What makes you so certain? In your own words, he is Raintree's enforcer."

Kathy's face clouded. "Mazy just couldn't, that's all."

Chambers Elliot turned and started for the door, his patience exhausted. "I wish you well, Kathy."

Before he could pick up his wet raincoat, the doorknob turned. A moment later the door opened and Sheila Clifford staggered in. her shoes soggy with water and caked in mud, her hair stringy and wet from the rain.

"Oh, God, no!" Sheila screamed, when she spotted Chambers Elliot.

He reached out and caught her arm as she tried to turn and run. "There's no place to hide, Sheila."

The young blonde gave out a terrified cry, broke free from Elliot's grasp and rushed over to Kathy. "He's dead, Kathy!"

"Don't say anything more," Kathy warned.

"George Pierce!" Sheila blurted in a panic. "Murdered!"

Elliot closed the door and then went over to where the women stood. "Who killed him, Sheila?"

Sheila jerked toward Elliot, wide-eyed in terror. "Milton!"

"Sheila, no!" Kathy shouted.

Elliot pointed to the loveseat, "Sit down, Sheila."

"Don't tell him anything!" Kathy moved away from the loveseat.

"I have to get out of here!" Sheila locked her eyes upon Chambers Elliot. "Don't you understand? I'll be arrested for murder!"

"Nobody's going anywhere," he declared. "What happened at the Pierce ranch?"

"All I know is, Milton told me to wait in Kathy's car," Sheila replied. "The butler let Milton in the ranchhouse. I waited and waited. It seemed like forever. Then I heard shots—that's when I panicked. I crawled behind the wheel of Kathy's Corvette and raced out of there. Look, Mr. Elliot, I didn't know what Milton was going to kill anybody."

"Why was he going there if not to murder George?" asked Elliot.

"To tell George about us getting married," Sheila replied.

"While wearing a dress?" scoffed the lawyer.

"He had on his disguise…" Sheila started.

"Don't be a fool, Sheila!" Kathy Martin barked. Her face was suddenly ugly with a horrible sneer. "Everything you tell him, he'll tell the cops!"

"Tell me all of it, Sheila!" Elliot demanded.

"I don't know anything else."

"How did Raintree expect to get in to see George?"

"Milton told the butler there had been a terrible accident and he needed to call the police." Sheila dropped her handbag to the floor, went over and sank down onto the loveseat. "Then he just pushed the butler aside and went in."

Elliot stepped over to where Sheila sat, towering over her. "Where is Milton Raintree?"

The blonde's face twisted in confused surprise. "Didn't the police arrest him when they got there? They must have."

"No," Elliot told her. "Where is Mazy Wilson?"

Sheila leaned back, her hands knotted in her lap. "I don't know."

"I can see where Raintree would want some help when dealing with the Portellos, but why get Mazy Wilson involved with George Pierce?"

The blonde's eyebrows flickered. "Mazy was a pal of Edward Pierce. That's how my mother met Edward. Milton thought we could use what Mazy knew about Edward to convince George that I was Edward's kid."

"What's Mazy's end?" he demanded.

A shiver went through her. "A third of whatever I get."

"Was Mazy at the Pierce ranch, tonight?"

"Don't say anymore, Sheila!" Kathy Martin shrilled.

"You've got to help me, Mr. Elliot. Milton's not about to take the fall for what happened to George." Sheila's face dropped. "He'll dump it on me—after I left him stranded, there."

Chambers Elliot smiled sardonically, his questioning eyes impatient. "Love has died so soon?" Then the attorney looked over at Kathy Martin. "Have you ever been arrested?"

Her arms cross over her breasts, her fingers clutching her elbows. "None of your business."

"There's an arrest warrant out on her," declared Sheila.

Elliot stared steadily at Kathy Martin. "What for?"

Kathy avoided his eyes. "Armed robbery."

"Should I assume guilt, or innocence?"

She looked up at him in mirthless complacence. "Assume what you like."

"Was Milton Raintree involved in that, too?"

Her eyes faltered away from his stare. "No. It happened ten years ago. Long before I met Milton."

He made an impatient gesture. "Was anyone hurt?"

Kathy Martin shook her head, blankly.

"Did you remain in Texas during that entire time?" he pressed.

Kathy gave him another look, nodding. "What difference does it make?"

Elliot's voice showed his impatience. "Ten years on the run is a long time. How did you survive without being arrested?"

"I used several names and social security numbers to get jobs. I lived with men when I couldn't find work. Happy, now?"

Elliot's eyes went from women to woman as he asked, "Does Milton Raintree own a gun?"

Sheila shrugged. "Pistol. She opened her purse pulled out a pack of cigarettes, lit one and then dropped it to the floor and crushed it under her heel. "Damn patches!"

"What caliber?"

"I don't know anything about guns," Sheila said.

The lawyer returned his attention to Kathy Martin. "I could be a big help to you," he began cautiously. "For example, the statute of limitations has run on that robbery charge—assuming you've told me the truth about it. I could get it dropped."

Kathy smirked suspiciously, "In return for what?"

"Honest answers," he replied.

The brunette moved closer to him. Her eyes locked on his in pleading. "You mean that?"

He nodded. "But no more lies." Then he turned to Sheila and said, "You saw George, tonight, didn't you?"

Sheila nodded her head several times.

"What time?" he asked.

"A couple of hours before Milton drove me back to the Pierce ranch in Kathy's car."

"Why did you meet with George?"

"I was scared." Sheila's cheeks bulging into a melancholy smile. "I kept thinking about what Milton had said about George getting killed. I wanted to warn George."

Elliot asked, "What else did you and George talk about?"

Sheila dipped her eyes away from his stare. "You're not going to believe me."

"Try me!"

"George said he was going to protect me and Sydney by putting everything into a trust. I was terrified. I knew Milton would blow his cork when he found out."

"But you told Raintree, didn't you?"

Sheila Clifford shook her head. "No. But he knew. Milton knew all of it."

"How?" Elliot asked.

Sheila splayed her hands. "He just knew."

He rubbed his chin and gazed at Sheila with suspicious eyes. "Then what happened?"

"Milton dressed up in women's clothes, told me to meet him three blocks away in fifteen minutes," said Sheila. "He said if I didn't show, he'd find me and have Mazy kill me. Then he took the keys to Kathy's Corvette and left. I waited out the time and did as he'd told me."

Chambers Elliot looked over at Kathy Martin.

"She had no choice, Mr. Elliot," said Kathy, suddenly cooperative.

"Milton picked you up as promised?" asked Elliot.

"I got in the car and he drove us out to Pierce's ranch," Sheila said in a flustered voice. "Didn't say a word the whole time. Didn't even look at me. Just drove. Then it went down like I already told you."

"George Pierce was shot once," said Elliot. "But there were several shots fired. Was Raintree wounded?"

Sheila heaved her shoulders. "All I know is I heard shots and left."

Elliot spoke slowly. "What's your relationship with Sydney Pierce?"

"I've never met him," Sheila said.

Outside in the hallway came the sound of rapidly approaching footsteps. Chambers Elliot went over to the door grabbed up his raincoat, and waited. A few seconds later the door burst open and Lt. Herbie Mann strode in, followed by two uniformed police officers.

"You get around, Chambers," Mann remarked. Then he pointed at the two women before speaking to the uniformed officers, "Read them their rights and then cuff them."

"Don't say a word unless I'm present, Sheila," Elliot instructed.

"What about me, Mr. Elliot?" pleaded Kathy Martin.

Chambers Elliot gave a reluctant nod. Then he turned to Lt. Herbie Mann. "Where are you taking them?"

"My office—to be booked on suspicion of murder."

"Who tipped you to them being here, Herbie?" Elliot asked.

Lt. Mann grinned. "An anonymous caller."

"Male?" asked Elliot.

"Are you sure you want to get involved in this, counselor? I thought George Pierce was a friend of yours."

Elliot looked over at the frightened women. "I'll be there by the time you arrive," he told them. "Remember, not one word unless I am present – both of you."

Chapter 13

Lydia Marshall was standing next to Maggie Sharp's desk when Chambers Elliot arrived at the office, just before noon. "Those checks are as phony as that priest."

"Sounds like I'm running true to form," he muttered, sleepily. Then he looked down at Maggie and noticed her red, swollen eyes. "Cats?"

"It's not my allergies," Maggie sniffed.

Lydia said, "According to my favorite drive-time radio-channel, Sheila Clifford and Kathy Martin were arrested. Martin was brought in on an outstanding armed-robbery warrant. Clifford is being questioned in connection with the murder of George Pierce."

"Any mention of Milton Raintree?" asked the lawyer.

"He's being sought by the police as a person of interest in the murder." Lydia narrowed her eyes. "You look like death warmed over, Chambers. Don't you ever sleep?"

"I was present during Sheila and Kathy's bookings—which lasted until a shave, shower and a drive ago." He refocused upon Maggie, with concern. "What's wrong with you?"

"Ramón," the receptionist sobbed.

"You're actually going to defend those two creeps, Chambers?" demanded Lydia.

"Stranger things have happened, Lydia." The lawyer tilted his head, indicating the petite, redheaded receptionist. "What's going?"

"Ramón's in the hospital," Maggie hiccupped.

Elliot gave Lydia an optimistic, questioning look. "Dying?"

"Ramón had another romantic setback, Chambers," Lydia explained, trying with great difficulty to stifle a laugh. "Our fearless intern will be unavailable for the next few days. But it's nothing serious."

Maggie gave Lydia a scolding look. "What do you mean, 'nothing serious'?" the receptionist demanded. "He's completely bald!"

"Bald?" Elliot echoed.

Maggie nodded her head before breaking into a tirade of wails. "She tried to kill him, I know she did!"

"Who is *she*?" asked Elliot. "And, more importantly, am I defending Ramón against a murder-charge?"

"Ramón called this morning to say he was in the hospital and therefore would not be in," explained Lydia. "Since you did not have any appointments scheduled, Maggie and I drove over to see him."

"When you say hospital, are we talking padded rooms or the usual?"

"I'm afraid nothing about Ramón involves the usual, Chambers. But he's not in the psyche ward."

The lawyer made a disgusted face. "Are you telling me that Ramón's contracted some strange form of venereal disease hitherto not inflicted upon mankind?"

Maggie's eyes widened in horror. Then she jumped to her feet and raced out of the office, sobbing hysterically.

The legal assistant put her hands akimbo at her hips. "Not as far as we know. But you could have phrased your question better. Maggie is absolutely distraught over this."

The lawyer pointed in the direction the receptionist's retreat. "I thought I'd made myself clear to both of them that I would not tolerate any personal interaction that disrupted this office."

Lydia covered her face with her hands. "That's part of the problem. Ramón told Maggie that it was best if they never got involved."

His mouth fell open. "You mean he actually has ethics?"

Her hands dropped to her sides and she gave her boss a pleading look. "Chambers, Ramón idolizes you. If you'd just give him half a chance…"

He batted at her words with one hand. "What about this bald thingy that I'm praying is not mange?"

"Ramón's latest dating-club encounter owns a hair-salon."

"Can I assume this deranged and obviously desperate woman shaved his head with a chainsaw?" The lawyer set his briefcase upon the desk.

"No. She offered to straighten and dye Ramón's hair—to give him that beach-junkie look," explained Lydia. "Unfortunately, while she was applying the hair-straightening cream the woman's rather ample cleavage hit Ramón in the face and—well, nature took its course right then and there."

Elliot rolled his eyes. "I'm going to get a lock for his zipper."

"Unfortunately," Lydia continued, "hair-straightening chemistry has some rather nasty side effects if not monitored properly."

"Ergo the baldness?" He rubbed the side of his jaw with his fingertips.

Lydia made a vague motion with one hand. "The hair dissolved right off his scalp."

Elliot shivered. "Ramón must look a cast-member from *Night of the Living Dead*. Will his hair grow back?"

"It's not permanent." She made a disgusted face. "At least that's what the doctor thinks. Ramón should be back in a couple of days—once the blisters subside."

The lawyer fumbled with his lower lips while considered her words.

"That means I'm going to have a bald guy with scabs on his head running around here?"

"Not entirely bald." She looked at him quickly and then looked away. "Ramón is missing one sideburn, half his moustache, most of both eyebrows plus one eyelash."

The lawyer clapped both hands over his eyes. "Only one eyelash?"

Lydia bit her lip. "I requested that he not go into any detail."

Elliot gave her an understanding nod. "A wise decision. Particularly on an empty stomach. Nevertheless, we have our clients to consider. They cannot be subjected to Ramón and his—his…"

"It won't be that bad, Chambers," she interjected, her eyes once more upon his. "I've already purchased a wig, for him. As for the eyebrows… I guess we could mascara the parts that are gone."

Chambers squared his shoulders and planted his feet. "I suppose expecting you to cut them off at throat-level would be asking too much?"

"You know you don't mean that." Lydia jabbed a thumb toward Elliot's office. "You've got bigger worries than Ramón in there."

He gave his private office door a fearful look. "The Portellos are back?"

"No. Your favorite detective's showed up about an hour ago and has been snoring on the couch, since. One last thing, Chambers. I got a call from Parker Jones. He wants to speak with you."

A worried look flooded across the lawyer's face. "Crazy-Leonard Jones is still incarcerated isn't he?"

"Yes," said Lydia. She laced her fingers together tightly, and then pulled them apart. "But Parker claims he's uncovered evidence which all but guarantees his brother a new trial."

"Leonard Jones is as guilty of murder as sin is black, Lydia," Elliot declared. "I went to bat for him only out of friendship for Parker. I lost the case due to overwhelming evidence, not through any lack of effort. Tell Parker I'm sorry but he'll have to find someone else."

"Parker is offering a half-million retainer, no matter the outcome. He claims he can prove the judge prejudiced the jury so his brother didn't get a fair trial."

Elliot shook his head. "A defendant is denied a fair trial only when a conviction occurs as the result of a breakdown in the adversarial process rendering the trial-result unreliable. I grant you Magistrate Whitaker is an odd sort—Ramón is bloodline-proof of that. However Elmo Whitaker faithfully followed courtroom procedures during Leonard's trial."

Lydia Marshall waggled a scolding forefinger at her boss. "So far this Zamoyski case has cost you a fortune. If you continue like this, all three of us will be in the soup-line."

The lawyer offered her a crooked grin. "I've never seen you and Maggie eat soup."

"Chambers, the offer from Jones would put us in the black and keep us there for two or three years," Lydia Marshall pleaded. "It's foolish to pass it up."

"I had all I could do to keep from strangling Leonard Jones during the trial," Elliot retorted, impatiently. "I seriously considered murdering him in the midst of the appeals-process. I couldn't possibly avoid arrest should I go to court with him, again. No, Lydia. It's out of the question."

"We'll get the judge to order Leonard gagged and shackled, for the duration," Lydia quickly suggested. "All you'll have to do is go through the motions. The prosecutor wins, as before. You'll pocket half a million. And best of all, you'll never hear from the Leonard Jones again. Chambers, it's a win-win situation."

The lawyer shook his head very slightly. "What you're suggesting is completely unethical." Then Elliot's brows furrowed with pleasure as he added, "I never realized you'd acquired the unmitigated scruples of a litigator. Well done, Lydia."

"Chambers, our bank balance is nearly as low as a snake's belly."

"As may be." He picked up his briefcase. "But we'll pass on the Leonard Jones' defense anyway."

Lydia pointed toward his private office. "I finished the motion for the supplemental briefing in Judge Laggard's disciplinary hearing, for this afternoon. It's on your desk. Don't get sidetracked with Jason and forget about signing it."

"Nag, nag, nag." Elliot headed into his office. After closing the door, the lawyer gave the davenport upon which Jason Taggart was sleeping, a nudge with a knee. "Up and at 'em, bright eyes."

Taggart jerked awake with a groan.

Elliot surveyed the detective's disheveled appearance. "Jason, that suit looks like you showered in it."

In a thick, clogged voice the detective said, "I think I did. What time is it?"

"Nearly half past twelve. What have you got for me?"

Taggart struggled to his feet. Then he staggered sleepily over to one of the customer armchairs in front of Elliot's desk. "My sources claim that Salvator Portello is not only onto Kathy Martin's hookup with Harry Farmer and Milton Raintree, but he's offered a reward to get his not so gentle hands on her."

Elliot frowned thoughtfully. "Why would Salvator offer a reward?

His snitches must've informed him about her arrest. Did you let Herbie know?"

The detective nodded. "He's stashed Kathy in a cell by herself. But inmates have died under more inaccessible circumstances."

The lawyer went over to his desk, and dropped his briefcase on top of it. "What about the Forty Winks Motel? Were they storing anything for Harry Farmer?"

Taggart gave his head a yawning shake. "Or so they claimed. But from the worried look on the owner's face when I questioned him about Harry, I think Salvator's people got there before me and made the same inquiry. If so, anything that might have been stored is gone and nobody's going to complain about the loss."

"What about George Pierce? Did you get confirmation on his death?"

"Yes," said Taggart. "George was shot once – probably with something along the lines of a .32 caliber pistol."

The line of the lawyer's jawbone stood out very distinctly for a moment. "Probably along the lines?"

Taggart splayed his hands. "The bullet shattered as it went through George's skull."

"Just like Harry Farmer?" Elliot mused.

"Exactly. So far, forensics can only make a 'guestimate' based upon the bullet's weight and the probably diameter of some of the pieces. They've asked the coroner to go back and look for more fragments."

"Will they be able to match bullet to a gun?"

The detective nodded slightly. "In time. But nobody's bragging at the moment. I've got a request in for a copy of the metallurgy results on both George and Harry Farmer." He took out a cigarette and lit it. "Since similar metals were used in both projectiles I'm guessing there will be a match. If so, there's a strong likelihood both men were killed by the same shooter although the gun would still be an open item. Just so you know, the wound was at the base of George's skull up in the hairline. It severed his spinal cord, cleanly. George died instantly."

"Luck or experience in terms of location?"

The detective's broad shoulders heaved. "Either way he's dead, Chambers."

Elliot went around the desk to his chair and sat down. "The round fired into Michael Douglas's head also shattered, didn't it?"

"I was afraid you'd remember that," muttered Taggart. "Chambers, why in hell would Dominic Portello kill George Pierce? I agree he had a good motive against Harry Farmer and possibly Michael Douglas. But

George?"

"Kathy Martin claimed she saw Dominic Portello at the Pierce Ranch threatening to kill George."

Taggart's eyes went wide. "What for?"

"To coerce George's cooperation in a stock transfer." Elliot wrinkled his nose. "Is it possible the evidence from the Douglas case is still around?"

"Not a chance." Then in a softer voice the detective asked, "Chambers, how can you believe anything Kathy says?"

The lawyer's face twisted in sudden confusion. "I agree she could be lying. But why? It's certainly within the realm of possibility that Dominic tried something like that with George." Chambers Elliot paused a moment to think. Then he said, "Why was more than one gunshot heard when George was killed if George was shot once in the back of the head?"

"Lt. Mann wanted the same explanation. So he had Forensics do an acid-wash on Pierce's hands. They found nitrates. This means, George Pierce fired a gun quite recently—probably at his killer."

"Was a pistol registered in George's name?"

Taggart shrugged. "Not officially. But that's no guaranty he didn't have one. Or the killer may have brought the gun, and George got hold of it. Herbie's theory is George had the gun and shot or shot at, his attacker or attackers. Then the attacker or attackers got the gun, killed George and took the weapon with they fled."

"Were there any bullet holes in the room?"

"Not according to my sources—which has Herbie running up a wall."

"Then there must've been blood. No bullet-holes means the rounds lodged in the person or persons shot at by George."

"Your logic is sound. But only George's blood was found and he had been shot only once."

Elliot smiled quietly to himself. "His killer or killers were wearing tight, heavy clothing that absorbed all the blood as these wounded people escaped?"

Taggart yawned. "That is also Herbie's theory. But, then, he's been eating nothing but carrots for a week."

The lawyer stood up, went around to the side of his desk and began to pace. "There's something wrong with this whole thing, Jason."

"So why not cut your losses and walk away from it?"

"Not until I get Milton Raintree. What about a connection between Harry Farmer and Junior Billings? According to my sources, Harry

Farmer stayed at the Billings home after leaving the Forty Winks Motel until after Billings died."

"Chambers, why do you bother hiring me to find out this stuff when you do it on your own?" The detective made a frustrated spread of both hands. "Yes there is a link. The two men were half-brothers."

Elliot looked annoyed. "I've also been told that Billing's daughter—Elvira—sold the DVD to Harry Farmer and Milton Raintree."

The detective nodded slightly. "That may well be true. I spoke with Elvira. She's a money-grubbing type with three ex-husbands, a penchant for seeing search-warrants, a closed mouth unless bribed with cash and a brand new Cadillac. By the way, the five hundred she got from me to get her talking will be on my next expense report."

The lawyer stared at him quietly for a moment. "That new car is a recent benefit from her latest marital upset?"

"Nope," said Taggart. "Her last hubby left years ago and Elvira's had no serious takers since. I asked about the new car. She told me it was none of my business how she got it—but in more colorful terms. So after I left Elvira, I went to the dealer who sold it to her. The Credit Manager told me that Elvira dropped twenty grand in cash—new bills—as the down-stroke for the car's financing."

"Thrifty saver?"

"I doubt it. Her fingers were stacked with cheap rings, and there was a pile of lottery tickets on the kitchen table as high as a toaster." Taggart's face tightened. "Who told you Elvira sold the DVD to Harry and Raintree?"

Elliot said slowly, "Kathy Martin. But if Raintree and Harry paid Elvira twenty grand, where did that money come from? Kathy told us she'd pawned jewelry to keep them afloat."

The detective rolled his eyes. "Stolen jewelry taken by Sheila from George, no less. Should I assume you're defending Kathy Martin?"

Chambers Elliot nodded thoughtfully. "Billings and Harry were close?"

"According to Elvira, Junior Billings couldn't have cared less about Harry Farmer, or Harry about Junior. The two never got along since they were kids."

The lawyer stopped and stared at Taggart. "Then Harry cut his living arrangement with Elvira?"

"Exactly. Cash on the barrelhead."

"Why didn't Elvira try to make a touch on the Portellos? She must've known what was on the DVD."

"Elvira is money-hungry but not stupid, Chambers," said the

detective. "My theory is, Elvira went snooping for whatever she could sell after her father died. When she discovered the DVD and played it, she realized what her father had been sitting on. But she was too scared to peddle it on her own. So, she gave Harry a peek. He saw potential, but Elvira wanted cash. So Harry called in Milton Raintree. Then the two of them made her an offer she could not turn down."

Chamber Elliot resumed his pacing. "Did anybody outside the family visit Billings while he was dying?"

"According to Elvira, her father had no visitors."

The lawyer stopped pacing and faced Taggart. "Were Father Zamoyski and Junior Billings friends?"

"Absolutely. According to Elvira, Zamoyski was a drinking buddy of her father's. Each night after work, Junior and Zamoyski would get together in the Priest's office and tipple for an hour or so." The detective tugged on one earlobe. "I'm only guessing. But I think it was during one of those imbibing sessions that Zamoyski said more than he should."

The lawyer wagged his head. "I think it must've been the other way around."

Taggart took a pocket nail-clipper out and began to use it, looking down. "I don't get you."

"Why did Father Zamoyski leave this country?"

"Nobody knows."

"So why would a Russian immigrant give up a cushy job here to go to Poland?" mused the lawyer.

"Okay, I'll bite. Why?"

"Because Junior Billings had the VHS tape of Michael Douglas' killing and told Zamoyski what was on it."

The detective shrugged. "Possibly. But why would that send Zamoyski running?"

"Because Zamoyski knew who'd made the confession about that killing," said Elliot.

"Rita Portello, yes. But…" He dropped the nail-clipper away back into his pocket.

"Until that time, I suspect Zamoyski assumed that Rita's confession concerned a little girl's imaginings. Considering her family, the girl likely had terrible nightmares," Elliot said, said almost gently. "But Zamoyski knew this was no fantasy when Billings confirmed what had been confessed by telling what he saw on the tape. At that point, Zamoyski realized how tenuous his hold on life had become. I think that revelation was so shocking, the priest blurted out what he knew."

"But Billings already knew who did it," objected the detective. "He had the tape, remember?"

"Junior Billings had the tape," agreed Elliot. "But odds are he didn't recognize Dominic. Remember, Dominic Portello was still too young to take an active role in the family business. Therefore it's not likely he was known to Billings."

"But why hang onto the tape if he didn't recognize anybody? Doing so would not get Billings any money and could land him in jail if police investigators found it."

"Because there was one person on the tape he did recognize."

"Who?"

"Barbara Pierce."

"Barbara?"

"That's what Kathy told me. That's what Milton Raintree was holding over George."

Taggart's eyes glistened with surprise. "Barbara killed Michael Douglas?"

"I don't think so. But both Sheila and Kathy said a woman appeared in the video after Michael Douglas dropped to the floor." Chambers Elliot stopped and looked over at the detective. "Did Billings actually collect anything for his blackmail effort?"

"Elvira claims her father was the epitome of innocence from cradle to grave," said Taggart. "But my people checked on the deed for the property bequeathed her. The house was paid-off thirty years ago - about three months after Michael Douglas' murder. So somebody coughed nearly fifteen thousand in Billings' direction."

"Did you ask Elvira if Rita Portello had confided anything concerning Michael Douglas' murder?"

"I asked. Elvira denied it, in all the living colors of our varied and much-maligned tongue."

The lawyer scratched the end of his nose, thoughtfully. "Both Sheila and Kathy told me that Michael Douglas simply dropped while Dominic was yelling at him."

"What's your point?"

"Neither said anything about Dominic going behind Douglas and shooting him in the head."

"Chambers, I remember distinctly that the gun used on Douglas had been pressed against his skull when fired. The DVD must've been edited leaving out the actual shooting."

"Why? That would be the most damning evidence," Elliot said, slowly.

Taggart shrugged. "Maybe Dominic struck Douglas and after the man dropped, Dominic bent down and shot him?"

"Maybe. But there was another man in the video, according to both women. His face was shielded by a hood."

The detective got to his feet nodding. "But we'll probably never find out who he is. In any event, Barb or George probably paid Junior Billings to keep quiet. She made enough TV appearances during her fund raising efforts for anyone who lived in the area to recognize her."

"I agree. But why didn't Billings return to the well?"

The detective dragged one hand across his unshaven face. Then he said, "He probably did. But what he got from the Pierce's on subsequent demands was likely pocket-money. That's the weakness in blackmailing if the blackmailer's identity is known. Once the blackmailer collects, he or she becomes an accessory to whatever is to be kept quiet. Ongoing extortion will continue. But the amounts paid invariably get smaller and smaller. That's because the one being blackmailed and the blackmailer both know that exposure will put each of them behind bars—or worse."

Elliot stopped pacing and tugged at his bottom lip, thoughtfully. "What happened to the will I brought out to George?"

Taggart shrugged. "The police must have it."

"No. Had Lt. Mann's people discovered it, Herbie would have mentioned it when Sheila was arraigned. It would've sealed his case against her."

The detective gave a slightly disappointed look. "Maybe George hid it?"

Elliot shook his head. "I saw him put it into his desk."

"Then I'd guess that Sydney Pierce came upon the new will between the time his father died and the police arrived, and disposed of it."

"That's probably an accurate assessment." Elliot started pacing, again, his forehead furrowed in thought. "When I was interrogating Sheila Clifford before Herbie arrested her, she told me that Raintree knew of her conversation with George Pierce earlier that evening— before George was murdered."

"Raintree must've bugged Pierce's bedroom." Taggart snuffed out his cigarette in the ashtray stand between the chairs.

"I don't think so. Lt. Mann and his people are very thorough. If there were bugs in there, Herbie would've found them."

"Maybe Herbie did and is holding-back?"

"No. Herbie would've made a point of mentioning it at the booking, hoping to frighten Sheila into thinking he had a tape-recording of the murder. It follows, therefore, that Raintree has someone in the house— for my money it's got to be Sydney Pierce, rather than one of the servants."

"Don't jump to any conclusions, Chambers. Armistice told several versions of when and where he heard the shots."

"But Sydney had everything to gain by killing his father before Sheila could be confirmed as a Pierce. Armistice did not. Put Sydney under surveillance – around the clock." The lawyer made a fist and thumped it into the palm of the opposite hand. "If he and Raintree are paired in George's killing, they'll meet at some point to settle up."

"I think Salvator Portello is of the same mind. Which could make grabbing Raintree alive more than a tic dangerous. Why not just hang loose and let the Portellos deal with him?"

"I'll do the grabbing and to hell with Salvator." Elliot returned to his desk and settled back into his chair. "I asked Kathy Martin who else was involved in Raintree's scam. She told me that Mazy Wilson was a player." He half-closed his eyes and watched the detective. "But what if there was someone else? Someone like Sydney Pierce?"

Taggart blinked. "Why would Sydney bother? He was the heir apparent."

Chambers Elliot opened his eyes and raised a meaningful finger. "Until Sheila showed up. What if George threatened to cut Sydney out of the Will?" The lawyer leaned back and propped his feet atop the desk. "What if George promised to hand the entire estate over to Sheila as punishment for Sydney's laziness?"

"I doubt George would do anything like that. But if he did, I think Sydney would've killed George rather than involve Raintree."

A faint metallic smile showed at the corners of the lawyer's lips. "What if Sydney couldn't bring himself to kill his father? He'd hire someone like Raintree, wouldn't he?"

"Chambers, speculation isn't going to get us anywhere."

The lawyer dropped his feet to the floor. "See if you can get a peek at Sydney Pierce's bank records. If I was Milton Raintree and Sydney wanted me to kill George, I'd demand some money up front." He laughed under his breath. "I'd want to make damn sure there was a link between the murder and Sydney—just in case the police tumbled to my involvement. I'd want to be able to use that to bargain against a death-sentence."

"You know damn well that without a court-order that information in inaccessible."

The lawyer spread his hands and looked down at them. "I'm certain you can figure a way around the rules, Jason."

The detective's chin moved an inch. "Your growing confidence in my criminal expertise is beginning to worry me."

Elliot said in a tone that meant nothing, "Sometimes rules have to be bent just a little to give justice a chance."

"Speaking of justice, I have a plan to smoke Raintree out."

"How?"

"You'll make a press-release announcing the results of Sheila's DNA test as a match for the Pierce family-line. Raintree will immediately try to make contact with her, hoping to rekindle their love in order to get his hands on her millions."

"First of all she's in jail," protested Elliot. "Secondly, the current will does not provide a bequest for Sheila Clifford under any circumstance. With the exception of a few minor handouts, Sydney Pierce inherits everything. Thirdly, Austin P.D. has a warrant out for Raintree's arrest. He's not about to show up at one of their jails on his own."

"For a chance at fifty million, I'm betting that Raintree will make his move, anyway." Taggart made a whistling sound with his lips and teeth. "I'm also betting there is another will. One that favors Sheila Clifford. One that will miraculously appear very shortly."

"On that we agree. But, assuming Sheila Clifford is willing to stick her neck out, which I doubt, if I announce she's a Pierce I can't very well dump her someplace where we can easily protect her," said the lawyer, thoughtfully. "Raintree would expect Sheila to move into the Pierce Ranchhouse."

"Not if we announce that she refuses to live there alone with Sydney."

"Is there anything criminal in Sydney Pierce's past that might worry a woman?"

"If there is, my people haven't found it. Sydney Pierce is a jerk of the third water and as lazy as a tic. But that's about all anyone can say about him." He made a soft popping sound with his lips. "He has no sexual perversities. He has no skeletons in the closet."

Chambers Elliot shrugged his shoulders. "Maybe claiming she refuses to live there will work." Then Elliot shook his head in silence as if arguing with himself. Suddenly he blurted, "Wait a minute... There's something wrong with the timing!"

"What timing?"

"George's murder."

The detective's palms came out. "I told you that Armistice..."

"I don't mean the butler's perception of events. How long did it take us to walk from the top of the steps on the second floor to George's bedroom?"

"Less than a minute. Why?"

"According to Sydney, the butler and he were together in Sydney's room and heard the shots. Sydney's room is right across from the landing."

"That would fit with Armistice's last claim that he was upstairs when he heard the shots," Taggart said, thoughtfully. "Still…"

"Never mind that for the time being. Armistice ran to George's room after hearing the shots—just sixty or seventy feet down the hall. This, according to Sydney Pierce's statement to Herbie. Giving consideration to Armistice's advanced age; he would have arrived at George's room probably within thirty seconds."

"Agreed."

"So how did his killer get away without being seen by the butler? Jump? The windows were locked from the inside."

Taggart's eyes widened in realization. "Tape recording. The shots were a blind played through a loudspeaker system to confuse the time of death."

"That wouldn't explain Herbie's people finding nitrates on George's hands."

"The nitrates could've been added posthumously to further confuse the death-scene."

"Von Drake stated that Kathy's Corvette entered the Pierce property, and left about twenty minutes later. Sheila Clifford admitted to me that she was the one driving the car when it left the Pierce ranch. She also confirmed the amount of time Von Drake estimated between her arrival in the Corvette and her departure."

Taggart thrust a finger through the air between them. "Which pretty much confirms that Armistice deliberately lied to protect Sydney Pierce."

"I'm not so sure. I don't recall Armistice having anything good to say about Sydney." Chambers Elliot paused in thought. "I want you to question Armistice, again. Take your time. Get him relaxed and trusting. We need to get the timeline correct." Chambers Elliot let got a disgruntled sigh. "Mazy Wilson. Have you ever seen him?"

"I arrested him several times when I was with Bunko Division at Austin P.D.," Taggart said. "Shaved head, gold teeth and a penchant for plaid."

Elliot went behind his desk and settled back down in his swivel chair. "I like your idea of luring Raintree from his hiding-place. But I don't think we can trust Sheila Clifford. We need to hire a woman to pose as Sheila. Someone…"

Taggart pointed toward the reception area. "We could ask Lydia or

Maggie to pair up with Sheila to keep an eye on what's happening."

"Not a chance, Jason. It's too dangerous."

He hesitated. "Not if one of them wears a wire. I'll have my people within yards of them at all times. I'm sure I can talk Maggie into it."

"Leave Maggie out of it, Jason. I mean it. She's too upset at the moment over baldness and bare eyebrows…"

"Then Lydia. That woman could frighten Dracula away from a blood-drive."

"Maybe," the lawyer said, giving consideration. Then Elliot shook his head. "Nope. It's not a job I could expect Lydia to do. There must be a female private investigator you can bring in."

Taggart gave his hands a beseeching spread. "But Lydia's perfect for the job. What if I got her to volunteer?"

The lawyer laughed. "You obviously don't know Lydia Marshall, Jason."

"Trust me, Chambers," Taggart said, adjusting his tie. "With my *special something* when it comes to women, by the time I finish sweet-talking her, Lydia will be begging for the job."

"You're an expert on women, are you?" Elliot asked in mock-awe.

"Absolutely." Taggart gave an unabashed grin.

Elliot pointed to his office door. "Well, in that case, there's no time like the present to get it settled. But remember, Lydia must volunteer."

With a self-confident strut, Jason Taggart headed out to the reception area.

Elliot leaned back against his desk softly chuckling, "'Special something when it comes to women', my ass. She'll tear him to shreds."

A moment later Lydia shouted, "Are you completely unhinged?"

There were more mumblings. Then the sound of heavy footsteps coming toward Elliot's office. A moment later, Jason Taggart stuck in his head.

"Complications?" Elliot was not able to hide a smile.

"A couple of rough spots to smooth over," Taggart declared in an embarrassed tone. "Otherwise, it's as good as done. Won't be a tic."

Elliot made a vague gesture. "No hurry."

Taggart's head disappeared. There were more mumblings.

A second later Lydia barked, "Not if you put a gun to my head, pulled the trigger, and dragged my bloody corpse to that ranch!"

Chambers Elliot laughed softly, almost under his breath.

More footsteps. Then Taggart entered Elliot's office.

"Smoothed over already?"

The detective's feet spread wide on the floor. He looked down at his shoes as if assessing the need for a shine. "There's one minor issue that will take some working-out."

Elliot pretended to weigh his words. "Is there any chance your tact with women has become rusty?"

Jason Taggart wagged his head, decisively. "I've still got it, Chambers. But I'm thinking I should have fed Lydia before broaching our plan."

"*Our* plan?"

"Yeah, you know." The detective put his hands to his hips. "Where we sort of use her as bait."

Elliot nodded in mock understanding. "Ah, *our* plan. The one that you came up with."

Taggart cleared his throat. "That's why I'm thinking I'll take her to lunch—before pressing the issue, further."

"Didn't Lydia just eat?"

"Trust me, Chambers. That woman can eat anytime." The detective waved a finger in the direction of the reception area. "Her and Maggie have been banned by every Chinese Buffet in Austin."

"Just so *our* plan does not create an irreparable breach in your relationship with Lydia, might I suggest a small change in tactic?"

A fleeting smile touched Taggart's lips. "I've already tried telling Lydia you'd pay any resulting medical bills."

"I think we need to announce that your detective agency located another pretender to the Pierce estate. With Sheila incarcerated and the potential of her being convicted of murder, I think our Mr. Raintree will cut Sheila loose and try to worm his way into the confidences of the newest aspirant."

"But my people aren't even looking for Edward Pierce's daughter, Chambers." The detective spread one hand in a large gesture. "Frankly, considering everything, I think it's a little late to start."

Elliot pointed toward the reception area. "Lydia, remember?"

He half smiled, and half shook his head. Then lights came on in his eyes. "Ah. I see what you mean. She would just pretend to be a pretender."

Elliot nodded. "And to make sure Lydia cannot come to harm because of *our* plan, we'll put her up in a suite at the Double-Oak Hotel. You'll bug her room and occupy an adjoining one. If Raintree arrives you'll be able to get to him in seconds."

"I think I can sell Lydia on the Double-Oak—provided I mention room-service."

Chambers Elliot nodded. "I'll contact the TV and radio stations to let them know of your success." The lawyer glanced at his watch. "I've got a hearing this afternoon. I should be back in four hours. Presumably you will have Lydia fed and contentedly agreeable by then?"

"I'm think that might be cutting it a bit close, but I'll try."

Taggart stared to leave, and then looked back. "Oh, uh, I think this little outing to the diner across the street should fall under legitimate expenses, don't you?"

Elliot chuckled, "Absolutely."

Chapter 14

Three evenings later, Chambers Elliot hurried into the Double Oak Hotel lobby, his brow furrowed with concern, his fists knotted. He rushed over to the elevators and took one up to the fourth floor. Then he trotted down the hallway to room 427.

The door was partially ajar and he bolted in. The room looked like something right out of Better Homes and Gardens gone explosive. The furniture was of traditional design and stained a monotonous blond—the parts that were not spotted with blood. Some of it was still usable, although mostly it looked like kindling-wood. The floor was carpeted from wall to wall in pale green shag. That remained quite nice except for its newly acquired piles of shattered porcelain. The walls were beige and decorated with colorful Japanese prints. In several places the plaster was in pristine condition, but mostly it was full of dents and holes. Sliding glass doors offered an inviting access to an expansive patio, at least the sections that had not been turned into shards.

"About time you got here, Chambers," Taggart was seated in the only upright chair. One of his hands clasped a bloody towel to the back of his head. In the other was holding his Glock pistol. Instead of his usual pinstriped suit, the detective was casually dressed in gray slacks, boat shoes, and a white polo shirt. The object of interest to his pistol was the man lying on the floor directly in front of Taggart. The unconscious fellow was squat, bald and dressed in a green, plaid sport coat and brown slacks. There were black penny-loafers on his feet with dimes in the slots.

"Where's Lydia?" Elliot's eyes darted wildly around the room. "Is she hurt?"

"No such luck," muttered Taggart.

The bathroom door opened and Lydia Marshall calmly strolled out carrying thick pile of gauze, and a role of adhesive tape.

"Are you all right?" Elliot rushed over to her.

"Barely," she chided. "Some great idea you had."

"I can't tell you how sorry I am, Lydia," pleaded the lawyer.

"I know I agreed to play bait," she continued. "But that was because the gifted-nifty gumshoe assured me there would be no danger."

"What about me?" Taggart demanded, waggling the bloody towel at Lydia. "I was nearly chopped into chum… by you!" He started to speak further but suddenly fell silent. Then he slapped with a bloody towel at a fly that had landed on his knee. "Damn pests!"

"What in hell happened?" demanded Elliot.

"She almost killed me, that's what happened," the detective

complained.

Elliot's gaze went to Lydia.

"Jason and the creep on the floor were fighting." She went over to where the detective sat. "Jason was not in the best of form, as usual. And after they busted everything in the room with no winner in sight, I decided to help."

"I'm lucky to be alive!" Taggart tossed the bloody towel at one of the piles of shattered porcelain littering the floor. "She brained me with that lamp!"

"It wasn't my fault, Chambers." Lydia taped the gauze to the back of Taggart's head. "I tried to hit the creep. Only, Taggart turned into the path of my swing."

"Then how is it he's lying there?" asked Elliot, pointing down at the man in plaid.

Taggart pointed a finger at the shattered remains of another lamp. "Because Lydia busted that one over *his* head."

"He's been unconscious since you called me?" asked Elliot, concern showing in his voice.

The detective pointed at a third pile of porcelain. "That's because she followed up the lamp by braining him with a vase the size of a bull-elephant. Still not content, Lydia jerked of her pantyhose and tried to garrote the guy with one of the legs. I had to drag her off him. I'm telling you, Chambers, that woman doesn't need a law-degree. Lydia needs forced, psychiatric care!"

Lydia started to open her mouth, but thought better of it and continued her ministrations of Taggart's wound, without comment.

Elliot went over to the fallen man and looked down at him for a few moments, studying the unfamiliar face. The fellow's figure was average, his face impish. There were brown welts under the eyes and his skin was like that of a filefish. His head was shaved. His nose was long and broad. His ears were rather large and jug-like.

"Anybody know who he is?" asked Elliot.

"That is Mazy Wilson," said the detective. "Pimp-extraordinaire and sometime car-booster."

Elliot squatted down and checked Wilson for a pulse. Satisfied the man was still alive, the lawyer rummaged through the fellow's pockets.

Finding nothing of note, he stood up.

"Nothing linking him to Raintree," remarked Taggart. "But I know damn well Mazy's working with him. Otherwise he wouldn't have showed up to rattle Lydia's cage."

"Did he make any demands?" asked Elliot, glancing over at her.

"He accused me of running a scam," said Lydia. "Then he stared pushing me around demanding to know who I was working for. I started screaming. That's when 'better-late-than-never' Taggart busted in."

"We had to get him talking," the detective said defensively. "Otherwise he could just claim he got into this room by mistake."

Elliot pursed his lips. "Did either of you telephone the police?"

"Not yet," said Lydia, as she finished taping the gauze to Taggart's head. "We thought you might want to question him before he was arrested."

Mazy Wilson made gurgling sounds.

The lawyer backed up several steps.

Wilson's eyes were not like those of normal people. His were mere holes through which to see; mirroring nothing; bereft of imagination and feelings; black like spider's eyes.

Wobbling to his feet like a newborn calf, Taggart aimed the Glock at the fallen man's head. "I'm looking for a reason to cap you, Mazy," the detective growled. "Move wrong and I'll give myself that pleasure."

Wilson made several attempts before managing to sit up. Then he muttered, "What the hell…"

"Where's Milton Raintree?" Elliot demanded.

Wilson's mouth worked in silence for many seconds. Finally he blurted, "Fuck off, Shyster!"

"Nice mouth," Lydia scolded.

Wilson shook his head as if trying to clear his thoughts, making a spray of blood from the split in his lower lip.

"I'd better cuff him, Chambers." Taggart holstered his pistol. "Then we'll get the locals on the horn."

A voice from the doorway said, "That won't be necessary, Mr. Taggart."

The detective looked toward the voice, his eyes widening with alarm. "Gun!"

Elliot whirled to face a long-haired, blond man. High cheekbones jutted boldly beneath the fellow's deep-set pale eyes and tufted blond brows. His mouth was a thin, hard line. A bulky, broad nose twisted down his long face. Below it was a close-cropped black mustache. He was immaculate in a creamy suit of heavy Irish linen, white-and-tan sports shoes, a white shirt, and a solid brown tie. In one of his gloved hands was an automatic pistol; the barrel extended nearly nine inches by a silencer. He aimed at Chambers Elliot.

Lydia made a small sound in her throat, but stood her ground.

A trace of a smirk appeared on the strangers face. "Please don't try anything foolish, Mr. Taggart." His voice was cold, confident and unafraid. "Make no mistake. I am quite willing to kill all three of you."

"Do as he says, Jason," Elliot ordered. He spoke out of the side of his mouth without looking at the detective.

Taggart reluctantly moved to one side of the room, stone-faced, angry, watchful.

The stranger smiled widely, exposing two rows of large white teeth. "That's a good boy."

Nervously, Lydia ran her fingers through her hair. "I knew I shouldn't have cancelled my long-term disability coverage."

Elliot smiled tightly at the gun-toting man. "Mr. Milton Raintree, I presume?"

"Mr. Elliot." Raintree bowed slightly. "It was not part of my plan for us to meet, again. But needs must outweigh intentions." Then he glared over at Mazy. "Good help is so very hard to find."

"Your disguise as Father Zamoyski was a bit overdone," Elliot remarked.

Raintree touched the wig's long hair with his free hand. "So's this. But some very nasty people are looking for me." His eyes darted to Lydia. "I should have suspected a setup from that televised announcement. Silly me. But as I watched the televised broadcast I didn't remember your beautiful face from my visit to your office."

"You'll pay for killing George Pierce," warned Elliot.

"Amen to that," chimed Taggart.

Raintree looked at both men out of cold, bleak eyes. "I can honestly say that Milton Raintree has never killed anyone." Then he glared over at his confederate. "Mazy, you couldn't fight your way out of a wet paper bag."

"If you didn't kill George Pierce, who did?" asked Elliot.

"Dominic Portello, I would guess. He threatened as much." Raintree sidled over to the man on the floor and nudged him in the ribs with the toe of one shoe. "Get on your feet."

Mazy let go a pained whimper as he struggled to his knees. "That crazy bitch tried to kill me!" Then his hollow, dark eyes shifted from Raintree to Elliot to Taggart to Lydia, before refocusing upon Raintree. "It was nothing but a fuckin' a setup."

"Why do I always end up with the ones who are a dollar short on brains?"

Lydia corrugated her forehead into a frown of concern as she watched, but remained silent.

Mazy's eyes shifted, and shifted again. His low, narrow brow was thickly furrowed. The muscles of his jaw worked nervously. His heavy square fingers played hide-and-seek with each other at his sides. Clearly, Mazy knew Raintree's temperament. He also understood the fine, tenuous thread upon which Raintree's nervous system vibrated, and feared retaliation over this mistake.

"Move!" barked Raintree.

Mazy tried to say something as he got to his feet, like a drunk on the fourth day of a three-day binge. But the words came out merely as complaining gurgles. He rubbed the back of one hand across his bleeding mouth. Then Mazy staggered past Raintree, out of the door and down the corridor.

Raintree smiled at Elliot and Taggart. "Don't try to follow." Then he laughed; a slow, insulting laugh. "It's not worth dying over, gentlemen."

Raintree backed over to the door. Then he waited until he heard the elevator purring. After which, he continued his retreat out into the hallway, pulling the door shut behind him.

Taggart jerked out his pistol and staggered after the Raintree. Elliot grabbed the detective's arm and held fast.

With a determined curse, Taggart jerked free. Elliot quickly moved in front of Taggart and held up a restraining hand, his voice sympathetic.

"You're not in any shape to do this, Jason," Lydia shouted.

"I'm not going to let those bastards get away!" The detective's eyes blazed and his face flushed with rage.

"And get yourself killed in the process? Not a chance. Not in my employ." Chambers Elliot turned to Lydia, "I'm so sorry about this."

"What are you apologizing to her for?" croaked Taggart, holstering his gun. "She's the reason I'm seeing double."

"What do we do now?" Lydia asked.

Elliot said to her, "Drive Jason to the hospital. Then go home and get some rest. Tomorrow we'll get together at the office and do a rethink."

Lydia looked at the lawyer as if he were feeble-minded. "Don't you comprehend the enormity of this situation, Chambers? Those two have killed twice: Harry Farmer and George Pierce. The next time it will be one of us. As far as I'm concerned, this case is closed."

"I can't let it go, Lydia," Elliot said, with determination. "This is personal between Raintree, and me. Don't worry. I won't put either of you in further danger." Then he faced Taggart. "You'll probably be kept overnight, Jason. Put the medical expenses on your bill to me."

"Assuming I live long enough to do so," Taggart groaned. "In any event, you might want to take Lydia's advice. Before Mazy arrived for our dance-number, my contact in Homicide rang me. Sheila Clifford or Raintree or whatever her current name is, made bail."

"She can't have," Elliot gaped. "I purposely told her to remain there where she would be safe."

"Sydney Pierce arranged it."

"Sydney?" the lawyer demanded in surprise. "What in hell for?"

Taggart fumbled for a cigarette. "I'll see what I can find out, tomorrow – assuming I'm not embalmed, by then."

Elliot gave the detective a reassuring pat on the arm. "Leave it to me."

"There's more, Chambers, and it isn't good," Taggart said. "Tipton French, the well-known ambulance-chaser and funeral-follower, is now Sheila's attorney-of-record."

Elliot gritted his teeth. "I don't mind being fired by a client. What bothers me is being fired in favor of Tipton French! The guy chews his moustache when he talks. How in hell did she hook up with him?"

"No details, yet."

"Are you ready to call it quits, now?" Lydia took one of Elliot's hands between hers. "Do this for me, Chambers, and I swear I'll never ask for another pay-raise."

"I've still got Kathy Martin to consider." Elliot pulled his hand from her embrace.

"Chambers, that woman has done nothing but lie to you," the detective complained. "You don't owe her anything."

Elliot's mouth turned up at the corners. "I plan to change her ways once and for all. In any event, I think I'm entitled to an explanation as to why Sheila Clifford terminated of my services."

"To what end?" Taggart scoffed. "What's done is done. Let's chalk this up to experience and move on."

"If you continue on with this lunacy I'm resigning, Chambers," Lydia vowed.

"I hope you don't mean that, Lydia," Elliot countered. "But I'll understand if you do."

Taggart said to the lawyer, "Do you think getting yourself killed will help anybody? In case you've forgotten, Salvator Portello is after that clown."

"Better get going. I imagine I'll be here for a while trying to explain to the management of this hotel how all this happened. I hope they'll take a check."

"You'd better use a credit card," declared Lydia. "Because as of today, we are all but tapped-out with our bank."

"Don't expect me any time before noon, Chambers." Taggart staggered toward the door. "Because I'm thinking I'll be dead before ten."

Four hours later, Chambers Elliot was knocking on the door to apartment 312. Moments later, Sheila Clifford answered, dressed in red Chinese pajamas not unlike those he had seen on George Pierce. They covered her completely from throat to toes. Her blonde hair hung straight down her back. It was damp and smelled of flowers as if she had just gotten out of the shower. Sheila lowered her golden lashes and caught a seductive lower lip indecisively between her teeth in what Elliot assumed was an effort at maidenly embarrassment.

"We have to talk." He walked into the apartment without waiting for an invitation.

She stared at him askance, as though she expected Elliot to make a pass. "About what?"

The lawyer's tone was icy. "Tipton French, for starters. We'll work up to the niceties from there."

"I thought you'd be happy to be rid of me."

Elliot turned to face her. "Whose idea was French? Raintree's?"

"Milton's." She gave Elliot a pitying smile. "Milton said I couldn't trust you to get me off."

"And you believed him?"

She shrugged faintly. "You left me to rot in jail."

Losing the battle to conceal his annoyance Elliot blurted, "I told you to stay there for your own damn safety!"

"I'm just as safe here… safer!" she retorted.

He studied her a moment noting her emotional frustration. "Have you consummated your marriage yet?"

"No, as if it's any of your business. I'm beginning to think he likes his pal better than me."

"Ugly Mazy to you? That is embarrassing. Particularly when Mazy used to be your pimp."

"Go to hell!"

He laughed grimly. "When a newly-married man has no interest in a wife who looks like you, he's got murder in mind. His wife's."

Sheila was quiet for a few seconds. Then she walked slowly over to where Elliot stood. "Why would Milton want me dead? The new will cuts me in for half of the hundred million—no questions asked."

"There is no new will!" Elliot scoffed.

She tilted her nose up, grinning. "Yes there is. I saw it. It makes me an heir on equal footing with Sydney Pierce."

"When did you see that document? Where?"

"Milton showed it to me, after getting me out of jail."

Elliot paused a few seconds, reconciling her statement. "Was it signed?"

She nodded. "Witnessed, notarized – the whole shebang."

"That's impossible. Even if George hired another attorney to draft such a document..." Elliot abruptly fell silent, rolling his lower lip between his teeth. "Where is Raintree?"

Sheila crossed her arms as she offered Elliot her back. "I have no idea. Around, I guess."

"Is Sydney Pierce in league with Raintree?"

She moved off, stretching lazily. "I don't know anything about anything."

Elliot dragged his hands across his face in frustration. "Tipton French has neither the experience nor the dedication to provide you with an adequate defense in a Capital-Murder case. I'm surprised he was even successful at arranging your bail. Sheila, if you keep following Raintree's guidance you'll end up in the death-house—if not dead before then."

She shrugged, went over to the loveseat with a long-legged strut, and curled upon. "According to Tipton the police don't have a thing. I'm as good as acquitted."

"Words so oft springing across that man's lips when scamming a new client." Elliot strode after her, his impatience growing. "Lt. Herbie Mann isn't some newbie at murder-investigations, Sheila. You wouldn't have been charged if he didn't have a rock-solid case. Was Sydney Pierce behind George Pierce's murder?"

Her eyes casually studied the red polish on her fingernails for a few seconds. Then she said, "All I know is, the charges against me won't hold. That's all I need to know."

"Did Raintree tell you what happened at the ranch?"

"George was dead when Milton got there. If you don't believe me, check with the coroner. The time of death was an hour before Milton arrived at the Pierce Ranch." She let her pink tongue flutter across her lower lip. "And if that doesn't convince you, talk to Kathy. She found George's body before anybody else." The words were casual as if she were talking to herself.

"Kathy?" Then he muttered a curse. "Why am I not surprised?"

Sheila uncoiled her legs, once more grinning. "See what I mean? I was out in the car—your detective pal who was following us can vouch for that. Milton, dressed as a woman, was on the main floor of the house with the butler when the shots were fired. When Kathy arrived, before me and Milton got there, George was already dead. That leaves the cops with nothing—unless they want to fit Sydney Pierce for the dirty deed. But I doubt he's got the balls for that."

"You knew you were being followed to the Pierce ranch?"

"Of course. We had to slow up a couple of times so he didn't lose me. Milton thought that was the biggest joke."

"What makes you think Sydney Pierce killed George? Did George mention something to you about Sydney?"

She laughed. "Not to me. But it would be perfect if Sydney did it. Milton says Sydney can't collect under the will if he's convicted of murdering George. That would leave everything to me."

"Unless you're convicted," Elliot sneered.

The corners of her mouth drooped into a frown.

"Why it arranged for Kathy to go to the ranch?" asked Elliot. "How did she get there? You had her car."

She allowed the silence that followed his words to gel for a while before saying solemnly, "I don't know. I don't know, anything."

"Did Kathy go there to warn George?"

"What difference does it make?"

There was another moment of awkward silence. Then Elliot said, "Did Raintree say who killed George? Was it Dominic Portello?"

"I don't know and I don't care." She leaned back and crossed her arms in defiance. "Me and Milton are gonna' get millions. That's all that interests me."

He studied her face for many seconds before gritting, "I hope you're this nonchalant on the gurney in the death-house. Don't worry. Tipton will be there to offer moral support. That's his duty as your attorney. I will also be there. But I'll be grinning as I watch the last shudder of life leave your body."

Her arms fell away and Sheila tilted toward him. "That's not going to happen!" she shouted, her eyes suddenly wary, her jaw muscles flexing as she swallowed and re-swallowed her fear, again. "Tipton said…"

Elliot went over to the chair across from her, and settled down. "Tipton hasn't won a criminal case in the last five years. Don't believe me? Ask around. Any lawyer in town will tell you the same thing. Tipton French couldn't beat a Jaywalking ticket handed to the Pope. The rubber hoses are nearly wrapped around your arms to pop up the veins, Sheila."

Her fingers leaped in an involuntary frantic gesture to her throat, as though she felt a noose tightening around it. "You're lying about him."

"To what end? My contract with you ended when you hired the brain-dead bozo. As for me expecting payment for services rendered, you owe me nothing. So how do I benefit from lies about Tipton French?"

"You're lying because you expected a boatload of money for defending me and you're mad that you won't get it." Her voice held a thin, hollow, metallic ring.

"You haven't got a dime," said Elliot.

A mirthless smile tugged at her lips. "I will when I inherit!"

"I wouldn't count on that—or anything else for your future. You're going to die as poor as you are now—in Huntsville."

She jumped up and began to pace. "Stop threatening me. Why would Milton lie to me about Tipton? Milton needs me. Without me, he'll get nothing."

"That's what's bothered me about your husband's motives," said Elliot. "There is no rational explanation for him putting you on death-row. And, yet, I'm certain that is his intention. Otherwise, why cancel my services in favor of Tipton French? I win nearly all of my cases."

She stopped and glared at Chambers Elliot. Her lips were drawn to straight lines as though about to curl back into a snarl. "I'll be alive and free long after you're rotting in your grave, old man."

"Not with Raintree charting your course," Elliot said, crossing his legs. "Did Tipton French discuss his defense plans with you?"

"He said I shouldn't worry," she said sharply.

"A good lawyer could easily muddy the trial-waters by building a case against Sydney Pierce. Armistice is confused about when he was actually with Sydney, that night. So that alibi is toast. Did Sydney hold a grudge against his father?"

"I don't know." She studied a thumbnail. "I've never talked to Sydney."

"You must have. I was told he arranged your bail."

Her breath caught sharply as she looked over at Elliot. "He did. But it was Tipton French who was there when I was released."

"George never remarked on Sydney's lack of interest in working in the family business?"

"George was mad at Sydney about that." Her arms went to her hips and she offered the lawyer her back.

"Was George mad enough to cut off Sydney's allowance?"

Sheila tossed Elliot a furtive glance over one shoulder. "George might've mentioned something like that."

"Or cut Sydney out of the Will?"

"He might've said that, too," she agreed, turning to face the lawyer.

"What's Kathy Martin expecting from this? Raintree must've promised her something to keep her around town."

She winced. "I guess she'll get a share. Milton said we owed her something."

"You and Kathy don't get along, do you?"

"She didn't want me getting ideas about Milton." She folded her arms. "So what?"

"Because she was in love with Raintree?"

A spot glowed in each of her cheeks. "Maybe."

"I'll give you any odds you want that Raintree's already handed Kathy the script of her testimony. She'll claim how you planned all along to kill George Pierce. She'll fall into tears as she explains how you tried to entice her help."

Sheila laughed soundlessly. "Not if she leaves town like Milton says she's gonna' do."

"Not before you're convicted," said the lawyer.

Her arms dropped as Sheila looked over at him, startled. "I'm not going die! Milton said…"

"Close your eyes and listen, Sheila. If you try real hard you can hear the hinges creak on your coffin-lid."

"No!" she screamed, her voice breaking in terror.

Elliot gave his head an impatient nod. "Tell Tipton French you want to see the witness list for the prosecution when it's delivered to him. If Kathy doesn't head that list, I'll pay for your funeral."

She came over to Elliot, her hands knotted at her middle. "Milton loves me!"

"He loves nobody but himself. Look how he dumped Kathy after you came along because you offered better financial pickings."

Her head shook. "Milton didn't dump her. Kathy ran out on him—after getting her hooks into Sydney Pierce."

Elliot gave her an amused smile. "Raintree told you that?"

Sheila smirked. "You don't get much right, do you lawyer? Kathy and Sydney are engaged. She told me. Bet you didn't know that."

Elliot crawled from the chair more than a little surprised by her last statement. He started to say something but fell silent when the apartment door opened and a man wearing thick makeup, an ice-cream suit, black penny-loafers on his feet with dimes in the slots, and a long wig walked in.

"You're getting on my nerves, Elliot," the man growled, his voice thick-tongued with anger, his lower lip swollen.

Elliot stiffened. "I'm glad we share a common assessment of each other, Mr. Raintree. Where's George Pierce's Will?"

Sheila tightened her lips and made her voice hard. "He said you're going to get me executed, Milton!" Then, she rushed over to her husband and wrapped her arms about his neck. "Tell him to leave. Tell him…" Her eyes bugged. "You! Where's…"

Raintree gave Sheila a shove, sending her staggering away from him. "Keep your mouth shut. This Shyster's on his way out, right now."

"Where is it, Raintree?" demanded Elliot.

He waited a few moments, studying Elliot, then he patted his suit with one hand. "Where I can get at it."

Elliot said grimly, "I'll prove it was forged, no matter how long it takes."

"Tough talk from a guy holding an empty sack. Now, beat it."

"I think Salvator Portello would pay plenty to get his mitts on you," said Elliot.

Raintree's smile remained. But it had sagged at the corners. "I can handle that blowhard." He gave Sheila an impatient glance. "Get me a drink." Then he moved easily across the room, and dropped onto the loveseat.

The young woman made a strangled sound, too scared to move.

Chambers Elliot stuck his hands in his pockets and grinned at Raintree. "A real lady-killer aren't you?"

"Do it, Sheila!" He twisted his made-up face into a hideous scowl to show how angry he was.

Sheila gave Elliot a worried glance, then darted into the kitchenette. There she dragged a bottle of Pinch and a glass from the cupboards. Then she poured several ounces of the liquor into the glass, and hurried with it back to Raintree. He snatched the drink from her hand and smirked proudly at Elliot.

"Salvator shares your view on being all-controlling," remarked Elliot. "Only his extends to both sexes."

"They do what I tell 'em or else."

"Sheila and I were just discussing the merits of Tipton French as her defense counsel. You must've dug deep and long to find an attorney of his low stature."

"You sound frustrated, Shyster," he said, over the rim of the glass. "You know I'm about to pull off the biggest swindle this town has ever seen but you haven't figured out how I'll make it work."

Elliot's shrewd eyes studied the other man in critical appraisal. There was something slightly wrong with the fellow's appearance. But he could not work out what it was.

"You'll be dead long before that. I wouldn't be surprised if the Portellos are outside waiting for me to leave."

The other man's eyes turned frosty, his confidence continuing to fade. "Try sending him my way and you won't live out the night."

Chambers Elliot was inured to such threats, so he offered up a casual grin. "I don't have to send him. He's had his men following me all day."

"You don't scare me, Shyster!" The other man scrambled to his feet, his hands shaking, his face like boiled pork through the thick makeup. Then he shouted at Sheila, "Look out the window, dammit! See if anybody's around."

Sheila laughed suddenly, a hollow, bitter laugh.

Its unexpected sharpness startled Raintree. He whirled toward her.

Elliot moved forward intending to stop Raintree, but the frightened man countered the lawyer's efforts by jerking out his pistol and taking aim at Elliot's head.

"Do as I say," Sheila!" the gunman growled. "Look outside!"

She hurried over to the nearest window and peered outside. "Nobody," she said, after a moment.

"You won't see them," Elliot told him, evenly. "Salvator Portello is a man who understands all the intricacies of surprise visits. He's not going to do anything until you and Sheila are alone. Then you'll hear the elevator whine as it comes up from the first floor. After that you'll hear slow, heavy footsteps coming down the hall. There will be a knock on the door. And while you're wondering what to do, someone will appear from the bedroom—having come in through the window."

The man's eyes dipped to his glass, the hand holding it shaking uncontrollably like he was standing naked in a freezer. "You're bluffing." His eyes came back up to Elliot's. "You figure you can scare me into backing off on this gig." He raised the glass slightly. "But I've invested too much time and effort into this to walk away empty handed."

"It's too late for that," warned Elliot. "With the Portellos after you, you have no option but to run and keep running."

Raintree licked his lips. "And leave a hundred million behind? Not likely." Then he reholstered the gun. "Everything's going as planned. All I have to do is wait it out."

"Not this time, Mr. Raintree."

"You'd like to know who killed George Pierce, wouldn't you?" Raintree spoke the words in a low, tense, bitter voice. "I know. And that's what's going to keep you shut about me for as long as I think it's necessary. Once I get what I want out of this gig, I'll tell you who did it. I'll even give you the proof necessary to make the charge stick." He took a heavy draw on the glass. "What say you now, Shyster?"

Elliot stuffed his hands into his pockets besotted with frustration.

"Don't make promises you can't keep."

Raintree tossed his glass across the room, shattering it on the wall; his face darkening under the makeup with rage."

"Mr. Elliot thinks I'm being sold-out," Sheila whimpered. "He thinks…"

"Shuttup!" The man didn't shift his eyes from the lawyer. "I decide what goes. Me! Understand?"

Elliot looked over at Sheila with a mean expression, his words quick and sarcastic. "Say your prayers with unbridled fervency, Sheila. You're going to need all the help you can get to endure your forthcoming nightmare."

"You keep shut, too!" the other man warned. The veins in his neck showed purple under the makeup.

Elliot turned and strode over to the apartment door. After opening it he turned in the doorway. "Or what? You'll haunt me from the grave?"

Elliot hurried down the hallway and took the elevator to the lobby. As he started across it, Sydney Pierce stepped from behind a large potted palm. There were dark circles under the man's eyes as if he had been up for days. His face was gray and unshaved. The tan suit he wore was badly wrinkled, as if he had slept in it.

"What the hell," the lawyer said, in surprise.

Sydney Pierce said grimly, "I saw Raintree go up. Is Sheila okay?"

"She would've been fine if you'd left her in jail." Elliot returned, sharply. "What in hell are you playing at?"

"Sheila called and begged me. What was I supposed to do? If she really is my niece…"

"Worried the newlyweds will kill each other?" Elliot taunted. "Or is that what you're hoping for? Did you know that Raintree has a will that cuts her in for half?"

Pierce shrugged. "But I thought…"

The lawyer reached out and tapped Sydney's chest. "If it is legitimate, you're out fifty million."

"Is it legitimate?"

"Tell me something, Sydney," said Elliot, crossing his arms. "Have you made any recent plans to marry?"

Pierce pinked. "Not as such."

"Kathy Martin comes to mind."

"I guess I might think about it with her."

"Sheila claims you and Kathy are engaged."

Pierce's chin dipped with embarrassment. "Not officially. I did buy a ring. But there's the pre-nup to sign, you know."

"Another lover of women." Chambers Elliot dropped his hands into his pants-pockets. "I seemed to be surrounded by your types, today. Tell me something, Sydney. How well do you know Milton Raintree? Well, enough to cut a deal for him to kill your father?"

Pierce tried to laugh. But the sound died abruptly. "With my father's money coming my way, why should I get involved with someone like Milton Raintree?"

"Why, indeed? Unless George was going to cut you out of the will." Elliot withdrew his hands from his pockets and gave Sydney Pierce a tap on the chin. "Before I go, I'll give you some advice. Married or not to Kathy Martin, she'll sell you out."

Sydney blanched. "I don't know what you mean?"

"Simply this: If you killed George and Kathy knows it, you'd better be prepared to make good on her demands."

The younger man swallowed several times, his eyes suddenly wide and worried. Then, Pierce said slowly, "No matter what you think, I had nothing to do with father's murder."

Elliot jabbed a thumb over one shoulder toward the elevators. "Sheila told me that your father was dead long before the shots were fired. If that's true, your alibi is toast."

Pierce's head wagged. "Dominic Portello killed my father."

Elliot's eyes bored steadily into Pierce's. "What makes you say that?"

A muscle in his jaw did a nervous tap-dance. "A few months ago," the younger man said, almost to himself. "I'd intended to be gone the whole weekend. But I came back Saturday night. I saw Dominic get into his car and drive away. Later, Kathy told me what happened. That he had threatened to kill my father. I couldn't believe…"

"Had the Portellos done business with George, before?" Elliot cut him short.

"Not that I know of." Pierce's voice trembled and broke with the questions. Then a slight shadow flitted across his face. "If you're correct about when my father was killed, then there's no question that Dominic did. Ask Armistice. When he discovered my father's body he caught a glimpse of Dominic crawling out my father's bedroom window. Talk to him."

The lawyer's mouth fell open slightly. "Why didn't he say as much to the police?"

"Afraid, I guess. Most people wouldn't fink on the Mafia."

"Have you told this to Lt. Mann?"

"I'm not about to put my head in a noose held by those gangsters."

Elliot muttered a low curse. "You say your father was murdered by

Dominic Portello and there is evidence to substantiate at least opportunity, and you do nothing?"

Pierce looked down at his feet, embarrassed. "I'm not a coward."

"Then do the right thing," said Elliot. "Take Armistice to see Herbie Mann. Get Armistice to tell what he saw."

Sydney Pierce waited dramatically, licking his lips while he fashioned his next statement. "I will. But not because of the way you're trying to shame me. I'll do it because I loved my father." A vein throbbed at his temple as his eyes reconnected with the lawyer's. "Now, you'll have to excuse me. I'm going up to see Sheila. It probably won't do any good, but I'm going to try to get her to leave Raintree."

Elliot's eyes narrowed suddenly, as if realization had came upon him unexpectedly. "I'm certain Mr. Raintree is no longer there."

Sydney Pierce started for the elevators. But Chambers Elliot grabbed his arm and pulled him to a stop. "You're about Mazy Wilson's age. Did you know him from school?"

"I knew him. We weren't friends. He wasn't exactly in my social sphere. Considering what he does now, I don't expect to renew our acquaintance."

The mention of social sphere thrust another idea into the lawyer's head. "You must've been pals with Dominic Portello, too."

"Me? Of course not."

"But you must've. You were a member of the Los Gatos Canyon Car Club when he was also a member."

"I know who he is—then and now. But I never really knew him in the sense of friendship. I'd never hang out with a gangster—then or now."

"But Dominic wasn't a gangster, then. Regardless, you were in high-school, together."

"No. He was never in any of my classes."

"It also follows that you knew Michael Douglas."

Sydney's chin tilted downward, slightly. "So what?"

Elliot smiled. "You didn't like him, did you?"

"I didn't dislike him."

"Why didn't you go to your father's room to see what had happened when you heard the shots?" Elliot asked. "Why send Armistice? He's old enough to be your grandfather. Surely you must've considered the possibility that your father's killer was still there?"

Sydney Pierce thought it over for a few seconds. "I intended to go. But Armistice rushed out before I could. I was going to follow. Actually, I started after him. But my father and I had argued earlier. If there was nothing to worry about, my barging into his room would only start the argument all over again."

"So you waited in your room?"

The younger man nodded. "When Armistice came back he said my father was dead, said it was best to remain where I was until the police arrived."

"If I had been told my father had been murdered, I think I would've gone to his room to see for myself," remarked Elliot. "My love for him, if nothing else, would've compelled me to do so."

The younger man's eyes dipped.

"Michael Douglas was having an affair with your mother, wasn't he? Isn't that why you disliked him?"

Pierce's eyes darted back to Elliot's, burning. "Of course not! And if you say one word about that, I'll sue!"

Elliot grinned wryly. "'The man doth protesteth too much, me thinks.' I won't rest until I find George's killer. No matter how long it takes, I will find him." With that Chambers Elliot turned and stalked out of the building.

Chapter 15

That evening, Chambers Elliot arrived home with a bucket of takeout chicken tucked under one arm. When he entered the house and got to the kitchen, the lawyer spotted a woman smoking a cigarette in the shadows of the living room.

"Lost?" He set the fast-food container on the kitchen table.

Rita Portello stepped into view. She was clothed in a slinky black dress, matching high-heels and was carrying a small, black clutch-purse. Like a shadow, Rita continued across the living room until she stood in the kitchen doorway, one hand perched on a cocked hip.

"You're the last person I expected to see," he remarked. "But welcome just the same." Elliot went over and turned on the kitchen light. Then his eyes darted past Rita, as if expecting death to be her silhouette. "Alone, I hope?"

Rita made a half-smile, like someone who really enjoys a prank. Her teeth came together in a sharp little click before gleaming through half-parted lips. Then the smile dropped like a stick holding a bucket of cement. After a moment she nodded without saying anything.

"Hungry?" he asked, pointing to the takeout-meal. "There's plenty. The joint was having a half-price sale. I'm a sucker for a bargain. So I waded in waving a credit card."

Rita moved across the kitchen as soundless as fog floating across sand. She dropped her cigarette into the sink then went to the table, set her purse down, and settled into a chair.

"They claim that stuff is loaded with herbs and spices." Elliot hoped to entice a verbal response from his unexpected guest. "I'm thinking the cook does that to cover the flavors of excessive cholesterol and high-growth hormones."

Failing to draw Rita out of her silence, Elliot went over to the cupboards and took down place settings for two, including wine glasses. Then he spread one of them out in front of Rita. The other setting he placed directly across the table.

Her eyes followed his every movement, seemingly curious about the attorney's living-habits.

"Does Salvator know you're here?" he asked.

Her reply was purposely vague. "This is strictly between you and me, Lawyer."

Elliot smiled, still ill at ease but relieved that she was now communicative. "Are you going to give me a hint as to what is between us? Or should we play spin-the-bottle?"

Rita regarded him impassively for a moment. "What will it take to back you off the Michael Douglas killing?"

"Dominic was there with a gun. Michael was shot. That's hard to ignore."

Her eyes flicked away from his. "We all have our price."

"So, I keep hearing and hearing." Chambers Elliot went to the refrigerator and took out a bottle of white wine. "I prefer my non-beef, fast-food with white wine. *Viognier* is my favorite. Okay with you?"

Rita shrugged with disinterest.

He took a corkscrew from a drawer and wrestled-out the bottle's stopper. Then he went over to the table, poured two glasses of wine and set down the bottle. Elliot set one glass in front of her and the second glass in front of the other place-setting.

Rita eyed the filled stemware for a few seconds as if suspicious of its lineage. Then she picked up the glass and raised it to her lips. After tasting the amber wine she gave a perfunctory nod of approval.

"My price might be more than you can pay," said Elliot.

"My cash-holdings might surprise you, Lawyer," she said, in an even tone.

"What if I asked for payment in Salvator's blood?" the lawyer quipped.

Rita offered him a crooked smile. "I would have to mention it to my brother. I don't think you'd enjoy his response."

"I'm certain I wouldn't." He indicated the container of chicken with a tilt of his head. "Shall we talk while we dine? Feel free to prop elbows on the tabletop and belch as needed. The napkins are supposed to be under the cover. But I can't swear to it."

Rita pulled the top from the cardboard bucket and took out a stack of napkins. After tucking one in her palm, she dropped the remained on the table before helping herself to the chicken.

Elliot settled across the table, picked up his glass of wine and took a sip. Despite her less than amiable nature, his eyes could not help but admire Rita Portello's sultry beauty.

"Might I ask how you got into my house?" he said, offering her a coaxing smile.

Her face shifted a little, but it didn't relax. "Considering my family's history, do you really find my presence surprising?"

His head wagged. "I'm sure your brothers have a stable of expert house-breakers. My curiosity centers on whether you got past my alarm system on your own, or if you had help from someone who might be waiting in the other room—holding something that goes bang in the night."

She offered him a wintry smile with just a hint of spring in it. "I'm fully trained—in all categories."

He hesitated. "Even murder?"

Rita studied him for a few ominous seconds. Then her elbows rested casually upon the table as she said, "Let's hope, for your sake, you never find out. But to address your real concerns, the Sicilian Brothers, two of Sal's bodyguards brought me here. And, yes, they do carry things that go bang in the night."

Elliot made an involuntary gulp as he glanced toward the dark living room. "Are they hungry? I think we've got plenty."

"They're outside."

"Thank God, for that."

She laughed softly. "I believe I scared you, Lawyer."

"I certainly know when I'm outgunned." Elliot set down his glass. "Since you and I are alone—and in this nearly-romantic setting—why don't you break a few family rules and tell me what happened to Harry Farmer?"

She nibbled at the chicken, ignoring his question.

"You were at the Double-Oak with Dominic," pressed Elliot, tossing out a throwaway accusation, based upon what Taggart had told him concerning Dominic's presence. "There were witnesses."

"I'm surprised you don't have a video camera in my bedroom," she grated.

"I'm working on that. Has Lt. Mann questioned you about Harry?"

"I'm not going to be high on his to-do list. But if there were witnesses, as you say, he'll come by. He enjoys ruffling my Sicilian feathers."

"Did you see who killed Harry?"

Rita paused in her eating to offer him a surprised look. "You don't suspect Dom and I of doing it?"

Chambers Elliot shrugged. "You tell me."

"We Portellos have long-understood the need for an unbreakable family union—that includes silence."

"Meaning Dominic did do it?"

Her brows arched. "Meaning the police would not even know that Harry was dead if we had been involved."

"The problem is all the evidence points to your family as Harry's killer." He scowled. "Strike that. On the surface it points to your family. When I delve deeper into what I've learned, I can't help but wonder if I'm being led down the garden path."

She was silent for a moment. Then, "What have you learned?"

"Three men were shot using a smallish caliber pistol that fired a round made of materials so brittle that the bullet shattered going through bone. All three of those men—Michael Douglas, Harry Farmer and George Pierce—had links to your family. All those men were threatened directly or indirectly by someone from your family."

Rita shook her head. "My family would not be that careless."

He nodded agreeably. "Dominic might."

She stared at him coldly. "He had nothing to do with those hits."

"I've never owned a gun. So I'm no expert on shooting. But I have spoken with someone who knows a great deal about weaponry. He tells me that the type of bullet used on those three men is unique. Rather than lead being used, it was cast from old wheel weights."

"I don't get your point."

"It means there is likely only one shooter." He raised his hands and counted off fingers as he spoke. "Someone who killed Michael Douglas thirty years, ago. Someone who killed Harry Farmer. Someone who killed George Pierce. Someone who is not finished killing."

"It wasn't my brother," she said smoothly.

His hands folded upon the table. "I've spoken with two people who've viewed the video Salvator is after. The same video Dominic denied receiving as part of an extortion demand. Both my contacts agreed on what took place during the video as well as the number of people involved. Both described an argument between a young man who is a physical match for Dominic and a man slightly older who I've been told was Michael Douglas. Both agreed that during this argument, Michael Douglas abruptly dropped to the floor." He cocked his head and gave her sidelong look. "I have not personally viewed the DVD so I cannot attest to those claims. But I suspect, based upon the consistency of both claims, that I've been told the truth."

Rita picked up the napkin and daubed her lips. "Salvator's taken quite a liking to you. Admittedly he would like you dead, best of all. But you made an impression on him like no other." She paused a moment to chuckle menacingly. "Five times, Sal told the Sicilian Brothers to pack you in cement and dump you out at sea. Five times Sal changed his mind. That's how close you came to reacquainting yourself with your maker, Lawyer."

His brows arched in question. "Is that your way of telling me the information I've received about the video is correct?"

Rita looked across the table at him, steadily. "I'm telling you to stop pressing your luck."

Elliot nodded without meaning and splayed his hands. "Tell me about Michael Douglas?"

"Why?" she flared.

He made a magnanimous gesture. "Call it my price for this elegant feast."

"So you can run with my words to the cops?" She waggled a finger at him. "I don't think so."

"I give you my word that everything you share will remain between us."

Her dark eyes widened. "Till death?"

Without hesitation he nodded.

She took a bite of chicken, set down the remaining meat and chewed thoughtfully. "I'm going to hold you to that." She wiped her hands on the napkin and then folded them gracefully on the table, in front of her. "If you tell a single soul, I shall come back here and cut your balls off— just before I slice your throat. Understood?"

Elliot winced, crossed his legs and nodded. "I never dreamed you would be such a fun date."

She leaned back smiling, genuinely amused. "You're nicer than I thought you'd be."

"I'm always nice to nice people," he declared, enjoying her beauty. "How is it you met Michael Douglas? Based upon what I've learned, he was not someone your father would introduced to you."

"Dom is the reason." The corners of her mouth drooped. She opened her purse and took out a pack of cigarettes and a small lighter. Rita stuffed the cigarette between her lips, and lit it. Then she blew smoke toward the ceiling. Her actions were slow and deliberate. When her gaze returned to his it was thoughtful, neutral. "Michael came to the house to see my father one evening—business. At that time Dom was having young fantasies—about cars. Michael Douglas had a souped-up number that could blow dust on anything with wheels. Naturally Dom wanted to see it. So while Pop and Michael were talking, Dom wandered outside and gave that fancy car a good looking-over. I tagged along because it seemed like the thing to do—not that I ever gave a shit about cars. After a while, Michael came out. When he saw how much Dom liked the car, Michael offered to take us for a spin. Dom and I went."

Her eyes partially shut leaving only the slightest gleam below the lids, as if she were replaying a special memory that open eyes might betray. After a few seconds the lids rose, and tears formed. Her voice choked. She swallowed and then started again, back in control. "During the ride I got whiffs of Michael's cologne and close-ups at his handsome face.

God, he was so beautiful. By the time Dom and I were back at home, I was having my first romantic fantasy about a pretty man with a pretty car. It was wonderful!"

"Dominic joined the car-club Douglas belonged to, didn't he? Los Gatos?"

Her brows arched in surprise. "If you know everything why pump me for information?"

"I don't know everything. What about the car-club?"

She shrugged. "Michael, wanting to make points with my father, invited Dom to the club's next rally. Naturally, Dom was more than ready to go. I, of course, begged to go along. I still didn't care about cars, but being at the rally would mean being close to Michael. So, a few weeks later we went. Dom paid his fees and signed the membership roster. Then we spent the entire afternoon walking around looking at cars, with Michael as our guide. For me it was the biggest thrill of my young life because I got to hold Michael's hand." She took a puff on the cigarette and chuckled during the exhale. "Every woman we met gave him a hungry leer. And I loved the envy I knew they felt. Because I was the one with him, the one he was hanging onto. You can't imagine how proud I felt."

He smiled.

"I was just beginning to develop," she went on, in the tone of a woman who was unaware of her surroundings and thinking of other things, past things. "You know. Training bra filled with a little of me and a whole lot of Kleenex." Rita offered Elliot a level stare filled with sadness. "I wanted to be noticed as more than just a kid."

He took a sip of wine. "Did Michael notice?"

She tapped the ash from her cigarette onto her plate. "To him, I was just a little girl. But I was not going to let Michael's lack of participation in my romantic ideas curb my fantasy."

"What do you mean?"

"As the weeks went by Dom and Michael became pals, of sorts. I think Michael was just using Dom to get in good with my father. But each time they got together, I went along. Each time I went along, I made a point of sitting as close as I could get to my pretty, fantasy-man." She wiped a tear from her cheek. "The last time was just a few hours before Michael was killed."

"What happened that night?"

"Dom and I drove to Winston Liquors to see Michael. Dom wanted advice on a car he was planning to buy and hoped Michael would take a look at it." She took a puff on her cigarette and blew smoke off to one side. "Junior Billings was there buying a pint when we walked in. Dom suggested Michael come with us for a quick bite. Billings offered to watch the place. Michael agreed. Then the three of us went to an IHOP a few miles away."

"Junior Billings? Elvira's father?"

She nodded. "He did the janitorial work, there, and filled in if Michael needed extra help."

"What time of the day was this?"

"I don't remember," Rita said with a neutral shrug. "Probably around five or so—that's the time I usually get hungry and I remember that I was starving. Why?"

"Because it's unlikely Junior Billings left after the three of you got back from dinner, only to return later to do the cleaning. A more likely scenario is that he was there when Michael was murdered."

Her eyes flashed. "A lot of good that information does now. Junior Billings is dead."

"But he might've told someone about the shooting—someone who is still alive. What happened while you and Dominic had supper with Michael?"

Her lips quirked at the corners. "I was feeling more than a little romantic, in my young way. I thought if I worked it right, I might get a kiss from Michael. So I made a point of leaning against him in the booth. Then every chance I got, I pressed what I had for breasts on his arm. I tried to be tactful. But at that age girls aren't very discrete. Michael ignored me. Dom, however, caught on right away."

"Your brother reprimanded you?"

"Not then. But after we got home that night, Dom went ballistic. He demanded to know what was going on between me and Michael." Her eyebrows jumped. "I told him the disappointing truth—that nothing was going on." She paused a moment to smile sadly. "Anyway, Dom threatened to kill Michael. The next day Michael was dead. I spent the following week in my room crying. I blamed myself for it."

"Dom returned to the liquor store after confronting you?"

Her head shook. "It was just talk. Nothing would've come of it. But later that night there was a phone-call. It was for Dom. He talked on the line for a few seconds. Then he went out."

Elliot cleared his throat carefully. "Why would you assume he went to Winston Liquors? Isn't it more likely Dominic would've gone to meet a friend?"

"I heard Dom on the phone. I heard him mention Winston Liquors."

"Did Dominic ever tell you who called him?"

"When he came home afterward, yes. He said it was Michael—trying to set things straight, about me."

"That doesn't fit," commented Elliot. "If Dom didn't confront Michael until after dropping you at home, why would Michael Douglas feel the need to explain anything before hand?"

She gave him a quick resentful frown. "I'm not a psychiatrist. That's what Dom told me."

The lawyer paused a moment in thought. Then he said, "Think back to the restaurant you, Dominic and Michael visited. Was anyone there that you knew? Anyone who Dom greeted or remarked about?"

"Lawyer, it was over thirty years ago. How in hell do you expect a love-struck eleven year-old to remember anything but the guy she was hung-up on?" Then Rita frowned. "Wait a second. There was someone —a kid about Dom's age. Dom waved at the kid as we sat down in the booth."

"Who?"

"I don't know who. He was sitting with a man and woman— probably his mother and father."

"Was there anything unusual about those people?"

She snuffed out her cigarette in her plate. "Do you really think I would notice?"

He shrugged. "Dominic got that call and went out. What happened then?"

"When he got back Dom was scared to death. He came to my room, stood there and cried like a baby. I asked Dom what had happened. He told me Michael Douglas was dead. I couldn't believe it. Not the pretty man of my dreams. Then I became angry. I accused Dom of doing it—of killing Michael. But he swore on all that was holy he hadn't. I wanted to believe him. But I couldn't. Not then. I told Dom to tell me the truth. I told him I'd take it to my grave no matter what he said. Dom swore on our mother's life he had not touched Michael in anger. Still I didn't believe. I asked who had killed Michael if not him. He said he didn't know."

Chambers Elliot made a disappointed face. Then he asked, "What prompted you to make a confession to Father Zamoyski?"

Suspicion crawled across her lovely face, like a snake. "How in hell did you figure that out?"

"Until this moment it was just a guess."

"Smart ass." She took another sip of wine. "I was so sick with guilt about Michael's death that after awhile I had to talk to someone— anyone. I had a girlfriend—Elvira Billings. I went to her and pretty-much spilled my guts about what I'd felt for Michael and how it haunted me now that he was dead."

"You told her you suspected Dom of killing Michael?"

Her head wagged. "Of course not. But I did tell her I was worried plenty about my brother. Like a good Catholic girl, Elvira told me to tell everything to Father Zamoyski. So I went to St. Michael's Rectory. I was too ashamed over my efforts at getting Michael's attention to admit anything, directly. So I decided to make a confession. That's when it came out. What I had done trying to interest Michael. What I assumed Dominic had done. No names, you understand. But that a murder had been the result, and I feared for my brother's soul."

"If you didn't mention any names how did Father Zamoyski know who you were?"

"How could he not? I was a regular in the confessional." She laughed. "My mother used to take me to confession at least twice a week."

Elliot scoffed. "At age eleven she thought you were so full of sin?"

Rita thought, remembered and then formed the words. "My mother kept a close eye on me. She knew I spent most of my waking moments thinking about boys. Not to mention her suspicions about my sleeping hours being filled with dreams of handsome knights who would adore me forever. I know it sounds hokey, but every girl has fantasies along those lines." She paused with a sad smirk. "When you're that age, love is pure and beautiful because of its innocence. It's not until later that you find out how lousy it can be." Her eyes leveled on him. "Weren't you ever in love with an older woman?"

Chambers Elliot nodded. "I was sixteen and she was a forty year old stripper with the biggest set of…"

"I mean when you were a little kid."

He slowly shook his head. "Somehow I missed that. What happened after Dominic got to Winston Liquors?"

She wiped a tear away from one eye. "Dom said he waited until there weren't any customers. Then he went in and started yelling at Michael about keeping clear of me. Poor Michael. He wouldn't have understood any of it. How could he?" There was another pause as she took a ragged breath. "Michael must've thought I had lied to my brother. He must've died thinking it. Anyway, Dom said Michael suddenly dropped to the floor. Like somebody'd poleaxed him, from behind. Dom said he squatted down thinking Michael was having some sort of fit or a heart attack, or something. That's when he saw blood running from the back of Michael's head. Dom had been around the family business long enough to know that blood comes from holes in flesh made by bullets. He looked around. But the glass in the store's windows hadn't been broken. At that point, Dom figured the shot must've come through the open front door. It was hot that night. The air conditioner had been on the blink all week. So the door was propped open, to let in the night air."

"Did he take a gun there?"

Her eyes darted away from Elliot's. "The gun Dom had was Michael's. Dom took it from Michael's shoulder holster after Michael was dead. My brother thought the shooter had tried to kill him. He wanted protection."

Elliot's gray brows pulled together into a divot over his nose. "You saw the gun?"

She jerked her head face-on and gave him an impatient glare. "Of course not. My father would've killed Dom for coming to my room with a gun."

He looked down at the wineglass as if he were wondering how it got into his hand. "What happened to it?"

"How in hell would I know?"

"When you made your confession to Zamoyski, did you suggest the idea that Michael Douglas was philandering?"

"Of course not." Her quick eyes had gone wide, almost worried. "I wouldn't have known what it meant."

"The police assumed the motive for Michael' killing was robbery," reflected Elliot. "Considering who the Hendersons blamed, that was an easy thing to accept."

Her shoulders rose and fell with disinterest. "Jerome Petty didn't kill Michael Douglas. He couldn't have."

"How can you be certain?"

"Because Petty was with Sal and my father that night—during the time Dom was at Winston Liquor's. I know. I saw Petty arrive. I saw him being carried out after my father's men worked him over later. I was a little girl who didn't miss much, around our house."

The lawyer's eyes narrowed with doubt. "You're certain the man you saw was Jerome Petty?"

Rita nodded.

"But what makes you think he was at your house when Michael Douglas was killed?"

"Fists on faces make noise, Mr. Elliot. So do men being beaten. I learned that long before I hit puberty. My father's men were very good at their jobs. They had to be. And Jerome Petty was not the strong, silent type. Petty was there for about an hour—begging for his life and getting a face full of knuckles."

"Begging? Why?"

"Jerome Petty owed my father a great deal of money," explained. Rita. "Petty wasn't making payments because the last action he tried blew up in his face. My father was a very sensitive man—despite his less than delicate reputation. He took offense to being ignored by Petty. My father believed that when you lend a man money, he repays you without being prompted." She waved one hand as if the next words were commonplace in her life. "If payments are to be late, then my father expected that man to explain why—before the next payment fell due. Jerome Petty didn't think enough of my father to offer that consideration. My father had his men make certain there would never be a repeat of that failing."

"But after Petty was arrested why didn't somebody come forward with an alibi?"

He could hear her slow exhalation. "What better way to make an example to anyone else thinking of stiffing my father?" she asked.

"But a dead man cannot repay a debt."

She took another drink of wine. "That's the way it is in our business."

Elliot could see frozen intensity upon Rita's beautiful face. "I understand the psychological importance of making examples. But there's still the money to consider. How much did Petty owe?"

"Fifty grand plus the juice for the loan." She added with an uncomfortable smile, "My father felt that Petty would never repay the debt. So he told Sal to write it off. Writing off, meant resolving the problem to the satisfaction of my father. When borrowing money from my father you either paid or you died. Either outcome was considered satisfactory."

"Your family doesn't own any banks in the area, do they? I might be a little late on my house-payment, this month."

"Several. But don't worry. I'll put in a good word for you."

Chambers Elliot folded his hands and twiddled his thumbs for a number of seconds. "It was your father who arranged for Petty to be hanged in his cell?"

Rita made a face. "I don't know who did what. But if it happened, Sal would know. You could ask him. I don't think you'll enjoy his answer. But you can ask."

"Why didn't you come forward with Petty's alibi if you knew him to be innocent?"

"Sure," she sneered, with a flick of her hands. "I'll just show up at the police station in my knee-socks and braids to admit that my father was having the guy beaten silly. I was stupid enough to get absolution for

Dom. But betray my father? Even at that tender age I would've died rather than do such a disgraceful thing. My father was my world." Rita toyed with the cigarette butt on her plate, with one finger. "Have you ever been in love?"

"Not yet," he said. "But you've made me hopeful."

She grunted skeptically, "Then you've never been married."

"Your father never found out about your juvenile infatuation with Michael Douglas?"

"Are you kidding?" Rita wiped her hands on a napkin. "My father may have committed murderers. He may have ordered bones broken to get his ideas across. He may have bought and sold politicians like the trash they are. But he would not have understood what my heart and body were going through. My father, to his dying day, thought I was still a virgin—God love him."

"Did Dominic mention seeing Barbara Pierce that night at Winston Liquors?"

She abruptly became edgy. "I don't recall."

"Why would Dominic assume whoever killed Michael Douglas had been trying to kill him?"

"Dom is short on common sense and long on stupid impulse."

His eyes moved back and forth across his face slowly, studying each curve and crevice.

"Even then," she continued, "Dom had a list of enemies that could fill a phone book. I'm not talking about kick-in-the-balls types. I'm talking make-dead types."

Elliot helped himself to a chicken-leg. "How did Jerome Petty fit with Michael Douglas?"

"They were both women-chasers. The fact is, they'd grown up living next door to one another. Pals most of the time. Enemies once in a while —usually over women." She paused a moment, forming her mouth into a purse. "Petty had his own rackets. That's what connected him to my family. He came to us for financing when he needed it. Michael kept clear of bad business."

"Was Petty a killer?"

"Not that I ever heard. But I wasn't included in those types of discussions. What I learned came from overheard conversations and what Dom told me."

"Why would your brother share information about family business with you?"

"Because I asked." She gave the tabletop a firm tap with one of her lacquered nails. "I knew who and what we were. I also knew that I wanted to be more than just the little girl everybody coddled." Rita tilted toward him gracefully and smiled between her teeth. "I was making plans for my own future."

"Did Salvator answer your questions?"

She let go a sharp, bitter laugh, and leaned back. "Sal treated me like a nuisance. Asking the wrong question back then got me a slap—and I mean hard. It still gets me a slap. But he's more careful about how hard, these days."

"Why?"

"Because he knows I carry a gun in my purse and I'm willing to use it if he crosses the line." Rita wrinkled her brow thoughtfully. "I wouldn't kill him. But I'm not above giving my brother tit-for-tat in terms of pain."

"Did you view the DVD Dom received?"

"No."

"But he did get one?"

She nodded. "The dummy destroyed it before I could see the video."

Elliot tilted toward her. "What brought you and Dominic to the Double Oak hotel?"

"Dom got a call from somebody," she said. "A man. We now know the caller was Milton Raintree. But he identified himself to Dom as Father Zamoyski."

Elliot sat erect with new curiosity. "Why are you convinced the caller was Milton Raintree? Why not Harry Farmer? Or someone else?"

She smirked. "Because Salvator said it was Milton Raintree. Salvator does not make mistakes."

"What was said on the phone?"

"Raintree told Dom he was at the Double Oak in room 302, and wanted to talk—about Michael Douglas. Raintree said to be there at a specified time. Dom agreed, still believing he was speaking to Father Zamoyski."

"To talk about what?" he asked.

Rita leaned lightly on the table, tilting forward. The low round neck of her dress had a lot of play in it, exposing a tanned span of delightful cleavage to the lawyer's probing eyes. She seemed indifferent to the fleshy disclosure that caught and held Elliot's less than fatherly interest.

"Blackmail, of course," she said.

"You went there knowing that?"

A sardonic smile flashed across her face, and she sat upright. "You don't kill a snake until you find out how strong its poison is."

He looked quizzically at her. "Then you went to the hotel intending murder?"

"Dom and I weren't going there to kiss his ass." Rita grabbed another piece of chicken from the bucket. "But murder? Not really. At the time Dom came to me with the news about the call, we were thinking more along the lines of dragging his sorry ass off some place to beat the hell out of him before turning the bastard over to Sal."

"Why would Dominic risk involving Salvator at this late date? Wouldn't it be more likely that Dominic would kill Zamoyski on his own to limit Sal's exposure?"

She smiled quickly. It was an ungainly smile, but far from unpleasant. Not unlike something expressed by a little girl with a heart of tin who made a habit of throwing acid at kittens.

"Dom's no saint," Rita declared. "But kill a priest? Dom might want to. He might threaten a priest with murder. Dom might even consider demanding it done. But he wouldn't do it. Not a priest. Not if Sal put a gun to his head and ordered it." She shook a finger at Elliot for emphasis before adding, "Not a priest."

"But Salvator would?"

"Without so much as a grimace of regret." Her mouth twisted slightly as she thought. "Salvator is like my father—the consummate *Capo di tutti i capi*. You do remember my father?"

"Old Frank? Oh, yes, indeed. I think everybody who's lived any amount of time in Austin, remembers Old Frank Portello." Elliot ran a hand roughly through coarse gray hair and said, "Did your brother actually remember Father Zamoyski from thirty years back?"

She laughed. "You don't forget the priest who made a practice of scaring the shit out of you over sins you did not even understand." Both her arms flew outward as if she were beholding an angel. "I can still see Father Zamoyski standing behind the pulpit screaming bloody murder about infidelity and lust." Her arms dropped back to the table. "My mother, God love her, thought Zamoyski was a Saint and should be canonized when he died."

"Did you believe the real Zamoyski had contacted your brother?"

"Of course not. Not Father Zamoyski. Not the holiest man on earth. He would never threaten extortion. I knew it had to be a ringer." Rita paused a moment, staring at the lawyer, her face taking on a less hardened façade. Then her eyes dipped as she said, "I didn't want Dom to go to the hotel. He doesn't think before he acts. I didn't want him to do something stupid."

"Like shooting his extorter and tossing the man's body off the hotel roof?"

She tossed Elliot a warning glare. "I said I'd go and check it out. If Zamoyski was really there, we'd decide what to do. But Dom insisted that it was his problem and he had to face it."

"Did you have any inkling it was as setup?"

"Dom didn't. But I did." Her face hardened slightly. "First, I'd heard Father Zamoyski was living in Poland. Second, assuming he had come back, I didn't believe Father Zamoyski would betray what went on in the confessional." Her eyes closed. "Third, asking us to meet at a hotel was too easy; too convenient; and too damn exposed for a very nervous priest like Zamoyski."

He winked. "You're an expert on nervous men?"

She raised her dark lashes and gave him a long, silent stare. "I've had a lot of experience with men if that's your dig."

He made a dismissive wave with one hand. "Don't take it out of context, Rita. What happened then?"

"I told Dom we should let Sal know—just in case," she said, her hands once more becoming animated. "But poor Dom refused. Salvator is so... Dear God, that man! Dom is not what you would call a smooth guy. He operates strictly at gut-level. He's never scared—except when he faces Sal. But when he came to me about the call, it was like thirty years before. My brother was terrified. Dom knew that if a priest got on the witness stand and pointed to him as Michael Douglas' killer, there wasn't a jury in the world who would not convict."

"I am surprised you brother is so afraid of prison."

"Prison, hell! He was afraid Sal would think Dom actually had done it, and kill him."

"Did Dominic ever find out about you confessing to Father Zamoyski?"

She looked away. "I told him because I thought he would want to know that he had nothing to worry about, in terms of his soul. Dom couldn't believe I'd done that. It was like I'd betrayed him. He was so angry I thought he was going to hit me. But he didn't." Rita took a deep breath. "I told Dom that I would come with him to meet Father Zamoyski. I could see my offer was a relief. But still, he refused. I knew he'd screw it up. I knew something would go wrong and then Sal would come down on him like a load of shit." Her eyes drifted back to Elliot's. "So I insisted. I told Dom I was coming whether he liked it, or not. We went."

"The two of you went there alone – without help from the family-goons?"

Rita said, with a slow languor, "The one thing I did not want to do is get us in any deeper than we already were. Not with Sal." Then she tapped the tabletop with a finger. "For your information, Lawyer, Sal had Dom and me on the carpet 'til sunrise the night we left you. My kid has the chicken pox, my mother's in Sicily so not only did I have to try to calm down the little screamer with ointment and an oatmeal bath, but I had to explain all that could be explained about Michael Douglas to a man who believes nobody. All because of your snippy remarks."

Elliot grinned. "That's what you get for showing up at my office without an appointment. What happened when you and Dominic arrived at room 302?"

Rita studied him, her full dark brows pulled together as if she didn't like the way things were going. "The door was ajar. But I knocked, anyway. Nobody came, so we went in. The place had been tossed. Nobody was in sight. But that damn photo was sitting right on top of the frigging desk."

"What photo?"

"A print of a frame from the video. It showed Dom running toward the back of the liquor store holding a gun."

"When you arrived were the lights on in the room, or off?"

Rita took her lower lip between her teeth and held it that way while she thought. Then she shrugged, let go of her lip and said, "Off. I remember I had trouble finding the damn wall-switch."

"Was there any sign of violence—other than the place having been searched?"

"There was blood on the bedding." It was a flat statement, the kind a woman might make when discussing the merits of a deodorant. "We'd been in the room no more than ten seconds when there came a scream from outside. I looked toward the window in time to see something go flying past. Dom and I ran over to the window and looked out. There, squashed on the pavement below, was a man wearing a priest's cassock. I told Dom it had been a setup and we had to get out of there. He went out one way. I grabbed the photo and went another."

"Do you still have the photo?"

Rita dropped the chicken to her plate. "Do you think I'm stupid? I burned that damn thing in the car, first thing."

Elliot pushed the wine bottle near her. Rita grabbed it and refilled her glass. Then she picked up the stemware and touched its rim to her chin. Her upper lip rose for part of a second before settling down again. She took a drink and set the glass aside.

"Salvator said he knew the dead priest was actually Harry Farmer because of Harry's hands," Elliot said. "How could he assume that?"

"Years back," Rita replied, "there was a not so accidental explosion in one of the trucks from our distribution business. The Russian Mafia was flexing its muscles. They had found out that Sal would be along on that trip and figured to take him out. How, they found out nobody knows to this day. The bomb-blast knocked Sal unconscious. Harry burned his hands dragging Sal out of the truck."

"What made Salvator assume that Milton Raintree and Harry were behind the DVD business?"

"Elvira Billings," Rita replied. "Elvira called to warn me that Milton Raintree and Harry Farmer had a DVD that showed Dominic with Michael Douglas when Michael was killed."

"She sold that DVD to Raintree. Did she tell you that?"

Her eyes crinkled at the corners. "That little bitch!"

"What did you do for her in return for this timely warning?"

"I gave her twenty thousand in cash to keep what she knew to herself. If I'd known she was the one who'd sold that damn DVD to Raintree I'd…"

"Does Salvator know Milton Raintree by sight?"

"Both my brothers do—from way back. Milton had been one of Sal's numbers-runners—until he ran off with a pile of dough Sal had to make good on."

"That must've been embarrassing."

"Salvator ordered a hit on Raintree. But my father disallowed it— why, I can't explain. Maybe it was because at the time my family was under pressure from a new governor. One who could not be bought. Can you believe it? An honest politician in Texas?"

"They show their faces now and then. Have you ever seen Raintree?"

She reflected a moment before shaking her head. "But we always know when Raintree's in town."

"How?"

"He telephones Sal to gloat."

"How long has it been since Raintree worked for your family?"

Rita looked at a corner of the ceiling and drew her mouth down at the corners. Then she shrugged. "Ten or fifteen years."

"Then it's possible neither of your brothers would have recognize Raintree's voice?"

"Sal has a memory like an elephant. He would never forget. He could never be deceived. Dom on the other hand has a memory that lasts about ten seconds. He'll shake your hand after being introduced and wander off wondering what your name was. It is so embarrassing."

"Somebody paid Junior Billings thousands shortly after Douglas' murder," said the lawyer. "I think Billings extorted it from Douglas' killer."

"Then he collected from an amateur."

"How do you know?"

"Ask anybody who knew Junior Billings," she said stiffly. "They'll tell you he was a dumb as a post. He'd have demanded the money, collected and gone home grinning—leaving a trail a mile wide right to his own doorstep." Rita drained her glass, picked up her purse and stood up. "What about it? Are you going to leave Michael Douglas at rest?"

Elliot rose to his feet. "I'll think about it. But before you leave I have a request. I want Milton Raintree alive. Please tell Salvator that. Whatever he has planned for Raintree is none of my business. But I have to speak with Raintree."

Rita Portello studied Chambers Elliot for a few seconds, snapping and unsnapped her bag impatiently. Then her eyes went icy and her teeth came together sharply. "I'll think about it".

Chapter 16

At 10:00 o'clock the next morning, Chambers Elliot was seated at a small oak table in interrogation room 'B', at Travis County Jail. He stared at Kathy Martin, with justified impatience. She was dressed in gray prison garb studying her hands as they coiled and uncoiled in her lap. The single, overhead light flickered from time to time, as if annoyed with the couple.

"What part of the question didn't you understand, Kathy?" Elliot demanded, with a frustrated flurry of his hands. "Did you or did you not shoot George Pierce?"

Kathy raised her head and gazed at him, a plaintive pleading in her eyes. "I'm afraid if I tell you the truth, you won't help me."

He adjusted the lay of his gray, tweed suit. "Then, you did do it."

"No!" She put one hand to her mouth as if horrified by his assumption.

The lawyer's arms splayed in irritation. "Then what in hell *are* you telling me?"

"I was at the ranch the night George was killed, yes." She rested her wrists on the tabletop and tilted them toward Elliot, her eyes locked upon his. "Milton planned all of it. Mazy was to go there and pretend to rob George. I was to come in through the kitchen, go up to George's bedroom and get the drop on Mazy."

Elliot got to his feet roaring, "Stop lying!"

"I'm not lying, Mr. Elliot," she said, her voice breaking. "There were two ways of getting at George's money. Sheila inheriting as his granddaughter or me inheriting as his wife. Don't you see?" She leaned back, showing a lot of throat. "The play with Mazy would make me a hero in George's eyes. He was already in love with me—I'd made sure of that. My saving George from Mazy was to be the final stroke to get George to propose."

Elliot frowned and resumed his seat. "If marrying George was your plan, how do you explain Sheila Clifford's claim that you're engaged to *Sydney* Pierce?"

He heard the sharp hissing intake of her breath.

"Well?" he demanded.

"That, too, was Milton's idea." Kathy stared at him level-eyed, her jaws tight. Her eyes had an opaque look. "But I didn't agree to marry Sydney until after George's murder. You don't have to believe me. Talk to Sydney."

"Why did Raintree and Sheila use your car to drive to the Pierce

Ranch?"

"That was part of the plan with Mazy. Milton would force his way in dressed as a woman, screaming his lungs out about an accident. I was to get distracted by his screams." Kathy leaned towards him, her eyes pleading. "That was Mazy's cue to take a wild shot at me and then bust out of there. I was to pretend I'd been slightly wounded. The plan was for me to nick my wrist with a nail-clipper. That would leave a small piece of flesh gone and lots of blood. It was all intended to maximize George's feelings for me."

He dragged his hands across his face. "And Sheila's role in all this?"

"Sheila was to burst into the house a two minutes after Milton. She was to pretend that she'd been in the accident Milton was reporting and beg to see George. The plan was for me to hear her cries and urge George to go down to see her. He would assume that she had risked her life to see him even thought she should have gone to the hospital." She went limp as a rag, staring at Elliot. Her voice was full of shame. "That, Milton thought, would put George on such a guilt trip that whether she was a Pierce or not, Sheila would be included in George's will. But it all went wrong. Sheila heard gunshots, lost her nerve and drove away."

"I didn't see any injuries on Sheila."

"You would have if you had lifted her blouse," said Kathy. "That girl's ribs are as blue as a bottle fly."

"Makeup won't fool anyone," he scoffed.

"The bruises are real." A couple of red spots burned in her cheeks. "Milton gave her a good working over to make sure of it. Look, don't believe me. You said you'd spoken with Sheila. Go back and ask to see her bruises."

He dragged one hand across the back of his neck. "Okay, who fired the shots?"

She shrugged. "That wasn't part of the plan. Look, when I got there, I went directly up to George's bedroom. Mazy was supposed to be there holding George at gunpoint. But, George was dead and Mazy was gone."

"So Mazy killed George?"

"Why? Killing George wasn't going to get us his money. That was the last thing we wanted to happen." Her voice became anxious. "It had to be Dominic Portello."

Elliot leveled a finger at her. "Based upon what evidence?"

Kathy Martin made a defeated gesture. "I don't have any evidence."

He made an exasperated noise. "How did you get to the Pierce Ranch?"

"In Milton's car," Kathy said.

"If he had a car why take yours?"

"Because he knew you were watching for him." She paused to take a breath. "That's why he dressed as a woman and took my Vette—to fool whoever was watching."

Elliot tugged at his tie. "If Sheila stranded Raintree there, how did he get away?"

"He was sitting in his own car waiting for me when I got back to it."

"Have you spoken with Mazy about George's murder?"

Her hands clasped then she twisted her fingers nervously. "I haven't seen or heard from him since that night."

"What caliber gun was Mazy to use in the plan for George?"

"The one he carries, I guess." She pushed her little finger along the tabletop as if collecting dust. "Milton didn't say."

His hands became impatiently animated. "Big gun? Small gun? Automatic? Revolver?"

"Automatic—small." She once more folded her hands into her lap.

"You're certain George was dead when you arrived?"

Kathy's eyes rapidly opened and closed as she tried to keep back the tears. "He was lying on the floor. His eyes were open but not blinking. He had to be dead."

"But you must've been seen by Armistice."

"No." Kathy's lips became tightly compressed as her eyes went down. Then she said, "At the time I heard the shots I had already been up to George's room, saw that he was dead and was back downstairs heading for the kitchen door. Armistice was upstairs in the hallway. He was calling out George's name." She reached out touched his arm. "Milton was hurrying for the front door as fast as he could make his feet go in those high-heels."

A quick rush of anger overwhelmed him. "Kathy, if this is another lie to protect Milton…"

She jerked back her hand and looked at him very carefully, drawing her eyebrows down at the corners. "I'm being straight with you, Mr. Elliot." The next words came across her lips like pistol shots. "I don't know who fired the shots. George was already dead and neither Milton nor me was anywhere near George's room."

For several seconds he fumbled with his lower lip, thinking. Then, "Where can I find Mazy?"

"He's got a flop somewhere in town," she said distantly. "But I don't know where."

"Milton?"

Kathy Martin made a beseeching gesture with her hands. "If I knew,

I'd have told the cops."

"How did Raintree know George had asked for changes in his Will?"

She shrugged. "He never said. But he knew about it. He also knew that George was making plans to put everything into a trust." Her eyes went remote and bitter. "That's when Milton came up with the robbery scam. He said we had to act now, or that trust would screw us over from both ends."

"Raintree claims he has an executed will which dumps the Pierce Estate into Sheila Clifford's lap. Have you seen it?"

Her head wagged. "But it doesn't surprise me. He'd make a phony as a last-ditch effort."

Elliot got up and began to pace. "Something's not right. Are you certain you've told me who all the players are?"

"As far as I know it was me, Milton, Sheila and Mazy." She made a nervous face and cowered in her chair. "Don't be mad. But there's something I've not told you yet. Milton told me he had an ace in the hole —whatever that means. Only he said he couldn't play it unless there was no other way."

He stopped and glared. "You must have some idea what Raintree was talking about."

Her head shook. "He wouldn't say." Kathy brightened up a little. "But I got the impression, from what I overheard Milton and Mazy discussing, that George Pierce had some history. Something big that could land George in jail. There must've been something to it because Mazy was afraid that George might kill to keep it quiet. I heard them mention that name."

"What name?"

"The one Harry was hassling Dominic Portello over." She gave him a quick up-from-under look and immediately looked away. "Michael Douglas."

Chambers Elliot stuffed his hands into his pockets. "Did Raintree speculate on who killed George?"

She gave a nod the size of a fingernail. "Dominic Portello."

Elliot raised his eyebrows just a little. "I can see Dominic making threats. But taking a chance on killing George? Not at this time."

"I don't think Milton figures Dominic went there intending to kill George." She looked at her thumb. "But guns go off, as guns do. It might've been an accident."

The lawyer wagged his head. "I don't buy it. Dominic is in enough trouble with his brother."

Her eyes took on a new fear. "You won't walk out on me, will you?"

Chambers Elliot returned to his chair and leaned back. "Is there any way to get in or out of the ranchhouse other than the front and rear doors?"

Kathy gave her head a frantic wave. "Not that I know of."

He made a bewildered face. "What's Raintree's reasoning behind hiring Tipton French to defend Sheila?"

"I think to punish her because she stranded him at the ranch," Kathy explained, in a faint voice. "Milton isn't one to forgive and forget. He told me flat out that he already regrets marrying her."

"I suspect she feels the same way." He tilted forward resting his forearms on the table. His face was stony. His voice barely audible. "She's not going to do him much good if convicted in George's murder —phony will or not. So why Tipton French?"

Her lips rustled like velvet on sand. "Milton will see she gets off. But he's going to make her sweat plenty before it happens."

"How can he be certain of acquittal with French handling her defense? She'd do better defending herself."

Kathy looked at a point well above the top of his head. "Milton Raintree doesn't leave anything to chance. I wouldn't be a bit surprised if he has proof that Dominic Portello did it. He'll let Sheila worry until it looks like a conviction is coming down the pipe, and then Tipton will bring out the proof."

"Tipton French isn't smooth enough for something like that." Elliot stood up and began moving again. After several seconds he said, "When you heard the gunshots, from where did the sound come?"

Kathy gave him a confused look.

"Upstairs? Downstairs? Outside the house?" suggested the lawyer, his arms splaying wide with exasperation. "Everybody in the house heard the damn gunshots. You must have some ideas."

"The sound seemed to come from behind me, but upstairs."

"How did Mazy get to the ranch?"

Kathy Martin rubbed one palm on the tabletop. "His car, I suppose."

"Three cars used when one could've done the job. Why?"

She looked surprised at his question. "Because that's how Milton planned it."

"Why didn't I see Mazy's muddy footsteps on the carpet in the ranchhouse?"

She shrugged, her eyes faintly puzzled. The she said, "He must've taken off his shoes."

"I doubt that very much."

She laughed harshly. "I'm not lying to you, Mr. Elliot."

"How does Sheila get along with Sydney Pierce?"

"I don't think they've ever met."

"Isn't that odd—considering?"

"Sydney's not very happy about her being Edward's daughter. So I suppose he just makes a point of being gone each time she shows up, at the ranch."

He stopped and stared down at her. "There's nothing else I should know, Kathy?" he said, in a warning tone. "You're absolutely certain?"

Kathy's eyes dipped away, her head nodding.

Elliot pressed his psychological advantage. "There's a good chance you won't be prosecuted for that armed robbery."

Kathy half stood, in hopeful excitement. Then she dropped back into the chair. "You're sure about that?"

Elliot nodded. "The State may bluster a bit, but there's nothing they can do. As for my fee…"

"Anything. Anything you want."

"Assuming Milton Raintree is still alive," said the lawyer. "If he contacts you I want to know about it right away—night or day. Agreed?"

Kathy Martin pressed her hands together in prayer fashion. "Anything you say, Mr. Elliot."

"Just sit tight. If somebody offers to make your bail, refuse and call me. The safest place you can be is in here."

She looked at him as though he had instructed her to do the impossible, but remained silent.

* * * *

Two hours later, Chambers Elliot was pacing in his private office. Jason Taggart, his head wrapped in bandages, sprawled upon the davenport.

"Not so much as an apology," the detective whined.

"I told you I was sorry," Elliot retorted with obvious irritation.

"I mean Lydia." Taggart draped one arm over his eyes. "Not one word of encouragement, or remorse." His hands form a cross upon his chest. "And after all the trouble I went to, at the diner. An extra slice of apple pie—with cheese. Extra chocolate in her malted milk. You'd think she'd have some feelings of sympathy."

"Have your people made any headway in locating Raintree?"

Jason Taggart groaned himself into a sitting position. "No yet. After you called, I radioed Henderson. He'd been watching Sheila Clifford's apartment. I had him go up to her apartment and try to get inside and grab Raintree. He did get in. But the place was empty. No Raintree. No Sheila. Frankly, from the way you described Raintree's treatment of her, I doubt she'll hang around. Not with Pierce dead and no hopes of collecting as an heir."

"She'll stay. Sheila is convinced that Raintree's phony will is going to get her a payout."

The detective's brows arched in surprise. "Will it?"

"I didn't see the document so I can't attest to its quality. But forgeries are usually easy to prove." The lawyer hesitated as he fumbled fingers in pockets, thinking. "Still, there might be enough to it that Sydney Pierce would settle some money on Sheila just to be rid of them. What about Sydney Pierce?"

"We're still watching him around the clock." Taggart made a feeble wave with one hand. "Van Dyke tailed Sydney to Sheila's apartment from the ranch. So Van Dyke was outside when you left."

"Where did Sydney go after I did?"

"Lunched at some seafood joint on Anderson. But it took him some time to leave the apartment building."

"How much time?"

"Twenty minutes, or so."

"Henderson didn't see Sydney in the foyer?"

Taggart started to wag his head, caught himself and then groaned in pain.

"Then where was Sydney?" asked Elliot.

The detective shrugged. "After Sydney ate, Van Dyke followed him back to the ranch where, last I heard, Sydney still is."

Chambers Elliot tugged at an earlobe. "I thought I was closing in on this thing."

"When you do let me know because I can't figure any of it."

"What about Mazy Wilson?"

"So far, we can't pin down where he lives."

The lawyer stopped pacing and faced Taggart. "Was anyone watching the ranch after Sydney left?"

"How? Van Dyke tailed Sydney, as instructed." The detective made an impatient gesture. "He was the only operative I had there."

"Then it's possible Milton Raintree or Mazy or both got in there," Elliot said, sharply.

Taggart nodded absently. "Yes, Chambers. It's also possible those two clowns are living it up in the Taj Mahal. However, it's not likely. Look, I'm trying to keep the costs to a minimum on this screwy thing." With another groan, Taggart stood. "Why in hell would Raintree go to the Pierce ranch, anyway? Herbie and his team of Eagle Scouts could go back there for another search at any time. In fact, I'd bet Herbie has at least one car out there 'round the clock."

"I know, I know," Elliot grumbled. "I'm just frustrated. If Salvator Portello gets his hands on Raintree before we do, all my efforts will be for nothing."

"Take it from me, they're going to be for nothing anyway." Jason Taggart's eyes suddenly went wide and white. "Can I sue Lydia for brain damage?"

"In your case it would be impossible to prove," said the lawyer, dryly. The lawyer glanced over at the detective. "If I wanted to kill someone and I wanted to make it look like the murder had been done at point-blank range—but it had not—how would I go about it?"

"You'd shoot the victim from a distance. Then, using a blank with the paper-wad removed, you go over to the victim and press the gun to the wound and fire the blank." Taggart smiled faintly. "In the old days, that would do it. But today you'd still have to be careful enough to use cartridges loaded with the same gunpowder. Otherwise Forensics might tumble to the variation when the nitrate residue is analyzed."

"But wouldn't the powder fall out without a wad to keep it in place?"

Taggart spread his hands. "The end of the cartridge could be notched and then crimped closed. That type of seal is tight enough to keep the powder in place. When the gun is fired, the crimp pops open from the blast, letting the burning powder flare."

Elliot nodded. "I want you to search the Pierce ranch. You're looking for three things. First, I want to know if there is any reloading equipment, there. Secondly, if there are any pistols. Lastly, if there is a stereo speaker-system in the house."

"I'm not likely to get permission from Sydney for a search, Chambers," Taggart said listlessly.

"You don't need his permission. I, as executor of the Pierce estate, have sent you there to search for the missing will. You will do so, very thoroughly." Elliot went around to the side of his desk and resumed pacing the floor. Suddenly he paused to turn to the detective. "I just thought of something. Were Salvator's men keeping watch on Kathy Martin's apartment?"

"Actually, Van Drake spotted two men in a car—he recognized both as members of the Portello mob." Taggart leaned back and rocked on his heels. "But they left shortly before you came out."

Elliot dragged his hands across his face. "They must've spotted Raintree and Sheila when those two skipped out. You'd better have your people stop searching for Raintree. Salvator has him, by now. Salvator probably has Mazy and Sheila, as well. Damn!" The lawyer thought for a few seconds then he said, "Where was Sydney Pierce during those twenty minutes?"

"Do you want me to call off Van Drake, too?"

"No. I still want Sydney watched. It's just that he told me he was going up to Sheila's apartment. If they'd skipped out, what took him so long to find out? If they hadn't, why didn't your people see him right away? I'd bet anything that Raintree and Sheila were gone just after I left the apartment. And one more thing, get a DNA sample from Sydney."

"How?"

"A bloody nose or split lip works quite well—not that I'd ever ask you to do anything illegal."

Taggart rolled his eyes. "Since when?"

Elliot scowled. "If Sydney attempts to stop you from searching you do have the right to defend yourself. If not, bump into him. Also, get your contact at the morgue to let you take a sample for a DNA analysis from George's corpse. I want a lab to do a match on the 'Y' chromosome. Put a rush on the processing."

"You want to verify Sydney's paternity?"

"George Pierce's wills were always specific. Sydney's been a beneficiary in each. But each version stipulated 'My son, Sydney.' If Sydney is not George's son, Raintree has a very large club to wield in terms of getting Sydney's cooperation."

"You're assuming that Barbara Pierce's affairs went on for years prior to Michael Douglas' killing?"

"I agree it's a long shot, Jason. But I have to know."

"I'll get right on it."

"One more thing," said Elliot, as the detective hobbled toward the door. "If you were Milton Raintree and you married Sheila Clifford, would you skip your wedding night?"

Taggart looked back and grinned. "Not unless I was dead."

"So why would did he? Further, why would he still have not consummated their marriage days later?"

"The man is either gay, or very sick."

"Considering his previous relationship with Kathy Martin, I think we can rule out gay. The last time we spoke with him he was obviously not sick. So why is the man avoiding it?"

The detective shrugged. "Insanity?"

Chambers Elliot suddenly grinned. "I think Milton Raintree is as sane as they come."

After Taggart left, Lydia hurried into Elliot's office. "Ramón's been kidnapped by gypsies. It happened as he left the hospital."

He gave her a disbelieving stare. "Go ahead. Hit me with the punchline."

"Chambers, it's true. I just got the call from the head of the Peterson clan. You do remember the Petersons?"

He gave his head a weary nod. "Lydia, they scam people on roofing and driveway sealant. The Peterson's don't kidnap people, let alone sex-crazed lunatics like Ramón Whitaker. Somebody's playing a joke on you."

"No. They grabbed Ramón because of Helene Peterson—the leader's daughter." She breathed hard, with her mouth a little open. "Apparently Ramón trifled with Helene's affections and then refused to marry her."

"The Petersons spend eighty percent of their time in North Dakota," said Elliot. "There was no chance for Ramón to... to... trifle with any of them."

"Helen left the clan after she and her father had an argument. Then she joined Ramón's dating club." Lydia dropped his eyes a little. "That's why she stayed in Austin the last time the clan left Texas for North Dakota."

"And now she's gone back to her family?"

"They're a tightly knit group. The Petersons want half a million in cash, three goats plus a rooster as compensation."

"For what?"

Lydia looked up and held out both arms as if trying to encircle a pregnant woman. "Her lost innocence and support of Ramón's progeny. Otherwise, they're going to neuter him."

The lawyer grinned. "Considering Ramón's recent history I don't think that's a bad idea."

"The Petersons don't joke, Chambers," she said irritably.

He tapped his chin before blaring, "I've had it up to here with Ramón Whitaker!"

"What about Maggie? If something happens to him she'll never forgive you."

Elliot's hands went to his eyes. "Dear, God, why don't you get a gun and shoot me?"

"Because Maggie would never forgive me. Believe it or not, Chambers, she views you as the father she never had."

His arms dropped. "Maggie has a father. I met him. He's a Baptist Minister."

Lydia said indifferently, "She wanted one who's a lawyer."

"She'll have to make do, Lydia. Call the police. Then inform Magistrate Whitaker about the forthcoming end to his family line. He can deal with Ramón's latest twist to life's romantic path. We are out of it."

"Chambers, Maggie is in tears," persisted Lydia. "She's in love with Ramón." Her hands went back to her hips. "Look, I'm sure I can talk the Petersons down to a reasonable sum."

"I'm not getting involved and that's the end of it."

She turned to leave and then stopped and turned back. "I heard on the news that Harry Farmer's body was formally identified by Elvira Billings."

"I'm surprised she even bothered."

"After hearing that, I did some checking on her. Elvira is the beneficiary of an insurance policy on Harry. She bothered because she needed his body to collect."

His mouth opened in surprise. "How much will she get?"

"Sixty thousand is what the insurance agent said. Almost worth killing for, wouldn't you agree?"

He nodded.

"I don't suppose Ramón has insurance for lost..." Lydia smiled politely and let the words hang.

"Forget it."

Chapter 17

Davis Archer, Senior Prosecutor for Travis County, looked like a keg of beer on stilts, covered in brown tweed. His waist was wider than his shoulders and hips. His limbs were spindly like a spider's. He had a shaved head, a long face, deeply set brown eyes, a broad pitted nose, a bluish slit for a mouth and a heavy, jutting chin.

"Taggart's got a knob on the back of his head the size of a tennis ball," Archer chuckled. He was in his office looking across his expansive walnut desk at Chambers Elliot. "The way he tells it, Lydia Marshall tried to kill him."

"The rumors of Lydia's temperament are grossly exaggerated," Elliot declared.

"Bullshit!" Archer dismissively waved one hand. "I've heard her cut loose on more than one man. That young woman's got the tongue of a fishmonger with the blind staggers. What really happened, Chambers? Did Taggart try to sneak a little something off her lunch-plate?"

Elliot crossed his legs. "There was a small conflagration between Taggart and somebody named Mazy Wilson."

Archer's eyebrows arched in surprise, his amusement fading. "That half-baked pimp?"

"The same," said Elliot. "Lydia thought Jason was in over his head as far as the struggle was concerned. So she waded in with a lamp. Jason forgot to duck."

"I'll bet that brightened Mazy's day."

"Not for long," said Elliot. "She nailed him, too—with another lamp."

Archer leaned back, letting go a laugh like a barking dog. "Gotta' love that girl."

"What can you tell me about Milton Raintree, Davis?"

"History-wise, we've been after him for years. But he's always eluded capture." He smiled, softly. "However, we now have good reason to believe that Raintree was abducted by members of the Portello mob, and is dead. An investigation is in progress. Frankly, I'm not holding out any hope that it will lead anywhere. What's your interest in Raintree?"

"If he's dead it really doesn't matter," Elliot said, in a disappointed tone."

"He conned one of your clients?"

"It's a bit more complicated than that."

Archer squinted suspiciously. "Raintree being dead is really bothering you. How come?"

"Let's just say I had hopes an understanding was in place concerning Mr. Raintree. Were you aware he'd married Sheila Clifford?"

"Did he now?" The prosecutor's eyes went misty. "I'll have to have another chat with that young woman. Not that I mind. She's one lovely creature."

"How frequently was Raintree in Austin?"

"It's been over a year since the last trouble." Archer tugged at his big nose. "For some reason, the Austin area is his favorite picking ground. He runs short on cash and comes back here to scam a few hundred thousand before disappearing again."

"He and Harry Farmer were working a shakedown regarding a murder that took place a thirty year ago."

Archer leaned forward smirking. "I know. Michael Douglas."

Elliot's eyes grew round. "How in hell…"

"I was told that Harry Farmer was running that action. How did Raintree get involved?"

Chambers Elliot stared at him with his mouth open. "Considering he's dead, apparently for all the wrong reasons. Who told you this?"

"Do you have the DVD Harry sent to Dominic?"

Elliot wagged his head.

Davis Archer leaned back, opened the middle drawer of the desk, pulled out a DVD and slid it across the desk to Chambers Elliot. "That's a copy. Take a peek when you have time. At this late date, it's not enough to charge Dominic. But thirty years ago it might've been."

Elliot picked up the DVD, in shock. "Where did you get it?"

"Mazy Wilson."

"Do you have a good address for Mazy Wilson?"

"I might," the prosecutor replied cagily. He leaned back in his chair and folded his arms across his big chest. "What's your interest?"

"According to my sources, he was to meet with George Pierce the night George was murdered."

Archer nodded agreeably. "He said as much when I questioned him. Claimed the whole thing was a robbery ruse to convince George to marry Kathy Martin. Wilson also said George was dead when he arrived. Consequently, he made an abrupt exit out the back way. So far, everything he's told us fits."

Elliot jumped to his feet in surprise. "When did you speak to Mazy?"

"Not more than twenty minutes before you arrived. He asked to be taken into protective custody. In exchange, he told us about the business with the Portellos and George." Davis Archer looked down at his clean, shiny fingernails. "I might be able to fit him with a conspiracy charge, or two. But I'm not sure anything will hold together before a jury."

"Did you check the police archives for the investigation-file on the Douglas' murder?" Elliot slumped back into his chair.

"What still exists is on microfiche. I'm having a hard-copy made." He smiled. It was a rather tired smile. "Would you like me to send you one?"

Elliot nodded, and stuffed the DVD into his coat pocket. "Did Wilson mention that Harry Farmer was Sheila's stepfather?"

Archer's big head slowly shook. "I hate it when people hold out on me."

"I know the feeling."

The Prosecutor sat very still, looking at Elliot. "I remember how close you and George were as kids, Chambers. I know you'd like to be the one who nails his killer." He paused and swept Elliot with a hard, level look. "But I know for a fact that Wilson and Raintree had nothing to do with it."

"You've made my day," Elliot muttered bitterly.

"Dominic Portello killed George Pierce. I have irrefutable evidence proving it. Not only that, I can link him to Harry Farmer's death—no doubt about that, either."

Elliot's mouth dropped. "Are you certain?"

Archer rubbed his big hands together and chuckled. "Forensics' got enough of the pieces of those shattered bullets put together to make a match to a gun. Both men were killed with the same pistol—an old Browning .32 automatic. We found the murder-weapon in Dominic's apartment."

"What made you go looking?"

"The usual anonymous tipster," Archer replied, casually. "Mr. Portello was taken into custody this morning, without incident."

"You don't think that pistol being there was a bit too convenient?"

"Not when the gun was locked in Dominic's wall-safe. Not when his palm and fingerprints are on the weapon's ammunition-clip." Archer, made a vague gesture. "He wiped off the rest of the gun. Chambers, if it was a plant it's the best I've ever seen."

Elliot wagged his head in disbelief. "Why would a mobster like Dominic Portello hang onto a gun after killing two people with it? It doesn't make sense, Davis."

"Neither does tossing Harry Farmer from a hotel roof, after shooting him. But that's what happened. Dominic Portello does not hold membership in God's brain-trust, Chambers."

"I agree. But Dominic's had a lifetime of tutoring in the art of murder from two of the best in that business—Old Frank and Salvator

Portello." Chambers Elliot fell silent for a moment. "The first thing Dominic should've done is get rid of that gun—strike that. The first thing would be to dump the bodies where they'd never be found. That's his family's tradition. The second thing is getting rid of the gun. But he did neither. Why?"

Archer frowned. "I don't know and I don't care. I've got the bastard cold." He held up one hand and waggled four fingers. "I have four witnesses who put Dominic Portello at the Double Oak Hotel when Harry Farmer was killed."

Elliot's eyes narrowed with suspicion. "Do you have any who can place him at the Pierce ranch when George was killed?"

"I can." His long forefinger tap-tapped for emphasis, at each statement. "The guy's a tourist who got lost. He was driving past the Pierce Ranch when he heard a shot. He drove his car into the ditch swerving around a man. He came in the next day, after reading about George's murder, to report the incident. This morning, he identified Dominic Portello from a lineup as the man he nearly ran down."

"Someone he nearly drove over during a hellish rainstorm he's able to identify days later?"

Archer spread his hands. "Now don't start muddying the waters with suspicions, Chambers. He picked Dominic out without a moment's hesitation."

"I'd like to speak to your witness."

"Can't. He took a plane back to Minnesota. But he'll return for the trial."

"Sounds like you've got this locked down, Davis."

"It gets better." He lifted his eyes until the gaze rested on the top of Elliot's head. Then he lowered the lids until half the iris was covered. For several seconds Archer looked at Elliot. Then he smiled. "We found a pair of shoes in Dominic's closet splattered with blood from two different people. We've not gotten the DNA results yet, but forensic analysis of the blood in our own laboratory gives a clear link to Harry Farmer and a type-match on George Pierce."

"How is there a link to Harry Farmer?"

"Same blood type as Harry plus traces of opium. Harry was a hardcore opium addict." Archer turned in his chair, crossed his spindly legs and gazed thoughtfully towards one of the paired office windows. "In addition to that, there were two shirts in Dominic's laundry. Both were spattered with blood. Again, the blood on the shirts links him to Harry and gives a pointer to George." The Prosecutor twisted back to face Elliot, folded his hands on the desktop, and tilted forward eagerly.

"Care to make a little wager on the outcome of Dominic's trial?"

"Sounds like a fool's bet," said Elliot.

Archer jerked back in his chair laughing. "I've waited twenty some years to nail a Portello. By God, I'm going to enjoy it." Then he abruptly fell silent as he noticed Elliot's grim expression. "What in hell's eating at you?"

"Just bits and pieces that don't fit."

"Say, I understand Sheila Clifford fired you in favor of Tipton French?"

Elliot nodded. "Apparently I'm beyond trust."

Archer threw his chest out laughing. "That must've burned."

"I admit I was red-faced for awhile. Where do you stand with Kathy Martin?"

The Prosecutor shrugged. "There's no doubt she's guilty of armed-robbery."

"The statute of limitations ran on that several years ago," Elliot said.

"Depends on her residency during the time since, as we both know." Archer dragged one hairy paw over his naked skull. "My people are investigating. But right now I'm still intending to prosecute. Why on earth are you defending her?"

Elliot shrugged. "I'm still wondering that, myself. The woman spouts one lie after another."

"Even if we don't prosecute on the robbery charge, there's still the murder of Harry Farmer."

Chambers Elliot sat straight up with a start. "You have evidence linking Kathy to that?"

"Not directly. But a witness places her at the hotel about the time Farmer was tossed from the roof. Another witness claims she visited Harry Farmer several times during his stay at the Double Oak." Archer flapped his hands gently on his desktop. Then he closed his eyes almost, but not quite, shut. The cool gleam of eyeballs shone between the thick lids, glimmering straight at Chambers Elliot. He sat very still for many seconds, as he formulated his next statement. Finally Archer opened his eyes. "When questioned, Kathy claimed to know nothing about him. I asked her about Dominic Portello. Again she denied knowing. But I happen to have half a dozen witnesses who will testify that she and Dominic were hot numbers less than a year ago. If she wasn't involved in Harry's killing, why lie about Dominic Portello?"

"Why, indeed?" Elliot got to his feet. "Did you talk to Dominic Portello about his relationship with Kathy?"

"Yup. He admitted it."

"That idiot…"

"Oh, one more thing," Archer said, with a grin. "Tipton French requested an expedited pretrial-hearing for Sheila Clifford. That jumps it forward to the day-after-tomorrow—in case you're free. I think you might find it very interesting."

"But Tipton just took her case. He'll need weeks to prepare."

Archer nodded, still grinning. "I suspect he doesn't plan to offer a defense—ever. Regardless, based upon what I've got against her I saw no need to deter him."

"Tipton's rushing Sheila to the death-house."

"Rushing or not, she's all but cooked." Archer stood and let go a belly laugh that shook his entire body. "Speaking of interesting… I heard that Ramón Whitaker's been kidnapped by Gypsies. He's your summer intern, isn't he?"

Elliot nodded, grimly. "Thanks for your time, Davis."

As Chambers Elliot left Archer's office his mind was so immersed in what Davis Archer had told him he did not notice the two stocky men in black suits, who climbed from the car that abruptly pulled to the curb.

"Mr. Elliot," said Thomaso, the eldest of the Sicilian Brothers, as he barred Elliot's path. "Mr. Salvator requests your company at his offices."

"Yeah," chimed Pietro, the younger brother in a deferential tone. "He requests your company."

A long shiver rippled through Elliot from head to foot. "I should've checked my horoscope before getting out of bed, this morning," the lawyer muttered. "Do we walk or drive?"

"We drive. Mr. Portello prefers it that way," Thomaso said. "He says we make people nervous when we're walking around."

"Yeah, we make people nervous."

Elliot nodded. "I can believe it."

Thomaso went over to the lawyer and lifted his arms. "I gotta' check you for weapons." Then he fumbled through Elliot's pockets. When Thomaso came upon the DVD he pulled it out.

"Last year's office Christmas party," Elliot said, his voice going soft and dry. "I was going to have copies made for my employees."

"That's real nice." Thomaso pocketed the DVD. "We ain't allowed to take no movies at our office parties. Sometimes they get kinda' rowdy."

"Yeah, rowdy." Pietro pointed to the car. "After you, Mr. Elliot."

Twenty minutes later, Chambers Elliot was in Salvator Portello's office on the main floor of the Lester Hampton Building, just a few blocks from Elliot's offices.

"Christmas party," said Thomaso as he handed his boss the DVD.

Salvator took it and set the disc on his desk. Then he began to pace. "You heard about my brother, Shyster?"

Elliot nodded as he settled into a comfortable chair in front of Salvator's glass desk, his eyes involuntarily locked upon the DVD. "I also learned a great deal about the Federal Statute concerning abductions when I was in law-school. Shall we compare notes while I telephone the authorities to have you arrested?"

Salvator smirked and settled into the chair behind his desk. "I warned you what would happen if you turned the dogs loose on my family."

The lawyer's hands flew apart, and he leveled a long forefinger at Salvator. "I had nothing to do with Dominic's arrest."

The gangster cast a sideways glance at his bodyguards as if checking their reactions. "Like hell, you didn't!"

"You've got bigger worries than trying to pin me for fingering your brother, Salvator. Davis Archer has him cold. Even the worst lawyer in Austin—and I'm including Tipton French—could get a conviction."

Salvator Portello jumped up roaring obscenities. "Can't that numbskull do anything right?"

"I would hardly call Davis Archer a numbskull."

"I'm talking about my brother." Salvator pointed toward the door, his eyes on the Sicilian Brothers. "Out."

"Are you sure, Mr. Portello?" asked Thomaso. "Mr. Elliot is still a bit miffed about bein' here."

"Yeah," Pietro echoed. "Are you sure, Mr. Portello? Mr. Elliot is a bit miffed. We kept him from gettin' his Christmas party copied."

Salvator nodded.

After the Sicilian Brothers left, the Mafia Don came around the desk and settled into the chair next to Elliot's. "All right, maybe I got out of line accusing you. But I'm chasing my tail over this thing. Are you certain they've got an easy conviction?"

Elliot nodded. "The hard evidence links your brother to both killings. If he was framed, there's a chance that DNA science could create questions to make that evidence suspect. Unfortunately, your family is universally despised. So despite all efforts brought to bear, it's likely he'll be convicted."

Salvator slapped his hands on his knees and jumped up cursing.

"I was told that Dominic was trying to force George Pierce into a stock transfer," said Elliot.

The mobster gaped in shock as he looked at Elliot. "How? My idiot brother wouldn't even know where to start. Is that part of what the cops have?"

"Possibly. I couldn't very well bring it up without further compromising your brother's already untenable situation. Have you or he ever had business-dealings with George Pierce?"

"Or course not." The mobster made a vague motion with one hand. "Sure, we know who he is. But there's no need to do business with that guy. He's a straight-arrow."

"Was."

"What do you want from me?" Salvator took his handkerchief out, wiped his neck with it and stuffed the cloth back into his pants. "I know he was a friend of yours, but I had nothing to do with that hit."

"Archer's got witnesses to place your brother at both murder-scenes at the time of each killing."

"That stupid bastard!" croaked Salvator.

"Archer may be a lot of things, but stupid he isn't."

Salvator gave the lawyer a sharp look. "I'm still talking about my idiot brother!"

"Sounds like you don't believe the rumors concerning your family's loyalty, to one another," remarked Elliot.

Salvator Portello began to pace. "Do you know what my brother's cost this family? Do you know? A fortune, that's what! His first job with the family after getting booted out of high school was driving a truck for the liquor-distributor we own. What does Dom do?" His eyes became thoughtful as if not fully comprehending the words he was about to say. "Dom arranges his own hijacking. Smart, huh? His cut was two hundred bucks. My old man and I lost five grand worth of liquor and fifty grand worth of truck. For pocket-change! When Pop asked Dom why he did it, my brother said he wanted to prove that he was more than just a truck-driver. I could've broken both his legs."

"I'll grant you it sounds like Dominic's reasoning was a bit flawed. Nevertheless—"

"So Pop sends him to school to become a chef," continued Salvator, still pacing. "How much trouble can Dom make for us working as a chef?" He prodded his chest with a forefinger. "I'll tell you how much trouble. The brain-dead bozo burned down the entire fucking school, that's how much trouble. When Pop asked him why, Dom said the teacher had not shown him any respect. Respect! Who shows a mental-midget respect?"

"You've got me, there." The lawyer looked down at his hands.

Salvator stopped pacing and returned to the chair next to Elliot. "Just before Pop died, Dom gets religion. He tells the old man that he wants to dedicate his life to God and would the family help him? All he wanted was a little financing for the purchase of some land so he could build a church. Pop agreed." The gangster wrinkled his high forehead as he let go a sarcastic laugh. "After all, how much trouble could Dom get into working for God—in the middle of fucking nowhere? So we bought the land and turned Dom loose with our best wishes and prayers. A year came and went with Dom not saying much. I'd ask. He'd turn vague. I got concerned. This was not like Dom. Finally, I convinced Pop there was something wrong. So Pop and I go out there. Do you know what we found?"

Elliot looked up. "Dare I even ask?"

"I'll tell you what we found." Salvator managed a flat white grin devoid of meaning. "We found a fucking church dedicated to Satan where my idiot brother was pushing dope to the membership! Are you still with me?"

Elliot nodded. "Not that I'm enjoying it."

"After that, I spent nearly half a million setting him up in a furniture store. That was about the time Pop died. Half a million, it cost me." A tight little droop tugged down the corners of his mouth. His nose sniffed. "I had to buy a fucking warehouse for nearly two million to store the shit my brother bought, that nobody could afford to buy! Then..." He breathed hard for a moment before spread his hands helplessly. "Then Dom got the bright idea of raising bees. Ninety-six grand I laid out for fucking bees—from Greece, yet! They had to be from Greece. No others would do, he said. Like clockwork people, started being stung to death— by his fucking bees! Sweet Christ, the man is cursed. Cursed, I tell you."

"I sympathize, Salvator," Elliot said. "But I do have a business to run. Why don't I just take my disc and be on my way?"

The mobster stopped and glared at the lawyer. "This *is* business. Why the fuck do you think I had you brought here? You're going to defend my brother."

"Like hell I am!"

His grin was taut, welded on. "Like hell you aren't."

"I would've taken his case had you approached me directly. But no. You had to drag me down here and coerce my cooperation. Well, it's not going to happen."

"You'll do it or I'll pack you in cement and dump you in the sea!"

"Look Salvator," the lawyer said calmly. "I did you a small favor by pointing out a flaw or two in the prosecutor's reasoning. If I'm right— and I'm overdue for being right—your brother's been framed. But that's the end of it. I'm walking."

"Maybe you got hold of something there," the mobster said, "but I wouldn't milk it."

"I can recommend several excellent litigators. I'll also stick my neck out far enough to tell them who I think is behind this whole thing. But that's it."

Salvator tilted toward him in surprise. "You know who framed Dom?"

Elliot rose stiffly to his feet. "That's my business."

"You tell me or so help me God…"

"Mr. Portello," Elliot said in an even, voice, "you can bluster all you want. But threats will get you nowhere with me. Right now, your brother needs all your help and energies."

"You're going to defend him or you don't fucking leave here alive!"

Elliot shrugged. "Then kill me."

The mobster glared a moment before stalking back behind his desk. "I ordered you hit five times. Five times. And five times I called it off." Absentmindedly, he picked up disc and began rocking it between his hands. "No more calling off. Understand?" Then, as if he was having a religious experience Salvator stared down at the disc, his mouth gaping. "Christmas my ass! You were going to hand this over to the fucking cops!"

"No," said Elliot. "I got that from Davis Archer. If you don't believe me, call him."

"You're dead, Shyster!"

"Never mind that. You can kill me later. Do you have a TV and DVD player anywhere?"

The mobster reached beneath the desk. A moment later, the wall behind him opened and a large, flat panel television slid forward. On a tray beneath it was a DVD player. Salvator turned on the TV and then slid the disc into the player. A moment later a grainy image appeared on the television screen."

"Winston Liquors," Salvator said as he viewed what appeared to be a store's interior.

"This is it," Elliot whispered.

"Michael Douglas." The gangster studied the athletically built blond man behind the cash register.

Elliot moved closer to get a better look at the video.

Seconds later, the blond man grinned and moved from behind the counter as if about to greet an old friend. Then the smile died. A second later a dark-haired youth stepped into view, confronting the blond.

"Dom," murmured Salvator. A faint gleam came into his eyes, then.

Like a light far back in a dusty attic.

Although the video supplied no sound, from the sudden distortion of the youth's face it was clear he was shouting at the blond man. The blond started to say something several times, his eyebrows arched in obvious confusion. But in each instance the youth interrupted with more angry words. Suddenly, the blond man dropped. The youth looked around wildly. Then he squatted out of the scene. Moments later he reappeared. This time, both his hands were no longer empty. One held a small caliber pistol. The youth turned and fled toward the back of the store.

"The bastard did it," groaned Salvator. "Christ almighty, can't I ever get a break?"

"No he didn't do it," said Elliot.

The Mobster looked over at him with a trace of sadness in his eyes. "You saw the gun. Of course he did it."

"I also saw several shiny flecks burst through Michael Douglas' eyelids. Those were particles from the bullet as it shattered. Rewind it. You'll see what I mean."

Salvator lurched over to the DVD player and did as instructed. Then he pushed a button so the video would play in slow motion. Just before Michael Douglas dropped, his eyelids closed.

"You're right," the mobster purred softly, like a tiger after dinner. Then he reached over and pushed a button that stopped the DVD. "Maybe I did the right thing calling off them hits on you."

"I want to see the rest of it," said Elliot.

The mobster jabbed another button and the video resumed. It played the same empty scene for nearly a minute. Then another figure appeared. This one wore a hooded sweatshirt that he kept closed about his face. The figure went over to the cash register, opened it, took out the cash, and then raced out the way he had come in.

Salvator's cheeks flushed in anger. "That thieving bastard."

Not many seconds later a woman hurried in from the rear of the store. She carried a gun that looked exactly like the one Dominic had run away with. She went directly toward the camera, squatted down out of the scene, and then stood. She glanced down, making a disgusted face. Then she hurried out the back of the store. A few seconds later, the video went black.

"But that don't change anything," remarked Salvator. He shut off the television and player. Then he turned to face Elliot. His stare was level and mercuric. "You're going to defend my brother."

The door to Salvator's office burst open and Rita rushed in. When she saw Chambers Elliot she stopped short. Then she strode over and faced her brother.

"I want to talk with him," she told Salvator.

"So talk," he growled.

Her smile was crafty as a flat tire. "In private, Sal."

"What for?"

"In private is for what!"

The Mafia-Don began to say something. Then he looked at Eliot sideways. He studied the lawyer, then closed his eyes in thought. Then he reopened them cautiously and looked back at his sister. But instead of making a remark, his mouth clicked shut like a coffin-lid. A moment later Salvator Portello stormed out, slamming the door on his exit.

Rita turned to Elliot and said, "I want a favor."

"Do I owe you one?" said he, cautiously.

She came over and wrapped her arms around his neck. "I would like to owe you one."

He grinned and pulled her close. "I would like you to owe me one, too. But it's not going to get me behind Dominic's defense."

Rita stared at him a long dreamy minute. "Anything you want, Lawyer," she whispered. "*Anything.*"

"What I want is George Pierce's killer. But from what I was told today, that's your brother."

"It can't be," she said, evenly. Rita uncoiled her arms from his neck, shaking her head. She backed away, thumbing a lock of hair past one ear. "Dom was with me the night George Pierce was killed."

Elliot chuckled mirthlessly. "Your sweet lies to my deaf ears."

"On the life of my child, lawyer... Are you hearing me? On the life of my child, I swear my brother was with me."

Elliot studied her face seeing only truth and fear. "All right. On the life of your child. But your words won't count for much in front of a jury. Not with what the prosecutor has for evidence."

She pointed a finger at Elliot. "You can get him off."

"Rita, I like the way you look. I like the way you act. I love the way you smell. But I won't do this—not for any price. Not after the way your brother dragged me here."

"I'll make whatever Sal said or did right by you. I don't care if I have to be your slave the rest of my life."

He winked at her. "I might be able to forgive and forget. Are we talking sex or labor?"

Her hands brushed at her long dark hair, pulling the tresses away from her face. "You call it."

Chambers Elliot slowly said, "Okay. But I'm going to hold you to that offer."

Her eyes glittered. "It would be a lot more fun if I held something of yours."

"Yes, well…" Then he pointed to the DVD player. "There's something in there of mine. Take it home, look at it and have a good cry."

She glanced over at the machines in confusion.

"I'll need money up front," he declared. "A case like this takes a lot of cash."

"Will fifty thousand get you started?"

He nodded. "But I don't think Salvator will pony-up that much without my liver as security."

"You'll have a check in that amount at your offices before the day is out. Anything else?"

"Yes. I want you to be at each interrogation I have with Dominic. I need his absolute cooperation. I also want Salvator kept abreast of everything including what is discussed during our chats with Dominic. I don't want him to have any concerns about what's been said to me. I also want Salvator to tell Dominic to be open and honest with me—no matter what I ask."

"Done." She came closer. "What else?"

"You keep Salvator off my back—for keeps. That means for forever and a day hereafter."

"Done." She reached him and pressed her breasts against his chest. "What else?"

"That will do."

She smiled slightly, rubbing her body firmly against his. "Are we talking sex or labor for the rest of it?"

"You've met my price." He tugged at his tie.

Rita wrapped her arms about his neck and kissed his lips. Then she backed away from him, smiling like a little girl who had just won a new bicycle. "Not yet, I haven't. But I will."

"Lady, stop scaring me."

Chapter 18

Two days later, Chambers Elliot entered Magistrate Joshua Barton's court and took a seat in the back near the door. He was curious why Davis Archer had assured him that Sheila Clifford's pretrial hearing would be worth attending. Knowing Tipton French as a lazy lout, Elliot felt the hearing would be a twenty-minute travesty.

His eyes scanned the room. Off in one corner he spotted Tipton French and Sheila Clifford. They were huddled together, talking earnestly. French was an angular bug-eyed man with a long, wet face and a Charlie Chan moustache. As Elliot watched, he saw Tipton discretely slip something into her hands. Then he took Sheila by the arm and led her over to the defense table. Chambers Elliot crossed his long legs and got comfortable.

Magistrate Barton entered the courtroom and took his place upon the bench. He was as bald as a melon. His face was broad and careful—one that looked like it had been around the block more than a few times. In his usual decorous manner, Barton surveyed the courtroom.

After giving the bailiff a nod of approval, Barton sternly waited as the uniformed officer stepped forward and called the court to order.

Almost immediately the din of chatter and shuffling feet fell silent.

When satisfied the attention of all present were upon him Barton said, "The Court would like Counsel who are present to introduce themselves, beginning with the Counsel for the prosecution."

Thaddeus Kendall from the prosecutor's table rose to his feet. He was short, redheaded and thickset, dressed in an old gray suit and mismatched socks. He identified himself to the court and then added, "I am an Assistant Prosecutor for Travis County."

Barton gave perfunctory nod and Kendall resumed his seat.

"And Counsel for the defendant?"

Tipton French stood up magnanimously in his expensively tailored seersucker, stuck his thumbs into the pockets of the blue suit's red vest and declared with righteous fervor, "I am Tipton French, and I represent the accused." Then French pointed to Sheila Raintree, grinning, his mouth showing porcelain jackets on his incisors that were too white for his other teeth.

The magistrate smiled mirthlessly. "I remember you." Barton made the admission sound akin to claiming a social disease.

Tipton French slumped back into his seat nervously chewing his moustache.

Barton said, "Then Mr. Kendall, you may begin."

Kendall rose and in a loud voice said, "The State of Texas would call Lt. Herbert Mann."

"Lt. Mann," droned Barton, "you know the routine. Step forward, face the Clerk, raise your right hand and be sworn."

Herbie Mann rose from his seat among the spectators and approached the bench in his wrinkled, salt-and-pepper tweeds. After being sworn-in, he took a seat in the witness chair.

"State your full name and spell your last name," instructed Kendall.

Lt. Mann did so with his usual precision.

Kendall then began his questions of Mann with respect to the Lieutenant's professional experiences. These were followed by more pointed questions regarding George Pierce's murder. The whole time Tipton French chewed his little mustache, wiped his horn-rimmed glasses and squinted nervously at the witness.

"Did you have the primary responsibility in connection with the investigation into George Pierce's death, Lt. Mann?" asked Kendall

Herbie Mann moved his shoulders. "Yes."

"In the course of that investigation, have you spoken with other investigating agents and experts?

"Yes, I have."

"Tell us what happened on June 19, of this year at the Pierce Ranch, in Leander Texas."

"Mr. George Pierce was shot to death," replied Mann. "Then his corpse was hoisted-up by way of a rope affixed to the chandelier in his bedroom."

"Approximately what time did Mr. Pierce's death occur?"

"Approximately 1:00 a.m."

"Have the experts informed you as to the type of weapon?"

"Yes."

"Please describe it to the court."

Herbie took out a small notebook and thumbed past several pages. Then he said, "It was a .32 caliber automatic. The barrel of the gun was held directly against the victim's skull, at the nape of the neck."

"Did these experts tell you the typical outcome of such a weapon's firing into that location?"

The tip of Mann's tongue moistened his lips. "Yes."

"Please describe that to the Court."

"The spinal column would be completely severed, causing instant death. The projectile would lodged itself in the decedent's brain."

"But that isn't exactly what happened, is it?"

"Objection!" shouted French. "Leading the witness."

"Sustained," said Barton. "Rephrase, please."

"Is that what happened?" Kendall looked at French sharply.

"No," said Lt. Mann. "The bullet disintegrated as it went through the skull into the brain."

"Disintegrated? Is that usual?"

"Decidedly not. The projectile, we later discovered, was made of a zinc-lead alloy rather than pure lead, which is the norm."

"Were these pieces of bullet recovered?"

Mann nodded. "But the bullet is in such disarray that rebuilding it will take time."

"Did you make a search for the gun that fired that round?"

"Yes."

"Have you located the weapon?"

"Yes we did—in the apartment Dominic Portello," said Mann. "We found it in his wall-safe."

"Do you recognize Prosecutor's Exhibit 1?" asked Kendall, pointing to the exhibits table.

"Yes, I do," said Mann.

"What is Prosecutor's Exhibit 1?"

"A .32 caliber, Browning automatic pistol."

"If the bullet shattered, how did you match it to that gun?"

"One piece of the round was large enough to give us a match on the gun-barrel rifling."

"Has an effort been made to trace the weapon's owner?"

"Yes."

Kendall offered Tipton French a smirk before asking, "Has the owner been located?"

"In a sense."

"What do you mean by that?"

"The owner is Michael Douglas," explained Mann. "He was murdered thirty years ago."

"Do you know where the gun has been since that time?"

"Presumably with Dominic Portello."

"Did Mr. Portello admit that?"

Herbie Mann wagged his head. "But I viewed a video of Michael Douglas' murder in which Dominic Portello left the murder-scene carrying a weapon exactly like it."

"Your Honor," said Kendall, "the Prosecution moves Exhibit 1 into evidence."

"Any objection?" Barton gave Tipton French an impatient glance.

"No objection."

"Is your investigation into George Pierce's death, continuing?" asked Kendall

"Yes," replied Lt. Mann.

"Explain to us what that means?"

"There are a number of leads that have been—are being—investigated."

"So despite your belief that the defendant is responsible for the murder, you are continuing to gather and evaluate evidence?"

"Yes. We believe she acted in consort with Mr. Portello."

"Has Mr. Portello been arrested?" Kendall asked.

"Yes. He is currently being held without bond in Travis County Jail."

"Has he implicated the defendant in George Pierce's murder?"

"Not yet. But we know from several sources that Mr. Portello and the defendant have long been acquainted."

"How is the information gathered from these leads recorded?" Kendall asked.

"The resulting data is entered into a computer."

"Now, is this material all logged by you into that computer, then?"

"I enter portions of it," Mann explained.

"Objection, Your Honor," said Tipton. "This goes well beyond the scope of a probable-cause hearing."

"Overruled," said Barton, with a sneer of disgust. Then he looked over at Mann and said, "You may answer the question, Lieutenant."

French chewed his lower lip, pulled it out with a manicured forefinger and thumb and then nibbled on the inside of it, like he was testing its potential for supper.

The courtroom door opened and Jason Taggart leaned in far enough to look around. Chambers Elliot noticed him, quickly rose from his seat and followed Jason Taggart out into the hallway.

"How is it going?" asked Taggart

"Surprisingly well considering Tipton's usual inexperience and that Herbie Mann is the first witness," replied Elliot, dryly.

Taggart frowned. "Tipton French has been practicing law longer than you."

Chambers Elliot rolled his eyes impatiently. "I meant his lack of success at trial, Jason. What's going on?"

"I have confirmation that Milton Raintree was abducted by the Sicilian Brothers. My informant, Willie Freeborn, saw it go down. Mazy Wilson got away by jumping into the back of a passing garbage truck."

"Have you taken Freeborn to Archer so he can make a statement?"

"Chambers, the man's a snitch not an idiot. No way is he going to point fingers at the Portello mob. He called my office to let me know because he knew I was looking for Raintree."

"What if I bribed him?"

Taggart smiled in a vague manner. "You don't have that kind of money—at least you won't after you get my next bill."

"I guess things could be worse."

"Things are," said Taggart, casually. "Kathy Martin made bail and promptly disappeared – presumably into Salvator Portello's clutches. But that's just…"

Chambers Elliot cut him short with a gesture. "I told that woman… Who in hell bailed her out?"

"Tipton French." The detective offered a homely lopsided grin. "Which means you've been fired in favor of him, twice. Now would be another good time to call it quits. You'll never see Milton Raintree, again —nobody will. As for George's killer it's pretty clear that Dominic Portello did it. He'll be convicted of it, anyway."

The lawyer dragged his palms across his face with a dismal groan. "You're not helping my confidence, Jason," muttered Elliot.

Taggart's eyes narrowed a little. "I'm trying to make you see sense."

"The problem is, I've agreed to defend Dominic Portello. Which means, I'm in this for the duration."

The detective's eyes bugged. "Have you lost your mind?"

"I asked myself that same question, this morning," said the lawyer, gloomily. "Where do we stand with Sydney Pierce?"

"He's been home-bound since leaving you at Sheila's apartment. We did notice that the live-in help at the ranch have moved out—including Armistice. Von Drake cornered the cook and was told that Sydney had fired the whole bunch."

"Did you speak with Armistice about the gunshots?"

"Yes," said Taggart. "He claims he cannot be certain of anything. Apparently, he had a glass of sherry at the behest of Sydney Pierce in celebration of Sydney's reelection to the Los Gatos Car Club presidency. The small tipple caused Armistice to become completely confused, making the entire night's events a mix-mash in his recollections."

"One drink?"

"Normally, he does not imbibe. He remembers clearly hearing the shots. But he's confused as to when they occurred and where he was when he heard them." Taggart was silent for a moment, staring at the lawyer without expression. "He thinks he was both upstairs in Sydney's room and downstairs in the foyer. Obviously he couldn't be in two places at once. He does recall going to George's room and finding George's body. But that, too, is confusing. He thinks he was in George's room twice."

"Twice?"

"Both times George is dead. But in one recollection there was another man, there."

The lawyer's eyebrows arched with interest. "Did he recognize the man?"

"All he can recall is the guy was tall, dark haired and climbing out the bedroom window."

"Dominic Portello," Elliot muttered grimly.

"Exactly my thought."

The lawyer's mouth pinched shut. Then he said, "It almost sounds like the Sherry was laced with some sort of hallucinogenic."

"Or Armistice had a stroke. I questioned him about his medical history. He's had two strokes, neither of which were physically disabling. But he lost his ability to speak for several months after one of them. And in both instances, his memories became confused and unreliable."

"Did you let Herbie know what Armistice disclosed?"

"Yes," said the detective. His tongue pushed out his lower lip. "But with Dominic Portello all but convicted, I don't think he's going to retake Armistice's statement."

"Have you searched the Pierce ranch, yet?"

"Von Drake and I are on our way out there now. Look, Chambers, taking on Dominic Portello's defense is professional suicide. Possibly in the literal sense, as well. Salvator will kill you if you don't get his brother off."

Elliot reached out and patted the detective's arm. "Don't worry. I'll pay your fees before going six feet under. Now, get going."

As Taggart hurried off, Elliot took out his cell-phone and dialed his office. When Maggie answered he asked her to get him Salvator Portello's home phone number. When she did so, he noticed the emotion in her voice.

"Is there something wrong, Maggie?" the lawyer asked.

"It's Ramón, Sir," she said with a small sob. "He's been reduced."

"Dear God!" The lawyer's knees hit together as his imagination ran rampant. "Does that mean the Peterson's turned him loose after cutting off Ramón's... You'd better put Lydia on the line, Maggie. I can't talk to you when you're crying, like this."

A few seconds later, he heard Lydia Marshall's impatient voice. "I'm at the critical stage in my negotiations with the Peterson's, Chambers. I'm expecting Lionel Peterson, head of the Peterson clan, to call me back any second."

"What negotiations? I told you to leave it to the police."

"The police are not doing anything. Magistrate Whitaker told them that Ramón had not been kidnapped, that it was just another attempt by Ramón to draw attention."

"You did explain the Whitaker that his son might be—reduced?"

"Of course, I did. He said it would be a blessing for all concerned and hung up on me."

"There is nothing like the love of a doting father."

"Chambers, I've got to go. I've been going back and forth on the phone all morning with Peterson. I've nearly got him on his knees. I just have to find a mongoose."

"A mongoose? I thought he wanted half a million and…"

"I countered with fifteen hundred and a cat. The money was acceptable. But they're up to their eyeballs in cats."

"What kind of idiot goes from half a million down to fifteen hundred? Never mind. Lydia, Ramón Whitaker is not our problem."

"Somebody has to look out for him."

"Now, listen to me. I want you to call the F.B.I. Tell them what's going on with Ramón. After that…"

"I already called. But once the feds spoke with Magistrate Whitaker, they backed out. So it's either me, or Ramón loses his—his personality."

"Lydia, I'm ordering you to forget his personally and—"

"Hang on a second. Who, Maggie? I've got to go, Chambers. Lionel Peterson is on the other line."

"Wait! Did Rita Portello's check clear?"

"Yes. Now, I have to go."

"Forget Ramón! I want you to arrange a two-hour interview with Dominic Portello at Travis County Jail for tomorrow morning. Lydia? Lydia!"

After ringing off, Elliot reentered the courtroom. Sheila Raintree glanced back, at him. She sat passively, lips gleaming wetly, a tiny flame of mockery in her eyes. A stocky uniformed police officer was on the stand.

"Officer Ingles, do you know the defendant, Sheila Clifford?" asked Kendall.

The cop looked over at Sheila. She stared down at the table in tight-lipped rigidity, avoiding the officer's gaze.

"I arrested her for soliciting, last June," said Ingles.

Kendall said, "That's the first time you saw her?"

"Yes. It was her first offense. So she was released after paying a fine."

"She paid the fine? Or did someone else?"

"Mazy Wilson, her pimp, paid the fine."

"Did you see the defendant another time in the course of your duties?" asked Kendall.

"Not as such. I was off-duty the next time. I spotted her having a conversation with Mazy Wilson."

"You know Mazy Wilson by sight?"

"Of course. I've arrested him several times."

"Did you hear what was being said?" said Kendall.

"Some of it. They were arguing. Mazy told her to cough up some dough. She…"

"Objection," Tipton snapped. "Hearsay."

"Exception," Kendall countered. "Mazy Wilson is in the courtroom and can attest to the accuracy of Officer Ingles' statements." Kendall, turned toward the courtroom and shouted, "Mazy Wilson, please stand up!"

Mazy, his nose and cheeks completely concealed by smears of gauze and strips of adhesive tape, struggled to his feet. "I'm Mazy Wilson."

"Objection overruled," Magistrate Barton declared.

"That's all, Mr. Wilson, you may sit down" Kendall said, and turned his attention back to Ingles. "What was said?"

Ingles pointed to where Mazy sat. "He told her to cough up some dough. She refused. He took a swing at her, but missed. She took off running. He started to follow, spotted me and took off in the opposite direction."

"Did you observe or have any interaction with the defendant at any other time?" asked Kendall.

"No," replied Ingles.

"Nothing further your honor," Kendall informed the court.

Tipton made a dismissive wave of one hand and said, "No questions."

"Mazy Wilson, will you take the stand?" Kendall called.

The battered man stood up, hobbled forward and was sworn. Then he slumped into the witness chair, visibly in pain.

"Do you know Officer Herbert Ingles, the witness who just testified?"

Mazy nodded, glumly. "I know him."

"Did he give a fair and accurate accounting of the events he described?"

"Fair enough," replied Mazy. "The little bitch was holding out on me, see?"

"When you say holding out, what do you mean?" said Kendall.

"She was working for me," Mazy replied, with a lift of one eyebrow.

"You were Sheila Clifford's pimp?"

Mazy gripped the arms of the witness chair so hard that his knuckles stood out like rows of ivory buttons. "I was her manager."

There was stifled laughter throughout the courtroom. Magistrate Barton impatiently banged his gavel to suppress it.

"How long had she worked for you?" Kendall asked.

"A few weeks," replied Wilson.

"How much money did she owe you?"

Tipton said, "I object, your Honor, relevancy. The question is incompetent, irrelevant and immaterial."

Magistrate Joshua Barton said, "Sustained."

"Did Sheila Clifford ever discuss the murder of George Pierce with you?" asked Kendall, frowning at Mazy.

"Not as such," replied Mazy.

"Meaning?"

Mazy spoke without the slightest tremor, much as though he were discussing something that did not touch him at all. "She thought a muscle-job was needed to force Pierce to sign a phony will."

Elliot noticed Sheila lean toward French and speak rapidly, clearly denying the truth in Wilson's statement.

"You agreed to this?"

"Of course not. That's when she said if I wouldn't do it, she'd get Dominic Portello to do it."

"Who killed George Pierce?" asked Kendall.

Mazy pointed at Sheila Clifford. "Who else? Her and Dominic Portello." He then pointed at Tipton French. "He was in on it, too."

"Objection," Tipton said. "Move to strike."

"Overruled," responded Magistrate Joshua Barton.

"Mr. Wilson, are you acquainted with Mr. Tipton French, the attorney representing the defendant?" asked Kendall

Mazy nodded. "Yeah, I know him. He's as crooked as they come."

Tipton's eyes got round and scared. "Objection! Irrelevant."

"If the court will allow me some leniency," said Kendall, "I will establish relevancy."

"Not at this hearing, Mr. Kendall. Objection is sustained," said the magistrate.

"Mr. Wilson, did Dominic Portello approach you concerning the murder of George Pierce?" asked Kendall.

"Thirty grand was the offer to me if I was to do it," replied Mazy.

"What prompted that offer?"

"Portello said he was tired of working on Pierce to give over the stock transfers."

"What stock transfers?"

"The stock transfers Dominic Portello was trying to shake outa' him."

"Did Mr. Portello ever mention the defendant?"

Wilson pointed to Sheila Clifford. "Him and her was at it hot as minks—even after she married Raintree."

"Let the record show the witness is pointing to the defendant," Kendall said.

"Objection!" Tipton shouted.

"Overruled," Barton declared.

"Did Milton Raintree ever suggest killing Mr. Pierce?"

Mazy shook his head. "And kill the golden goose? Not a chance." He, again, pointed at Sheila Clifford. "It was Portello and her. She wasn't satisfied with half the money when Pierce died and she wasn't gonna wait on that. She wanted all the money and she wanted it now. That's why she and Dominic Portello come up with the idea of the stock transfers. Pierce would sign over everything, and her and Portello would have it all right away."

"Objection!" cried Tipton French.

"Sustained," declared Barton. "Witness will refrain from rendering opinions."

Kendall paused a moment as if to formulate a question then he said to Wilson, "You look like you've been in a terrible fight."

"Me and Raintree was jumped by a couple of Dominic Portello's goons. I got away. Raintree didn't."

"In fact, you were so frightened by the incident you requested protection from the police?"

"Damn right, I did. I wanted to make damn sure I was still alive to be here to testify—against Dominic Portello and her!"

Kendall indicated Tipton with one hand. "Isn't it true that he was instructed by Dominic Portello to relay Mr. Portello's orders so that you and Mr. Raintree would be abducted?"

"You're damn right, he was," grinned Mazy. "When I took a swing at one of them goons, I grabbed the guy by the pocket on his jacket. It tore. And what fell out? That bastard's business card."

Tipton leaped to his feet roaring, "Your Honor, I object to this attempt at slandering my reputation as incompetent, immaterial and irrelevant!"

Magistrate Barton grimaced suspiciously at Tipton a moment before sustaining the objection. "Personally, I beg to differ but the rules of evidence will apply. Sustained."

Kendall tossed Tipton a sneering glance. Then he asked Mazy, "Explain what you and Milton were doing when the attack took place."

"Objection," yelled French. "Relevancy."

"If the court will allow me some leeway," said Kendall, "I will link the question to this case."

"Overruled," said Barton. "Answer the question, Mr. Wilson."

"Me and Milton Raintree was talkin' out a problem—business, you know," said Wilson. "He was tellin' me how Sheila had been pushin' him to get George Pierce out of the way and how he wanted no part in it."

"Objection!" cried French. "Hearsay."

"I'm going to let the question be answered," said Barton. "Please proceed, Mr. Wilson."

"We was on the sidewalk outside a bar called, 'Joneses'," continued Wilson. "Raintree started tellin' me how she had brought in Dominic Portello to snuff Pierce and how he was worried he'd be blamed. Suddenly them two goons jumped out of a car. They tried to put the grab on us. I threw a punch. But them guys knocked me seven ways from Sunday. Raintree put up a fight, too. That's when one of the pair who were goin' at me went to help his pals. That's when I decked the goon I was dealin' with and made a run for it. I hopped into a garbage truck that was rollin' past, and got away." Then Mazy shook an accusing finger at Tipton. "That bastard is nothing but a Portello shyster!"

"Objection!" Tipton screamed. "Move to strike."

"Sustained," Barton grunted. "The last eight words of Mr. Wilson's testimony will be stricken from the record. Mr. Wilson you will respond to questions and only to questions."

"Did you go to the police after the incident?" Kendall asked.

"Damn right I did," Mazy Wilson said. Then he tilted toward Tipton grinning. "I been there tellin' all I know about everything."

"Have you had contact with Milton Raintree since that terrible occurrence?" Kendall asked.

Mazy wagged his head. "Raintree's toast. You can bet your ass he won't be seen around here, ever again."

Tipton recoiled as though Mazy had clacked false teeth in his face. Sheila's hands went to her face in horror.

"That's right, bitch!" Mazy shouted from the witness chair. "No hubby comin' home with sausage for you!"

"No more questions," Kendall said.

"No questions," muttered Tipton, suddenly timid.

Then Kendall approached the bench. "Your honor, the prosecution rests. We feel we have established a *prima-facea* case of murder against the defendant."

Barton nodded and then looked over at Tipton. "Mr. Tipton, do you wish to offer a defense at this time?"

Tipton French dismally wagged his head. "No, your honor."

"The defendant will be bound over for trial the date to be set forthwith."

Kendall said, "Your Honor, a warrant for the arrest of Tipton French has been issued. Considering this, I feel it is in the best interests of the defendant to delay setting a trial date until the defendant can seek legal advice from another attorney."

"On what basis am I to be charged?" shrieked Tipton.

"So ordered, Mr. Kendall," said Barton. "We will reconvene at a future date yet to be determined at which time the issue of a pretrial defense and a trial date will be addressed. Bailiff, take the defendant into custody."

As Barton banged his gavel, the courtroom doors swung open and two burly police officers rushed in. They handcuffed Tipton, read him his rights and then dragged him out of the courtroom. Sheila gave a long bewildered stare after him.

Chambers Elliot got to his feet and followed the officers dragging Tipton; the moustache-chewing attorney was literally foaming at the mouth with protestations.

"For years I've tried to get a witness to testify against the Portello mob, and nothing."

Elliot turned to see Lt. Herbie Mann staring after Tipton French.

"Now," continued Mann, "I got one who not only fingers Dominic Portello on a killing but links the mob to one of our local attorneys. Interesting, huh?"

"How long do you think Mazy Wilson has to live?" Elliot asked.

"I'd be surprised if he survived the night."

"I thought you guys were protecting him."

Herbie Mann took a baggie full of carrots from his coat-pocket. "Which is why I'll be surprised." Herbie withdrew a carrot from the bag and pointed with it to the Sicilian Brothers, who were standing a few yards away. "Something for you to think about—seeing as you're defending Dominic Portello."

* * * *

Lydia greeted Elliot's return to the office with, "Kathy Martin called.

She says to tell you, you're fired."

"Apparently my trustworthiness is extending," said Chambers Elliot. "What happened?"

"Did you arrange the interview?"

"Of course. Oh, Rita Portello called. She wanted to know if you'd thought of anything else she might provide. She said she was trying on something slinky, black, and lacy. Is there something going on between you and her?"

"Call her back," said Elliot. "Tell her to be at the jail on time tomorrow."

"Well, are you and she an item?"

"Of course not."

"Do you think Tipton French will face trial?"

"Of course not. Wilson's testimony against Dominic Portello means he's either got to leave the country, or commit suicide—before the Portellos kill him. Either way, the charges against French will be dropped."

"Meaning French is being framed?"

Elliot nodded. "Why I don't know."

"Why would Mazy Wilson put his own head in the noose by implicating Dominic Portello?"

"For a great deal of money, I suspect. Get Jason on the line. Tell him I want to speak to that snitch who allegedly witnessed the abduction. The guy's name is Willie Freeborn."

She nodded. "Is Sheila in on Tipton French's frame?"

"I don't think so. From the look on her face when Tipton French was arrested, she was completely surprised. Speaking of surprises, I want you to promise me that you are done with the Peterson's and Ramón Whitaker."

"I was able to negotiate his release," Lydia proclaimed.

"How?"

She giggled. "We settled for fifty bucks."

He gave her a disbelieving look. "From half a million down to fifty?"

"Lionel said he'd be willing to pay more. But Helene's getting married and the reception is busting his budget."

"Ramón agreed to marry her?"

"No, she's marrying a member of another gypsy clan, who, apparently, is the father of her baby—not Ramón."

The lawyer grimaced. "When is Ramón due back?"

"Not until after Helene's wedding. He's the best man."

"The best man?"

"Leonard Peterson thinks that's the safest way."

"I don't understand."

"He wants to be sure that she's married before he lets Ramón out of his sight. Just in case Helene begins to backpedal. I'll tell Jason where to make the pickup as soon as I know it."

"Jason?"

"Jason suggested he'd be a better choice to meet Ramón than you. Something about a recurring dream you keep having."

The phone rang and Lydia grabbed the receiver. After a few seconds she set it down, her face white. "That was Lt. Mann. Sheila Clifford was just found dead in her cell. Suicide."

"That's impossible."

"Poison is suspected. An autopsy is scheduled for tomorrow."

"I saw Tipton give her something in court. But I couldn't see what it was. Perhaps I've been underestimating him?"

"Why would Tipton French kill her?" asked Lydia

"Call Herbie back and let him know. It may be nothing. But I want Herbie informed."

"But why would Tipton French want to kill his client?"

"He may not have realized what he passed to her was poison," said Elliot. "I expect Tipton will explain how someone had instructed him to pass it on something to her."

"But if Milton Raintree is dead..."

"Milton Raintree is not dead. Of that I am certain."

Chapter 19

Chambers Elliot paced the length of the interrogation room and back at Travis County Jail as Dominic Portello spoke with ringing fury.

Rita Portello sat across from her brother at a small, rectangular table; her hands folded upon its top, her chin dipped in frustration.

"I keep tellin' ya, Archer's got nothin'!" Dominic proclaimed, his voice bouncing from the walls like hammer-blows on steel. "He's blowin' smoke up your ass, Shyster. So I don't say shit!"

"Then you're a dead man, Portello." Elliot glanced scornfully at the gangster.

The gangster's basalt eyes were bullets. "Says you!"

"You don't get it do you, Dominic?" the lawyer demanded. "There's no bulling your way out of this. And with your *sterling* reputation, any jury seated will jump at the chance to send you to death-row."

Angry red spots touched the gangster cheeks. "I got nothin' to say!"

Rita's eyes went hot as she glared across the table at her brother. "Stop being stupid, Dom. Mr. Elliot is the only chance you've got."

Elliot stopped and looked down at Dominic, his attitude softening slightly. "Do you cooperate and honestly answer my questions, or do I get Salvator in here to offer you incentives?"

Dominic Portello squirmed in his chair as if his backside was being heated by an iron. "I can't make a fuckin' turn without shit flyin' my way," he grumbled, with a sullen shrug.

"Then do yourself a favor, Dom," Rita chimed, "play it smart for a change. Tell the man what he wants to know."

"And what if he goes to the cops?" Dominic demanded.

"How many times do I have to tell you?" his sister screamed. "He can't! You're his client. He can't tell anybody anything."

"I don't trust him," the gangster growled.

"Tell him anyway!"

Chambers Elliot stretched his arms and then went to the wall on the left side of the table, and leaned back against it. "Call Salvator, Rita. Tell him he comes down here and makes your pet-idiot talk, or I walk. Tell him if I walk, I won't be back."

She jumped to her feet, glaring at her brother. "Is that what you want, Dom? Sal here? Haven't you got enough trouble?"

Dominic Portello dipped his eyes away from hers and a faint humming tremor went through him. He sat for a while with his head down. Then he looked up at her. "How do I know this room ain't bugged?"

"For the hundredth time, it's not bugged!" she shouted.

"It's do-or-die, Dominic," Elliot chided.

The gangster's face darkened. "All right. "I'll do it your way, Rita." Then he looked at Elliot stonily. "But I still don't like it."

She slumped back into her chair, cursing softly.

"Let's start again." Elliot's voice once more became even. "The night Michael Douglas was shot, you where at Winston Liquor Store. Who else was in the place besides Michael?"

Dominic Portello considered the question. "I didn't see nobody." The mobster's eyes remained full of suspicion.

"You're certain?" pressed Elliot.

The gangster shrugged. "No, I ain't sure. But I didn't see nobody." Then he gave his sister a pleading look. "How come I can't get outa' here? Didn't you tell Sal to fix it?"

"There's no fixing it this time, Dom. You have to do this Mr. Elliot's way." Her voice betrayed the pity and love she felt for her brother.

"What happened that night, Dominic?" The lawyer left the wall and came over to the table.

The gangster thought and then shrugged. "I was giving Mike what-for about Rita," explained Dominic. "I know different, now. But then… Well, I figured somethin' was wrong, that's what. So I was givin' him what-for."

She jumped up screaming, "Because of you that poor man went to his grave thinking I'd shamed him!"

"I'm sorry, Rita." Her brother spread his hands in beseechment. "I did what I thought was right."

Rita sat down, wiping tears from her face and sniffing.

"Was Douglas talking to you when he dropped to the floor?" asked Elliot.

"Nope. He was lookin' at me like I was crazy. Then he just dropped. Thump. Right down on the floor. I thought, maybe I'd given him a heart attack, or something. So I crouched down and gave him a shake. But he didn't groan or nothin'. That's when I saw blood coming from his head. I figured if he was dead I was in deep shit with Pop. I'd have to explain why and how and everything else. So I lifted Mike's head to take a look at what happened. That's when I saw blood dribbling from a small hole."

"You knew it was a bullet-hole?" asked the lawyer.

Dominic nodded. "I knew it, all right. Fat Tony, one of Pop's bodyguards, took me on some business. Things got tough and Tony had to cap a guy. He showed me all about it." He shrugged loosely. "That's why I figured maybe somebody's trying to take me out. So I grabbed the

Mike's gun from his shoulder-holster. I jerked out the clip to make sure it was loaded. It was full. So I slammed the clip back into the automatic. Then I made a break for the back exit."

"You didn't hear a shot while you were talking to Michael Douglas?"

The gangster's head wagged. "Not a peep. Mike just dropped."

"Why didn't you call the police?" asked Elliot.

"I don't call no cops, ever," Dominic bellowed. "I had my jalopy out back. I was gonna' get the hell out of there and tell Pop."

"Taking the gun with you?" pressed Elliot.

The gangster made a defeated gesture. "If somebody's gunnin' for you, you don't go nowhere without no gun."

"Okay," said Elliot. "Then what happened?"

Dominic gave Rita an embarrassed look. "Does *she* have to be here?"

"Dammit to hell..." Elliot checked the harsh outcry. "What happened?"

"I, uh, saw somebody," stammered the gangster.

"Who Dom?" Rita demanded, impatiently. "He has to know who."

Her brother leaned back in the chair looking ashamed. "I don't want to say, in front of Rita."

"You'll say or so help me God I'll call Sal!" she warned.

Elliot watched the gangster collect himself.

"Barbara," Dominic finally muttered.

"Barbara, who?" she shouted. "For God's sake, there must be a thousand Barbaras in Texas!"

Black grief seemed to envelope the gangster, under his sister's gaze. "Barbara Pierce," Dominic murmured.

Chambers Elliot looked down at the gangster. "How is it you knew Barbara?"

The gangster shrugged.

"Tell him!" Rita shouted.

The gangster looked away from his sister for a long moment before he turned his head toward Chambers Elliot. "I, uh, you know.... Her and me...."

Rita rolled her eyes. "And you were worried about what I might be doing with Michael? Hah! While you were screwing some guy's wife you're thinking I'm dirt because I wanted to hold Michael's hand?"

"You were having an affair with Barbara?" Chambers Elliot asked, in disbelief.

Dominic Portello made a pleading motion with his arms. "She... We..." His dark eyes glanced over at Rita, ashamedly. "I liked her, okay?"

"Sweet Jesus, Dom!" Rita snapped. "You were sixteen. Haven't you ever kept your damn zipper closed?"

Elliot turned one of the chairs around, and sat down, straddling it. "You left Winston Liquors with Barb?"

"No," said Dominic. "She could see I was scared. She could see the gun. So she asked. I told her about Mike."

"Before or after you got it off with her?"

"Rita, you're not helping," Elliot scolded.

Angry dark eyes glared out at him from under her fluffed out black hair. "You told me to be here." One of her hands thumped her chest. "I'm here. This is what you get when I'm here."

Elliot shifted his eyes back to Dominic. "What happened?"

"Barbara accused me of whacking Mike," said the gangster, gloomily. "I couldn't make her believe. I tried. I swear to God, I tried. But she wouldn't. So I gave her the gun. I told her if she really thought I'd done it, to kill me. She took aim. I thought she was going to do it, sure. But she suddenly ran past me into the liquor store.

"I jumped into my heap, and burned rubber outa' there."

Chambers Elliot lowered his voice to a soft intensity. "Did you speak with Barbara after that?"

Dominic wagged his head.

"So the gun she carried into the store was the one you took from Michael Douglas?" pressed Elliot.

He nodded.

Chambers Elliot stood up and looked over at Rita. "I blew it."

"What do you mean?" Rita asked, her voice taut with concern. "I pay you fifty grand and you're giving up?"

"I meant, I've had it all wrong," the lawyer said, almost under his breath. "In all three killings I was certain there was only one shooter."

"I don't understand," said Rita. "One shooter? Two shooters? What are you talking about?"

"Michael Douglas was shot twice," Elliot said, making his tone emphatic. "The second time was with the Michael's pistol."

"Who shoots a dead man?" Rita demanded, in disbelief.

Elliot looked over at her. "Did you look at the DVD?"

She looked away, wiping tears from her cheeks. "Yes, damn you for it. I cried all night."

"Then you remember the video showed Barbara coming into the store carrying a gun. She was wearing gloves. She squatted down. When I saw that I assumed she was checking for a pulse. But when she stood up and left, she was no longer carrying the gun."

Rita glared over at her brother. "You lied to me? You shot him and she covered up for you?"

"I didn't do it, Rita!" Dominic bleated.

"But there would've been two bullets in Mike," Rita said, abruptly.

"Two shattered bullets," said Elliot, his brows furrowed in thought. "The first breaking apart as it went through the skull going in. The second shattered after it went through the brain and hit the interior of the skull. But there was only one bullet hole. When the coroner did not find a complete bullet, just pieces, he thought there was only one round. In the video, some of the pieces from the first round went out Michael's eyes. That's how I knew Dominic had not done it. What remained of the two rounds probably weighed up equivalent to one, misleading the coroner."

"Who in hell were these shooters?" Rita demanded.

"I don't know who shot Michael Douglas when he was being addressed by your brother," replied the lawyer, "but Barbara Pierce fired the second shot."

"But why would Barbara do it? The man was dead, for God's sake," Rita said, her voice rising in frustration. "She must've realized it."

The lawyer looked over at her and smiled slightly. "To blame Dominic. That's why she left the gun behind. The police would find it and assume it was the murder weapon."

"But Dom wasn't arrested," said Rita.

"Because someone took the gun away after Barb left it," said Elliot.

"Who?" she persisted.

"Someone trying to protect her," the lawyer replied. "Or blackmail her. Someone who was there and saw the whole series of events."

"The Petersons?"

"Maybe. Regardless, I'm convinced she knew who had been the first shooter. Her effort to blame Dominic was to protect that other person."

"So you got me off the hook, huh?" asked Dominic, grinning like a Cheshire cat at the lawyer.

"Not by any means," said Elliot. Then he asked, "Where's Milton Raintree?"

"Sal put a contract on him," the gangster replied casually.

"My suspicion is that Raintree is alive," the lawyer pressed. "Is that true?"

The gangster hesitated. "Alive, I guess. Sal ain't said nothin' 'bout bustin' Raintree."

"Would he?" asked Elliot.

Dominic Portello grinned. "You bet. He's gonna' spend a week dippin' Raintree."

"What's Raintree to do with anything?" Rita demanded.

"Milton Raintree is the key to everything." Elliot stretched uncomfortably. "Rita, call Salvator."

"I've been talkin'!" squealed the gangster, in terror.

"Tell Salvator that Dominic's life depends on Milton Raintree remaining alive and my being able to speak with Raintree. Make sure he understands that."

Rita stood up and then hesitated. "What if it's too late?"

"I don't think it is." Elliot leaned back rubbing his face with his hands. "In fact, I'm all but certain it isn't. But tell you brother I *must* speak with Raintree."

She hurried to the door of the interrogation room, and knocked. A uniformed police officer opened the door, and let her out.

"That's it?" asked Dominic, affably.

Chambers Elliot shook his head. "You and Sydney Pierce used to be friends."

Dominic's gloom returned. "In school. So what?"

"What ended that friendship?"

The gangster tossed a shameful glance toward the door, as if to make certain his sister was out of earshot. "Sid found out about me, and Barb."

"Did Sydney know about you and Barbara before Michael Douglas was killed?"

"Yeah. It really broke him up. He said I'd crossed him." Dominic gave a rueful shrug. "Maybe I did. But at that age when a guy gets offered… Well, you know."

Chambers Elliot let go long sigh. "Let's talk about the DVD."

The gangster's eyes dropped to the table. "What DVD?"

"Don't start playing games again. I know you received a DVD in the mail."

The gangster looked reproachful. "You're like the fuckin' C-I-Eight. You got spies everywhere."

"It's C-I-A, you simple-minded…" The lawyer regained his composure. "Did anything come in the mail with the DVD?"

"A note. It said I was to lay my hands on five mill to keep the lid on." Dominic splayed his hands.

"Was the note signed?"

"Nope," said the mobster. "But Sal knows who's behind it. Raintree."

"The DVD video doesn't show Michael Douglas on the floor."

"That's 'cause the angle was too high on the camera," said Dominic authoritatively.

"Yes, I know. My point is, did anything else take place that the DVD didn't show, other than what you've told me? For example, did you see a car drive into the parking lot while you and Mike were talking?"

Dominic Portello considered the question for some time. Then he shook his head.

"Did you speak with Sydney about what happened at Winston Liquors?" asked Elliot.

Dominic Portello made a face. "What was to tell? He was there."

Elliot gaped. "There? But I just asked you…"

The gangster shifted in his chair as he interrupted, "That was him in the hooded sweatshirt on the DVD."

"How can you be certain? The face was concealed by the hood."

"His hand.' Dominic raised his left hand and pointed at the back of the thumb with his right hand. "I saw the scar. He got that when we was just kids. He stuck his hand down gopher hole and the gopher bit him. It was Sydney, all right. It was him what copped the cash. Sal's gonna' be real sore about that."

Chambers Elliot suddenly smiled, as if having a revelation. "Okay. Let's get back to Milton Raintree. My understanding is, he worked for your family. Is that correct?"

Dominic nodded. "He was one of our runners."

"Numbers?"

"Yeah. He picked up the bets from the bookies. Then he delivered 'em to Sal." Dominic speared the air between he and Chambers Elliot with a forefinger as he said, "Only the last time he picked up the bets and just kept runnin'." The gangster winced a little. "Cost Sal over fifteen grand. My brother was not happy with me about that."

"Has he ever been happy with you about anything?"

Dominic paused a moment to think. Then he shook his head.

"Why did Raintree skipping out mean trouble for you?" asked Elliot.

"I got Raintree the job," the gangster replied.

"Was Milton with one of the local gangs?"

"No," said Dominic. "He worked for the Pierce's. Ranch manager. That's what she called him."

"She?"

"Barbara Pierce. She asked if I'd help get Raintree a job."

"Not five minutes ago you told me you had not spoken with her after the Winston Liquors incident."

"I didn't speak with her. This was a note from her."

Elliot went stood up groaning, "Sweet Jesus grant me patience."

"Anyway," continued Dominic, "I told Pop about Raintree and after some talk he agreed to give Raintree a chance. Sal was dead against it."

"Did you ever meet George Pierce?"

"Me?" the gangster asked, touching his chest with a finger. "Hell, no. I knew who he was. But we never talked. I wasn't about to get cornered by him in case he knew about me and Barbara."

"So shortly before George was murdered you didn't attempt to force George into a stock transfer?"

The gangster's eyes went as blank as white porcelain. "What's that?"

"It's complicated. Never mind. Let's jump to Harry Farmer's killing. When you received the call from someone claiming to be Father Zamoyski, did you recognize the voice?"

Dominic wet his seamed lips with the pink tip of his tongue, thought for a moment and then shook his head. "Just a voice. A guy's voice, you know."

"So when this voice identified himself as Father Zamoyski you didn't believe him?"

"What do you think I am?" Dominic demanded, in sudden furry. "Stupid?"

"That is self-evident."

The gangster grinned. "You gotta' tell Sal that. He don't think I got a brain in my head."

"Rita gave me the impression that you believed you were speaking to Father Zamoyski."

Dominic's eyes flickered. "At first, maybe. Just a little, maybe. But after I talked to Rita I un-believed right off. I figured it for a scam. But I just wasn't sure—but only at first. Anybody'd been fooled. Just anybody."

"Salvator swears it was Milton Raintree posing as Father Zamoyski who called you. Do you agree with that?"

The gangster blinked, dully. "What did Rita say?"

"Just answer my question."

Dominic's eyes dipped to the table. "I ain't sure. What Sal says, goes. Unless Rita says different. Then, what Rita says goes."

"Dominic, if you were the only one this voice contacted by phone and you are not certain of that voice's identity, why would Salvator think it was Milton Raintree?"

The gangster looked up, his face twisted in confusion. "What was that, again? Only slower."

"We'll come back to that. It's my understanding that Milton Raintree telephones Salvator each time Raintree's in town. Is that true?"

"He thinks he's such hot shit cause of that one boost. Dominic Portello made a vague move of one hand.

"I'll take that as yes. Tell me about your relationship with Sheila Clifford?"

"She was a tumble I used to pick up when I visited Houston. Nothing special."

"You dated her in Austin?"

"What for? I got plenty of action, here." The gangster raked his fingers through his hair so forcefully that his eyes slanted, giving him a Eurasian look. "She's just one of my out-of-towner's."

"What about Kathy Martin?"

Dominic grinned. "I see her around, sure. That's one who really likes her mattress-work. Special, you know?"

"When did you last see her?"

"A few days back. She was staying at the Pierce Ranch, that night. But the old boy couldn't get it up, you know?" Dominic tilted his head in Elliot's direction. "So she asked me to come out there and well, you know. Only it was raining dogs and pigs. So I told her I'd pass. But she really begged. So I said, I'd be there."

"That was the night George Pierce was murdered?"

The gangster thought for a moment and then nodded. "Yeah. That's the night." Then his mouth fell open. "But I didn't whack him!"

"You and Kathy got together that night, excuse the pun?"

"No. She told me to sneak in the back way. So Pierce wouldn't spot me. So I did. She told me to go upstairs and to this room. But when I got there..." His voice trailed off in a mumble.

"When you got there what?"

Dominic leaned across the table and whispered, "I spotted this dead-guy."

"George?"

The gangster nodded. "I was gonna' split, you know. Because people would think that I—well, you know. Only then I heard these two guys talking in the hall. It sounded like they were coming to where I was. So I crawled out on the roof through the window. That's when I slipped and fell off the roof. Landed in the mud."

"What happened then?"

"I lit out. Only I got turned around in the storm and ended up at the front gates. They opened up as I reached 'em. So I ran out."

"Almost getting hit by a car?"

Dominic's mouth fell open. "How'd you know that?"

"I'm a mind reader. Where's Kathy now? Is there any chance Salvator had her picked up?"

"Not Sal," said Dominic. "He walks the straight and narrow since gettin' married."

"I mean, there were rumors that your brother was looking for her in hopes she could lead him to Milton Raintree."

"Not that I know of." Dominic pulled a partially crumpled cigarette from his pants pocket and stuffed it in his mouth. Then he fished out a book of matches, and lit it. His eyes locked on Elliot's face. "Who said that? Was it that bastard Mazy Wilson?"

"Rumors."

"Well, you can tell Rumors from me, that he's in deep shit!"

For nearly a minute there was silence, except for Dominic's nasal breathing and smoke-spewing.

Elliot asked, "How well do you know Mazy Wilson?"

"That bastard's toast after what he said about me in court," declared the gangster.

"As may be, but you didn't answer my question. When did you first meet him?"

"Mazy used to hang around with me and Sydney when we was pals. Mazy was Mazy—no class. But we used to let him hang with us." He took a long drag on the cigarette and then exhaled as he said, "After Sydney and me parted ways, I never saw much of either."

"But he and Mazy were close?"

Dominic splayed his hands. "I guess they might've gotten close—what with me no longer 'round. But that was then. I ain't kept in touch."

Elliot stared at the table a moment, weighing his options. Finally, he got to his feet. "Your pretrial hearing will be in the next few weeks. I'll tell you the exact date when I know it. I want you to think over everything we've discussed. Everything you know about George Pierce. Everything you know about Milton Raintree. Everything you know about Harry Farmer. Understand?"

The gangster made a worried face. "All at the same time?"

"We'll talk again in a few days. When we do, we're going to go over everything, one more time. Under no circumstances do you speak to anyone unless I'm there. No one. Not even another prisoner. No one."

The gangster's eyebrows arched in pleading. "What about getting' me outa' here?"

"No judge in his right mind would turn you loose. You're too big a flight-risk—not to mention the rest of your hazardous potential for society."

Dominic made a bitter face; and then it vanished. "This ain't the

Ritz."

"No, I grant you it isn't. But it'll have to do. Thank you for your cooperation, Mr. Portello."

Dominic smiled slightly. "*Mr. Portello...* Sounds like I finally got respect from you."

Elliot nodded. "You earned it."

Out in the parking lot Chamber Elliot found Rita pacing next to his car. "What's the word on Raintree?" he asked.

She looked at him, and her eyes were not warm. "Sal says he doesn't have him—yet. He says if Raintree's so important, you'd better not take too long on getting Dom cleared. Because he wants to spend a month dipping him. Regardless, he says if he gets him he'll tell you."

"Charming hobby your brother has."

"Not much. You can't imagine the stink, and the screams." She made a sour face. "What gives with Raintree? What makes him so important? Or are you just shining me on?"

"When I can prove what I suspect, I'll let you know." Elliot unlocked his car. "In the meantime, you and your brothers will just have to trust me."

"Sal doesn't have my sense of humor, lawyer. I'm letting you know that now. One way or another what Raintree's got coming he's going to get."

"I have no interest in the matter except as it pertains to Dominic. Have a nice afternoon, Ms. Portello."

* * * *

When Chambers Elliot got back to his private office, Jason Taggart was waiting. "What did you find at the Pierce Ranch, Jason?"

"It's a big place." The detective crawled from the couch. "Von Drake and I didn't finish until a few minutes ago. By the way, Mazy Wilson showed up while Von Drake and I were there."

"He saw you?"

"No. But Von Drake spotted him. You think maybe he's trying to hustle Sydney Pierce?"

"I think he probably came by to collect what's due him before the Portellos get hold of Wilson. Did you find the Will?"

"Nope." The detective grinned as he pulled a handful of badly tarnished wheel-weights from his coat-pocket. "But I found a whole box of these, out there." He stacked the weights on the desk. "The old horse barn's been converted to an indoor shooting range. Pretty fancy."

"Recently?"

Taggart wagged his head. "Long time back. Still, by today's standards it's got most of the bells and whistles. There's a reloading area at the front. That's where I spotted the weights and some other stuff. There's also a melting pot. It's been used very recently. The residue is nice and shiny."

Elliot pointed at the weights. "Weights like those were melted in it?"

"I chipped off a sample from the walls of the pot and dropped it off for analysis. But as brittle as the stuff is, I'm certain it's not pure lead."

"What about a sound system?"

"It's there. Newly installed from the looks of the wiring. The system, according to Sydney, was intended to double as a fire or intruder alarm. That is why each room in the place was included in the speaker setup. Music or warnings could be transmitted to every room or selected rooms. It's quite sophisticated."

"Could it give the illusion that gunshots were being fired in one area of the house while they were occurring in another part?"

"No doubt about it. That's why I looked for a recording of gunfire. But I didn't find anything."

"I didn't think you would."

"There was something interesting about it," said Taggart. "The system was set up to receive as well as transmit."

"You mean like bugs?"

The detective nodded. "But not in the typical sense. You see a speaker, when properly hooked up to an amplifying receiver, can act as a microphone."

"How?"

"All you have to do is connect the two wires from the speaker into an input device such as a tape recorder, computer, or amplifier. The speaker then acts as a microphone and picks up sound. The downside of that is the sound quality. It is not as good as a true microphone."

"But it would be clear enough to understand?"

"Absolutely."

"So that's how discussions with George were passed on to Milton Raintree."

"Possibly. It doesn't tell us who did it. But we now know how it could've been done. It's also why Herbie's men didn't notice it. They would've looked for a typical bugging setup. In this case the extra wires, soldered to the speakers that went to a computer, were the only indication."

"Computer?"

"In the garage." He reached into his pocket and withdrew a rectangular piece of electronic gear. "Its hard drive."

Elliot smiled as he took the device. "Naturally we suspect that George must have used this drive as part of his business therefore I, as executor, am allowed to make use of whatever information may be on it."

The detective rolled his eyes. "Naturally."

"Well done, Jason."

Lydia came into Elliot's office. "Salvator Portello's on the phone. He wants to know why you can't arrange bail for his brother?"

"Tell that killer to think about it. Even with his lack of brains, the reason should come to him," the lawyer snapped.

"Chambers…" scolded Taggart.

"Strike that, Lydia," said Elliot. He went over to his desk and put the hard drive into a drawer. "Just politely advise Mr. Portello that I've gone out. If he asks where, tell Mr. Portello that I'm investigating something of extreme importance to his brother's case and that you will inform me of his call upon my return."

"He's not going to like hearing either version of your response," she warned.

"Nevertheless, if I'm not here he'll have to accept it. I'll call him back when I have time."

"Maggie isn't back from lunch," Lydia said with concern. "It's not like her to be late. I tried calling her cell-phone, but she doesn't answer. You don't think the Portellos…"

"What would they want with the Fearless Virgin?" Taggart questioned.

Lydia made an angry face at the detective. "Why do you always refer to her as that, Jason?"

"She is, isn't she?" Taggart protested. "A virgin, I mean."

"What her sexual experienced may or may not be," Lydia retorted, "is none of our concern. And I think it is extremely rude of you to decry her moral convictions."

"I wasn't doing anything of the kind," the detective objected.

Chambers Elliot stepped between the arguing pair. "I doubt the Portellos had anything to do with her disappearance. But she may have been involved in an accident. Telephone the police."

After Lydia hurried out Taggart said, "That woman's never liked me. Not since I took that French Fry from her plate, at that Cheesecake joint."

"So you admit you are losing your touch with women?" Elliot teased.

"Don't be ridiculous!" He pushed out his lips in a small pout. "I'm as smooth as I always was—with normal women, anyway."

"What about Kathy Martin?"

He nodded. "I'd say she's very normal. In fact, if she wasn't married I'd like to…."

"Married? Who in hell did she marry?"

"Sydney Pierce," said Taggart with a snicker. "Von Drake also spotted her at the ranch."

"You're absolutely certain they're married?"

The detective nodded. "My contact at the State's Licensing Division called when he saw their names come across his computer-screen. They went through a civil-ceremony before Magistrate Whitaker."

"Whitaker?" asked Elliot in surprise.

"I thought it was odd, too. He's usually above such lowly duties. But my contact had a chat with Whitaker's Clerk-of-Court. Sydney Pierce made the request of Whitaker, personally. And used whatever was necessary to gain the Magistrate's cooperation."

"You're not suggesting a bribe?"

"Of course I am."

"I didn't release that Sydney Pierce had connections to the Whitaker family."

"Something you may want to address with Ramón, after I get him back from the Peterson's," the detective said with a worried smile.

"Did you have time to talk with Willie Freeborn?"

Taggart shook his head. "And it's too late, now."

"Too late? Why?"

"Willie was hit by a rental-truck. Killed. Hit and run. I heard it on the radio on my way here." Taggart reached into his inside pocket and drew out a plastic evidence bag within which was a small vial of colorless liquid. "Then, there's this which I find extremely interesting."

Elliot reached for it but Taggart jerked it away. "It has no smell. It's very toxic," said the detective. "Liquid nicotine. I found it at the Pierce Ranch."

"Nicotine? From tobacco? I thought it would be brown."

"You're thinking of the tars from tobacco. The bottle this came from had a cracked top. It apparently had been tipped on its side, which cause a good bit to leak out. There was a big collection of dead mice, rats and insects near the fluid that had seeped out."

"I take it the original bottle was labeled?"

"Not at all. In fact it was entirely unmarked—looked to be a new bottle."

Elliot pointed at the bottle in the detective's hand. "Then how do you know that's nicotine?"

"I stopped by the lab I'm using to process Sheila's DNA profile. While there, I described all the dead things around the original bottle. That's when their chief chemist asked to see what I'd taken. He did a quick test and that confirmed it."

"Did you get her profile?" Elliot asked, excitedly.

Taggart withdrew a large envelope from his pocket and passed over to the lawyer. "She was definitely Edward Pierce's daughter."

Chambers Elliot reviewed the lab report and then dropped it upon his desk. "Why would anyone want liquid nicotine?" Elliot asked.

"Old habits die hard?"

"Your pun is well-taken. Nevertheless, does nicotine offer any properties that make it a better pesticide than those currently available?"

"Not according to the chemist when I asked him the same thing," Taggart said. "But he speculated that if insects in an area had developed a resistance to the stuff sold over the counter, nicotine could make a good substitute. It's not been in use in a very long time."

The lawyer rubbed his eyes sleepily. "Could I buy nicotine locally?"

"I doubt it. Do you want me to check?"

"No. I'm just curious about how something like that can be acquired."

"Nicotine can be extracted from tobacco leaves using a relatively simple chemical process."

"Simple? Meaning you and I could do it?"

The detective wagged his head. "But a high-school chemistry teacher could manage it."

"That nicotine," said the lawyer, pointing a finger at the bottle. "It's what's used in stop-smoking patches and gums, isn't it?"

"Exactly." The detective looked at the lawyer from the corners of his eyes. "In fact, hundreds of kids each year get sick from chewing that gum."

"I'll wager an autopsy prove will prove that Sheila Clifford died from nicotine poisoning."

"The bottle I found. It was Milton Raintree's doing?"

Chambers Elliot nodded. "Exactly. He doctored up a patch and had Tipton French deliver it to Sheila."

"But why kill her? The DNA profile would've put her in George's will."

"Had George been alive to execute it."

"So you no longer think Raintree killed George Pierce?"

"Quite the contrary. I'm more convinced than ever he is responsible."

"Chambers, you've lost me. If Raintree knew that Sheila was Edward Pierce's daughter, why kill George?"

"Was Mazy Wilson still at the Pierce Ranch when you left?"

"I don't know. Probably." Taggart plucked at the hairs in his nose. "It's not like he can show his face around town without risking a swim in the dip-tank. Why?"

"I think it's time I had a talk with him and Milton Raintree."

"Milton Raintree was abducted by the Portellos, remember?"

"If I'm right, Milton Raintree's at the Pierce ranch," said Elliot.

Taggart rolled his eyes. "Dare I ask if you want me to come along?"

"I think a gun would be suitable in this type of situation don't you?"

"Chambers, if you think Raintree is there tell Herbie so he can arrest the guy."

Chambers Elliot grinned. "Not a chance. I want the pleasure of bringing Milton Raintree to task. Give me twenty minutes and then follow."

As the lawyer headed for the office door Lydia burst in. "I just heard from Maggie. She's okay. She had an appointment with her doctor and forgot to tell me."

"That's a relief," said Elliot.

"No it isn't," the legal assistant countered. "Maggie's decided to devote her life to Ramón. She feels with her love and care he won't feel the need to explore the rest of the female population."

"So she went to the doctor to get immunity injections, in case he's contagious?" asked Taggart.

"Birth control pills," she grimly explained.

The detective gave Elliot a stunned look.

"Well," the lawyer responded. "Would you want to have Ramón's child while devoting your life to him?"

"Chambers," Taggart replied. "After what I saw of Ramón, I wouldn't even consider marriage." Then the detective gave Lydia an embarrassed look before adding, "Assuming I was a woman of a desperate and deeply confused nature."

Chapter 20

The cast-iron gates to the Pierce Ranch entrance were open when Chambers Elliot arrived. He parked the Lagonda in front, got out, and hurried up the walk to the door. There he rang the bell and waited. A few seconds later the door opened and Kathy Martin looked out.

"I'm please to see that you're still here," Elliot said. He brushed past her into the house.

"What do you want?" Kathy demanded.

He looked at her dispassionately. "That is between me and Sydney."

"He's busy."

"So am I. Please tell him I'm here."

She cocked one hip, an angry sparkle lighting Kathy's eyes. "You should've telephoned for an appointment."

"That is not for you to decide."

The ghost of a smirk trembled at one corner of her mouth and then vanished. "Obviously you have not heard."

"That congratulation's are in order on your wedding?" The lawyer squared himself. "Oh, yes, indeed. But as I said, it's not for you to decide."

She smoothed her dark hair, and then shut the door. "I'm Sydney's wife. Half of everything he has is mine. Therefore I do make decisions."

He nodded curtly. "Completely accurate. Unfortunately, Sydney owns nothing. Half of nothing was, is and always will be nothing. I presume you see my point, now? Whatever decisions you may make, they do not concern this property, its contents or anything else that is part of George Pierce's estate."

Kathy drew in a deep, jagged breath. "There's another will, isn't there?"

"Where is Sydney?"

"Upstairs." She tilted her head toward the nearby staircase. Her face suddenly became sick. Her lips began to shake, kept on shaking as if she were about to cry. "She got it all, didn't she?"

"You should've stayed clear of it, Kathy. There's no statute of limitations on murder."

"Murder?" Kathy flashed her hands in denial. "Sheila killed herself."

The lawyer smiled faintly. "Is that what Raintree told you? What about Harry Farmer and George Pierce? Did your husband tell you they committed suicide, too?"

Her throat bobbed up and down as if she were trying to swallow her own tongue. "You know, don't you?"

He nodded. "The question you should be asking me is whether you can save yourself, from a death-sentence."

Her hands went to her face and Kathy began to sob.

Chambers Elliot could not repress a little smirk of triumph as he noted her terror. "Your only hope is to cooperate."

Her hands dropped away and she stared askance at Elliot. "If I tell you all I know…"

He stopped her with a gesture. "Is Mazy Wilson still here?"

Kathy gulped, again. "He's upstairs with Sydney."

"Was it you who bribed Willie Freeborn into telling Jason Taggart the tale of Raintree's convenient abduction?" Elliot asked.

Her brows lowered defensively and her hands became animated. "They forced me to do it. Sydney and Mazy."

"Kick me, whip me, make me write bad checks. A common claim to so many judges in check-kiting cases. Unfortunately, no jury believes it. Was it sex or money that caused Willie to lie for you?"

Her lips quivered so badly that Kathy could not utter a word in her own defense.

Chambers Elliot tilted is head toward the other end of the hallway. "I'll be waiting in the library." With that, the lawyer turned and strode away.

Kathy Martin watched him a moment before scurrying up the staircase, to the second floor.

In the library Elliot went over to George's Desk and sat. He proceeded through it drawer by drawer. In the middle one he came upon a *Last Will and Testament* document. It was signed 'George Pierce' and properly notarized. But the autograph was not as Elliot remembered it. The signature was close. But there was something wrong about the way the 'r' was formed, in each name. He let his eyes quickly scan the document. With the exception of minor bequests to several nonprofit organizations, the entire estate was to go to Sydney Pierce. It was dated the day George Pierce died.

"How nice I found this after Taggart did so thorough a search," he muttered, with a smile.

The door to the library burst open. Sydney Pierce and Mazy Wilson rushed in. Following behind them, almost reluctantly, came Kathy Martin.

"You should've telephoned, Mr. Elliot," Sydney declared impatiently. The veins in his forehead distended as if he were choking on his own words. "I'm too busy to deal with you, today."

"As executor of your father's estate I am not obliged to do any such thing. Until your father's Will is probated you are allowed to live here only by my sufferance." Then Elliot held up the document he had found. "This was in your father's desk."

Sydney Pierce shrugged, his face taking on a venomous twist. "So what?"

The lawyer pursed his lips dubiously. "I hope you weren't planning to claim it as your father's Last Will and Testament."

"Why shouldn't I?" demanded Sydney.

Elliot dropped the document to the desktop and leaned back in the chair. "It's a forgery."

"My father signed that in front of witnesses. I was there."

"Someone certainly signed it," Elliot agreed. Then he smiled languidly before adding, "And I do believe you were there—Mr. Raintree."

"I told you he knew everything," whimpered Kathy.

Sydney blanched, backing up a staggering step. "Shuttup, Kathy."

"Milton Raintree," continued the lawyer, with a faint show of humor. "That's your alter-ego, Sydney. The name by which you've spent decades conning Texas citizens and tormenting Salvator Portello. How he would love to get his hands on you."

"You can't prove anything," Sydney sneered.

"I can prove that you, Mazy Wilson and Kathy Martin were involved in three murders," countered Elliot.

Kathy's fingers coiled at her cheeks in horror as she looked at her husband. "*Three* murders?"

"Harry Farmer, George Pierce and Willie Freeborn," Elliot explained. "You de remember those men, don't you Kathy? Or is murder so commonplace in your life that it no longer torments your soul?"

"Willie?" Her head shook as her hands fell away, and she looked back at Elliot. "No, you're mistaken. Not Willie."

"Which one of you drove the rental truck that ran Willie Freeborn down?" asked the lawyer.

"Dear God!" she groaned. Then she pointed over at Wilson. "Him. Mazy must've done it. He rented the truck."

Wilson jerked a gun from his coat pocket. His voice was harsh, grating and insulting. "Shuttup you stupid bitch!" Then he pointed the weapon at Chambers Elliot. "You just outsmarted yourself, Shyster. The question is, what do we do with him?"

"No," Elliot asserted, raising a warning finger. "The question is whether Sydney married Kathy in the mistaken belief that marriage would stop her from giving testimony against him?" He paused dramatically, looking at Kathy Martin with interest. "You see she knows all your dirty secrets."

Sydney Pierce's lips pinched together in irritation. "You can't force her to say anything! A wife can't testify against her husband."

The lawyer's eyebrows rose. "That was a common rule of law during antiquity," admitted Elliot. He watched Kathy rock back and forth on her heels, sobbing. "It was held that one spouse could testify neither for nor against the other, in a criminal action. That reasoning was intended to protect marital tranquility. However Shores v. United States, 8th Circuit Court of Appeals in 1949, held that a wife's testimony against her husband is competent evidence, and may be allowed." He gave his chin a lazy scratch. "We have the death-penalty in this State, Kathy. You're going to be executed right along with your husband."

Mazy smirked. "There are a hundred million reasons for her to do as she's told—by us."

"You mean Sydney's inheritance?" Elliot flicked the will with one finger. "Sydney will never see dime-one. How much did he offer you, Wilson? How much were you to be paid for putting your life in jeopardy by testifying against Dominic Portello and for killing Willie Freeborn?"

"What's he mean, you won't get anything?" Mazy glanced over at Sydney Pierce.

"He's bluffing." Sydney fairly spit out the words. "We'll bury his body, ditch his car and claim he never showed up. Once that will is read I'll get it all—no questions asked."

One of the lawyer's eyebrows arched the merest trifle in the direction of Mazy Wilson. "Lies are easy. The truth is you did it all for nothing, Mazy. Even if you aren't convicted for killing Willie, the Portellos won't let you live."

"Another murder, Sydney?" Kathy suddenly shouted. "I'm not going to die for you."

"I told you to shuttup!" Sydney blustered.

"You don't think I came alone, do you?" Elliot pointed a long index finger at Mazy. "I expected you to pull a gun. That's why I brought some help."

Wilson glanced around, suddenly wary. "I don't like this."

Sydney went over to Mazy and took the pistol. "Check around outside. I'll keep an eye on him until you get back."

Mazy Wilson swallowed hard. "But if there's trouble I won't have a gun."

"Trouble in spades is waiting out there for you, Mazy," Elliot taunted. "I'm told that Salvator Portello has a secret place where he keeps something he calls the 'Dip-Tank'. It's full of acid. He uses it to torture his enemies by slowly dipping them into it. Rumor has it they don't die until the acid eats away the bottom of their heart. It takes a long time for acid to dissolve flesh and bone from the bottom of feet up to the heart."

"Just give a yell if you see anybody, I'll come running," Sydney promised.

"By the time Mazy sees the Portellos men it will be too late for yelling or running," the lawyer declared.

"He's right, Sydney," Mazy reached for the gun. "You go. They're not after you."

Sydney swung the weapon like a club, raking the barrel across Wilson's face, leaving a bleeding trail in the other man's cheek, and sending Wilson spinning. "Get going!"

As Mazy Wilson scurried from the room, Chambers Elliot propped his feet atop the desk.

"Dominic claims that Salvator intends to spend a week dipping Milton Raintree, too. He will be so pleased to find out the object of that quest is conveniently here." Elliot's voice was studiedly calm. Then the lawyer focused his attention on Kathy. "Which one of you killed George Pierce?"

Kathy pointed at Sydney without hesitation. "Him. He killed his mother, too." She began talking fast. "George found out that Sydney had gotten the DNA report on Sheila, and substituted another so George wouldn't believe Sheila was his granddaughter."

"Shuttup, you stupid bitch!" Sydney yelled.

"Go ahead and kill me, Sydney!" she countered. "After what you got me into I'll feel better dead."

"I'll see that you don't die with him, Kathy." Elliot calmly raked his fingers through his hair. "Who fired all the shots that night?"

With an effort that crumpled up his face, Sydney Pierce brought himself under control. "You're the only one who's going to die, lawyer."

"Mazy." Kathy swayed slightly on the balls of her feet, and blinked hard. "He put a gun loaded with blanks into George's hand and fired it. Later on, to screw with how the cops figure the time of death, Sydney played a recording of gunshots."

The lawyer bit his lip thoughtfully. "How did Mazy get upstairs without Armistice seeing him?"

"After Sydney killed George, he waited for Mazy to arrive. Then he called the butler upstairs and gave him a drink doctored with LSD," Kathy said. "It was while that was going on Mazy went up there."

Sydney Pierce laughed harshly. "No sense keeping it a secret any longer. Not with big-mouth over there spilling her guts. I gave the old fool a microdot of LSD. So what?" His features molded themselves into an expression of delight. "After that Armistice didn't have a clue. He saw and understood what was happening. But he couldn't keep it straight in his head as to when or the order of things."

"So," Elliot suggested, "Mazy's role in George's murder was limited to tampering with the evidence?"

Pierce nodded, still grinning. "I killed my father. He was putting everything into a trust. For the rest of my life I'd be limited to whatever allowance the trust meted out. I wanted it all. I deserved it all."

"You did," Elliot said agreeably. "The shame is you didn't wait for it. The trust would not have lasted long. Once your father realized how much it limited his business activities, he would've revoked it. There was no need to kill George."

"Sydney told me nobody would get hurt." Kathy glanced distrustfully at her husband. "I didn't know he was going to kill George."

Sydney Pierce snorted with impertinence. "Lying bitch."

"You invited Dominic Portello here, Kathy." Elliot puckered his brow with a thoughtful frown. "To implicate him in the killing. Whose idea was that?"

She licked her lips, nervously. "Sydney made me do it."

"Liar!" Sydney Pierce shouted.

"It sounds like Sydney has a lot to answer for," the lawyer remarked. Then his brows furrowed in confusion. "But if Sydney killed George and you played no part in it, who wore Sheila's clothes during the killing? They were spattered with George's blood."

Sydney Pierce laughed. "Explain that, Kathy."

"I didn't want to," Kathy screamed. "He made me."

"It then follows," Elliot persisted, "that you also wore her clothing when Harry Farmer was shot. His blood is there, as well."

"She pushed him off the roof," Sydney giggled, "just as I shot him. She laughed the whole time he fell to the ground."

Kathy chewed her lower lip a moment. "I had no choice. Sydney would've killed me if I hadn't done it."

"You were eager enough when you thought you'd get your greedy mitts on millions!" Sydney's face flushed angrily.

"It was quite clever the way you implicated Dominic Portello in those killings, Sydney," Elliot said. "Wearing his clothing during each murder and then returning the soiled garments to be found by the police was brilliant. I guess I should say, almost brilliant. You see, as part of my defense of Dominic, I will be having his clothing and shoes tested for another's DNA. I might not find yours on the clothing. But the shoes will be no problem. Our feet sweat as soon as we put shoes on. You won't be able to explain your DNA without implicating yourself, will you?"

"You won't be doing any testing." Sydney Pierce strutted over to the desk. "Admit it, Elliot. Admit I had you completely fooled." He smiled confidently. "All that's left to do is fool the Portello's into thinking Milton Raintree is dead. And, of course, to get rid of you."

"I assume you plan to make Mazy Wilson the patsy?" said Elliot. "He will assume your role as Raintree albeit postmortem?"

"Mazy's about my size," grinned Sydney. "You know what they say about necessary collateral damage."

Elliot got to his feet. "I must admit that you completely took me in at the offset. Your portrayal of Father Zamoyski put me into a mindset that I couldn't shake. I kept trying to link Michael Douglas's murder to George and Harry's. It wasn't until I heard Dominic's recollection of the events of that night, that I realized there were two killers. Your mother and you. It was you who picked up the gun she left at Winston Liquors."

Sydney Pierce shrugged. "I thought the stupid cow was trying to commit suicide by getting herself arrested for killing him. My mother hated my father so much that she'd talked often about killing herself. So, I grabbed the gun and brought it home."

"Which horrified your mother so much, realizing that you knew what she had done, that she threatened to turn herself over to the police," surmised Elliot. "But then the Jensens came into the play. They'd been outside of Winston Liquors, watching. They'd seen the whole thing. They wanted money. In return they promised to lay the blame on Jerome Petty."

Sydney nodded. "Otherwise, they would implicate both me and my mother in Mike's murder."

"Why did your mother kill Michael Douglas?" asked Elliot.

"He said he wasn't interested in her anymore," said Sydney. "Mother was furious. Mike was her best chance to get clear of father."

"So you and your mother came up with a plan for the Jensens," said Elliot. "She would learn to maintain helicopters. At least enough to cause one to crash. The idea was to kill the Jensens but make it look like they died in a terrible accident."

"Why did she bring you with to Samoa?"

Sydney shrugged. "Because I wanted to go."

Elliot smiled. "As good a reason as any. The Jensens were already there? Or did you wait for them to arrive?"

"We waited. Mother offered to pay them a million dollars in a lump sum, final payment. The condition was, they had to accept payment in Samoa where my mother said the money was. They were stupid, greedy people so they came."

"The Jensen's were given money and air-travel tickets," said Elliot. "They flew there expecting to return home rich. Little did they suspect what was in store for them with you being there."

"They deserved what they got," Sydney declared.

"Perhaps," Elliot agreed. "But did your mother deserve what she got?"

"She was going to confess to all of it," explained Sydney. "She got back from Samoa and went crazy. I had to stop her. I dumped sleeping pills into her drink. She'd become such a lush she didn't even notice."

Elliot looked over at Kathy. "Telephone the police."

"Stay put!" Sydney's eyes shrank to pinpoints of death.

"He'll kill you anyway, Kathy," Elliot asserted calmly. "You heard his plans for Mazy. You will be treated no different."

She bolted for the door.

Sydney turned toward her and raised the gun to fire.

Chambers, with a quick, cat-like movement, dove across the desk, knocking Sydney to the floor.

As the gun roared, Kathy raced out of the room leaving the two men to battle for it. Sydney Pierce was younger. But Chambers Elliot was heavier and stronger. He slugged Pierce, and then scrambled across the floor to the gun.

Sydney scrambled after it like a three-legged cat.

Chambers sank a fist into the side of his neck. Sydney toppled over sideways, still trying to crawl over to the gun. Elliot hit him again, sending Sydney sprawling. Then the lawyer stood, grabbed the gun, and then turned to face his adversary.

Sydney came up on all fours, glaring. He coughed and shook his head as if trying to clear his brain of cobwebs.

"Come any closer and I'll shoot," Elliot warned.

Sydney Pierce's face went expressionless, but his whole body shook with rage. "You haven't got the guts."

The lawyer's eyes twinkled. "That's to be seen."

There was the sound of hurrying footsteps.

Elliot twisted toward the doorway pointing the gun in that direction.

A moment later, Jason Taggart stepped into view. He had Mazy Wilson by the collar with one hand and was holding his pistol in the other. Kathy Martin reluctantly trailed behind.

"I didn't expect you for another five minutes, Jason." Elliot lowered the gun.

A look of blank amazement spread over the detective's face. "I left early, figuring I'd be saving your bacon. You're usually in over you're your head."

Elliot waggled the pistol. "As you see, I am in complete control this time."

"I guess there's always once." The detective gave Mazy Wilson a shove. "I called the locals after grabbing this one. They're on their way."

"Take my advice for a change, Kathy," said Elliot. His tone was unmistakably firm. "When the police arrive, tell them all you know and offer to testify against these two. You'll face charges. But you won't be looking at Capital Murder."

"Will you defend me?" she whimpered.

Chambers Elliot nodded.

"Chambers, for crying out loud..." the detective began. "Forget it. There's no changing you, is there?"

The lawyer's eyes glinted with amusement. "Not in my lifetime, anyway."

Chapter 21

When Chambers Elliot entered his offices the next afternoon, Maggie was sitting at the reception desk sobbing. Lydia stood beside her, offering vague reassurance.

"What happened?" The lawyer looked from woman to woman.

"Ramón's dead!" Maggie sniffed.

With one hand, the lawyer quickly covered the smile forming upon his face. He leaned toward his legal assistant. "How did it happen? Or are the details something you should convey to my privately because they are too gruesome to describe in front of her?"

"We don't know that it *did* happen," Lydia proclaimed. "About an hour ago, I sent Taggart to the pickup-point Leonard Peterson stipulated. Instead of finding Ramón, there was an open coffin sitting on top of a huge fire-ant mound."

Elliot straightened up, more than slightly disappointed. "Then why is Ramón presumed dead?"

"Because Taggart found blood in coffin and coyote tracks all around it," Lydia replied. "His assumption being that Ramon's body was dumped fit for burial, and the coyotes dragged it away. Taggart contacted the Texas Rangers and they've sent out an investigative team with a cadaver dog. Jason's assisting as needed."

"They can't find Ramón's body!" Maggie sobbed. "Those horrible coyotes took it."

Elliot's face took on a worried expression. "Maybe you'd better send her home, Lydia."

"I've tried," Lydia said. "But Maggie insists on being here."

"In case someone has to identify him," Maggie wailed.

"But if coyotes took his body…" the lawyer began.

Jason Taggart hurried into the office looking grim-struck. "I'm sorry, Maggie," the detective said gravely, as he stopped in front of her desk.

Maggie looked up at him through tearing eyes. "You found Ramón's body?"

The detective gave Elliot and Lydia a swift look, before nodding. "Unfortunately, it's still alive."

"Jason!" Lydia scolded. "You didn't have to put it that way!"

Maggie leaped up shrieking with delight.

"You mean I've still got Ramón for the rest of the summer?" the lawyer whined.

Taggart shrugged. "Apparently, even coyotes are allergic to him."

Elliot made a disapproving noise with his tongue and lips.

"What happened?" Lydia demanded.

"Yes, what happened?" Maggie chimed.

"According to Ramón, the Petersons were delivering a load of coffins to one of the cut-rate funeral parlors," the detective explained. "You know the kind. The boxes are made of cardboard but painted like wood. Since there wasn't enough room in the truck for Peterson and his troop plus Ramón, they stuffed Ramón into one of the coffins."

"Well, at least they had part of a good idea," Elliot muttered.

"As the truck reached the point where Ramón was to get off," Taggart continued, "it skidded on some spilled oil. The coffin Ramón was in fell off the truck. He remembers that the Petersons, stopped, went back and opened the coffin. But after they took one look at Ramón, they ran off. Probably because of the blood they thought Ramón was dead. Anyway, he passed out at that point. Which was not a good idea considering his proximity to the world's largest fire-ant mound. I found Ramón wandering around in a daze, trying to bat off the fire-ants."

Maggie scrambled over to the detective. "Where is Ramón? Please, I have to help him."

"I dropped him off out front," said Taggart. "He's getting insect-bite ointment at the pharmacy on the main floor. The detective gave Elliot a warning look. "He's pretty badly stung so scratching is more than just a hobby with him."

With a shriek of concern, Maggie raced out of the office.

"I think I need a drink." Chambers Elliot turned and headed dismally into his private office.

"Champagne is definitely in order," Lydia declared, with a grin.

"I was thinking more along the lines of hemlock."

"Oh, Lydia," Taggart said. "Ramón is using the fifty the Petersons gave him to give to you to pay for the ointment. From the looks of Ramón, he'll need the extra large bottle. So they're probably won't be much left in the way of change."

She shrugged. "Easy come, easy go. My big worry is that damn Mongoose. It keeps eyeing my cat in a way that sends poor kitty right up the curtains. I don't suppose you'd like a pet mongoose?"

With an unsympathetic arch of his eyebrows the detective turned and hurried after the lawyer.

"What about Dominic Portello, Chambers?" Taggart settled into one of the chairs fronting Elliot's desk.

"I spent most of the morning getting the case dismissed." Elliot was settled in his swivel chair, twiddling his thumbs. "The rest of the time I was with Sydney Pierce."

"Pierce? You're not going to defend him!"

"No." Elliot leaned back. "But I wanted to listen to as much as he would be willing to tell me about this case."

"Lies," Taggart muttered laconically.

The lawyer stretched with a sigh, as if the whole weight of the world was on his shoulders. "In any event, Dominic Portello is a free man—God help Texas."

The detective snickered. "Turning that thug loose must've burned Davis Archer."

Elliot nodded. "Archer did some blustering about arresting the entire Portello clan on conspiracy charges. But there's no case in it."

"You must be a hero amongst the Sicilian ne'er-do-well set."

"I earned my fee," Elliot protested. "It's not like I've fallen in with them."

The detective winked. "According to Lydia, you might be about to—at least with Rita Portello."

The lawyer shook a threatening finger at Taggart. "It's rumors like those that keep detectives in the unemployment line."

"There's no need to overreact, Chambers." He took out a cigarette and lit it. "Just when did you realize that Sydney Pierce was Milton Raintree?"

"Not for some time," Elliot replied. "I knew the Father Zamoyski characterization was a phony, before he left my office. Still, his emphasis on Michael Douglas kept me on the wrong course—which is what Sydney Pierce intended. When Harry Farmer was murdered, once more I made an erroneous assumption, as Sydney intended. Based upon the description you gave of him, I jumped to the conclusion that it was he who posed as Zamoyski. It wasn't until you had that battle with Mazy Wilson at the Double Oak Hotel, that Sydney's clever plan went astray."

"How? I had no idea who he was in that disguise."

"Neither did—at the time. But shoes were Sydney's downfall."

"Shoes?"

Elliot leaned forward, folding his hands on the desk. "What's the first thing you notice about a man when you first see him?"

The detective spoke with a touch of malice. "Not his tattoo, I can tell you."

Elliot chuckled. "With the exception of Ramón Whitaker."

The detective pondered the question a moment. Then his eyes widened and he nodded. "Shoes."

"Women notice other women's hair first. Men, invariably, notice the other man's shoes. When Milton Raintree confronted us at the Double

Oak Hotel, he was wearing tan saddle shoes. Mazy Wilson was wearing black penny loafers with dimes in the niches."

Taggart nodded. "I remember."

"But at Sheila Clifford's apartment, the Raintree who showed up there was wearing penny loafers with dimes. The general disguise was good enough to keep me off balance, except for the shoes. Those told me that I was dealing with Wilson. Was Wilson really Milton Raintree or vice versa? I wasn't sure at that point. Nevertheless, I doubted that Wilson had the brains for the action Raintree was running. So I assumed someone else must be backing his play. Then I left Sheila's apartment and Sydney appeared in the lobby. Again, I noticed his shoes. This time, I spotted the tan saddle shoes. Ergo, Sydney Pierce must be the mysterious Milton Raintree."

"But how could he know that you would go to Sheila's apartment?"

"That was the reason behind my being fired in favor of Tipton French. Sydney knew my ego would be bruised. He knew that I would confront Sheila and demand an explanation. So with Mazy in the wings disguised as Raintree, they waited for me to arrive."

The detective's voice took on a loathing tenor. "Sheila was his niece and yet Sydney married her."

"Yes," said Elliot. "Marrying Sheila Clifford was intended to take away any apparent motive from Sydney when she was killed, later on— which Sydney knew must be done."

"But he had the best motive."

"When investigating a homicide where the victim is a married woman, who immediately becomes the primary suspect?"

"Her husband. There's a ninety-five percent chance that he did it."

"Motive or not, Sydney was counting on the police to suspect the terrible Milton Raintree."

Taggart nodded. "Which they would've. But why bother marrying her at all?"

"So that I would believe Kathy Martin. Kathy gave us that song-and-dance about Raintree dumping her in favor of Sheila. The implication being that Kathy would have no loyalty to Raintree. I might've assumed that she was playing a part for our benefit when we first questioned her."

"Which she was."

"But when Raintree married Sheila, any implication that Kathy's words were just a ploy went out the window."

"That still doesn't explain the phony abduction story we got from Willie Freeborn."

"Sydney wanted to be rid of the Raintree persona. He also wanted the police to stop looking for Raintree as a suspect in Sheila's murder. He wanted the police to close the case, as they had done with Michael Douglas' murder when Jerome Petty died. So, he had Kathy arrange for Willie to contact you. Unfortunately for Willie, doing so meant a death-sentence. He was a loose end and had to go. As was his killer, Mazy Wilson."

"Sydney planned to kill Mazy?"

"Absolutely. But he needed a fall-guy."

"Dominic Portello."

"The Portello clan, in general. Which is why Sydney promised Mazy millions to testify against Dominic at Sheila's pretrial hearing."

"Mazy dies and Portello revenge is assumed," the detective muttered in agreement. Then he gave Elliot a questioning look. "But the Portellos never leave bodies behind."

"Sydney didn't know that."

"Why not just let the Portellos take care of Mazy? Why would Sydney risk killing him?"

"Because once the Portellos had Mazy, he would've tried to bargain for his life—by telling Salvator Milton Raintree's real identity. Sydney could not afford to have that happen."

"Did he explain his reasoning behind using the Michael Douglas murder as bait?"

Elliot nodded. "Sydney wanted revenge against Dominic Portello."

"Over a brief affair that took place thirty years ago?" Taggart scoffed. "I find it hard to believe that Sydney is the type to wait that long for revenge."

"He isn't. In fact, he'd all but forgotten it. Then he saw the DVD that Elvira offered for sale. It all came back to him. That is why he was eager to help Harry Farmer by pretending to be Zamoyski for my benefit. He wanted to loop me in but using a specific killing. One he still had one piece of evidence that would link Dominic to it. The gun Sydney's mother used to shoot Michael the second time. The same gun he purposely used to incriminate Dominic further by killing Harry and George with it."

"But there's nothing in the way of forensics still around for the Michael Douglas killing."

"But Sydney didn't know that. He was basing his assumptions upon what he'd seen being acted-out on television and in the films. Still, the prints on the gun did successfully tie Dominic to George and Harry's murders. Sydney nearly got away with putting his old pal in the death-house."

The detective thought for a moment. Then he reflected, "I wonder if Herbie will be able to trace where Sydney bought that poison?"

"The nicotine he used to kill Sheila? I suspect Sydney manufactured it himself. Remember, he had a degree in chemistry."

"So Sydney killed Harry Farmer because Harry knew Sydney was Raintree?" asked Taggart.

"No," Elliot said. "Harry did not know that Sydney Pierce was Milton Raintree. Harry was simply being a good father by trying to stop Sheila from marrying Raintree. Harry was so determined to do so that he threatened to point the Portellos to the man he believed was Milton Raintree. Making the situation even more difficult for Sydney's plans was Sheila's willingness to do as Harry demanded. Therefore, Harry had to go."

"What happens to the Pierce fortune now that Sydney's been charged in his father's murder?"

"It will go to the State of Texas if Sydney's convicted," said the lawyer.

"Couldn't Sheila Clifford's family, if she has any, make a claim?"

"It would not hold up because at the time George died she was not a beneficiary to the Pierce estate. If she were still alive, she could make a valid claim as the granddaughter of George Pierce."

"I'm still confused as to why did Barbara Pierce shot Douglas twice."

"Initially that was not part of her plan," said Elliot. "Michael Douglass dumped her and Barb killed him for it. But when she was driving away after shooting Douglas, she spotted Sydney sneaking into the liquor-store. At the time, Barb assumed he had just arrived. She was afraid the police were on their way and he would get blamed. So she parked in the back lot and got out, intending to go in. She intended to drag Sydney away pretending to have spotted him in the store, as any mother would do to an underage son. But as Barb headed for the store's rear entrance, Dominic Portello came running out. She assumed he had seen her kill Douglas and intended to detain her using Douglas' gun— which he was carrying. But when Dominic started in about what had happened she realized he had seen nothing. Barb also realized that she had an unexpected opportunity to frame Dominic for the killing. All she had to do was take the gun, which Dominic handed over to her, go back inside, send Sydney home, fire the pistol into Douglas' head, and then leave the gun behind for the police. Dominic's fingerprints were on it. She assumed the bullet for the pistol would be found and linked to the pistol. The round she had fired that actually killed Michael, she assumed would also be blamed on Dominic. When she got into the store, Sydney was already gone—much to the betterment of her plan. After shooting Michael with the pistol, Barb dropped the gun on the floor and left."

"But Sydney was still nearby and saw his mother?"

"Sydney saw the whole thing," said Elliot. "He went back into the store and grabbed the gun, thinking he was protecting her."

"Enter the Jensens from Leander?"

Elliot nodded. "They saw everything and began their short-lived blackmail. Petty was chosen as the fall-guy because the Jensens knew he was a crook. Curiously enough they felt blaming someone innocent of criminal dealings to help their blackmail plan was wrong."

Taggart pulled a thick envelope from his pocket. "This is the DNA profile on Sydney Pierce." He tapped it against his knuckles. "Do you still want it?"

"Was he George's son?" asked Elliot.

The detective tossed the envelope onto the desk. "I'd rather you decide that for yourself."

There was a commotion out in the reception area. Then the two men heard Lydia say, "Dear God, what happened to you?"

"Must be Ramón," Taggart said with a sympathetic shake of his head. "He looks worse than he is. Those ant stings can really make you swell up."

Lydia entered the office and went over to Taggart.

"I hope you told the Rangers to arrest those horrid Petersons," she declared. "Maggie is in a panic because that poor man out there is nearly dead."

"The Petersons are probably in Oklahoma by now," the detective said. "Regardless, what happens to them is beyond my control."

"Oh, Ramón!" Maggie exclaimed from the reception area. "Are you sure that's where it hurts the worst?"

"Maggie is a natural caregiver," Lydia explained proudly. "Ramón is so lucky she cares so much about him."

A few seconds later Maggie's voice was heard to utter, "The tip looks so purple. Is it bruised?"

Lydia glanced over her shoulder toward the door, smiling. "She's got the ointment out doing her best to ease poor Ramón's suffering—not that you two give a damn about him."

"Nonsense," Elliot protested. "We've just been discussing how that poor young man has suffered."

"Amen to that," Taggart agreed. "He had his hands down his pants scratching the whole ride here."

"Oh, Ramón," Maggie's voice echoed, again. "Should it be getting bigger, like that? I mean, it's not allergic to the lotion, is it?"

Lydia crossed her arms and smiled at the two men. "I'll give you any odds you want that Maggie will turn Ramón from the world's biggest jerk into someone this firm can be proud of."

"Oh, Ramón!" Maggie's voice came more excitedly than before. "When it moves on its own like that is it feeling better, or worse?"

"Is it just me or do you think somebody should go out there and see what those two are doing?" suggested the detective.

Lydia made a disgusted face. "That is so like you, Taggart. You are always thinking the worst of people." With that Lydia turned and strode out of the office. A second later her voice cried, "Dear God, Maggie! Ramón! What in hell do you two think you're doing?"

"I was just trying to make him feel better," the receptionist protested.

"I can see that," Lydia declared. "Now, put that damn lotion away. And, Ramón, put your damn tattoo away!"

"Do we want to know any details, Chambers?" Taggart asked.

The lawyer shook his head. "In situations like this I believe a firm dedication to prolonged ignorance is the best course of action."

Jason Taggart got to his feet. "Well, I'd better get back to my office and finish filling out my expense reports."

Elliot nodded his head. "I thought you might."

There was the sound of muffled voices from the reception area. Then Lydia's head appeared in the doorway.

"I'll be gone for about half an hour, Chambers," she said. "You don't have any appointments, so I'm going to drive Ramón home. Maggie's coming along."

"With the ointment?"

Lydia blushed. "That is staying here."

"Has Maggie ever met Magistrate Whitaker?" Elliot asked.

Lydia shook her head. "Not that I know of. Why?"

"Be sure she does, will you? And make certain Maggie is wearing her glasses when she does. I think that might cure her infatuation with his son. Lock the door when you leave. I think I'll have a short nap until you and Maggie get back."

"I know it would cure me," Taggart said as he followed Lydia out.

Elliot leaned back in his chair and propped his feet on the desk. He was just about to doze off when the telephone rang. He dropped his feet to the floor and grabbed up the receiver.

"If this has anything to do with Ramón Whitaker, I'm going to hang up."

From the other end of the line he heard a sultry laugh. "It has to do with me."

A smile crept across his face. "Rita? What can I do for you?"

"I was thinking about fried chicken," she said.

His eyes began to twinkle. "Where would you like to meet?"

"Where I am. Your house."

He stood up. "Alone?"

There was another giggle. "Of course. I changed the sheets on your bed. I was thinking we could have our little nibble there."

"Regular or extra crispy?"

Rita laughed naughtily. "Definitely extra everything."

"Give me thirty minutes. Whatever you do, don't start without me. I'll just leave a note for my legal assistant that I'll be taking the rest of the day off and I'll be on my way."

"Better take tomorrow off, as well."

He nodded, and hung up the phone. "Should I claim I fell ill and will need a couple of days to recuperate? Or will Lydia more likely believe that I'm investigating another case? No. I'll just write that I'm pulling a Ramón Whitaker."

As he tore the page from the pad he noticed the envelope Taggart had left. Elliot opened it, and unfolded the report.

"Just as I thought," he said, and dropped the report into the trash can next to his desk.

The End

www.ingramcontent.com/pod-product-compliance
Lightning Source LLC
Chambersburg PA
CBHW070331260626
47160CB00003B/1010

* 9 7 8 1 6 0 2 1 5 1 1 4 7 *